Bad at Love

AIMEE NICOLE WALKER

Bad at making decisions or bad at love? Either way, Kendall Blakemore doesn't trust his judgment. He falls too hard, too fast, and always for the wrong guy. Needing a major shakeup, Kendall moves into his own place for the first time and seizes a new career opportunity. But everything he thought he wanted turns out to be the last thing he needs. When loneliness threatens to derail Kendall's good behavior, he decides to rent out his spare bedroom. What could go wrong? Try a tenant who's temptation incarnate.

Bad at commitment or born to roam? Either way, US Deputy Marshal Kurt Dandridge feels trapped. Maybe staying in one place for too long is the source of his unhappiness, or maybe it's because he's engaged to the wrong person. Finding his fiancé in bed with another man takes care of one problem but creates another. Ridge needs a place to live. He'd leave Savannah altogether if not for his vow to apprehend an elusive fugitive. Renting a room from Kendall Blakemore seems like the perfect solution until Ridge finds himself falling for the alluring man. Would one kiss derail his course? And could he stop at just one?

Hurts so good. Chemistry burns between them—hot, consuming, and impossible to ignore. And why should they? Kendall and Ridge are consenting adults who know the score. Being bad has never felt so good, but it's a slippery slope to navigate. One misstep could have disastrous consequences for both men.

Bad at Love is a standalone novel within the *Sinister in Savannah* universe where both characters first appeared. It is not necessary to read that series first. *Bad at Love* is a romantic suspense that's heavier on the romance than the suspense.

For Cheryl Kaiser
Thank you for patiently answering all my questions and making me fall in love with Ridge's beloved Montana. You're a doll, and I appreciate you so much!

Chapter One

US Deputy Marshal Kurt Dandridge shook his head at the fugitive covered in cake and frosting. "You shouldn't have come to your grandmother's birthday party, Tiggy."

"Didn't I tell you I always catch my guy?" Zack Beaumont asked as he assisted the handcuffed man into the back of the SUV.

Zack reminded Ridge of a tawny lion, but not just because of his unique hair and eye color. Strength and power radiated off the man. And like the majestic cat he resembled, Zack had patiently stalked his prey until Tiggy Barnes had made a fatal mistake. He shouldn't have stopped at his favorite watering hole for a drink because Zack, along with Ridge and Eddie Chandler, had been there, in the tall grass, waiting to pounce.

Every lawman has an unsolved case that consumes their thoughts, and most criminals have a soft spot for at least one person. The key to capturing the bad guy was discovering their weakness and setting a trap. Timothy "Tiggy" Barnes was Zack's elusive fugitive, and Tiggy's soft spot was Beulah Barnes, the grandmother who'd raised him. Zack had stalked the social media accounts of Tiggy's known relatives and had known it was time to strike when he saw the announcement for the birthday party in Tallahassee.

They'd set up shop on the street behind granny's house a few days before the party so they could watch the people coming and going. After three days with no Tiggy sighting, it had seemed Zack had overestimated

Beulah's importance to the arms dealer until the man stepped out of the house carrying an enormous birthday cake. Living on the run hadn't been kind to the fugitive. Tiggy had gained at least fifty pounds and lost most of his hair. Ridge might've thought it was a close relative if not for his distinctive tattoos.

Joy and relief flashed in his friend's golden-brown eyes as he high-fived Ridge and Eddie after a successful mission. Ridge knew he'd look just as dopey on the day he finally slapped handcuffs on Sheldon Harris's wrists.

Eddie ducked down to look at Tiggy. The marshal's white-blond hair and vibrant green eyes gave him a youthful appearance that made it easy for fugitives to underestimate him. Tiggy had learned his lesson the hard way when he'd dropped the cake and made a run for freedom after the trio of marshals identified themselves. Eddie, a former defensive end, had tackled him to the ground just as he'd done to the quarterbacks in college. Slamming into a brick wall at full speed would be softer than running into Eddie. Maybe the cake had softened the impact a little. "That must've been some cake for you to risk your freedom. What was it? Marble with whipped cream icing?"

Tiggy scowled at the suggestion. "Hummingbird cake, and fuck you, man. My granny means everything to me, and she might not be around much longer. I planned on turning myself in tomorrow."

"Sure you did," Zack said.

Tiggy had been on their most-wanted list for over three years. He'd had ample time to turn himself in and hadn't done it. None of the marshals believed his bullshit for a second.

Eddie sighed. "Hummingbird cake is my favorite. I probably would've gambled on it too."

Ridge looked over at the porch where the ninety-year-old woman was holding court with about two dozen family members. The white-haired lady met his gaze head-on and lifted her chin a few notches. "Sorry about your ruined party and cake, ma'am." Beulah Barnes flipped him off. Stifling a chuckle, he said, "She'll outlive us all," then slid into the back with the gunrunner. "What kind of name is Tiggy, anyway?"

"My baby sister couldn't say Timothy and called me Tiggy. She'd been on a big *Winnie the Pooh* kick, and Tigger was her favorite character." That explained the tattoo of the cartoon tiger on his forearm. "I was a super hyper kid, always bouncing around, so maybe she thought I was like him. The name just stuck all these years, even though I resemble the chubby bear these days."

Ridge spent most of the four-and-a-half-hour drive in speculative silence. As happy as he was for Zack, he couldn't stop thinking about his elusive fugitive. He cycled through the steps he'd taken to locate Sheldon Harris. Unlike Tiggy, Ridge had been unable to find a soft spot for the Cardoza cartel hitman.

"What's your problem?" Tiggy asked, breaking into his thoughts. "You the strong silent kind or something?"

"Man troubles," Eddie said from the front seat.

Tiggy's eyebrows arched toward his forehead. "You like dudes?"

Ridge glared at the man. "Is that a problem for you?"

"Hell no," Tiggy said quickly. "To each their own, my granny always said. You just look so…um…masculine."

"It's called butch," Eddie said.

"Are you one too?" Tiggy asked.

Eddie pivoted in his seat and leveled a menacing look at the arms dealer. "Am I *one* too?"

Tiggy had the decency to look properly chastised. "Sorry," he said to Ridge. "I didn't mean any offense. I'm never sure what I'm allowed to say these days."

"You sell illegal guns to motorcycle gangs and drug cartels, and you're worried about using politically correct language?" Ridge asked.

Tiggy shrugged. "I used to be a nice Southern gentleman." Ridge was curious to know what had happened to set the man on this course but refused to ask. "It's okay to ask someone if they're gay or queer."

"Really? That last one used to be an insult."

"They're reclaiming the word," Eddie informed him. "And context matters. Using those words in a derogatory way isn't cool."

"You sound like an HR video," Zack said. Eddie flipped him off.

"Are you gay too?" Tiggy asked.

"I'm not," Eddie replied, "but my best friend is, so I made an effort to learn the language."

Ridge chuckled. "He's perused the urban dictionary. I have never used the term *butch* to describe myself or anyone else."

"What kind of man troubles are you having?" Tiggy inquired.

Ridge scowled at him. "I am not discussing my boyfriend with you."

Zack snorted from the driver's seat. "For starters, Dandridge can't seem to remember he has a fiancé."

"Huh?" Ziggy asked. "You're juggling two guys?"

Eddie laughed. "The boyfriend *is* the fiancé, but for some reason, Deputy Marshal Dandridge can't remember the status upgrade."

"*Upgrade,*" Zack grumbled. "He can't remember because they're not right for each other."

"Not this again," Ridge said under his breath.

"Oh, this sounds interesting," Tiggy said, straightening in his seat. "Lay it on me."

"First of all, a carnivore and a vegan have no business being together," Zack said. "It's the same as someone wanting kids marrying someone who can't stand them. How does anyone think there's a suitable outcome there?"

"It's not the same thing at all," Ridge countered.

"Oh, really? Where's the compromise?" Eddie asked. "He expects you to give up all meat and animal byproducts. What are you supposed to dunk Oreos in?"

"Almond milk," Ridge replied, proud he kept the horror out of his voice.

"Gross," the three other men in the car said simultaneously.

"What's his sacrifice?" Zack asked.

Ridge tried to come up with a response to defend Todd but mentally flailed. His boyfriend—*fiancé*—was an all-or-nothing guy. Compromise wasn't in his repertoire.

"That's just the tip of the iceberg," Eddie said. "I've never seen two people so ill-suited for each other."

"Then why did you get engaged?" Tiggy asked.

Ridge pinned him with a dark look. "I think you should worry more about yourself right now."

Tiggy just shrugged and changed the subject, leaving Ridge to look out the window and contemplate the conversation he needed to have with Todd. His friends were right. They weren't a good fit. They weren't in love, and Ridge doubted they'd ever experienced anything deeper than infatuation, but that had been in the beginning, and those feelings had long since faded. Getting engaged had been a mistake. Ridge could see it clearly now, and he even understood what had prompted it. He'd have to untangle the mess he'd made of his personal life.

"Aw, that's so sweet," Tiggy said, yanking Ridge back to the conversation happening around him.

He noticed both Tiggy and Eddie were looking at him while Zack glanced at him in the rearview mirror. "What?"

"Your friends have already picked out your next fiancé," Tiggy replied.

Ridge rolled his eyes. "There won't be another fiancé." He'd never allow himself to get tangled in someone else's vines ever again. Loose and free would be his motto going forward. "And I'm not having this conversation again."

Zack and Eddie had taken every opportunity to mention a guy named Kendall, who they'd met at a barbecue at their inspector's house. Ridge had gotten in trouble with Todd for eating chili at Asher's house the last time he'd attended a cookout there, so he'd been banned from attending.

"So sensitive," Tiggy grumbled.

Ignoring him, Ridge said, "How'd you like it if I kept pushing other women at you guys?"

Zack snorted, and Eddie laughed. Ridge loved Emma and Jess, their respective girlfriends, and they both knew it. He flipped them off and stewed the rest of the way back to Savannah.

"You go on home," Eddie told Ridge once they parked at the field office just after midnight. "We'll get Tiggy booked."

He started to protest but saw the determined look in his best friend's eyes.

"Fine," Ridge said as he unbuckled his seat belt and opened the door. "I'll tell my boyfriend you said hello."

"Fiancé," his friends and Tiggy replied.

Fuck.

Ridge's adrenaline started to wane not long after he pulled out of the parking lot. The upscale apartment he shared with Todd had felt more like a battlefield lately, but their soft bed beckoned.

Ridge collected his gear from the back of his SUV and headed toward the building. Their apartment complex was exclusive, elegant, and expensive, which came with some excellent security features. Most of the residents were young professionals, so it was always quiet when he came home in the middle of the night. That explained why the doorman was fast asleep at his desk when Ridge entered his code and stepped inside the lobby. He cleared his throat to wake the man and continued to the elevators.

Ridge's tension ebbed as he rode up to the fourth floor, and it had nearly disappeared by the time he unlocked the door and stepped into his apartment. His stress returned tenfold when he was immediately greeted by a throaty *meow*. Samson, Todd's cat who looked more like a miniature lion, leaped onto the foyer table, knocking the mail onto the floor. Ridge set his bags down and reached for the tawny beast who'd stolen his heart.

"Hey there, big guy," Ridge said as he scratched behind the cat's ears, earning a rumbling purr as a reward. "What are you doing out here?" Sammy always slept in bed with Todd. The only exception was when they were—

The adrenaline that had left him for dead on the side of the road reappeared suddenly. "I don't fucking believe it." Ridge gently set Sammy down and cut across the room and down the hallway to the master bedroom. Sure enough, the door was closed. Should he knock to alert the lying son of a bitch he was home or just open the door and confirm what he'd known for weeks, maybe months?

Ridge chose the latter option and flipped on the light switch. "Honey, I'm home," he said, his false cheer echoing in the still room.

Two men jackknifed into a sitting position on the bed. Todd's mouth gaped open in surprise while Todd's boss, Richard, clutched the sheet to his chest and trembled in fear.

Todd recovered first and said, "You're not supposed to be home for a few more days."

"Obviously," Ridge quipped. He shook his head and went to the closet to remove his suitcase and garment bag. He didn't own much, so it wouldn't take him long to pack and leave—something he should've done a long time ago. Ridge swung the luggage onto the bed, not caring if he clipped Richard's legs in the process.

"What are you doing?" Todd asked.

"Oh my god," Richard said. "Is that where he keeps his guns?"

Ridge met the older man's gaze. The signs had been there. The late dinners, the constant texting, and the almost possessive exchanges during the few times Ridge had attended events at Richard's art gallery. He'd known something was going on between the two men but hadn't listened to his gut. Todd had spent way too much time accusing Ridge of nonexistent infidelity, and now he realized his soon-to-be ex-boyfriend was projecting his guilt.

"I wouldn't risk a life sentence or the death penalty on either of you," Ridge said.

Richard heaved a deep sigh and sagged against the headboard while Todd attempted to murder Ridge with his furious gaze. He'd have to try harder because Ridge was tough to kill.

Throwing back the covers, Todd advanced on Ridge. "That's all you have to say?"

Ridge spared him a glance before he started emptying the dresser drawers into his suitcase. "It's all I'm willing to say right now." Once finished, he started toward the closet again to retrieve his suits.

Todd slid in front of him, blocking the way. "This is all your fault."

Ridge breathed deeply through his nose, unwilling to participate in the fight Todd wanted to have with him. No matter what he said, Todd would turn his words around. His fiancé had been gaslighting him for months. *Now you remember he's your fiancé?* The thought put a smile on his face, which apparently dumped gasoline on Todd's fire.

"Oh, you think this is funny?" Todd asked, shoving against Ridge's chest. He was too heavy to move with such a pitiful attempt. He'd more than lived up to his family's built-like-a-mountain moniker, so Todd's feeble efforts made him chuckle.

"Honey, I don't think it's wise to provoke the man," Richard said from the bed.

Ridge quirked a brow at the pet name the older man had used but didn't remark. His silence only made Todd angrier, and Ridge was starting to enjoy the show. Todd's pale skin was turning a shade of red he'd only seen in cartoons. Would steam come out of his ears next?

"If you were here more, I wouldn't have started looking for another man to keep me company," Todd said.

It was apparent Todd wasn't going to step aside until he'd had his say. Ridge wasn't about to forcibly move him and risk ending up with Todd filing allegations of domestic abuse. He also realized he couldn't ignore the man forever, so Ridge braced himself for the confrontation and met Todd's gaze.

"You knew I was a marshal when we met," Ridge said. "Not once have you ever asked me to change careers. Besides, this is the first time I've left town in months."

Todd snorted. "You wouldn't have switched jobs, and I didn't feel like wasting my breath."

"You weren't concerned about your personal air conservation when you spent every free moment accusing me of fucking around," Ridge said.

His former fiancé tilted his chin up. "I wasn't referring to your career, anyway. In fact, it's the only fun thing about you."

Ridge snorted. "Nice deflection."

Todd crossed his arms over his chest. "I was talking about your absence when you were home. You might've physically been in the same room with me, but you weren't here. You were never engaged in conversation or…sex. You're selfish, Ridge. I need more—in and out of bed."

Ridge refused to let Todd's blow land. "Then why are you blocking my way to the closet? Why not let me collect my things and leave?"

"He asks a good question, dear," Richard said.

Honey? Dear? Were they suddenly in an episode of an old sitcom?

"Not now, Richard," Todd said snidely. "I have things I need to say."

"I don't care to hear them," Ridge replied.

Todd spoke over him and said, "Once he leaves, I won't get another opportunity."

"You got that right," Ridge agreed.

Ignoring him, Todd added, "And I want closure so this isn't hanging over our relationship."

"Fine," Richard said. "I'll just get dressed and go into the living room."

"No," Todd and Ridge said at the same time.

"Stay where you are, Dick," Ridge said.

"This won't take long," Todd added. "It *never* does with him." That insult landed hard, but Ridge must not have shown it outwardly because Todd's smirk melted like an ice cream cone in August. Todd shook his head and sighed. "Never mind. I'm not going to waste my breath." Todd stepped aside, clearing Ridge's path to the closet and gesturing for him to continue.

Instead of retreating to the bed, Todd followed Ridge into the closet and did the opposite of what he'd just declared. He wasted a ton of air and energy berating everything about Ridge, from how he dressed to what he ate. The verbal abuse continued through clearing out the bathroom and his nightstand, but Ridge didn't engage. He just smiled, shook his head, or laughed at the incredibly ridiculous complaints.

Once finished, Ridge stopped at the foot of the bed and faced Richard, who managed to look both shell-shocked and remorseful. "Good luck, pal," Ridge said, then headed for the door.

"You asshole," Todd said, following him down the hall into the living room.

Ridge stopped by the front door long enough to work the apartment key off his ring. He dropped it onto the foyer table and reached for the doorknob, only stopping when he heard Sammy meowing by his feet. He could blow off everything about the apartment and even the man he'd shared it with but not the fluffy little guy. Ridge set his bags on the floor and hoisted the cat into his arms.

"I'm going to miss you, Sammy."

"His name is Samson," Todd said. "Jesus. You show more affection to my cat than you ever did to me."

Ridge met Todd's furious gaze. "Damn right I do," he said calmly. "He's more deserving."

Todd tilted his head to the side. "Why aren't you angrier?"

Ridge dropped a kiss on Sammy's head and set him on the foyer table because he knew it would infuriate Todd, who was too stupid to realize you couldn't train a cat. They trained you. Ridge stroked his hand over Sammy's sleek back, and the furry bastard arched up into his caress, purring loudly beneath his ministrations. The sound had always brought him comfort after long days on the job.

"I asked you a question," Todd said.

Ridge took a deep breath, opened the apartment door, and picked up his luggage from the floor. "I'm plenty angry." He allowed Todd to wallow in his aggrandized victory before he lowered the boom. "I'm pissed I let you gaslight me when you were the one fucking around. I'm furious I allowed this farce to continue for as long as I did. I resent the times I felt guilty for eating meat behind your back. It wasn't just chili at that one barbecue."

Todd glared. "So you are a cheater."

"It's not the same thing, and we both know it." Ridge stepped out into the hallway. "Mostly, I regret the day we met. There's nothing I can do about that now, so I'm going to move forward and have a wonderful life. Best of luck to you and Richard."

Todd responded by slamming the door in his face. Ridge walked away without looking back. The doorman had fallen asleep again when he reached the lobby. Ridge just shook his head and kept walking.

The reality of his situation punched him in the face when he stepped into the muggy night. Where the hell was he going to go? He knew Zack and Eddie were still awake, but they would be reconnecting with their girlfriends. Besides, thirty-five was a bit old to be crashing on his buddy's sofa.

A hotel was the sensible solution, so he got into his SUV and headed toward the closest one. A sign with a giant neon airplane caught his attention like a flashy beacon in the dark. It was reminiscent of something Ridge would expect to find in Vegas, not Savannah.

Ridge drove past the hotel and the next one too, heading toward the club as if on autopilot. The Cockpit was a popular gay club that happened to serve the best wings, or so he'd heard from Zack and Eddie, who'd soaked up adoration from the waiters as they'd mowed through wings and fries without him. *Assholes.*

A cute brunet dressed like a sexy flight attendant stood at the host station when he walked in. He lit up like a firecracker when his gaze met Ridge's. He opened his mouth to talk but was interrupted by a waiter who spoke in a low but urgent tone. Ridge didn't mind because it allowed him to check out the club's interior.

Holy hell. He'd expected an over-the-top theme, but this was like nothing he'd ever seen before. The warehouse had been converted into a multi-level club with ceilings so high in the main section actual planes hung suspended from the metal rafters. The stage was constructed to look like a giant airplane wing, and male dancers wearing angel wings and silver G-strings gyrated to the loud music on platforms above the crowd. The waiters wore pilot hats, aviators, mesh crop tops, and navy-blue booty shorts with gold wings on the crotch and the club's name on the back. Ridge glanced over at the bar and saw the bartenders all wore green flight suits like military pilots.

"Hi. I'm Seth."

Ridge glanced back at the host station and smiled. "Hi, Seth." He didn't offer up his name, causing the flight attendant to pout prettily.

"Will you be dining alone, or is someone joining you?"

"Just me, but I plan on eating enough wings for three people."

Seth smiled. "This way," he said, tilting his head toward the dining area.

Ridge followed him to a table in the center of the room. "Colt will be right over to take your order. I hope you enjoy, handsome."

Ridge smiled and shook his head when the flight attendant walked away, then scrubbed his hands over his face. What a fucking night. Hell, what a fucking week. A waiter stopped at the table across from his, and Ridge got a whiff of something spicy and sweet. His mouth watered as he looked at the heaping plate of wings the waiter set down.

The cute guy turned and smiled at Ridge. "Well, hello. My name is Colt, and I'll be taking *excellent* care of you tonight. Can I start you off with something to drink?"

Ridge ignored the flirtation and pointed to the neighboring table. "What flavor are those wings?"

Colt smiled coyly. "Regret."

How fitting. Ridge chuckled, then said, "I'll start with a dozen."

Chapter Two

THE KEY TO GAINING FREEDOM LAY IN WAIT AT THE END OF THE corridor. All Kendall had to do was traverse the thirty or forty feet to the employee breakroom and clock out. Easy peasy. He'd be home in bed by twelve thirty and could log six solid hours of shut-eye before starting his day job. The thought of spending eight or ten hours at the law office made his stomach pitch. *But this is what you wanted. A respectable career as a paralegal to prove Stanton wrong.*

Kendall slammed on the mental brakes and steered his mind in a healthier direction. His stepfather was the opposite of good for his health. *I am enough. I am enough.* Maybe he'd start to believe it after adequate repetition. One more time for good measure. *I am enough.*

And how long was this damn hallway? Was he trapped in a bad dream? Kendall's legs were moving, but he wasn't gaining any ground. With each step, his legs felt heavier and more sluggish. Six hours of hauling a heavy food tray at The Cockpit while avoiding handsy patrons wore a guy out more than leg day at the gym. Damn, the men in Savannah were hungry and horny—for both the wings and the waiters who delivered them. Kendall had discreetly tossed out the phone numbers written on napkins a few of the bolder men had given him. Old Kendall wouldn't have hesitated to use them or spend his break time with a cutie in the parking lot, but he wasn't that guy anymore. He'd turned over a new leaf…or was trying to.

Rapidly approaching feet and hushed whispers reached Kendall's ears as he neared the breakroom door. He recognized the voices and knew they'd only cause him trouble, so he willed his tired feet to move faster. He cleared the doorway and had made it to the computerized timecard system before the duo of doom burst into the small, nondescript room. The owner had put a ton of money and detail into the rest of the club, but the employees were stuck with metal folding chairs and a rickety-ass card table someone must've found at a yard sale.

His pursuers panted heavily in the small space, and against his better judgment, Kendall turned to see what Colt and Carey wanted. The two buff waiters, both with dark hair and dark eyes, had arms braced against the wall while they caught their breaths. Their looks and mannerisms were so similar that most people thought Colt and Carey were brothers. Their frequent petty squabbles did nothing to dispel the opinion. Kendall knew better because he'd taken the time to look beyond the obvious or misleading in this case. He'd gotten to know them and learned they'd been best friends since childhood. Where one went, the other followed. Over time, they'd started assuming one another's habits.

"Fellas," he said jovially, "maybe you need to spend more time on the cardio equipment and less time weightlifting."

Colt scowled. "We're in great shape." This was said between pants, so Kendall quirked a brow to silently refute his statement.

Carey straightened to his full height and stuck out his chest, looking more like a Chippendale dancer than a waiter. "I'm fine as fuck."

"And I don't disagree," Kendall said, hoping to soothe the guy's ruffled feathers so he could clock out and go home.

"You just move so fast," Colt commented. "Jesus, I thought the building was on fire."

"Probably has a hot date," Carey added.

Kendall smiled at the best friends, choosing to keep them guessing rather than tell the sad truth. The only date he had was with his bed and pillow. It was his favorite threesome of late. Maybe his fist would make a brief appearance, but that wasn't likely. Working two jobs had caught up to him, making Kendall duller than dull—in and out of the bedroom. Regardless, he didn't have time for their antics.

He could clock out, but he'd have to walk through them to get out the door. It would be so much easier to find out what the hell they wanted, so he asked.

"We need you to settle a bet," Colt said.

Kendall didn't bother hiding a groan. "No way." He punched in his employee number, accessed the menu, and clocked out at the stroke of midnight. Kendall had zero interest in getting involved in one of their stupid bets on a normal night and was especially averse to the idea when he had an important deposition to attend in eight hours. "I gotta go," he said and headed toward the door.

Carey turned and looked at Colt. "If a guy doesn't respond to my flirting, then he's straight. Plain and simple."

"Not this again," Kendall grumbled at the same time Colt let out a shocked gasp.

"What are you saying? You think I'm ugly?" Colt asked, turning his body and stepping so close they formed an immovable wall of muscle. Kendall bit back another groan, not that they'd have heard it. The men had forgotten he was even in the room.

"No," Carey replied quickly. "You're just more subtle in your flirtation."

Colt snorted. "While you take the bull-in-an-antique-store approach."

"China shop," Kendall said.

Colt looked at him. "Huh?"

Kendall shook his head. "Never mind. What's it going to take for me to settle this argument peacefully?" He had both men's attention.

Carey smiled. "Check on the patron at table twenty. Flirt a little." Carey turned to Colt. "If he doesn't hit on Sugar, we'll know for sure he's straight."

"I agree," Colt said.

Sugar. Oh, how he hated that nickname.

"Get out of here," Kendall said, rolling his eyes at their ridiculous claim.

"You're irresistible," Carey said.

"Like sugar," Colt added, sounding earnest and sweet. The wicked gleam in his eyes betrayed him as the manipulative little shit Kendall knew him to be. "Guys want to lick you like—"

Kendall held up his hand to cut him off. "Yeah, there's no need for a metaphor. I got it."

"Meta what?"

"Never mind," Kendall said. "Table twenty?"

Colt clapped his hands. "Yes. I can't wait until you prove the hottie *is* into guys."

"What will you win?"

Colt smiled. "I'm not telling."

"Let me get this straight," Kendall said, placing his hands on his hips. "You want me to go out there and make an ass of myself, but you're not willing to say what prize is at stake?"

A dark blush bloomed across Colt's cheeks. "It's private and personal."

Ahh. Kendall heaved a heavy sigh. "Move." The two friends did as he demanded, leaving enough room for him to squeeze through. Kendall paused at the threshold but kept his gaze forward. "And the two of you should fuck already. Everyone around you would be grateful."

Colt gasped, and Carey chuckled. How Kendall knew that without looking was a testament to how much time he'd spent in their company. He heard the friends following behind him but could tell it was at a distance.

"Slow down," Carey urged. "We need to be in position so we can spy on your progress."

"Or you could just call the whole thing off," Kendall said over his shoulder.

"No way," Colt said.

Ignoring them, Kendall headed back out into the dining room section of the club. Colt and Carey were ridiculous, but they had hella good taste in men, so Kendall was expecting a looker. The mountain of a man with short, dark hair was beyond handsome, even with wing sauce smeared on the corner of his mouth. Dark assessing eyes glanced in his direction and held, raking over Kendall from head to toe as his long legs made quick work of the distance between them. Full lips parted, and his brawny hand stilled in the air. A chicken wing swayed between his fingertips but didn't fall to the plate. Big, broad, and beautiful took his time trailing his gaze back up to meet Kendall's face.

The guy definitely wasn't straight, but maybe he was still questioning or denying his sexuality.

Kendall stopped at his table and smiled. "Hello."

The swinging chicken wing slid from his sauce-slicked fingers and fell. Kendall imagined Colt was cheering from his hiding place while Carey groaned. And just what the hell was the payout going to be? Kendall might've given the bet more thought if the sexy man at table twenty hadn't swallowed hard. The bobbing of his throat had a strange effect on Kendall, and he found himself reaching for the glass of water on the table. Enticing a man like that could go to a fella's head and cause him to do stupid things.

"Um," the guy said when Kendall put the cup to his lips and took a long sip. "I was drinking that."

Too late to change course, Kendall shrugged and studied the man over the rim of the glass. He couldn't tell if his eyes were brown or dark blue, but the bouncing lights from the disco ball revealed dark red strands of hair instead of brown or black as he'd first thought. More chestnut than auburn.

Kendall set the glass down with a clink. "Sorry. Long night."

Ridge barked out a dry laugh. "You can say that again."

Instead of repeating himself, Kendall pulled out the chair across from the stranger and sat down.

The man continued to stare intently for a moment before speaking. "What are you doing?"

Kendall returned his scrutiny, noticing the weariness creeping into the handsome guy's expression. Shrugging, Kendall said, "Hell if I know." His remark earned him a half smile. "What's your name?"

"Ridge."

Kendall quirked a brow. "What a unique name. I think that's a character in the soap opera my elderly babysitter used to watch." The comment triggered memories of the simpler times he longed for. Rather than wallow in sadness, Kendall turned all his attention to the handsome stranger mowing through another wing. "Is Ridge a nickname or short for something else?"

Ridge dropped the cleaned bone onto his plate and took a napkin from the pile. He wiped his hands thoroughly but didn't remove the smear of sauce from his face. "Nickname. My name is Kurt Dandridge, but my friends and family call me Ridge. It's both a family joke and a shortened version of my last name."

Kendall planted his elbow on the table and dropped his chin onto his upturned palm. "I'm curious about the family joke part."

Ridge tilted his head to the side, then looked around the club. "Shouldn't you be checking on patrons in your section?"

"I've already clocked out, so I'm all yours." A flash of heat washed over him at the montage of suggestions his libido wanted to make. All of them were dirty and delicious but entirely off the table. *Damn it.* He was about to clear the air in case Ridge thought Kendall had offered himself up as dessert, but Ridge smiled wickedly.

"Good to know," he said, dropping his gaze to the name tag Kendall still wore. "Sugar, huh?" Ridge picked up another wing and sank his teeth into it. Kendall couldn't recall a time he'd been so turned on. He wanted the big bruiser to manhandle him like a chicken wing.

He took another sip of Ridge's water, earning an incredulous glare. *Oops.* Drinking after strangers was gross, yet he'd done it twice in a row without a single thought for his health or safety. He didn't want to delve too deeply into his actions because the repressed parts of him would start suggesting other things belonging to Ridge that Kendall could stick in his mouth.

"About this nickname…"

"I look just like my dad, who everyone refers to as a mountain of a man."

"Ah, I see," Kendall said. "That made you his little mountain ridge."

Without thinking, Kendall reached across the table and wiped the smear of sauce off Ridge's lips, then brought his thumb to his own mouth to clean it. "Mmmm. Tastes like Regret."

Ridge stared at Kendall's mouth for much longer than appropriate before looking back up. The penetrative stare made Kendall want to wiggle like a worm on a hook or Kendall on a big cock. He was an unapologetic size queen, and this guy…*No. No. And hell no.*

"The sauce perfectly describes my mood."

"Uh-oh," Kendall said. "Sounds like trouble."

Ridge's answering smile was diabolical. "Something tells me you're intimately acquainted with trouble."

"We have a love-hate relationship," Kendall admitted. "We're not on speaking terms right now."

"Pity."

Don't I know it. "So what brought you to the point where you're scarfing down extremely hot chicken wings with no regard for your safety?"

"You drank all my water," Ridge said, nodding toward the empty glass.

"So I did. I'll get you a clean glass." Kendall pushed his chair away from the table, but Ridge reached out and snagged his wrist before he could stand up.

"Stay. I like you."

"Thank you."

Ridge chuckled. "Not going to return the sentiment?"

"I don't know you, so how do I know if I like you?" Kendall leaned forward and dropped his voice. "I like what I see a whole lot, but I'm not the answer to whatever is bothering you." Kendall cocked his head. "I'm a good listener, though."

Ridge's expression turned momentarily dark until he blinked it away. "What happened to the other guys, Frick and Frack?"

Kendall's mouth fell open in surprise. Once he caught his breath, he flopped back in his chair and laughed until tears filled his eyes. "Frick and Frack?"

Ridge just shrugged. "Suits them."

"Maybe so," Kendall agreed. "They, um…" Kendall turned and looked to see where they might be hiding and was surprised the two knuckleheads were nowhere in sight.

"What?" Ridge asked, pulling Kendall's attention back to him. "Let me guess. They placed a bet about me."

"How'd you know?"

"I know the type," Ridge said casually. "Their egos won't allow them to believe I'm not attracted to them, so I had to be straight. Am I right?"

"They don't mean to be insulting. They're young and—"

Ridge waved him off. "I'm not offended, but I am curious. Why'd they send you to the table?"

"They claim I'm irresistible," Kendall replied with a dramatic eye roll.

Ridge's nostrils flared on his next inhale. "Yeah, I can see that."

The compliment heated Kendall's cheeks, and he suddenly wished he hadn't drained the water glass. "You're too sweet."

Ridge snorted. "That's a word no one has ever used to describe me."

"Really?"

"Yep." He pointed to Kendall's name tag. "With a nickname like Sugar, I'm willing to bet plenty of people think you're sweet."

"How do you know it's a nickname?"

Ridge quirked a brow and dropped another bone to his plate. "You expect me to believe your mother named you Sugar?"

"She said I had the sweetest little face she'd ever seen."

"Okay," Ridge said, "I'll bite. What's your full name?"

"Sugar And Spice."

Ridge blessed him with a full belly laugh. "Kind of like this sauce. The person who named it must have a wicked sense of humor."

"I'll be sure to pass your kind words along," Kendall said.

"And they're excellent at pairing flavors too. It starts out sweet, then comes on strong at the end."

Kendall reached across the table and helped himself to a french fry Ridge was ignoring. "Much like regret the emotion." He bit through the perfectly fried potato.

"True." Ridge ate another wing before wiping his hands and mouth. "So, what are the special ingredients?"

"They wouldn't be special if I told you," Kendall said.

"I'm not here to steal the recipe and start my own business."

Kendall winked at him. "Good to know. I still can't share the recipe with you."

"Can't or won't?"

"Can't."

"Fine," Ridge said, but Kendall saw the fierce determination in his eyes.

Yes, baby. Tie me up and bang the truth out of me. Kendall nearly choked on his own saliva as soon as the thought crossed his mind.

Ridge pushed a glass of milk toward him, but Kendall waved it off.

"Not choking, just clumsy."

"Doubt it," Ridge said. "I watched you glide to my table."

"It was more of a saunter."

"It was graceful and fluid." Ridge's eyes darkened, and Kendall was quite sure of the direction his thoughts had gone.

Damn it. Kendall's mind followed down the same path. He'd definitely invite his fist to the slumber party when he got home. He needed to head in that direction and catch as much sleep as possible, but thoughts of never seeing Ridge again kept his ass planted firmly in the chair.

"What sorrows are you trying to drown in a plate of wings?" Kendall asked, hoping to steer the conversation in a safer direction.

"I feel like this is all give and take here," Ridge replied. "I'm doing all the giving while you're lying back and..." His cheeks turned bright pink. "That wasn't very appropriate."

"Please," Kendall said, casually waving him off as if his dick weren't stiffening in his spandex boy shorts. No, he wasn't imagining himself at the mercy of Ridge's big body as he rammed into him over and over.

"I'll show you mine if you show me yours."

Kendall met his gaze once more. "Really? That's the cheesiest pickup line ever. It's almost a dad joke."

Ridge winced. "Ouch."

"Sorry." Kendall took a deep breath. "You have a deal, but you're going first. Spill."

"I caught my fiancé in bed with his boss about twenty minutes ago."

Whoa. "Seriously?"

"Uh-huh." Ridge's lips curved upward at the corners.

"And you're smiling?" Kendall couldn't imagine something so awful.

Ridge tilted his head for a second as if considering his circumstances. "Yeah, I am. The asshole did me a favor. I mean, I'm not thrilled about finding a new place to live, and I'm going to miss Sammy."

"Who's that?"

"Todd's cat."

"Todd, huh?" Kendall asked. "That's the male equivalent of Karen."

Ridge laughed. "So it is." He took a deep breath and released it slowly. "I really loved that cat."

Kendall leaned closer. "Want someone to steal the cat for you? I'm not qualified, but I know a guy who knows several guys."

Ridge assessed him through narrowed eyes. "You really are trouble."

Sighing, Kendall said, "I don't try to be."

"It just comes naturally?"

"Something like that."

Ridge continued to study him for a few moments before his lips curved into a wry smile. "I don't believe you."

Kendall ate another fry. "You should because, while I'm bad at many things, being honest isn't one of them."

"Okay, I'll play. Name one thing you're bad at."

"Love," Kendall replied without hesitation.

Ridge flopped back against his chair and laughed.

"What's so funny?" Kendall asked.

Ridge wiped his mouth and hands. "We make quite a pair."

"Oh? How so?"

"You're bad at love, and I'm bad in bed," Ridge said.

His remark was so ridiculous Kendall could only blink for a moment. He raked his gaze over the man's big, thick body and refused to believe it.

"You're not bad in bed. Who told you that? The loser you caught cheating with his boss?" Kendall snorted. "How fucking original, by the way."

"I'm selfish and inattentive," Ridge countered. Were those insults his ex had thrown at him or things he actually believed about himself?

Kendall extended his hand across the table. "Hi, I make brash decisions and give my heart away too easily."

Ridge smiled and shook his hand. "Is this a weekly occurrence for you?"

"Nah. Only when I'm lonely."

"I see," Ridge said.

Kendall heaved a sigh. "And I'm fast approaching the intersection of lonesome and reckless. How's that for honesty?"

"Refreshing," Ridge replied. "Reckless, huh? I never would've guessed."

Kendall shrugged. "You still win the trophy for the shittiest night."

"Not a contest I asked for."

"It's still the hand you were dealt," Kendall countered. "But you're in luck."

Ridge's hand flew to his chest. "Luckier than earning a trophy I don't want?"

Kendall found it impossible not to be charmed by the boyish smile on such a masculine face. "Way luckier." He nibbled on another fry to allow the suspense to build. "I'm going to impart my hard-earned wisdom about how to recover from a broken heart."

Ridge reclined against the back of his seat and crossed his arms over his chest. "I don't have a broken heart."

"Fine. A bruised ego then," Kendall replied, raising his hand when Ridge started to protest. "No one leaves a situation like yours unscathed."

The big man drew in a deep breath. "Fine."

"Do you want to take notes?" Kendall asked.

Smirking, Ridge tapped his temple. "I have an excellent memory." He lifted his glass and took a long drink of milk.

"Suit yourself," Kendall quipped. "Option number one is to engage in a glorious rebound fuck. Todd's nemesis would be a good place to start."

Ridge choked and sputtered for a few seconds. "I can't wait to hear the other options."

Kendall laughed. "They're tamer, I promise."

"Do tell," Ridge said and gestured for him to continue.

"You could write a poem or a song about your feelings."

Ridge snorted. "Not gonna happen. What else do you have in your bag of tricks?"

"You could lie around in baggy sweatpants and eat junk food while binge-watching true-crime documentaries."

"I'm now homeless," Ridge reminded him.

"Yes, well, that is an issue."

"I can crash at a buddy's or stay at a hotel," Ridge said. "Don't worry about me."

Relief washed over Kendall. "Oh, good."

"But my very existence revolves around crime," Ridge added, "so I'll take a pass on the true-crime documentaries."

"Law enforcement?"

"Yep. What else do you have?"

Kendall considered the options. "There's all kinds of trashy reality television available. Nothing makes you feel better about your life than watching someone else's shitshow."

"Hard pass," Ridge said. "Sports is the only reality show I watch."

"Hmmm. You could discover a new podcast." Kendall snapped his fingers when the perfect solution came to him. "There's this one out of the UK where a guy reads the erotica novel his dad wrote while his friends react."

Ridge chuckled. "*My Dad Wrote a Porno*, right? I've heard of that one. My best friends won't shut up about it."

"Glad to see they have good taste," Kendall said.

Ridge tapped a finger to his lips for a second before lowering his hand. "These are all things you've tried?"

"To cure a breakup? God no. I firmly fall into the rebound-fuck camp." Kendall pointed at his chest. "Bad at love. Hell on the heart. I want better for you, though."

"Do as you say, not as you do?" Ridge asked.

"Something like that."

Ridge shook his head and tore into another wing.

"Well, I guess it's my turn to come clean, but my secret ingredient feels anticlimactic after your story," Kendall said. He looked to the right and left, then behind him. Tilting forward, he said. "Habanero pepper is a secret ingredient."

"A hot pepper in a hot sauce is supposed to be a secret ingredient?"

"There are many varieties of peppers. Now you know which one was used in this sauce you love so much."

"I feel cheated," Ridge proclaimed. "Oddly, I'm more upset about this than Todd screwing his boss."

"Yikes. I think that says a lot about your relationship."

Ridge chuckled. "And you don't know the half of it." He aimed another boyish smile at Kendall. "Are you sure I can't coax you into telling me what the secret sweet ingredient is?"

Kendall shook his head.

"How about your real name?"

"It's best if I don't," Kendall said, letting regret tinge his voice as he pushed his chair back and stood up. Ridge didn't attempt to stop him a second time. "It was nice meeting you, Kurt Dandridge."

"You too, Sugar And Spice."

They continued to stare at one another for a few more seconds before Kendall gave himself a mental kick in the ass. "Take care."

"Maybe I'll see you around."

"Maybe," Kendall replied noncommittally.

He winked before walking away, feeling Ridge's hot gaze all over his body as viscerally as if the man were touching him. Kendall fought off a shiver and the urge to look over his shoulder. It was best to keep walking. Instead of heading straight for the exit, Kendall stopped by the register and paid for Ridge's dinner. He pulled out the receipt and wrote a message.

"So, he's gay," Colt said from behind Kendall.

"Or bi at least." He would've asked about Colt's prize, but his puffy, just-kissed lips gave it away. "Do you mind delivering this receipt to table twenty?"

Colt looked down at the receipt and smiled. "Not at all."

Kendall headed out then. He'd lived in Georgia his entire life, but the humidity still caught him off guard sometimes. Standing in the dark parking lot of the club was one of those times. He shook his head at his silliness and headed to his car. Instead of climbing into bed at twelve thirty, Kendall didn't pull into the driveway until one fifteen. Lights on in the kitchen meant Jonah or Avery, his roommates, were up. Kendall just hoped they weren't naked. Things were getting serious for the lovebirds, and he knew it was beyond time for him to find his own place.

He'd just never lived alone before. Who'd keep him on the straight and narrow? *You will, dumbass.* Kendall unlocked the front door and inched it open far enough to poke his head around. The first floor was empty, even though some of the lights were on. There was a partially open package of chocolate chip cookies on the counter next to a glass with the barest trace of milk at the bottom.

Kendall shook his head, then closed the package of cookies and rinsed the glass before putting it in the sink. A crash sounded above, followed by Jonah groaning and Avery giggling. A rueful smile tugged on Kendall's lips as he made his way to his bedroom.

Yep. It was definitely time to get his own place.

Chapter Three

RIDGE POURED A GENEROUS AMOUNT OF CREAMER INTO HIS coffee and stared at the French vanilla swirl forming in the black brew. It reminded him of fluffy white clouds, the bluest skies he'd ever seen, snow-capped mountains, and a stretch of green valley as far as the eye could see. It reminded him of home.

The mountains had been on his mind a lot lately since he'd taken Sugar's advice and started drawing in his sketchbook to relieve stress. The Bitterroot Mountains and Sapphire Range had been his biggest inspiration since his family moved to Corvallis, Montana, right before Ridge started high school. His dad had just retired from the army, and for the first time in Ridge's life, his family planted roots in fertile soil—literally and metaphorically. While his mother, father, and sister had adapted quickly to ranch life, Ridge, an awkward, gangly teenager, had taken longer to adjust. Riding out to the valley and gazing up at the mountains had calmed his soul in ways he'd never predicted. All these years later, Ridge still craved the ranges whenever his life felt tumultuous. His mother claimed they had magical healing power, and he had to admit she wasn't wrong.

The ranges weren't the only thing lingering in Ridge's mind over the past seven days since he'd moved out of Todd's apartment. A certain guy with platinum hair, pale blue eyes, and the prettiest mouth he'd ever seen kept popping into his thoughts when Ridge least expected it. The receipt with the note from Sugar burned a hole in his wallet, and he had an urge to reread it, even though he could recite the words from memory.

Give me a call if you want help rescuing the cat or maybe want to prove Todd wrong.

He'd signed off with *XOXO* and given his phone number. Ridge had stuffed the receipt into his wallet without hesitation but hadn't entered Sugar's number into his phone. He had no intention of calling the man and couldn't figure out why he hadn't just thrown the damn receipt out.

Yesterday at lunch, it had fallen out of his wallet when he'd pulled out cash to tip the waitress.

"Whoa, ho ho," Eddie had said, snatching it up before Ridge could. "What do we have here?"

"Sugar?" Asher had asked. Their inspector sat back in his chair and quirked a brow. Ridge considered himself to be a big man, but Asher made him feel puny. He crossed his brawny arms over his chest and smirked. "Cause he's sweet?"

Ridge shrugged. "So he claims."

Eddie waggled his brows. "Looks to me like he's offering up a taste. Why aren't you sampling? Nothing is holding you back."

"Leave him alone, Eduardo," Zack said before leveling Ridge with a curious gaze. "But why aren't you? Isn't he your type?"

Without permission, an image of Sugar had come to the forefront of Ridge's mind—the slender man reaching across the table and wiping a smidge of sauce off his face before licking it off his thumb. Ridge had been fascinated by both his boldness and the raw sexuality that pulsed from the man. He'd wanted to lean across the table and kiss his lips to see if they were as soft as they looked. He hadn't acted on his instinct, and it was nearly impossible for Ridge to name anything he regretted more.

Eddie laughed. "Would he have saved this cute little note with the guy's phone number if he wasn't interested?"

Zack nodded. "Yeah, you're right."

"So," Asher asked, "what's the deal?"

Ridge shrugged. "The guy is big trouble. I can feel it in my bones."

Eddie snorted. "Yeah, I bet you did."

"He said bones, not boner," Zack pointed out.

Oh, there'd been plenty of that too. Ridge had fantasized about taking Sugar in every conceivable position and some he wasn't certain were possible. Heat crept up Ridge's neck, and he took a big sip of water before his reaction gave his thoughts away. He felt in better control of his emotions afterward, even though Zack lobbed a knowing look in his direction.

"Why keep his number if you don't plan to use it?" Eddie had asked. A loud thump sounded from under the table, and Eddie flinched. "Sorry, Ridge. It's none of my business." Eddie handed the receipt back to him.

Ridge had briefly considered wadding it up and leaving it with the trash on the table, but he couldn't. He silently tucked the slip of paper back into his wallet and winked at Zack when he'd changed the subject to something less embarrassing than Ridge's horny schoolboy crush on a stranger whose real name he didn't even know.

He wanted to say the lunchtime conversation had shaken some sense into him, but Ridge had zoned out before bed the previous night and sketched half of Sugar's face before he'd become aware of what he was doing. Now he'd followed that up by thinking about the man while gazing at creamer clouds in his coffee. *Christ.*

"Morning," Jess sang out as she entered Eddie's tiny kitchen.

Jess was tall, curvy, and beautiful with a riot of red curls cascading to her waist, green eyes that always danced with mischief, and a dusting of freckles over her nose and cheeks. She and Emma, Zack's girlfriend, worked in the marshals' asset forfeiture department. Eddie had taken one look at Jess on her first day of work and announced to everyone, including her, that he would marry her someday. Jess had rolled her eyes, told him not to hold his breath, and vowed not to give him the time of day. Two months later, Zack won the office pool when she finally agreed to one date with Eddie. Ridge's entry had been "when hell freezes over" but being wrong had never felt so right.

"Morning," Ridge said.

Three months after their first date, Jess had practically moved in with Eddie, so Ridge crashing in the guestroom was a horrible idea. The couple was still in the honeymoon phase and didn't need Ridge cramping their style.

Jess poured herself a cup of coffee but didn't doctor it as he had. She leaned against the counter, crossed one leg in front of the other, and studied him over the rim of her cup.

"You look lovely," Ridge said, hoping to delay the inevitable. *Fucking Eddie and his big mouth.*

Jess looked down at her plum pencil skirt and old-fashioned ivory blouse with a high neck and a neatly tied bow at the top. "Thanks. It's one of my favorites."

"I don't know how you walk around in those," Ridge said, gesturing at her nude heels.

A smile tugged at her lips, but Jess took another sip of coffee before answering. "It's not like I run down fugitives."

"I wouldn't make it ten feet in those things."

Jess tilted her head. "Have we killed enough time so I can ask about Sugar now?"

Ridge heaved a sigh. "There's nothing to tell."

Taking pity on him, Jess patted his bicep and headed back toward the bedroom. "I tried, Eddie," she hollered.

Ridge was still grinning when he headed out of the apartment a few minutes later. His phone rang when he pulled out of the parking lot, and he smiled when the caller's name popped up on his dashboard display. Ridge hit the green phone button on his steering wheel. "Morning, Pop. How'd you know I was daydreaming about my mountains this morning?"

His dad's warm chuckle filtered through the speakers, filling Ridge's heart with relief. The man he'd always seen as indestructible had suffered a heart attack a little over two months ago. It had shaken Ridge to his core and left him reeling.

"Fathers know best, right?" Something in his dad's tone let Ridge know this was a setup.

"And if I agree, you'll use my words against whatever order Mom has given you?"

"Damn, you're smart."

"I get more than just my good looks and broad shoulders from you," Ridge said.

"Well, you get your intuitiveness from your mama. And speaking of the warden…" His father then rattled off a list of reasons why his mother needed to relent and let him get back to ranching.

"What does your cardiologist say?"

His dad grumbled. "She's got him on her payroll."

"Dad, will you listen to yourself? Do you really think Mom and Dr. Thorne are in cahoots? And to what end? To keep you alive longer? How dare they."

"I think Dr. Thorne is sweet on your mother. He says I'm not allowed to have sex for a while longer still. I think he wants her to get lonely and turn to him."

Ridge snorted. "She's quite the catch, but if Dr. Thorne wanted you dead, wouldn't he let up on your restrictions sooner? He'd encourage you to jump right back in the saddle and…" Yeah, he couldn't finish the thought.

"Stop being logical," his dad said, sounding like a bear denied honey for far too long. Considering his dad's biggest complaint, Ridge figured the analogy wasn't too far off the mark. Then he cringed because thinking about his parents' sex life, or lack thereof, wasn't something he wanted to do. *Ever*.

"Something else is bothering you," Ridge said. "Are you still convinced your heart condition will ruin Mom's dreams of seeing her organic bison and hummus in grocery stores across America?"

His dad sighed. "I'd hoped to keep my condition under wraps, but she said it was sneaky and underhanded."

"And you have nothing to be ashamed of," Ridge said. "Dr. Thorne said your stent placement was the result of a genetic condition and not your life-style choices." No plaque or cholesterol would dare to build up in the man's arteries. His dad sighed, and Ridge thought he was making a breakthrough, so he kept pushing. "No one looks at you and sees an unhealthy man, Dad. For fuck's sake, turn it around and make it part of the narrative. If you can have a heart attack, anyone can. You can be the face of the company."

An indignant snort came through the car speakers. "Can you imagine? Me hocking hummus?"

"You'd do it in a heartbeat if it would make Mom happy."

"Your mother *is* my heartbeat, Ridge. That's why I don't want to be the reason her dreams are crushed."

Ridge nearly sighed. Why had he thought he could settle for a love less than theirs? "You won't."

"You sound as certain as your mother."

"Because we're intuitive," Ridge reminded him. "Why do you trust our instincts on every issue besides this one?"

"I've turned into a grumpy old goat like Gus."

Thinking about his dad's beloved goat made Ridge smile. The little guy followed him everywhere and often charged other animals or people who got too close to Ridge's dad, including his wife.

"He saved my life, you know."

"Gus?" His mother hadn't told Ridge, but then, she probably didn't want to relive the terror she'd felt that day.

"Yeah. I collapsed in the barn, and Gus found your mom in the greenhouse. Kept ramming into her legs until she followed him. If not for Gus, I might not be here."

The pain in Ridge's chest was so swift and severe he had to pull over and pinch the bridge of his nose to keep the tears at bay. "I just can't…"

"Hey, I'm still here," his dad said. "And I have no intention of going anywhere soon, which is why I'm following the doctor's orders. I just needed to gripe about it to someone."

He loved being the person his father turned to but maybe not so much when his complaint was about not having enough sex with Ridge's mom. "Honor the goat by not acting like one," Ridge said. "Take the time to properly heal so you don't have setbacks. I'm sure Gus is looking forward to continuing your adventures."

His dad laughed. "Didn't Mom tell you she's moved Gus into the house? He has a doggie door that allows him to come and go as he pleases. He has a plush bed by the fireplace and everything. Gus is mom's goat now."

"Uh, no," Ridge said. "She failed to mention Gus's upgraded status during our conversations."

"Can you see why I doubt her judgment about other things right now? She's still fixated on losing me and not focusing on the future of her business."

Back to this again. Ridge eased back into traffic and continued on to work. "Dad, she can't envision a future business without you," Ridge said. "Your health is Mom's top priority right now, so stop making things harder on her. No one said you have to like being cooped up in the house, but it's temporary."

His dad sighed heavily. "You're right. I need to stop being an insufferable ass."

"I don't think that's what I said."

"No, I did," his dad said. "And maybe your mother said it too."

Ridge laughed. "If Mom called you an insufferable ass, then you probably had it coming."

"Yeah, maybe. Guess I'll try to find something to read. Have you stumbled on any new mysteries or thrillers lately?"

They chatted for a few minutes about books before disconnecting. A few seconds later, Ridge's phone rang again. He figured it was his mom calling to offer her side of the story and accepted the call without checking the name on the display.

"You really moved that old goat in with you?" he asked. Dread washed over him when silence greeted his question. He glanced over at the display and saw Todd's name. *Fuck.*

"Richard isn't that much older than I am," Todd said snidely. "And, no, he's not moving in. Yet."

"I thought you were my mom calling."

"She's moved a goat into the house? Is that a euphemism for something, or do you mean an actual barnyard animal?" He sounded disgusted by the idea. How in the hell had Ridge ever thought Todd was the man for him?

"I mean an actual goat. It's a long story," Ridge said.

"I have time."

"I don't," Ridge replied. "Not to be rude, but why the hell are you calling me, Todd? What could we possibly have to talk about?"

"You don't want to be rude, yet you say the rudest thing that pops into your head."

"No," Ridge said, "much ruder thoughts came to mind first. Trust me. I went with the kindest one."

"And to think I've actually missed you." Todd's voice was low and silky but not enticing in the least.

"Well, I can't return the sentiment." Ridge slid his thumb over to the disconnect button on the steering wheel. "If that's all you—"

"Sammy misses you," Todd blurted before Ridge could end the call. "He's not himself."

Ridge's heart squeezed painfully. "What's wrong with him?"

"He just lies around and mopes."

"He's always been a little on the lazy side," Ridge countered. God, he missed Sammy's purrs rumbling against his chest.

"This is different," Todd claimed. "He's not eating much. I think he's depressed."

The vise around his heart tightened. "Have you taken him to the vet?"

"Not yet," Todd replied. "I was hoping maybe you'd stop by for a visit. Maybe seeing you would boost Sammy's spirits."

"That's not going to happen." Ridge didn't believe for a second the cat was wasting away while pining for him. Todd was using Ridge's affection for the cat for his own selfish gain, but to what end? Ridge didn't know, and he wasn't interested in finding out.

"I thought you loved Sammy."

"I do. How will seeing me for fifteen minutes make the situation better? Won't it just give him false hope?"

"It doesn't have to." Todd's voice was low and full of pout.

Ridge pictured the matching expression his ex wore like an accessory. Instead of feeling moved, Ridge was irritated. It was time to shut this down. "I don't know if you're referring to the time limit for a visit that will never happen or the false hope claim. And it doesn't matter because neither is up for debate. Take Sammy to the vet or give him to me." Todd gasped in outrage, but Ridge kept talking. "As for the false hope. We are never getting back together. Don't call me again unless it's to make arrangements for me to pick up my cat."

Ridge disconnected the call before Todd finished sputtering, then whipped his SUV into the parking lot at work. He pocketed his keys and headed into the building with a heavy heart and a brain filled with dozens of possibilities as to why Sammy was acting up. None of the options were good, and he had a crazy idea to call Sugar and accept his offer to help steal the cat.

What the hell is wrong with you, Dandridge?

"Want me to answer that?" Zack asked as he joined Ridge by the elevators.

Ridge sighed. "I wasn't aware I'd spoken my thoughts out loud."

His friend clapped him on the shoulder, and they rode up to their floor in silence. Zack liked to tease, but he rarely needled a person like Eddie did. Ridge was glad for the reprieve so he could pull his head out of his ass and focus before Eddie showed up and started dissecting his surly mood. As it turned out, his best friend strolling into the bullpen with a plum lipstick kiss on his cheek was the thing that broke through Ridge's gloom.

He recognized the color of lipstick since Jess had been wearing it during their brief chat. Not wanting to tip Eddie off, Ridge hid his smile by taking a sip of coffee. He almost told his friend about the lipstick print but decided to wait until after their morning debriefing so everyone in their unit would get a chance to see it. Unfortunately for Eddie, no one else clued him in either. Asher stood in front of the room doling out assignments and somehow managed not to smirk at Eddie. Ridge snapped a discreet picture but didn't text it to his best friend until the meeting was over.

"You assholes!" Eddie yelled after opening the message. He glowered at everyone in the room as he snagged a tissue from the box and scrubbed at his face. "Did I get it all?"

"Uh, sure." Ridge stared in disbelief at the bold lipstick still staining his cheek. Eddie's efforts hadn't so much as dimmed the color or smeared it.

"No the fuck I didn't," Eddie said, then launched out of his chair and headed out of the office. His voice filtered in from the hallway, and Ridge could tell by his tone that he'd called Jess. "Babe, what's in the lipstick you wear, and how do I get it off my face?"

The room burst into laughter, and Eddie ducked his head around the door and flipped them all off. With his friend no longer distracting his thoughts, Ridge returned to mulling over his options. It didn't take him long to determine his only choice. Staying with Eddie long-term was a no-go. He still had every intention of leaving Savannah once he busted Sheldon Harris, but there was Sammy to consider now. Todd might've just been screwing around to lure him back to the apartment for…His brain stumbled there. Ridge couldn't think of a single viable reason why Todd would want him there. If Todd had wished to keep Ridge, he wouldn't have been sleeping with Richard. Maybe Sammy really was depressed and missing him.

Ridge pulled out his phone and scrolled through a list of apartments he'd found in Savannah. He filtered out the ones requiring long-term leases, cost one arm and two legs to rent, or didn't allow pets. Ridge found a listing toward the bottom with a price he didn't hate and clicked on it to see if a lease commitment was required and if cats were allowed. The information provided for Tranquil Breezes didn't mention a commitment and clearly stated cats and dogs were welcome. Ridge felt hopeful about the prospect and clicked on the Schedule a Tour button at the bottom of the page. He filled in his contact information before he could talk himself out of it and crossed his fingers that he'd hear from them soon.

Chapter Four

"**K**ENDALL, A MOMENT OF YOUR TIME, PLEASE," CHET DAWSON called out from his office when Kendall passed by.

Fighting off a cringe, Kendall stopped in his tracks and changed direction. Entering the office that had once belonged to Vivian Gross, the rising-star attorney who'd hired and mentored him for five years, hadn't gotten any easier.

His former boss and dear friend hadn't just died, though. Vivian had been murdered by a woman who'd become obsessed with one of her clients, and Kendall had been the person to discover her. He felt her absence every day. He couldn't believe two years had passed since he'd heard her laugh or call someone out on their bullshit. Vivian had believed in him when no one else had. She'd offered him a home when he'd had no place to go and had given him her friendship without any expectations from him. Vivian had encouraged him to become a paralegal because she'd believed Kendall was capable of so much more. To give up on this career would be letting her down. But staying someplace that made him miserable was letting himself down.

He still expected to smell her favorite gardenia perfume when he crossed the threshold, but all traces of his friend were long gone. Elderwood, Johnson, and McClary had hired a shark disguised as a man as Vivian's replacement, and he smelled like sandalwood and brimstone.

His chest tightened when he entered the office, and he shoved his hands into his pockets to prevent himself from rubbing the ache. "Sir?" Kendall asked coolly. They weren't close and never would be.

Chet's attention was focused solely on his computer screen, putting his face in profile. He was a handsome devil with his dark hair and eyes, swarthy skin, and impeccable bone structure. He wore designer suits and smelled like sin, but that was all Kendall knew about the man. They'd never had a single personal conversation since they'd started working together, not that Kendall was complaining. His new boss was a constant reminder of how much he missed Vivian. Chet glanced briefly in Kendall's direction before returning his attention to the computer. The attorney's fingers danced over the keyboard, making Kendall curious about what had captured his attention so completely.

"You did an excellent job during the deposition last week. You're a real asset to the firm." Chet's compliment was given in his courtroom voice—smooth like honey—but without the slightest attempt on the attorney's part to make eye contact. It felt insincere and empty.

With anyone else, Kendall would've been pleased with the high praise. He'd smile and force the tension from his body. But with Chet, Kendall suspected the man wielded compliments like a weapon to unarm and manipulate others.

"What can I do for you, Mr. Dawson?" Kendall asked, preferring to get down to business rather than play games. He figured he could go toe to toe with the likes of Chet, but he was short on time. He had an appointment to tour an apartment in thirty minutes, and he was already cutting it close. According to the property manager, there was only one vacancy and several people were vying for the apartment.

A shiver of terror and excitement raced through Kendall's body. He'd never been on his own before. He'd lived with his mother and stepfather until the latter had made him choose between living under his roof or living openly and honestly. Kendall had packed his clothes and moved into the decrepit car he'd bought with the money he'd squirreled away. It had been a piece of shit, but it was the first thing he'd bought all on his own, and it provided shelter for a few days until Vivian had found out about his situation and swooped in to rescue him. After she passed, Kendall moved in with his friend Jonah. He'd been content there, but Jonah and Avery deserved their privacy, and Kendall needed to grow the hell up. This was a big step, and he didn't want to blow it by missing his appointment.

"I've decided to take on Bobby Jack Dennison as a client. He and his parents will be here soon to sign the attorney-client representation agreement," Chet said without looking away from his computer. "I need you to make some amendments to a few sections."

"Bobby Jack Dennison?" Kendall asked flatly. "The kid who bullied his gay classmate until he ended his own life?"

Chet's fingers stilled, and he finally met Kendall's gaze. "Alleged bullying."

Screenshots of Bobby Jack's vicious texts and videos of him harassing Joshua Jones had been splashed on every media outlet for the past month. Bobby Jack had set up fake social media accounts and pretended to be gay to lure Joshua out of the closet, then shared every message the two had exchanged. The bastard was pure evil, and Kendall felt sick to his stomach. He'd been the kid who'd gotten picked on and beat up. Some kids could hide their queerness while others had it stamped on their foreheads for the world to see. Kendall had fallen into the latter camp and had decided if he was going to get his ass beat, he'd go down in style. Since he'd attended a private school, there was little variance permitted with his uniform, but he found ways to circumvent the rules. Eventually, he caught the eye of the biggest baddest dude in the school. The bigger they are, the harder they fall to their knees to suck your cock or beg to tap your tight ass. Maybe Kendall's allegory veered away from the familiar saying, but it was no less true.

"But, sir, he—"

Chet's scowl cut off his protest. "I do not get paid to like my clients, Mr. Blakemore. I get paid to represent them." It didn't hurt that the boy's parents could give Midas a run for his money. "If you have a problem with the clients I bring into the firm, I suggest you take it up with Mr. Elderwood. If this is nothing more than a personal grievance because you can't separate your emotions from your job, then perhaps you'd be better suited doing something else with your life." Chet raised an arrogant brow, daring Kendall to reveal his hand.

It was on the tip of his tongue to tell the prick to go fuck himself, but he straightened his spine in response to the gauntlet thrown. "What clauses would you like me to change, sir?" He could whip the contract out in no time and still make his appointment to tour the apartment.

The right side of Chet's mouth crept up into a sneer. "My retainer fee, for starters. I want a hundred grand upfront." It was more than twice his usual retainer. Kendall didn't say anything, but his face must've betrayed his surprise because Chet's sneer returned. "If Stuart and Denae want me to represent their little asshole, then I will be handsomely compensated."

Under normal circumstances, Kendall might feel a modicum of respect for the man, but his disdain for Bobby Jack was deeply personal. "And your hourly rate, sir?"

"Fifteen hundred. And I'm still not sure that will cover the amount of bleach I'll need to purchase."

Despite his better judgment, Kendall let down his guard a little. "So why do it?"

Chet gave Kendall his full attention, coolly assessing him. "Do you think only innocent people deserve legal representation?"

"No." Though Kendall did wrestle with the win-at-any-expense attitude prevalent at the firm. Winning wasn't everything when it meant awful people were free to harm others. "But I think we disagree on what fair representation means."

Chet leaned back in his leather chair and studied him curiously. "I'm listening."

Kendall knew he should let it drop; he did have that appointment after all. "It doesn't really matter what I think, and my personal beliefs won't interfere with my professional judgment."

Chet narrowed his eyes, and Kendall thought the attorney wasn't going to let their disagreement drop. His moniker wasn't Bull Shark for nothing. After a moment, Chet nodded curtly and said, "See that it doesn't."

"Any other clauses you'd like me to amend?"

Chet ran through a few more changes, focusing on the type of behavior he demanded of Bobby Jack until the civil trial ended. He insisted Bobby Jack deactivate all social media accounts under his name and promise not to open anonymous ones. If Chet had the slightest suspicion Bobby Jack was harassing, stalking, or engaging with Joshua Jones's friends or family, the contract would be void. "Make sure they know I'll retain the fee, and payment for all billable hours will be due immediately upon the severed contract."

"Yes, sir."

Kendall hurried to his office and made the required amendments before sending them to Chet for approval. Once he received the go-ahead, Kendall finalized and emailed the final contract. He wanted to be gone before the asshole and his parents arrived but nearly collided with them when he exited his office. An apology was on the tip of his tongue until he saw the fury on Bobby Jack's face.

"Watch it," the bully snarled as he stepped toward Kendall. The seventeen-year-old towered over him and probably outweighed Kendall by seventy pounds. The blond ogre with menacing green eyes would find out just how vulnerable his kneecaps were if he came one step closer.

"BJ," Denae Dennison bit out as she gripped her son's arm and made futile attempts to pull him back. Her blue eyes widened in alarm as she stared up at her son in horror. Denae glanced at Kendall pleadingly, but he wasn't moved—physically or otherwise. Her artfully styled blonde hair swished around her flushed cheeks when she snapped her head to stare at her husband. "Do something, Stuart."

Stuart Dennison was deep in conversation on his phone, seemingly unaware of the scuffle about to occur, until Denae said his name again but much louder and with more alarm in her voice. He glanced over, then did a double take. "Bill, I need to go. Something has come up." Yeah, his son's temper. "I'll call you after we finish meeting with BJ's attorney. Yeah, I'm hoping he can make this all go away." *Good luck with that, asshole.* "Talk soon."

Stuart tapped his phone, slid it into his pocket, and gave the trio his full attention. He was slightly shorter than his son but just as muscular. He was dark to Denae's fair, and BJ had inherited the strongest features from both his parents. "What's going on here?" Stuart asked authoritatively while glowering at Kendall. *Pompous asshole.*

"I'll tell you what's happening," a new voice chimed in.

Kendall turned his head as Chet strode toward them in a powerful stride.

"Mr. Dawson," Stuart said, shifting his attention to the man he'd pinned all his hopes on.

"We're not getting off to a very good start, Mr. Dennison," Chet informed Stuart before turning to Kendall. "I see that you're on your way out, but I'm afraid I need you to make another amendment to the client-attorney agreement."

Kendall bit back a groan. So much for landing the apartment. "Yes, sir. How can I help?" Kendall's frustration nearly turned to glee when Chet outlined the behavior he expected Bobby Jack to exhibit in the law office and in the courtroom. Abusing the staff would automatically negate the contract.

Chet turned to assess Bobby Jack's reaction and sneered at the bristling bastard. "Am I understood?"

Bobby Jack's nostrils flared like a bull, but he nodded curtly. "Yes, sir."

Kendall ducked back inside his office and made the necessary changes before emailing them to Chet. The attorney approved them within seconds and included a message that made Kendall smile.

Knee the asshole in the balls if he charges you again. Then we'll keep the fucker's money. Have a good night.

Chet

Kendall logged out and was more circumspect when he exited his office, picking up the pace as he neared the employee door at the rear of the building. If traffic cooperated, Kendall could make his appointment on time. Three blocks later, someone rear-ended him at a red light.

"Fuck me," he groused. Maybe it was a sign the apartment wasn't meant to be. He released his seatbelt and got out of the car, taking out his frustration by slamming the door shut. He walked around to the rear bumper and was relieved to see the damage was minimal.

A gangly teen with frizzy brown hair, acne, and braces got out of the driver's seat and approached him. "Sorry, man," he said sheepishly. "Are you hurt?"

Kendall gave the kid points for inquiring about his health first. "Nah. It wasn't much more than a tap. You have insurance, right?"

"Yeah, but I couldn't tell you who we're with because my parents handle all that."

"You probably have an ID card in your glovebox," Kendall told him.

"Oh, I'll look," the kid said.

Before he could head to the car, a few short siren blasts sounded from nearby. Kendall saw a police cruiser several cars back, trying to cut through traffic to reach them. At least they wouldn't have to wait long to complete the report. Except the cop was a rookie, so his trainer went into excruciating detail on every part of the form.

Forty minutes later, Kendall drove off with the information he needed to file a claim with the kid's insurance company and was twenty minutes late for his appointment. Instead of giving up, he drove to the Tranquil Breezes apartment complex. Hopefully the property manager would take pity on him.

Kendall checked his appearance in the mirror, popped a piece of gum into his mouth, and headed to the front entrance. The lobby was spacious, but the tile floor looked a little worn.

A redhead sat behind the desk, snapping her gum and looking bored to tears. Her nameplate identified her as Missy. "Can I help you?" she asked in a monotone voice.

"Uh, yes," Kendall said as he approached the desk. "I had an appointment with David to view an available apartment. I got rear-ended on my way here, the cop took forever, and now I'm late. Is there a chance he'll still show me the apartment?"

"Nope," a familiar voice said behind him.

Kendall turned and locked eyes with Ridge. The man was even more gorgeous in daylight. A lock of chestnut hair had fallen across his forehead, and Kendall was dying to know if it was as soft as it looked. His eyes were a warm brown, not dark blue, and Ridge let them rake over Kendall from head to toe just like he had the first night they'd met. What was it? A week ago? Kendall had finally stopped hoping the guy would call or return to the club.

"Are you okay?" Ridge asked gently.

Better now. "Yeah. It was a minor fender bender." He tilted his head. "You're not David."

Ridge smirked and stood up. Mountain of a man, indeed. His legs stretched on forever, and his thick thighs looked immovable. An ember of lust sparked in Kendall's gut. "No, I'm definitely not David, but it's my turn to view the apartment."

"Oh man," Missy said, her dull voice not shifting in pitch. "Will I need to call the cops?"

"Already here," Ridge said, lifting his shirt to reveal a silver star clipped to his belt.

Kendall quirked a brow. "A marshal, huh?" Unable to stop himself, Kendall leaned forward. "Where are your handcuffs?"

Ridge chuckled. "In my vehicle."

"I—" Movement on the periphery pulled his attention. A lanky, balding man with a hassled expression ambled toward them. Kendall was grateful for the interruption. He'd been on the verge of making a fool of himself.

"Sorry to keep you waiting," the man said, splitting his attention between Kendall and Ridge. "Which one of you is Mr. Dandridge?"

Ridge waved his hand.

"Are you Dave?" Kendall asked.

"David," he corrected. "And you are?"

"I was your six o'clock appointment," Kendall said. "I'm—"

"Late," David replied flatly. "You can schedule another appointment with Missy if you wish."

"I'm very sorry, but I was involved in an accident, and—"

"That's unfortunate, Mr. Blakemore," David said. "But—"

"Aha!" Ridge said abruptly. "I know part of your name now."

Startled, David looked between the two men. "Do you know each other?"

"Sorta." Oh, how Kendall would love to upgrade that to a *fuck yes*.

"You know," Ridge said, leaning closer, "if you tell me your first name, I'll let you tour the apartment with me." Kendall bit his lip to keep from moaning. Ridge's gaze shifted down toward his mouth, then snapped back up. "What do you say?"

"My name is Sugar," Kendall said calmly, waiting to see if David would blurt out the truth.

"Uh," the property manager said. "I don't mean to be a dick—"

"Here comes the but," Kendall said to Ridge, who chuckled.

David scowled at Kendall before shifting his gaze back to Ridge. "I have several other appointments after yours. If you want an opportunity to see the unit, I suggest you come now." The lanky man pivoted and headed toward the elevator bank.

"Show him your badge," Kendall whispered.

Ridge rolled his eyes and gestured for Kendall to precede him.

"You're such a gentleman."

A rumble of laughter followed him down the hall. Moments later, Ridge's body heat engulfed Kendall as the large man caught up.

"Just enjoying the view." Kendall looked around at the dingy tile and faded wallpaper. "I wasn't referring to the building," Ridge said huskily.

Oh. Kendall wasn't sure how to respond, so he said nothing as the trio boarded the elevator. The climb wasn't smooth, and Kendall feared the contraption would get stuck before they reached their destination. While he could think of many things he would like to do with Ridge in a small space, he'd prefer to do it without a bystander.

"How often are the elevators serviced?" Ridge asked David.

The property manager glanced up from his phone and offered what he probably thought was a reassuring smile. It reminded Kendall of the car salesman who'd sold him his first crap car. "The elevators are inspected according to state laws."

"And that's how often?" Ridge pressed.

"I'd have to look, but I think it's annually."

Ridge narrowed his eyes and hummed. He looked like he wanted to say more, but their ascent came to an abrupt halt, knocking Kendall off-balance and into Ridge.

"Maybe this elevator isn't so bad," the hunk whispered.

"Right this way," David said, ushering them to the left. The available apartment was only a few doors down. David had a tough time unlocking the door and grinned sheepishly. "Easy fix."

"Uh-huh," Ridge said.

Kendall had already seen enough to know this place wasn't for him, but he wasn't eager to part ways with Ridge yet.

David opened the door with a flourish and stood back. Kendall looked at Ridge, who placed his hand at the small of Kendall's back and guided him over the threshold. Kendall's mouth fell open when he saw the apartment was about the same size as his small bedroom at Jonah's.

"A thousand dollars a month for this?" Kendall asked.

Apparently, David mistook his astonishment as a positive because he nodded and smiled. "Isn't it great?"

Great? Kendall looked around, noting the cracks in the cigarette smoke-stained walls. The lingering smell made him want to gag. So much for the claims it was a smoke-free building. The carpet under his feet crunched and made him want to shudder. Not even his desire to learn more about Ridge was going to keep him in the disgusting space a second longer. He started to back up and crashed into a solid wall of muscle. Ridge placed his hand on Kendall's hip to steady him. Ridge's fingers tightened, and Kendall felt branded. Well, maybe he could stay a few minutes longer. He should at least check out the bathroom and bedroom.

Bedroom turned out to be a generous term. Though there were four walls and a door, Kendall had seen bigger linen closets.

"Cozy," Ridge said, his breath ghosting over Kendall's neck.

Kendall gasped and nearly swallowed his gum. Behind him, Ridge chuckled and returned his hand to Kendall's hip. His touch was somehow hotter than the first time. David's phone rang, and he excused himself to take the call. He stepped out of the apartment, leaving them all alone.

Kendall turned around to face Ridge but resisted the urge to press against his broad chest. "This feels like something out of a horror film."

"Want to place a bet on the bathroom's condition?"

"What do I get if I win?" Kendall asked.

Ridge briefly glanced down at Kendall's mouth before meeting his eyes once more. "Anything you want."

His pulse galloped at the myriad ideas flitting across his brain. "A kiss."

Ridge quirked a brow. "Bold. I like it."

"And what will you claim?"

Ridge leaned in until his lips were a hairsbreadth away. "I want to know your real name. First, middle, and last."

"So you can run me through the system?"

"Not hardly." Ridge quirked a brow. "Should I?"

Kendall laughed. "No, but I don't agree to your terms."

"Fine. I'd settle for the secret sweet ingredient in the Regret wing sauce."

"Deal."

After agreeing on prizes, they each stated what they expected to find on the other side of the door. Kendall had guessed a stained toilet and a disgusting shower. Ridge had simply assumed a dead body.

"Are you throwing the bet?" Kendall asked.

Ridge took a deep breath. "Well, I can't stop thinking about your mouth and wondering if your lips are as sweet as they look."

"Like sugar. So, should we have our kiss now without traumatizing ourselves by opening the bathroom door?"

Ridge reached around him and gripped the knob. "After you."

"No way in hell."

Ridge maneuvered around him and flipped on the light. "Looks like I win."

"Shut up," Kendall said, spinning around to see that his predictions were accurate and were the least of the problems in the tiny space. "This is gross," he said as he brushed past Ridge. His body tingled, feeling more alive than he had in two years. He yanked back the paper-thin shower curtain and grimaced at the rusty stains at the bottom. The stench coming up through the drain was enough to make him gag, but he staved off the urge. "There is nothing tranquil about this breeze."

"You can't even open the linen closet without shutting the door," Ridge said.

Kendall snapped his head around. "Don't—" his protest was drowned out by creaking rusty door hinges. *Shut the door.*

Ridge waggled his brows. "Want to claim your kiss now?"

"In here?"

"The monster inside the linen closet will kill us both."

"Yeah, I've seen that movie," Kendall agreed.

Ridge slowly licked his lips. "Looks like it's now or never."

"A more compelling argument, I've yet to hear."

A faint whimper filtered into the bathroom, and for a second, Ridge and Kendall just stared at one another in shock. Then Kendall realized the sound was coming through the wall separating the apartment from the one next door. Heat crept up Kendall's neck when a steady thumping shook the wall hard enough for grout to shake loose from between several shower tiles. The faint whimpers became guttural moans.

"Oh god," Kendall said and buried his face in his hands.

"That's what he said." Kendall spread his fingers and peeked between them to catch Ridge smirking. "Seriously. One guy said, 'Fuck me harder.' The other said, 'Oh god.'"

"You were able to make out the words?"

Ridge held up his shirt again, flashing his badge and cut abs. "I've developed a keen ear after years of surveillance. Fairly sure one of them is named Manuel."

The thumping turned into hardcore banging, and the groans became shouts. Kendall rubbed the back of his neck and implored his body not to respond to the stimuli. He crossed the room and yanked open the closet door so hard the handle came off in his hand.

"Oops."

Ridge took the knob from his hand and set it on the vanity. "We'll say the banging next door caused it."

"Good idea."

"And I'll happily pay up that kiss but preferably in a place where we're not likely to pick up bed bugs or something else."

Kendall grimaced as he looked around. "Also a good idea."

"We'll just—" Ridge's voice cut off when the bathroom door wouldn't open. "Oh shit."

"Is the handle stuck?" Kendall asked, elbowing the bigger man out of the way.

The knob turned easily, but the door didn't budge. Kendall turned the lock, hoping it had just slipped when Ridge shut the door. He tried the handle again with no luck.

"Christ," Kendall groaned. He turned toward Ridge. "Use those big shoulders and get us out of here."

"Won't work. The door swings in, not out."

"I bet you could blast a hole in the door," Kendall said.

Ridge shook his head. "This building appears to be cheaply constructed except for the doors." He knocked on it for emphasis. "Solid wood. I'd have more luck running through the wall."

Kendall quirked a brow to ask what he was waiting for.

"I think a better use of my time is to give you the kiss you won fair and square."

"I thought you said we'd get lice or scabies in here?"

Ridge took two steps forward, pressing Kendall against the very solid door. "I said bed bugs, but we have to find some way to pass the time until David gets off his call and realizes we're trapped."

When Ridge placed both hands on his hips, Kendall forgot any protest he could've made. The only thing that mattered was feeling Ridge's firm mouth against his. The big guy didn't move fast; he took his time, allowing Kendall to call a halt at any moment. He didn't. The first press of lips was tentative and gentle. Ridge pulled back and looked at Kendall, sizing up his response. Should he proceed or back off? Kendall gripped Ridge's thick neck, stood up on his tiptoes, and settled any debate. Ridge's mouth met his, and this time, his kiss was bold and confident. Kendall parted his lips, and Ridge licked into his mouth, tangling their tongues together.

Kendall moaned as loud as Manuel, Michael, or whoever was next door. Ridge answered with a growl that made Kendall's toes curl.

A loud knock sounded on the door by Kendall's head, jarring him out of his lusty haze.

"Hey!" David shouted. "What's going on in there?"

Ridge recovered first. "The door's stuck."

"Did you try twisting the lock? Sometimes they're a little tricky."

"I didn't twist it in the first place, so there's no need to try it in the other direction," Ridge argued.

"Just try," the property manager said.

"That was the first thing I tried," Kendall replied. "I think you're going to need maintenance to come up with a screwdriver."

"Damn it. I don't have time for this shit."

"Gotta tell you, Dave," Kendall said, "we're not really happy about this either."

"The name's David, and you two didn't sound real pissed a moment ago."

"I'm a US deputy marshal, Dave," Ridge said. "You really don't want to push me or find out what I look or sound like when pissed off."

"I'll make the call," David said.

Moments later, a cell phone started ringing on the other side of the wall. The bed knocking stopped a second but quickly resumed.

"He's not answering. Damn it. He must be out for dinner."

"What's his name?" Ridge asked.

"Manuel."

Kendall fought off a snicker. "Try next door."

"What?" Dave asked. "How would you know that?"

"Trust us," Ridge said. "The apartment to the left."

Manuel freed them a few minutes later. The man had taken the time to put on pants but hadn't buttoned his shirt, putting his sculpted, sweaty chest on display.

While Dave braved the elevator, Ridge and Kendall took the stairs down to the lobby.

"Well, I guess the apartment comes with unexpected perks," Ridge said.

Kendall smirked and shook his head. "No hot maintenance guy is worth risking your life."

Ridge laughed. "I meant the sketchy elevator would ensure frequent use of the stairs." He nudged Kendall. "I see you had a different kind of cardio in mind."

"And it's all your fault," Kendall said.

They stopped and faced each other when they reached the sidewalk in front of the building. Kendall was about to share his real name when he noticed Ridge was chewing gum. *His* gum. He'd been so caught up in the kiss he hadn't realized it was missing.

"You stole my gum."

"Not purposely. It happened when David banged on the door. I almost choked on it." Ridge smiled and lifted a hand to his mouth.

"I don't want it back," Kendall said. "Still want to know my name?" He started walking backward.

"You know I do."

"Then use the phone number I gave you and ask for it."

"What makes you think I still have it?"

"That silly smile on your lips."

Ridge reached up and touched his mouth. "Huh, what do you know?"

Kendall took a few more steps to put distance between them. "It's chocolate, by the way."

"Excuse me?" Ridge said.

"The secret sweet ingredient in Regret."

Ridge put his hands on his hips, and Kendall could tell he was mentally running through the flavor profile from memory. "Really?"

Kendall nodded.

"I never would've guessed. Thanks for trusting me with the secret."

Kendall winked. "Goodbye, US Deputy Marshal Kurt Dandridge."

"Goodbye, Sugar Blakemore."

Kendall smiled as he drove to his second job, but his humor fizzled as he put on the spandex shorts and mesh crop top. His paralegal gig wasn't working out the way he'd hoped, but slinging wings and beer wasn't a long-term solution, even though the tips were great. He was twenty-seven-freaking years old. Why couldn't he get his shit together?

Outside the locker room, he ran into their general manager. "Shit. I'm sorry, Drew."

"Is everything okay, Kendall?" He loved that Drew didn't call him by his silly nickname, even if it was the one on his name tag.

"I've had better days." Though he wouldn't complain about running into Ridge.

Drew crossed his thick arms over his chest. "Anything I can help with?"

"Do you have a crystal ball to help me decide what kind of career I should pursue?"

Smiling, Drew said, "No."

"Are you able to fix my car that some kid crashed into?"

"Oh no. Are you okay?" Drew asked.

"Yeah. It's just a minor annoyance. I might just bang out the dents in my bumper with a hammer and not mess with filing a claim. I don't want the kid's rates to go up." Kendall took a deep breath. "But I don't suppose you know someone who's renting a house or manages a decent apartment complex."

Drew rubbed his chin as he considered Kendall's situation. "I think I have a solution to two out of three of your problems."

"Dare I ask which two?"

Drew laughed. "A management position opened up today when I fired Erik for abusing his role."

Kendall blinked at him. "You think I'd be a good manager?"

"I know so," Drew replied. "I also happen to know someone who has an adorable little house for rent."

Kendall grimaced. "I just toured a shitty apartment that cost a thousand bucks a month. I can't afford a house."

"It's more affordable than you think. Besides, you could always get a roommate and offset some of the rent. Can you give me fifteen minutes to chat?"

Kendall gestured to Drew's office. "Lead the way, boss."

Chapter Five

I'M NOT IN OVER MY HEAD. *I*'M NOT IN OVER MY HEAD. *I*'M SO FUCKING *in over my head.*

Kendall dropped his head into his hands and took a few breaths. Why had he given Drew's suggestion a try? Sure, he'd been unhappy at the law firm for quite some time, but to actually quit? Why hadn't he just tried to find work with another attorney? Managing the club? Yes, he knew the ins and outs after working there for nearly three years, but him…a manager…of people? What had Drew been thinking when he'd made the pitch two weeks ago? No sane person would put Kendall in charge of anything, least of all a business so heavily regulated by the government. God, if someone screwed up on his watch and cost them their liquor license… they'd be fucked.

Panicking over his career move kept Kendall from obsessing about Ridge and the hot kiss they'd shared. Their chemistry had burned hot enough to raze Tranquil Breezes, so why hadn't Ridge called or texted? Had Kendall misread the signs? Hell no. There was no mistaking the passionate way Ridge had kissed him. It had melted his brain and was probably the reason he'd accepted Drew's offer. And Kendall was right back to fretting over his first shift as the night manager.

A knock on his open door interrupted him before his worry could turn into a full-blown panic attack. Kendall jerked his head up and met the dark gaze of a man he'd never seen before. The guy with honey-blond hair wore a flight suit, identifying him as a bartender. Drew had mentioned a new hire the previous day when Kendall was shadowing him for the last time before flying solo. What was the new bartender's name? Eric? Elliot?

Full lips curved into a dazzling smile, distracting Kendall from his meltdown. "You look like you're freaking out." When Kendall continued to stare, the man stepped into the room and approached the desk, his hand out. "I'm Emmett by the way."

Emmett. That was it. Kendall stood up and they shook. "Kendall," he said. "It's nice to meet you."

"You say that now, but wait until you find out why I'm here."

Kendall stifled a groan and braced himself. Health department? Police? "Lay it on me."

Emmett's lips twitched. "Two of our waiters are about to come to blows over a patron. Javier said I should come to your office and let you know."

Technically, it was an office shared by the club management team. Moments ago, his ass was in the manager's chair. Therefore, it was his office until three in the morning when he could run screaming to his car.

I'm so fucking in over my head.

"Um, Javier said you're good at settling disputes."

I am? Since when? No time like the present, he guessed.

Apparently, Kendall hesitated too long because Emmett looked at him expectantly and said, "About the waiters…"

Kendall nodded and walked around the desk. "Right. Colt and Carey. Most people call them the twins."

Emmett fell into step with him as they exited his office. *His office.* That was going to take some getting used to…if he survived his first shift in charge. Colt and Carey seemed determined to put him to the test.

"Are they related?" Emmett asked.

"No. Just childhood friends. They've spent so much time together their looks and mannerisms are identical."

Emmett chuckled. "Sounds like they could probably stand a little separation. Perhaps make a new friend or two."

"I couldn't agree more. Please tell me Colt and Carey aren't arguing in front of our guests." And why were they still fighting over other men when they so obviously wanted each other?

"Nope," Emmett replied. "They're locking horns and creating havoc in the kitchen. I happened to catch the show when I returned from my break."

Kendall groaned. The last time those two had gotten into a catfight the fur, body glitter, and saliva had gone flying. "They'd better not taint the food again."

"Again?" Emmett asked. Kendall didn't need to see his face to know the man was cringing.

Kendall pushed through the swinging doors and stepped into the kitchen. Colt and Carey were midbattle and unconcerned about their audience. The argument hadn't turned physical yet, but their red cheeks and pinched expressions let Kendall know he'd arrived in the nick of time.

"I saw him first," Colt snarled.

Carey snorted. "So what? You were too busy batting your eyelashes at him to close the deal. I saw an opening and took it."

"Ha!" Colt bellowed. "And how'd he respond to you pushing your phone number toward him?"

Carey sniffed and lifted his chin. "His fingers were coated in sauce, so he ignored it."

"How convenient," Colt quipped.

Carey lifted his hands and shoved Colt's chest before Kendall could reach them. The effort was minimal at best, but Colt flailed his arms and took a few steps back, a cloud of body glitter wafting in his wake.

"Hey!" Kendall yelled, gaining both their attention. "Put the damn claws away, gentlemen."

Colt and Carey immediately launched into explanations about how the other had started the altercation. Kendall held up his hand and cut them both off.

"I don't care how the fight started. I'm ending it," he told them. "I want both of you to clock out and go home."

"What?" Colt said.

"You can't be serious," Carey added.

"You heard me. I know for a fact Drew gave you both verbal warnings last week." Kendall gestured around the kitchen to where the staff was guarding the food against contamination. "Clock out and go home. Make sure you come in early on your next shifts to sign and acknowledge your official write-ups."

Colt's gaze widened and filled with unshed tears. Kendall barely fought the urge to roll his eyes. *Jesus.* He'd perfected the kitten-stuck-in-the-rain look, and this kid had a long way to go. Carey crossed his arms over his chest, striking a defiant stance. It didn't budge Kendall a centimeter from his decision.

"You can go now and miss out on tips from half a shift, or you can miss two nights' worth. What's it going to be, gentlemen?" Though neither of them deserved the title, Kendall bestowed it on them anyway. He wouldn't give them a valid complaint to take to Drew.

Carey continued to scowl until Colt sniffled. Then his taciturn expression morphed into one of fierce protectiveness as he slipped his arm around Colt's shoulders. "Don't cry," he said. "I'm sorry I acted like an asshole."

Colt leaned into his friend and slipped an arm low around Carey's waist. "I'm sorry for overreacting. You were right. The guy was completely indifferent to my flirting."

"Well, there's something wrong with him, then," Carey said, "because you're perfect."

"Maybe our guest just wants to eat the best damn wings in town without getting harassed," Kendall suggested.

The newly made-up friends glared at him like he was public enemy number one. Oh well. His conscience was guilt free when he gestured for them to exit the kitchen.

"Fine," Colt said haughtily. He sailed through the swinging door with his head held high. Carey glared at Kendall once more before following his friend.

The kitchen staff erupted in a cheer. Chef Mike gave him two thumbs up and removed the plastic wrap from the sauce bowls on his station. Could this night get any weirder?

"I see Javier was right about you," Emmett said. "Nice job."

Maybe Kendall should classify his conflict-resolution style as picking his battles rather than avoidance. He was feeling stronger about his decision after receiving praise from the kitchen staff and Emmett.

"Still doubting your decision to accept the management position?" Emmett asked.

Kendall tilted his head and studied the handsome man. "Is everyone talking about me?"

Emmett chuckled. "Nope. I'm just very astute." The taller man stepped closer and said, "Even if I were a dim bulb, I still would've recognized the panic I saw in your eyes."

Mimicking Carey's stance from a moment ago, Kendall crossed his arms over his chest. "I think panic is a strong word."

"Drew took a big chance when he promoted you. I'd be more concerned if you didn't have doubts."

Kendall heaved a sigh. "You're not helping."

"It's not you I doubt. Promoting from within presents a unique set of problems for every manager. Yes, you put someone in charge who's familiar with the company and the employees, but—"

"The promoted person isn't always respected because the staff still sees them as an equal," Kendall said.

Emmett nodded. "And sometimes they see the person as inferior to themselves or someone else they believe should've been promoted instead."

Kendall blew out a breath. He'd had his share of battles with the other servers in the past. Did they see him as inferior or undeserving of the promotion Drew had offered him? Wasn't that fair if they did? Kendall had doubted his decision every other second since he'd accepted Drew's offer. Why would the rest of the club feel differently about his sudden rise in authority? "I can see your point."

The swinging doors opened suddenly, catching Kendall's right hip. Mateo, a former college gymnast, came through them, looking between his manager and the bartender. "Sorry, K," he said when Kendall ran a hand over his hip. "Um, who do you want to pick up Carey's and Colt's tables? It's a packed house out there, and we're now short two of our best waiters."

"Wow," Emmett said. "Word travels fast around here."

"Faster than gossip through a beauty parlor or church pew," Kendall quipped.

Emmett chuckled. "I'll take your word for it." He headed out to the club, leaving Kendall to sort out the newest problem.

"What's his deal?" Mateo asked.

"His deal?"

"Yeah, polite and professional."

Kendall gasped in mock horror. "Say it isn't so."

"Even to the customers," Mateo added.

"Oh." That was curious. "No flirting?"

Mateo shook his head. "There's a bet going."

"Already? Can't the guy even complete his first shift?"

"You know how it is around here, K."

Kendall nodded. "Dare I ask?"

"Three camps," Mateo said, needing no further prompting. "He's either straight, in a committed relationship, or doesn't need the money. If you want generous tips, you gotta flirt, but you know this. Your skills are legendary."

Kendall fought off the urge to preen. "I don't know about that."

"*Legendary.*"

He could think of a dozen things he'd rather be known for, but he let it go. Mateo had sought him out to solve a problem, after all. "I'll take care of the tables and divvy up the tips between all of you."

"Sweet!" the gymnast said before pivoting and leaving the kitchen.

Kendall headed out to the dining room, stopping by the computer to check which areas were assigned to Colt and Carey. They were next to one another, which had made it easy for Carey to witness Colt striking out. He wanted to check in with the patron the guys had fought over but wasn't sure which table it was until he got to Colt's section. The man was tall, broad, and looked like he could stop a freight train with a hug.

Kendall observed the man's behavior as he made his way to the table. The oak tree of a man kept his head down, avoiding eye contact as he mowed his way through chicken wings. Two empty plates were stacked at the edge of the table. Christ. It looked like the big bruiser was eating his body weight in wings.

"Let me clear these for you," Kendall said when he reached the object of Colt and Carey's obsession.

The man snapped his head up and scowled at Kendall. His black hair was shaved close to his head, but it wasn't quite a buzz cut. Kendall had heard of eyes so dark they looked black but hadn't thought they were real until that moment. A white scar slashed across the man's forehead, the bottom of the scar bisecting his eyebrow on the left side. The dark stubble dotting his jawline was a stark contrast to his pale skin. Two teardrops were tattooed under his left eye and three under his right. Had this man killed five people? And would he be opposed to adding a third teardrop under his left to balance them out? Kendall was a big fan of symmetry. A cruel sneer tipped the corner of the big bruiser's mouth, and Kendall was sure he'd done Colt and Carey a favor by getting them away. *You've watched too many true-crime documentaries, K. Not all jerks are homicidal maniacs.*

"What happened to the other two waiters? Was there a shift change?" bruiser asked.

"Of sorts," Kendall replied.

The guy smirked. "Did they get into a fight over me?"

Kendall figuratively bit his lip to keep from saying all the things that came to mind. Was the beefcake a closet case or just a cruel jackass? What was his goal? Getting the gay guys all worked up and fighting over him? Would he take the memory home and wrap it around his cock with his fist, or would he have used it as an excuse to harm them in the parking lot later? He let the thoughts bounce safely through his mind and land in the filter he was still honing.

"Can I refill your drink?" Kendall asked, refusing to take the man's bait.

Bruiser snorted. "Sure. Coke Zero."

"You got it," Kendall said, then started to turn.

"Wait," the man said before he took two steps. "Could I order another plate of wings? I've never had anything quite like these."

"Sweet chili lime?" Kendall asked.

"Yeah, but what kind of chili? It's more smoky than hot."

Kendall forced his lips into a flirty smile. "You really want to know?" The man blinked a few times before nodding. Kendall set the empty plates back on the table and leaned closer to him. Bruiser widened his eyes, but he didn't pull back. Just how curious was he about the ingredients in the sauce? "It's a secret."

The man swallowed hard, and a genuine smile played on his lips. Maybe his skills were legendary. "I promise not to tell anyone."

"While you put us out of business?" Kendall asked, straightening to his full height. "I don't think so. I'll be right back with your order." He picked up the plates and moved on to the neighboring table to check in with the other patrons.

Kendall fell into a familiar rhythm of bouncing from table to table, making sure guests were taken care of, racking up big tips as he went. He thought a lot about what Emmett had said and hoped the waitstaff realized Kendall was committed to being an excellent manager, even though he wasn't convinced the move had been the right one. His decision to send Colt and Carey home could still backfire, but at least he'd demonstrated a willingness to step in when it was needed.

He caught Emmett's eye during one of his trips to the bar. The taller man came over to fill his order and added a glass of water for Kendall.

"You're a natural," the enigmatic bartender said.

Kendall took a long drink, then handed the empty glass back. "I think the jury is still out on that one."

Still, Emmett's praise was a much-needed shot in the arm.

Maybe I'm not completely in over my head.

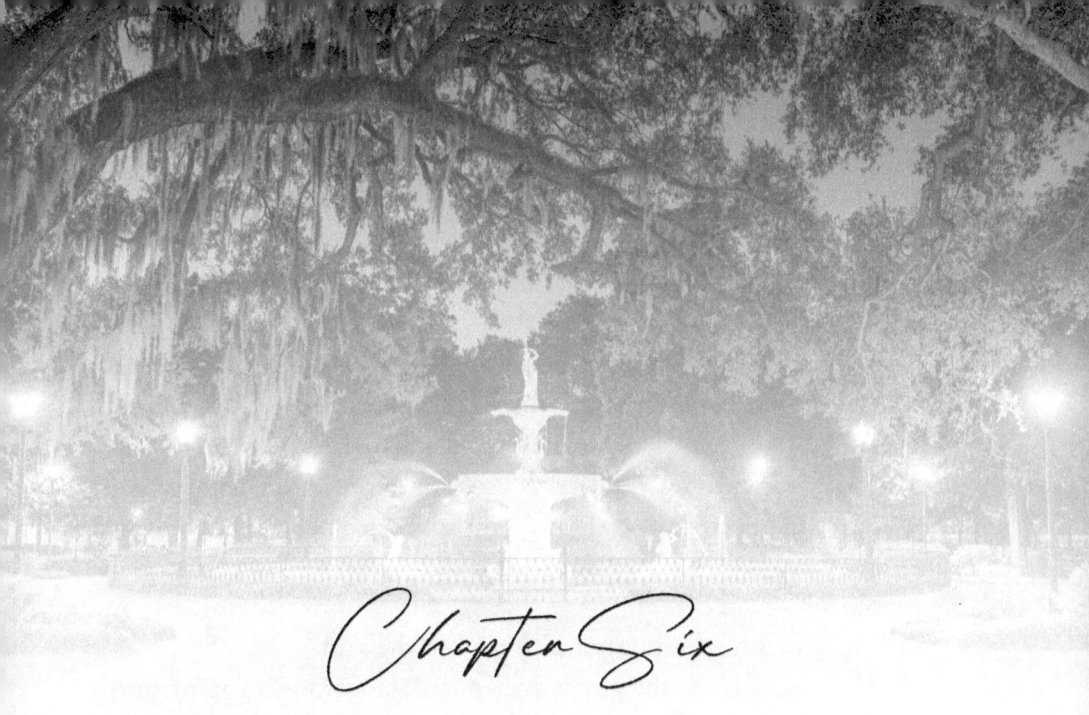

Chapter Six

RIDGE WHEELED INTO THE PARKING LOT AND SAW EDDIE AND
Zack had already arrived and were suited up and ready to go. He
hadn't asked any questions when Asher had called and told him to
report for duty. Ridge shifted his SUV into park and cut the engine, then
grabbed his gear and stepped out into the muggy summer air.

"What's up, fellas?" Ridge asked as his friends approached. Zack and
Eddie had been gone all day, transporting a fugitive, while Ridge and a few
others had been assigned to the federal courthouse. "I didn't know you guys
were back."

"Thank fuck," Eddie said. "Although I wish I were going home instead
of assisting the Miami field office. They uncovered a possible local connection to a fugitive on their most-wanted list. Asher reached out to SPD for
assistance, and a CI spotted our target."

"Another birthday party?" Ridge asked as he put on the last of his gear.

Zack snorted. "Not this time. We're heading to The Cockpit. Maybe
you'll run into Sugar."

"Maybe the bad guy *is* Sugar," Eddie countered.

"Fuck you both."

Zack paused long enough to have a good laugh at Ridge's expense before continuing. "Sergeant Locke from SPD major crimes is meeting us at
the club with a few officers from his unit to assist. Ready to roll?"

Ridge did a quick inventory. "Yep."

"I call shotgun," Eddie said and sprinted to the passenger side of Zack's rig.

"Asshole," Ridge grumbled as he slid onto the rear bench seat. "So, who are we looking for?"

Eddie handed him a fugitive sheet for Rodney James, a dark-haired, pale man with a vivid scar across his forehead and teardrops tatted beneath both eyes. The man's dark eyes looked as dull and lifeless as a shark's. Ridge whistled as he skimmed over the man's arrest and conviction history. "How does a man who's been convicted and sent to jail for burglary, aggravated assault, and possession of illegal firearms land back on the street to become a suspect in a homicide?"

"You're preaching to the choir, Ridgey," Eddie said.

"We have to assume the guy is armed and dangerous, so going into a crowded club with guns blazing isn't the answer," Zack said.

Ridge would've argued the club would be less crowded on a worknight, but he'd seen firsthand it didn't matter when the hottest waiters served the best wings on the planet. Like it had too many times to count, his mind shifted to a platinum-blond waiter with pretty lips and a wicked tongue. Ridge had been seduced by both the words that had come out of his mouth and the skillful way Sugar had kissed him. Two weeks had passed since they'd parted ways outside Tranquil Breezes, and Ridge had wanted to text or call him every single day. The urge was even stronger after finding out a dangerous felon was potentially among the crowd eating wings.

"Don't do it," Eddie said.

"Do what?"

His friend turned and looked at him. "A warning text could set off a disastrous chain of events. Let's just get to the club and assess the situation."

Ridge knew Eddie was right and nodded.

The ride to the club didn't take long, and Zack drove around back and parked in a far corner next to another dark SUV tucked away in the shadows. Where the front of the building was lit for Jesus, the back was pitch black save for a single light above a door. Ridge didn't want to think about the questionable activities that most likely occurred back there or who on the staff might be participating in them.

Eddie rolled down his window, stuck his head out, and made some weird bird sound. The back door of the SUV next to them opened, and

Detective Royce Locke stepped out. Ridge had worked with the blond man several times and liked him a lot.

"You big idiot," Locke said as he gripped Eddie in a headlock and gave him a noogie. "Why don't you broadcast to everyone that we're setting up a sting operation." Locke released Eddie, opened the rear passenger door, and climbed in beside Ridge. "How's it going, Smoky?" It was always fun to see which mountain range Locke would use to address him.

"It's always good to see you, Locke," he said, bumping the man's raised fist. "So, what's the plan?"

Before Locke could answer, a door opened at the back of the building, and a man stepped out. Platinum-blond hair shone brightly in the single exterior light. *Sugar.* After only a few steps, the guy was fully engulfed by the darkness.

"Is that Kendall?" Zack asked.

"Sure looked like it," Locke replied.

Son of a bitch. His Sugar was the same guy his friends had been eager for him to meet?

"Is he your CI?" Ridge asked, hoping his voice came out sounding normal.

"No," Locke replied, "I met Kendall Blakemore during a homicide investigation about two years ago. He came home after a weekend away and discovered his roommate had been murdered."

"How awful," Eddie said sadly. "Poor guy."

Ridge suddenly felt sick to his stomach. He hated that something so ugly had touched the beautiful man.

Locke rolled down the window and stuck his head out. "*Psst.* Kendall. Come here," he called out.

"Fuck no," came the reply. "I am not appearing on a future episode of *Disappeared.*"

Everyone in the car chuckled.

"Nice going, Locke," Zack said. "The guy is probably running for his life now."

Locke opened the door and slipped out. "Kendall, it's me, Detective Locke."

"Uh-huh," he replied sassily. "I don't want candy, and I'm not helping you look for a puppy." Though Ridge heard the uncertainty in his voice,

Kendall had sounded closer. He either recognized Locke's voice or was too curious for his own good.

Zack turned on his headlights, illuminating Locke long enough for the man to see him.

"Oh, it really is you," Kendall said, relief making his voice sound throaty. "Does Sawyer know you're lurking around in the dark trying to pick up guys?"

The driver-side window on the SUV beside them rolled down, and Locke's boyfriend, Sawyer Key, stuck his head out. "Yes, I do."

Kendall shook his head. "Perverts." He heaved a sigh. "All I wanted was twenty minutes of peace and quiet. I guess that's just too much to ask for tonight. What can I do for Savannah's finest?"

"Step into the SUV so we can chat," Locke told him. He opened the door for Kendall, who started to get in until he saw Ridge sitting on the bench seat.

Blue eyes widened, and soft pink lips parted on a gasp. "Oh," Kendall said, sounding a little breathless. "You could've just used the phone number I gave you. There was no need to stage a"—he waved his hand around—"whatever this is."

Ridge couldn't help but smile. "Hello, Sugar."

"Sugar?" Eddie and Zack asked. Ridge ignored them, but they snagged Kendall's attention.

"Oh, hey," he said cheerfully. "Zack and Eddie, right? You work with Asher." Then he turned wide eyes on Ridge. "I can't believe I didn't make the connection when you showed off your badge. I blame it on stress."

"When did he show you his badge?" Eddie asked.

"When we toured an apartment complex a couple weeks ago. I think Ridge was looking for an excuse to show off his hot body, though."

Ridge fought off the urge to squirm. "Was not." But maybe a little.

"Aren't you a little overdressed, Kendall?" Locke asked. "Where're your normal booty shorts." *Good question.* Not that Ridge hated the new look.

Kendall ran his long, slender fingers over the length of his tie. It was navy blue with gold pinstripes. "I've recently been promoted to manager. In fact, tonight is my first shift."

Something in his voice said it had been a real humdinger. Ridge wanted to probe for more details, but a round of congratulations filtered through the vehicle.

"Thanks," Kendall said. "So, um, not to be rude or anything, but if this isn't an elaborate scheme for Ridge to get me into bed, what's going on here?" Kendall directed his pale eyes to Ridge and whispered, "You wouldn't have to go to such extremes, by the way." The truth of his declaration was evident in Kendall's sultry smile.

Ridge would've responded, hopefully just as wittily, if his tongue hadn't been glued to the roof of his mouth. Kendall nibbled on his bottom lip while waiting for a reply.

"Ridge, show him the printout of our fugitive," Eddie said.

He'd forgotten all about the sheet of paper. Before he could react, Kendall scooted right up against Ridge and peered at the document. The man smelled like an intoxicating mix of crisp, citrusy cologne and chicken wings. Ridge wasn't sure what he found more alluring, and what the hell did that say about him?

Kendall snorted and shook his head. "I should've known." He rattled off the man's convictions out loud as well as his alleged crimes. "What a charmer."

"You recognize him?" Eddie asked.

"Oh yeah." He told them about two waiters getting into a fight while trying to gain the guy's favor. "He's put away at least twelve pounds of chicken wings."

"Ought to make him easier to apprehend," Zack said.

"Unless he's dripping in sauce," Kendall countered.

Recovering his ability to speak, Ridge said, "So he's still in there?"

"He was a few minutes ago, but he could've left since I stepped outside."

"We need to act fast," Zack said. "Can you get us a table near him?"

"We can't all go in," Royce said. "Just one of us needs to scout the club."

"We need a table close to James but not in his direct line of sight," Eddie added.

"Let me go in and see what's available," Kendall said. "Which one of you should I text when the coast is clear?"

"Ridge, stop playing hard to get and give the man your digits."

"Thank you, Eddie." Kendall held out his phone to Ridge.

Ridge accepted the device and entered his number. "Don't abuse it."

Kendall winked when Ridge returned the phone. "You should be so lucky."

Locke opened the car door and stepped out so Kendall could return to the club.

"Hey," Ridge said. Kendall stopped and turned around. "Be careful."

"I will."

Ridge watched him disappear into the darkness. "I don't like this," he said once Kendall had reentered the club.

"All he has to do is tell us if James is still there," Zack said.

A few minutes later, Ridge received a text from Kendall. *Found the perfect table. I'll meet you at the host station up front.*

"I'm up." Ridge pocketed his phone. "You guys get into position. I'll text you when he's on his way out so you can take him down in the parking lot."

Once Ridge stepped out of the vehicle, he removed his personal protection gear and tucked his gun into his waistband at the small of his back. His shirt was long and loose enough to hide the outline. After tucking his badge into his pocket, Ridge gave each of them a fist bump and headed toward the front of the building.

The wind kicked up, but the air was too humid to be a relief. Something skittered across the blacktop, and Ridge hoped it was leaves and detritus instead of rodents with beady eyes and sharp teeth. Faint moans echoed from the shadows but not the kind that stirred alarm. It wasn't Ridge's responsibility to police the activities going on in the dark. He had a fugitive to apprehend.

Kendall was at the host station talking to the same cute brunet he'd seen on his first visit. The guy batted his eyelashes at Ridge and said, "Well, hello. We meet again. May I—"

"This one is all mine, Seth." Kendall maneuvered around the station and stopped in front of Ridge. He rose on his tiptoes and pressed a firm kiss to Ridge's lips. Kendall eased back and looked into his eyes, and Ridge felt truly claimed by the possessiveness he saw there. He tried to remember this was all for show, but…was it? There was no denying the electrical charge between them. Kendall pulled back slowly and continued to gaze into Ridge's eyes. Want and need pressed heavily against him, and it felt like Ridge had been hit in the chest with a sledgehammer.

The flight attendant sighed heavily. "Lucky bastard."

Kendall laughed and led him deeper into the club. The dance floor was packed with bodies writhing together to a bass-heavy song Ridge didn't recognize. He used the loud music as an excuse to lean into Kendall. "Don't these people have to work in the morning?"

Kendall placed a proprietary arm around Ridge's waist, and he liked it a lot. "You're only young once."

As Ridge watched the clubbers, he wondered what a night of carefree dancing might feel like. Could he even dance? He couldn't recall a single time where he'd been enticed to try.

"James just started in on another plate of sweet chili lime wings," Kendall said, interrupting his thoughts. At least one of them was focused on the mission. "I found a table with the perfect vantage point so you can alert the others when he leaves."

Ridge's stomach growled. "Sweet chili lime?"

Kendall nodded and smiled. "It's our flavor of the week."

"The name seems a little tame compared to Regret," Ridge said.

Kendall gestured to an empty table, and they stopped beside it. He smiled up at Ridge, his eyes sparkling with mischief. "Though it lacks a snappy name, the sauce doesn't lack flavor. Maybe I'll send some home with you after you collar your perp."

"Collar my perp?"

"I watch way too many true-crime documentaries." Ridge sat down, and Kendall assessed him.

"Well, I definitely can't eat them now. The sauce might make it difficult to draw my weapon."

Kendall's lips quirked, and Ridge realized the double entendre he'd stepped into. "Well, you can't just sit here and look handsome. You're too conspicuous and will attract too much attention. What if I bring you an order of loaded fries? You can eat those with a fork and keep your hands clean and your head down to watch the per—um, the bad guy from the corner of your eye."

"You twisted my arm," Ridge replied. "Could I have a glass of water?" Beer was out of the question, and soda would keep him up all damn night.

"Certainly." Kendall cleared his throat and shifted his eyes to the left. "I'll be right back."

Ridge glanced to the left and saw Rodney James's table two rows over. He was positioned behind the fugitive and at an angle, providing Ridge the perfect vantage point. The man wouldn't see him unless he purposefully scanned the room, and his body language wasn't the least bit alert as he tore into a chicken wing. James was utterly at ease and enjoying his food.

Kendall returned a few minutes later with a plateful of crispy fries smothered in melted cheese, bacon, and chives. "I wasn't sure what you wanted to dip them in, so I brought you ranch and sweet chili sauce."

"Yes and yes," Ridge said, fighting off the urge to rub his hands together gleefully. *Focus on the mission, asshole.* He forced his eyes off the plate to look at Kendall. "I don't want you to do anything to tip James off, okay?" Kendall nodded. "Keep serving his wings and refilling his drink like normal. Don't over solicit, and don't ignore him. Any change could trigger his suspicion. Just give me a heads up after he asks for his bill."

Kendall released a deep breath. "Got it."

Ridge dug into his fries while sending a group text to Eddie and Zack. *Eyes on target.*

Yeah, but do you see James? Zack asked.

Ha fucking ha, Ridge replied. He glanced up to make sure his target was still in the same place.

Told you Kendall is the perfect guy for you, Eddie wrote.

I'll text you when James is on the move. Ridge speared a cheese-smothered fry and shoved it into his mouth. He had decent food, excellent scenery, and eyes on his target. As far as missions went, this takedown should be relatively easy.

So why was the hair on the back of his neck standing up?

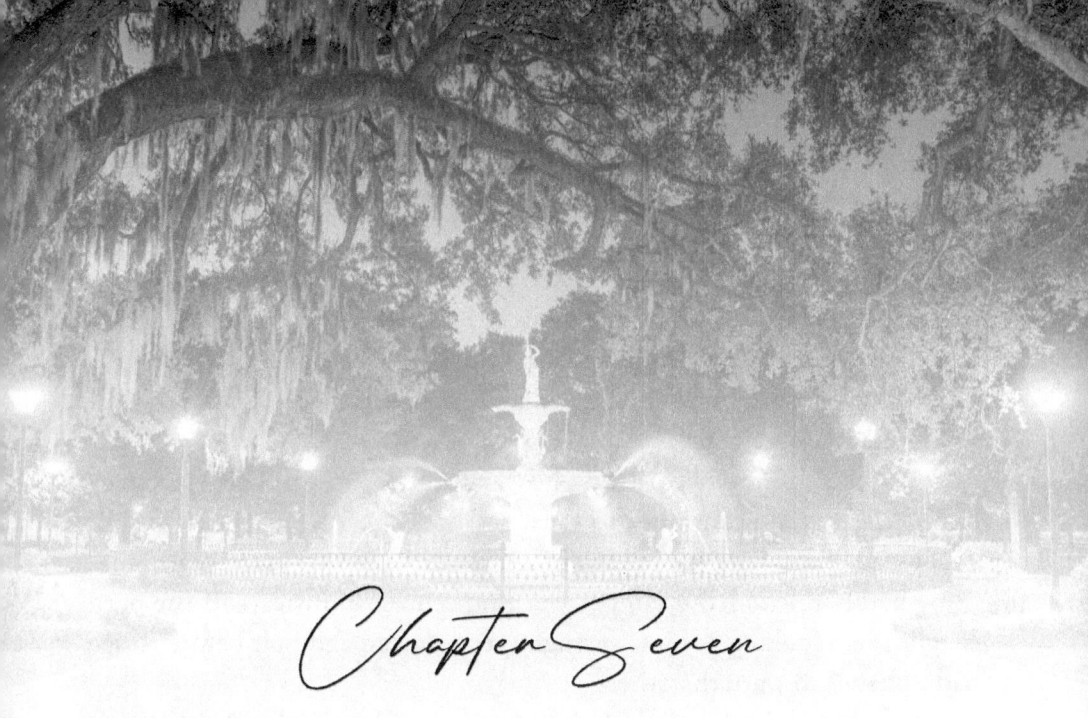

Chapter Seven

"**W**HY ARE YOU BACK FROM BREAK SO SOON?" EMMETT asked when Kendall stopped by the bar to place another order.

I was coerced into the back of an SUV where I reunited with the sexiest man on earth, and I'm now assisting SPD and the US Marshals with a fugitive takedown.

Except Kendall wasn't sure he could trust Emmett with the truth. Hell, Kendall wasn't sure he trusted himself with it either. So he shrugged his shoulders and said the next best thing—a half-truth. "I felt guilty for leaving the dining room short-staffed, so I came back early."

Emmett looked up from the tap. "You did the right thing sending those immature brats home."

Nodding, Kendall said, "Yeah, but doing the right thing doesn't mean I'm immune from second thoughts and regrets."

"I get it," Emmett said as he placed a mug of beer on Kendall's tray. "Try not to dwell on it, though."

Kendall gave him a mock salute, but the bartender didn't see it because he was too busy scanning the crowded club. Curious about what had snagged Emmett's attention, Kendall pivoted and followed the bartender's line of sight. A corner of the dance floor was visible as well as most of the dining room. The angle of the bar put the fugitive and the deputy marshal front and center for Emmett.

"I don't like him."

Kendall spun around and looked at Emmett. "Who?"

"The sketchy-looking dude Colt and Carey were fighting over. He's been here for hours and keeps shoving wings into his mouth."

"They're damn fine wings," Kendall replied. "This week's featured flavor seems to be a big hit."

"Maybe." Emmett's voice said he wasn't buying it. The bartender narrowed his eyes and continued to stare.

Kendall was tempted to look in James's direction again to see if something had happened, but Ridge's warning echoed in his ears. If the perp caught them looking at him, he might get spooked and bolt before Ridge had a chance to warn the others.

Jesus. How in the world had he landed in the middle of this mess? The truth really was stranger than fiction. Kendall's phone buzzed in his pocket, startling him from his pity party for one. He retrieved the device and groaned when he saw the caller.

"It's Drew," he told Emmett. "I bet the twins called him to complain about me."

"Without a doubt," the bartender replied. "Answer it. Best not to keep the boss man waiting."

Kendall stepped away from the bar to answer the call. "Hey, Drew," he said into the phone. "I can explain everything."

"Whoa," his boss said. "I was just checking in to see how your first shift as manager was going."

"Oh." Kendall's voice and energy resembled a deflating balloon.

Drew chuckled. "But you have my attention now."

Kendall grimaced, then told Drew about Colt and Carey's fight and his plans to formally write them up. All the while, he kept an eye on the fugitive scarfing down wings like it was his last meal. The thought made Kendall stumble over his words.

"Are you okay?" Drew asked once he finished.

"Me? Sure. Why do you ask?"

"Your voice sounded funny there for a second," Drew explained.

Kendall took a deep breath to focus his squirrelly brain. "Sorry about that. I'm just keeping an eye on my tables."

"Your tables?"

He explained his decision to pick up Colt's and Carey's sections and split their tips among the other servers. "I thought it was the right thing to do."

"Absolutely," Drew agreed. "This just proves I made the right decision to promote you to manager. Do you need me to come in and help?"

"No," Kendall replied, though he appreciated the gesture. "We only have a few hours left before last call."

"Let me know if you change your mind," Drew said.

"Will do."

The men exchanged goodbyes, and Kendall tucked his phone away as he returned to the bar.

"I added another soda for the sketchy dude," Emmett said.

"Thanks."

Kendall hoisted the loaded tray in the air and headed to the dining area. He plastered a smile on his face and began his rounds at the opposite end of the room from James, saving his soda delivery for last. His heart beat faster with every step closer to the scary man, and it was doing a damn fine impersonation of a jackhammer by the time Kendall reached his table.

"The bartender thought you might be thirsty," he told the fugitive.

James lifted his head, and dull, lifeless eyes stared back at Kendall. The man's lips slanted into a cruel sneer. "Does he want to fuck me too?"

A scathing remark was on the tip of Kendall's tongue, and only the worry he might blow Ridge's opportunity to capture the asshole prevented the words from escaping his lips. "Not that I'm aware of," he said instead. Before he could congratulate himself on his maturity and restraint, Kendall opened his mouth and ruined everything. "Do you want me to go ask him?"

The sneer turned into a scary scowl. "Fuck no. Gross. I'm just here for the wings, man." The guy pulled his napkin off his lap, proving even the worst people could use good etiquette, and wiped his mouth. James tossed the napkin and reached for his wallet. A shiver of anticipation raced through Kendall. *This was it.* The fugitive was going to ask for his bill. But instead of pulling out a credit card, James handed Kendall three crisp one-hundred-dollar bills. The man scooted his chair back and rose to his feet. "That ought to be enough to cover the food and provide a nice tip for the trouble I caused."

Kendall craned his neck to meet James's dark gaze. How fucking tall was this guy? The rap sheet he'd seen said six four, but he seemed much taller. "Trouble?" he asked. Kendall darted a glance in Ridge's direction to see if he was witnessing the interaction. A waiter had stopped at his table and stood directly in Kendall's line of sight, which meant Ridge wouldn't be able to see him either. *Fuck.*

James shifted closer to Kendall, pulling his attention back to the scary fugitive. "I'm like a magnet," he said.

With his adrenaline spiking, it took Kendall a moment to remember what they'd been discussing. *Trouble.* James was admitting to being at the center of it all the time. Kendall had to stall the man until he could tip Ridge off. Forcing a flirty smile to his lips, Kendall batted his eyelashes. "I know a little something about causing trouble."

James raked his dark gaze over Kendall before meeting his eyes once more. "I just bet you do."

Kendall was about five seconds away from pissing himself, so he changed tactics. "This tip is too generous. Are you sure you don't want change?"

James quirked a brow at the sudden topic shift, and Kendall worried he'd tripped his alarm. Instead, the man gave him another genuine smile. "Nah. You've earned it for putting up with me. I always tip servers and sex workers well."

Kendall wasn't shocked often, but James's offhanded comment caught him off guard. "Well, that's nice of you. How about a drink to go?"

"I—"

A loud crash in the dining room interrupted James's response. Kendall recognized the sound of shattering dishes and glassware and automatically turned in the direction of the noise to assess the damage. Unfortunately, James was equally curious and diverted his gaze as well. Two waiters had collided right in front of Ridge's table. The lawman looked up from the fray and locked eyes with Kendall before glancing at the fugitive standing beside him.

"A fucking cop!" James snarled just as Ridge shot to his feet with his gun drawn.

The fugitive probably had an embedded alarm system alerting him to the presence of law enforcement—copdar instead of gaydar. James's survival instincts must have kicked in. He hooked a beefy arm around Kendall's neck, yanking him to his chest as a human shield.

A metal click sounded near Kendall's right ear, and a second later something sharp pressed into his neck. His bladder spasmed and threatened to empty right there, but he held on somehow. The last thing he needed was James slipping in his piss and nicking an artery.

The guests and staff around them screamed and ran for cover, triggering a reactionary effect until everyone was screaming and scrambling toward the exit. It felt like it was only the three of them left in the bar. Ridge's face was hard as stone and laser focused as he aimed his gun at James.

"US marshal," he declared. "Drop the weapon and let the man go."

"Fuck you," James snarled, tightening the headlock until black dots swam in front of Kendall's vision. "Drop the fucking tray, or I'll gut you like a fish."

He'd forgotten he still held it but became acutely aware of his fingers clutching the rim. Kendall tightened his grip on the rigid plastic instead of letting go. If he could command his arms to work, maybe he could use the tray as a weapon.

"Do it right now," the angry man hissed, pushing the tip of his blade deeper into Kendall's skin.

A sharp, burning sensation was followed by warm liquid trickling down Kendall's neck, and the urge to vomit replaced the need to piss himself. If he was going to die, he wanted to do it with dignity. Letting go of the large round tray required a lot of mental energy and repetitive commands to his brain before his fingers loosened enough to let it drop to the floor. Kendall was utterly defenseless unless he considered his biting wit and sharp tongue, both of which seemed to have abandoned him.

James sidestepped a few feet to the right, forcing Kendall to come with him. "Stay back. I won't hesitate to kill him."

"You know damn well I won't let you leave here with a hostage," Ridge said. "I will shoot you."

James sidestepped a little more, but Ridge kept pace from two rows over. His gun never wavered. "And risk shooting the hostage?" James asked. "I don't think so."

Kendall would rather take his chances with Ridge's aim than face whatever James had in store for him.

A cocky grin tugged at the marshal's lips, distracting Kendall from his panic. "I never miss."

The fugitive paused for a second before continuing toward the exit. "I'll let him go as soon as I get outside."

No, he wouldn't. James would kill Kendall in the parking lot or force him into the car and dispose of him later. Neither option was desirable.

"Bullshit," Ridge said. "You're not going to leave a witness, James."

The burly man paused again. "So you know who I am."

"You thought he was here for his health?" Kendall asked.

James snorted. "The wings are excellent. Cops gotta eat too. Could've been a coincidence."

Ridge's jaw tensed, telling Kendall his distraction techniques weren't welcome or wise. "Yeah, I know who you are. I know where you're going too," Ridge said.

"Disney World?" Kendall guessed. *Fuck.* What was wrong with him? It was as if his brain couldn't control his bladder and his mouth at the same time.

James chuckled, but it wasn't a happy sound. "To hell," he replied.

"Eventually, I'm sure," Ridge agreed. "But not until you spend the rest of your life in a prison cell."

"I'll pass," James said and began moving again.

Panic rose inside Kendall with each step they took toward the front door. He could tell they were getting close to the edge of the dining room, which meant he was running out of time. Damn it. There were so many things he wanted to do and needed to say, and there was a deputy marshal he hadn't fondled. He couldn't die yet.

"Chipotle pepper!" Kendall blurted.

He must've startled James because the arm around his neck loosened, and the press of the knife eased. *Now or never.* Kendall swung his fist back as hard as he could, tagging the man in the balls. He didn't care how big and tough James was; that area was every man's weakness.

The knife clattered to the floor seconds before James buckled forward. Kendall took advantage of the momentum to slip free. Instead of running away like an intelligent person would, Kendall aimed a kick at James's knee, sending him sprawling to the ground where he curled into the fetal position. Kendall kicked the knife away and glanced up in time to see Ridge leaping over the last chair separating them. He started to breathe a sigh of relief until he saw James reach for a gun holstered at his ankle.

"Gun!" Kendall shouted as he frantically searched for a way to help.

His gaze landed on an abandoned serving tray on the table beside him.

Without thinking, he picked it up and swung it down on James's head. It connected with a loud *thud*, and the big man went completely limp.

"Christ," Ridge said as he reached them. He fished a pair of cuffs out of his back pocket and snapped them into place on James's wrists. He stood up, his chest heaving, and surveyed Kendall as he pushed a button on his phone. "You okay?"

Kendall opened his mouth but couldn't speak, so he shook his head. Concern washed over Ridge's features as he stepped forward and pulled Kendall into his arms. A man's voice came through Ridge's phone, but Kendall couldn't tell which one of the guys he'd called.

"I wasn't talking to you, Eduardo, but it's good to know you're okay. I got James. Get your asses in here to collect him, and call for an ambulance." He stowed his phone away in his pocket and gently pushed Kendall back a step so he could probe his neck.

"*You* got James, huh?" Kendall's voice sounded a little shaky, but who could blame him?

Ridge snapped his gaze up. His brown eyes were warm and soft where they'd been hard and cold just moments before. "Fine. You got James."

"I'll keep your secret." Kendall's head suddenly felt fuzzy and heavy. Something was off. How much blood had he lost? "Am I dying? Quick. Let me fondle your abs before I take my final breath."

"Hey, hey," Ridge said softly before pressing a quick kiss to his forehead. Kendall closed his eyes and sighed. No man had ever kissed him so tenderly. "Just breathe. You're going to be okay. The cut is superficial, but it is bleeding." He glanced around, then grabbed a stack of napkins off the table next to them. He peeled off a few and held them to Kendall's neck. "Can you hold these against the wound?"

Could he? Kendall couldn't seem to get his limbs to work at all.

"If you want to touch my abs, you'll need to put some pressure on that cut."

Kendall took a deep breath, dug deep, and applied all the pressure he could muster to the wound.

"I could've done without your smartass commentary," Ridge said, "but that was some fast thinking at the end. What was the deal with the chipotle pepper?"

Ridge's smile unlocked parts of Kendall's frozen brain. "James had asked me what pepper we used in the sweet chili lime sauce because it was more smoky than hot. Of course I hadn't told him, so I just blurted it out, hoping to catch him off guard."

"Well, it worked."

Thunderous footsteps approached, but Kendall couldn't force his gaze away from the sexy man in front of him.

"What the hell happened in here?" Eddie asked them. "One minute, everything is quiet and we're fighting off sleep while waiting for you to signal us…"

"And the next, everyone comes screaming out of the club," Zack continued.

Ridge smirked at them. "That *was* your signal."

"Couldn't you have just texted or called as we'd discussed?" Zack asked.

"No time," Ridge replied.

"And him?" Eddie asked, gesturing to the prone man on the ground. "What happened to James?"

"Kendall did," Ridge replied.

"Nice," Eddie said while Zack nodded his approval. They both bumped Kendall's fist.

He told them what happened, then told SPD and then the EMTs when they arrived on the scene. The marshals escorted James out of the club, and Kendall had overheard they were taking him to the hospital to rule out a concussion before taking him to lockup. Kendall had declined transportation after he assessed his injury in the bathroom. Mass pandemonium ensued when the staff returned to give their statements, and Drew showed up to make sure everyone was okay. It seemed like Kendall had rehashed the story at least a thousand times before he found a few quiet moments to himself in his office.

"There you are," Drew said, stepping into the room. His black hair was still disheveled, and his pale eyes studied Kendall from behind black-rimmed glasses. "Are you okay?"

Kendall inclined his head and smiled. "Do you think my answer will be any different than the previous hundred times I've given it tonight?"

Drew smiled and dropped onto the small couch tucked away in the corner. "I think you're going to tell me whatever it is you think I want to hear."

"Probably."

"Okay," Drew said, "I want the truth."

Kendall took a deep breath and released it slowly. "I'm as good as can be expected."

"Why don't you go on home and let me close up."

Drew hadn't wanted to reopen the club once the crime scene had been processed, but Kendall talked him into taking advantage of the buzz generated by the takedown. Maybe it was tacky, but Kendall was the only staff member involved, and he'd prefer to work through his adrenaline rather than go to an empty house. What Kendall wanted more than anything was to talk to Ridge again. Okay, maybe talking wasn't the first thing he wanted to do. Ridge had disappeared quickly and without so much as a goodbye. Kendall still had his number programmed into his phone, but it wouldn't be appropriate to text him. Would it? Besides, he would be busy dealing with James.

"Kendall," Drew said, interrupting his thoughts.

He met his boss's concerned gaze and smiled. "I'd rather stay here."

Drew raised his hands in surrender. "I can tell when I'm not going to win an argument. I'm going to insist you take a few days off, though."

"Okay. I'll let you twist my arm."

They chatted for a few minutes, then Drew left the club. Kendall resumed waiting tables, noting the club was busier than it had been before the showdown with James.

"I'm not going to ask how you're doing," Emmett said when Kendall stopped by the bar to place drink orders.

Kendall sagged against the long stretch of polished wood. "Thank goodness."

"I'm going to tell you," the bartender said. *Uh-oh.* "Pay attention to the expressions in the staff's eyes when they look at you. It's been a shitty night full of ups and downs, but the respect you've earned tonight is no small victory."

After he left the bar with his heavy tray, Kendall let Emmett's words soak in, and he allowed himself to really see what he'd missed in the winks and nods the staff had given him. Respect. It bolstered his energy when his adrenaline caught the last bus out of town.

I can do this. I can really fucking do this.

Chapter Eight

RIDGE MET ZACK'S GAZE IN THE REARVIEW MIRROR A FEW HOURS later. The twinkle in his friend's eyes and the crooked smile on his ruggedly handsome face spelled trouble.

"Don't start," Ridge warned.

"What? I wasn't about to say 'I told you so.'"

Eddie elbowed Zack. "*We*, jackass. *We* told him so."

"You guys are reading way too much into this," Ridge said. "Are we transporting James to Miami in the morning?"

Zack chuckled as he turned into the USMS parking lot. "Smooth, Ridgey."

"We hardly noticed the abrupt change in conversation," Eddie added. "And no, two marshals are in route from Miami as we speak."

"Thank goodness," Zack said. "James started whining and complaining the moment he came to on the gurney in the ambulance and didn't let up until we processed him at lockup. The Miami boys can have him." Zack pulled to a stop beside Ridge's SUV and met his gaze once more. "Do us all a favor and call Kendall."

"Can't you find someone else to harass?" Ridge opened the door and slid out, but Zack called his name before he could close it. He ducked his head back inside the vehicle. "Yeah?"

"Did Kendall really ask James if he was going to Disney World?"

Ridge heaved a sigh. "Yeah. That was just one of his smartass quips. I'm not sure how he's still alive."

"Bet you're glad he is, though," Eddie said, waggling his brows.

"Of course I am. The guy put himself at risk to help us. I wouldn't want any harm to come to him."

"Yeah, that's the reason," Zack said. "And Ridgey…" God, he hated that nickname. "We nag because we care."

Ridge rolled his eyes. "Thanks, Mom." He shut the door on their laughter and hit the fob to unlock his SUV, then stowed his gear and started the engine. They were going to be insufferable after this. He wouldn't even get a break since he was still crashing at Eddie's, except Ridge turned left out of the parking lot instead of going right toward his friend's apartment. He didn't bother trying to convince himself he was seeking the solace of a quiet hotel room.

"I'm just checking to make sure Kendall is okay," he said when he pulled into the club's parking lot a few minutes later.

Nothing more, nothing less.

He'd nearly had himself convinced by the time he reached the club's entrance. The heavy bass thumping through the speakers sounded louder, the crowd around the bar seemed larger, and more dancers were writhing on the floor than before the takedown. The same flight attendant was working the host station when he walked in.

The cute guy's eyes widened when he saw Ridge. "Oh, you're back." He stepped out from behind his post and glided over.

"Hi, Seth," Ridge said, then introduced himself. "I wanted to make sure Kendall is doing okay. Is he still here?" He scanned the club again but didn't see Kendall anywhere.

"Of course our hero is still here," Seth said. "Let me get you seated, and I'll let him know you're back."

"Thanks."

"This way," Seth said, tilting his head toward the dining room.

Ridge followed him to the same table Kendall had led him to earlier.

Seth looked around the club for a second before meeting his gaze. "I'll go find Kendall. Can I place an order for you on the way?"

"Nah," Ridge said. "I'm not staying long."

Seth winked. "That's what they all say."

Ridge chuckled when the flight attendant walked away, then scrubbed his hand over his face. What a fucking night. He wanted to call Seth back and place an order for a strong drink but didn't.

Instead of second-guessing his motives, Ridge passed the time watching people dance, laugh, and celebrate life. There was a sudden shift in the atmosphere, and Ridge knew Kendall was nearby without looking, but he searched the club for him anyway. Their eyes met and held, and a smile slowly stretched across Kendall's handsome face. Ridge returned the gesture and felt the answering joy spread through his chest.

Kendall wound his way over to the table, and Ridge was unable to tear his eyes away for even a second. Kendall's smile turned shy when he reached Ridge's table. Was this the same bold man who'd drunk from his glass and licked the sauce he'd wiped off Ridge's face the first night they'd met? Ridge understood the hesitancy. Something very drastic had shifted between them after the kiss during their second meeting. Before the tour at Tranquil Breezes, he'd been aware of Kendall, but after...it felt more like infatuation. Ridge shoved the annoying thought aside.

"Hi," he said.

Kendall tilted his head. "Hi back."

"How are you?" they both asked at once, then shared a laugh.

Kendall gestured to the empty chair across from Ridge. "May I sit?"

Ridge thought it was extremely odd Kendall's reluctance and vulnerability bothered him more than his boldness had. Both extremes were bothersome but for entirely different reasons. One fueled fantasies, and the other invoked a possessive streak that shocked him. All over a man he'd kissed once. Somehow that single kiss had felt more intimate than the sex he'd experienced with others.

"Please," Ridge said.

Kendall lowered himself into the seat and interlocked his hands on top of the table. The small space separating them felt like a wide gulf. Ridge's fingers itched to touch Kendall, so he tucked them under the table. Kendall's posture was relaxed, but his knuckles were white from the tight grip he had on himself. Was he fighting the urge to reach for Ridge too?

Fuck it.

Ridge reached across the table and gently skimmed a finger over the bandage on Kendall's slender neck. Kendall's mouth parted as a shiver rolled through him. Had he gasped? Ridge resented the hell out of the thumping music and was about to suggest they go someplace quieter to talk.

"It's nothing more than a tiny scratch," Kendall told him. "I'm okay."

Before Ridge could comment further, a waiter stopped by their table. He set a plate of wings in front of Ridge and a grilled cheese sandwich and fries in front of Kendall.

"I didn't order anything," Ridge said.

The waiter looked momentarily confused until Kendall spoke up. "I did. Thank you, Terry."

The guy nodded and left them alone again.

The scent coming from the wings was enough to temporarily hijack Ridge's thoughts and make him drool. Kendall must have mistaken his silence as rejection.

"Did I misread your reaction to the wings earlier?" he asked. "I can order you something else." He slid his plate toward Ridge. "Or I can share my sandwich."

Ridge cleared his throat. "No, this is perfect. My brain just short-circuited for a second."

Kendall picked up a triangle of bread and cheese and nibbled one corner. "Dig in."

Ridge picked up a wing and sank his teeth into it. Pure perfection—crispy on the outside and juicy on the inside. The sauce was a perfect harmony of heat and sweet but without the pungency of too much vinegar as was the case with many restaurants. "So good. The chef really knows his stuff."

Kendall smiled. "Sure does." He took another small bite of his sandwich before swirling a fry in ranch. Most people would pop the entire crinkly fry into their mouths, but Kendall only bit off a small chunk. Was he always such a fastidious eater or was it something else? He paid closer attention and saw Kendall seemed to swallow with great difficulty.

"You're not okay," Ridge said, tossing his napkin on top of the table. "I want to take you to the hospital."

Kendall dropped the fry and grabbed Ridge's wrist before he could rise. "You're right. I'm not okay, but I will be." He took a shaky breath. "I have, um…This is embarrassing."

Ridge smiled to reassure him. "More embarrassing than the time I came in and told a complete stranger about finding my boyfriend in bed with his boss?"

Kendall cocked his head to the side. "I thought you said he was your fiancé?"

"He was, but I kept forgetting, which is why Eddie and Zack...Never mind." Yeah, he wasn't going there. "We're talking about you now."

Kendall leaned forward and propped his elbows on the table. "Oh, I'd much rather hear the rest of that sentence. Eddie and Zack, what?"

Ridge shook his head. "Nope. Tell me what's wrong, or I'll toss you over my shoulder and cart you off to the hospital."

Kendall flopped back against his seat and crossed his arms over his chest. The little pout on his pretty mouth made Ridge want to kiss him. "Your story took a lame turn. I was all for you tossing me over your shoulder and carrying me away. But the hospital? You couldn't think of a better ending?"

As far as distraction techniques went, Kendall's was a damn good one. Ridge's brain had no problem conceiving an alternate ending to the plot. He reined himself in. "You look like you're having difficulty swallowing those tiny bites. Maybe we should—"

Kendall's pout gave way to the most seductive grin Ridge had ever seen. "Now we're talking."

"—have a professional check it out," Ridge casually continued as if his dick wasn't getting hard beneath the table.

Huffing a deep sigh, Kendall said, "Bummer. My swallowing issues have nothing to do with the squeeze James put on my throat."

"How can you be so sure?"

"Because I've been battling an eating disorder since I was ten."

A pang of guilt and something even more potent squeezed Ridge's heart as he imagined the boy he used to be. He had so many questions. "I'm sorry. I shouldn't have pried."

"Because you're not sure what to do with the information."

Gorgeous and perceptive. "Yeah," Ridge admitted. Kendall looked so sad he felt obligated to expose an uncomfortable truth about himself. "Not because I think you should be embarrassed or ashamed."

Kendall studied him intently, and Ridge read the unspoken question in his gaze.

"I hate the thought of you hurting. Then or now. I'm a fixer. I make things right."

Kendall's smile was sad but no less brilliant than the seductive one he'd given Ridge earlier. "You're just a big teddy bear. All burly and tough on the outside but squishy and cuddly on the inside."

Ridge snorted. "I don't cuddle."

"So you think." Kendall took another bite of his sandwich, slightly bigger than before. Ridge still gnawed his way through one and a half wings before Kendall finished chewing and swallowing his food. "My body acts up when I encounter extremely stressful situations and throws my ghrelin and leptin hormones into a tailspin."

"Did you say gremlin?"

Kendall chuckled. "Close enough. Ghrelin is the hunger hormone, and leptin is the satiety hormone. When stressed, my ghrelin is nearly suppressed while my leptin goes into overdrive. Because I'm not hungry, I don't want to eat. It becomes physically painful for me to eat, but skipping meals isn't an option. I just have to take tiny bites and work through my problems."

"Can I help alleviate the stress?" Ridge suddenly realized his question sounded like a proposition. "I mean, do you work out? Exercise is my go-to."

Kendall's smile was dirty and delicious. "I love a good cardio session, but I'm going to be fine. Drew is giving me a few days off to decompress."

"Is Drew the club owner?" Ridge asked.

"The owner's nephew. Drew is our general manager and a damn good one."

Ridge consumed another wing before he spoke again. "What are your plans?"

"Hmmm?" Kendall asked, then ate another tiny bite of his grilled cheese.

"For your time off?"

"Oh, um...I'm not sure. I've recently moved into a house and could use the time to decorate the place. Make it feel more like home, you know? Right now, most of my stuff is still in boxes in the garage."

"Ah, so at least one of us is spared from future apartment-hunting nightmares."

Kendall nodded. "I got really lucky. I was telling Drew—"

"Your boss?"

"Yeah, I was telling him about my plight, and he said his boyfriend had an empty rental property. They'd just fixed it up after the last tenants moved out and were debating putting it on the market and washing their hands of it."

"Why didn't they?" Ridge asked.

"The home has been in the family for a few generations. They decided to hang on to it and offered to rent it to me for a fraction of what Tranquil Breezes wanted for that crappy apartment. What about you? Still haven't found a place?"

"No, and I need to get my ass in gear." Ridge dropped a bone onto the plate and picked up another wing. "I need to find a place for Sammy and me."

"Oh," Kendall said, rubbing his hands together. "You're going to nab the cat."

Ridge laughed. "No sketchy vans and face masks necessary."

Kendall took a bite of his french fry and Ridge noticed he seemed to chew and swallow it easier than before. "What do you mean?"

Ridge explained the situation with Sammy and was stunned when Kendall burst into laughter. After a few seconds, he wiped his wet eyes and munched on his sandwich before popping a whole fry into his mouth. Ridge wasn't sure what Kendall thought was so funny, but he was happy to see him eating more. "The guy wants you back really bad," Kendall said.

"What?" Ridge's voice came out a higher octave than he'd intended. "No way."

"Oh, honey," Kendall said, reaching across the table to pat his hand. Ridge didn't care for his patronizing tone one bit. He would've said as much if the cutie hadn't burst into another round of giggles. "You should see your face. You look more like a grizzly than a teddy bear."

"Good. I don't cuddle."

Kendall snorted. "We'll see about that." *Would we?* "How frequently does dear Todd update you about the cat while you're hunting for a new place to live?"

Ridge narrowed his eyes at Kendall's cocky grin. "Frequently. And smug doesn't look good on you."

"Oh, it does in the right light. You'll see." *Would he?* "Anyway," Kendall continued, "how frequently? Let me guess. The texts started out every few days but are now arriving daily?"

Ridge thought of the ignored text on his phone from earlier in the evening. "Maybe."

Kendall's lips quivered before he schooled his expression. "So Todd is definitely reaching out once a day. Texts, phone calls, or both?"

"Texts."

"I see," Kendall said in a studious voice. "And how many of these texts contain pictures of the cat?"

Ridge huffed out a breath of frustration. Todd was fucking playing him like a violin, and he'd been too dumb to see it. "All of them."

"And how many include—"

"Yeah, yeah, yeah," Ridge said, cutting him off. "Todd includes himself in many of the photos. And before you ask, sometimes he's partially dressed and lying in bed."

"And the boss?" Kendall asked.

Ridge shrugged. "Beats me. I delete any picture that includes Todd and only save the ones of the cat."

"You've got it bad, my friend." Kendall considered him closely. "We are friends, aren't we?"

"Sure feels like it."

"And friends help each other out and give advice and shit, right?" Kendall asked. Unsure where his new friend was going, Ridge simply nodded. "Todd's tiny little…ego can't handle your lack of interest in him, so he's coming up with every excuse in the book to hold on to you. You don't own joint property, I assume." Ridge shook his head. "And you don't have children." Ridge shook his head harder. "Easy before you wrench something." Ridge forced himself to relax. "Todd's only line to you is through that cat."

Ridge scrubbed his face with his clean hand. "Son of a bitch."

"He is," Kendall agreed. "You gotta call his bluff, friend."

"How do you suppose I do that?"

"Find a place to live that allows cats," Kendall said. "Then you pick Sammy up, block Todd's number, and live happily ever after."

Ridge chuckled. "You make it sound so easy. You saw the shitty apartments available in the area. Tranquil Breezes was the best place I looked at unless I wanted to be locked into a long-term lease."

"Commitment issues?" Kendall asked.

Ridge glared at him. "I don't plan on making Savannah my permanent home. I hadn't planned to stay longer than a few years, but there's this case I can't let go."

"And you plan to leave once it's solved?"

"Yes," Ridge said, though the answer didn't roll off his tongue as easily as he'd have liked.

"I think that's admirable," Kendall said. "But you still need a place to live with Sammy until the big arrest occurs."

"I do."

"I think I have a solution to both our problems."

Ridge tilted his head. "What's your problem?"

Kendall pushed back from his chair and stood up. "Follow me."

Ridge polished off the last wing, wiped his hands, and hurried to catch up with Kendall. "Where are we going?"

"You'll see."

"I'm not exactly the kind of guy who goes into a situation blind."

Kendall stopped and faced him. "Do you trust me?" Ridge didn't even know him, but it somehow made sense to nod. He waited while Kendall approached the bar and had a brief conversation with a handsome bartender. The guy kept glancing over at Ridge, making Ridge wonder what they were discussing. He didn't like thinking the stranger knew what Kendall had in store for him when he didn't.

Did it involve a bedpost and Ridge's silk tie? Why had his mind immediately gone there? He wasn't into bondage. *Was he?* Damn, Ridge's mind was a jumbled mess, and the playful wink the bartender sent him spelled even more chaos. His brain urged him to run, but his heart stuttered at the mere thought of not knowing what Kendall had planned.

Kendall made his way back to Ridge, then quietly led him down a dark corridor to the same exit Kendall had used earlier. "Did you park out front?"

"Uh, yeah."

"I'll drive you to your vehicle, and you can follow me."

Ridge lowered himself into Kendall's small car and adjusted the seat to remove his knees from his chest. "To where?"

"The place you'll call home until it's time to move on."

A nagging suspicion began to form, but he forgot all about it when Kendall punched the gas and shot out of the employee parking lot like he was on the last lap of the Daytona 500. He careened around the corner on two wheels and sped through the customer lot.

"Which one is yours?"

Ridge was too shocked to speak, so he pointed to the hulking SUV on the far end of the lot. Kendall waited until he was right on top of the vehicle before applying the brakes and skidding to a halt.

Adrenaline made Ridge's heartbeat spike. "Holy shit," he said between panting breaths.

Kendall laughed like a Disney villain and said, "I'm a little much sometimes."

Ridge pushed open the door and stepped outside. He ducked back down and met Kendall's glittering gaze. "Understatement of the century."

He winked. "But it won't stop you from following me, will it?"

"Only if I can't keep up with you. Take it easy, Mario."

"As in Kart?"

Laughing, Ridge said, "I was thinking Andretti, but Kart works too."

"I'll take it easy on you." The wicked promise in Kendall's eyes said otherwise.

Ridge shook his head, closed the door, and unlocked his vehicle. True to his word, Kendall obeyed all traffic laws and kept all four wheels on the ground, even around corners, during the short drive to a cozy cottage in a quiet neighborhood. Ridge's headlights illuminated a soft yellow home attached to a garage by a breezeway. Security lights tucked inside the flower beds on both sides of the front porch showed off the lush, colorful vegetation. Someone had put a lot of time and effort into the property.

After killing the engine, Ridge stepped out of the car and locked the door behind him. The neighborhood looked safe, but he wouldn't risk his gear getting stolen out of his vehicle. The lights flashed when the locks engaged, and Ridge joined Kendall on the walkway leading to the porch.

"Pretty house," Ridge said.

"But can you see yourself living here?" Kendall asked.

There was no denying the home gave off a warm and friendly vibe. "Who lives here?"

"I do," Kendall said. "Silly me. How can I expect you to answer without seeing the rest of the property?" Kendall pulled a set of keys from his pocket and headed up the front steps. "Come on."

The reality of the situation kept Ridge's feet planted firmly in place. Kendall was asking him to move in with him? What the—

"Hey, big guy," Kendall called out. Ridge snapped his head up and found the enigmatic man standing in the open doorway. The porchlight made his platinum hair look silver and cast shadows over his face. "Don't get the wrong idea, okay? I'm not looking to tie you down or trick you. I just want to help you get Sammy."

Something in Kendall's voice sounded sad and wistful, and it unglued Ridge's feet, enabling him to jog onto the porch. "Back at the club, you said you had a solution for both our problems. How will I help you by moving in here?" Ridge expected the answer to be about cutting his expenses, but Kendall worked his bottom lip between his teeth like the answer was more personal.

Kendall dropped his gaze to the porch. "I'm having a tough time adjusting to living alone, and I don't want to rent my spare bedroom to a stranger."

Ridge tucked his hand under Kendall's chin and tipped his head up so he could stare into Kendall's pretty blue eyes. "I travel a lot and work weird hours. I'm not sure I'm the right solution."

Kendall straightened, and a look of determination washed over his features. Ridge nearly groaned as he wondered how he'd measure up against the smaller man's resolve. He'd seen similar scenes play out between his parents many times over the years, and his tiny mother always came out the victor.

"That's what I need," Kendall said. "Someone to help me transition to living fully on my own. Plus, as a tenant, you come with a wonderful perk."

"Um…"

Kendall heaved a deep sigh and flipped on a light switch inside the house. "Arrogant much? I was talking about Sammy."

Heat suffused Ridge's chest, neck, and face. "My bad."

Kendall chuckled as he backed into the house. "Are you coming?" Ridge smiled, and it was Kendall's turn to blush. "Inside," he added. Ridge chuckled as Kendall stumbled back a few more steps. "To see the *spare* bedroom!"

"Oh," Ridge said, "in that case, lead the way."

Chapter Nine

A FEW DAYS LATER, EDDIE BACKED UP TO THE LOADING DOCK OF the local furniture store and put his truck in park. Ridge wanted to knock the arrogant smirk right off his face.

"Don't say it, Eddie."

His best friend sighed, and Ridge thought he'd effectively silenced him. But a heartbeat later, Eddie angled in his seat to get a better look at Ridge. "I just want to go on the record and say I encouraged you to get to know Kendall. I said nothing about you moving in with him." He waggled his white-blond eyebrows, and humor twinkled in his green eyes. "Have you even made it to second base yet?"

"Eddie, we're not dating. Kendall has a spare room to rent, and I need a place to stay. My current landlord is an obnoxious prick, and we spend way too much time together."

"There is that," Eddie conceded. "Seriously, bro."

"Bro?"

Eddie rolled his eyes. "Fine. Do you like jackass better?"

"Actually, yes, I do."

"Okay, *jackass*, you're not rushing out of my apartment because you think you're cramping my style, are you?"

"No."

Eddie laughed. "Liar."

Ridge caught movement in his side mirror and watched as the bay door went up. "Here we go." It didn't take them long to load the bed frame, mattress, and small dresser into the bed of Eddie's truck. "Thanks for helping me today."

"No problem," Eddie said, wincing when one of the employees slammed his tailgate closed. "I'm just surprised they don't deliver."

"Oh, they do," Ridge said. "I didn't spend enough money to get free delivery, and there are better ways I can spend a hundred dollars."

"Such as?"

"Stuff for Sammy."

Eddie glanced over before he put his truck in drive and pulled away from the loading dock. "You're serious about getting the cat?"

"Of course."

Eddie chuckled. "You do realize the shit with Todd is nothing more than a ploy, right?"

"Yep."

"And?" Eddie pressed.

Ridge squared his shoulders and kept an eye on the mirror to make sure nothing flew out of the truck bed. "I'm calling Todd's bluff."

"How?"

"By finding a place to stay and picking up Sammy."

Eddie stopped at a red light and looked over at him. "Does he know you're coming over today and expecting to leave with his cat?"

"Yes, and Sammy is *my* cat. I told Todd I'd found a place and would be moving in today. I told him I'd be over to get Sammy after I got everything set up."

"You're just going to knock on his door and take the cat?" Eddie shook his head like he couldn't believe it.

"Kendall wanted to steal Sammy, but it's too much drama for me."

Eddie laughed. "I knew I liked that guy. So, walk me through the plan."

"We figure Todd plans to hand Sammy over today but will reach out in a day or so because he 'misses' him. He'll try to get us both back."

"*We?*" Eddie asked.

"I didn't realize what Todd was up to until Kendall pointed it out." He repeated the conversation they'd had, and Eddie had a good laugh at Ridge's expense. "Anyway, I'm taking a contract with me when I go to Todd's."

"It won't be binding without witnesses and a notary public."

"Kendall is a notary," Ridge said.

Eddie grinned. "And I'll be the witness."

"Are you sure? I've taken up enough of your Saturday."

"Shut the hell up. I wouldn't miss this soap opera if my life depended on it. Wait until Todd sees Kendall. The fur will fucking fly."

Ridge honestly hoped not. He just wanted to collect the cat and go.

Kendall's car was parked in the driveway when Eddie backed in. The bumper was still slightly crooked from the fender bender he'd been in because he'd decided not to make more trouble for the kid who'd hit him.

Eddie let out a whistle. "This is nice."

The house was even prettier in daylight. The paint color looked sunnier, making a nice backdrop for the vibrant flowers.

"I mean, if you're going to play house…" Eddie said.

"No one is playing house, and please don't say anything to Kendall about how you and Zack were trying to get me to ditch my boyfriend for him."

"*Fiancé.*"

"Yeah, whatever," Ridge said. "Please keep your commentary to yourself. It's one thing to embarrass me, but to mislead Kendall—"

"Give me some credit, Ridgey."

Eddie was right. They might play around and cut up, but they wouldn't purposely hurt someone else in the process. "Sorry."

"No worries. You're just going through a lot of changes all at once."

Ridge got out of the pickup, grabbed his duffle bag and suitcases, and headed up to the porch. Kendall had already given him a key, but he still felt like he should knock. Turned out he didn't have to because Kendall swung the door open when Ridge's foot landed on the bottom step.

"I figured you'd talked yourself out of moving in."

Ridge's brain had made a valiant effort while waiting for Eddie to finish getting ready, but he'd ignored the dire warning in favor of listening to his gut. "Nope," he said when he reached the door.

Kendall stepped aside so he could enter. Ridge had really liked the house when he'd first seen it, even though there had still been moving boxes stacked around. In just a few days, Kendall had completely transformed the space. "My home is your home," he said, gesturing to the living room, which had overstuffed furniture, a large television, and lush houseplants.

The kitchen was immaculate and included a tall table with four padded chairs. The back of the house had a screened-in porch, and the two bed-rooms and single bathroom were off to the left. The home was tiny but cozy and comfortable. If Ridge were looking to buy a house and put down roots, this would be the kind of house he'd want.

"Oh, this is nice," Eddie said when he stepped in behind Ridge. He pointed to the multitiered shelving units where the plants sat. "Sammy is going to have fun climbing that thing."

"I made sure all the plants were cat friendly," Kendall said. "I included some grass made specifically for cats to eat."

"The stuff that makes them high?" Eddie asked.

Kendall chuckled. "Not catnip. This is to aid their digestion."

"I never knew there was such a thing," Ridge said.

"Makes two of us, buddy." Eddie slapped Ridge's shoulder. "Ready to move the bigger pieces in? The sooner we get you set up, the sooner we can go over to the asshole's and get your cat."

"You're coming too?" Kendall asked.

"I wouldn't miss it for anything."

The three of them worked together, carrying in the furniture and getting everything set up. Eddie had brought a drill, but Ridge was surprised and even charmed when Kendall told him not to bother and retrieved one from the garage. Kendall wielded it like he'd been born with a drill in his hand.

When Kendall left the room to put the tool away, Eddie rounded on Ridge.

"Marry him. Even I got a little hot watching him work that drill."

"Shut up, Eddie." Ridge swung his garment bag on top of his newly made bed and unzipped it. "I'm not interested in a relationship, and I'm sure as hell not looking to hurt Kendall." He'd sensed the guy had been hurt enough. A ten-year-old kid didn't develop an eating disorder for no reason. Ridge craved Kendall with every fiber of his being, but he wouldn't act on it. He tugged the closet door open a little harder than necessary, then stared in shock at two large canvases resting against the wall.

The first one was a close-up of Kendall's face. His platinum hair was styled artfully to look mussed. Kendall wore a lacy black mask that beauti-fully contrasted with his pale blue eyes. It felt like Kendall could see right into Ridge's soul, and he couldn't tear his eyes away for several heartbeats. Ridge took a deep breath and dropped his gaze lower. Kendall's parted lips looked shiny and pink and oh-so-fucking kissable. Ridge imagined the little sigh of ecstasy he could coax out of that delectable mouth. Kendall's bare chest looked like it was covered in a sheen of sweat, and Ridge longed to lick a path from his collarbone to his ear, then along his jaw until he reached those soft lips.

The second image was of Kendall stretched out on a bed adorned with black satin sheets. He wore only a pair of skimpy lace boxer briefs, which left nothing to the imagination. Ridge was in jeopardy of choking on his own saliva as he stared at the erection straining the fabric. He took a shaky breath and allowed his eyes to roam over the full length of Kendall's splendid body. The sheen from the first photo was still present, making Kendall look thoroughly fucked and sated as he smiled sexily for the photographer. Who the hell had taken the photos? Someone Kendall knew intimately?

"Wow," Eddie whispered.

Ridge's heart was thundering so loudly he hadn't heard his friend move closer. "Shut up, Eddie." He quickly shut the doors.

His friend made a wheezing sound, and Ridge spun around to assess him. The asshole was trying his hardest not to laugh at him. Ridge knew Eddie wasn't mocking the provocative photos; the jerk was laughing at Ridge's reaction to them.

"You should see your face," Eddie said, then he raked his gaze down the front of Ridge's body. "And other things."

Ridge became aware of the growing problem just as he heard Kendall in the hallway.

"Good luck resisting him," Eddie said just as Ridge turned his back to hide his erection from Kendall. He spent an unusual amount of time removing his dress clothes from the garment bag and laying them out on the duvet while Eddie engaged Kendall in small talk.

"I saw a pretty plant in the living room I wanted to ask questions about," he said. "I think my girlfriend would like one for her office, but she's pretty low maintenance."

"I'd love to help you," Kendall replied.

Jess was beautiful but the opposite of low maintenance. She liked to look like a million dollars and didn't mind spending the time or money to make that happen. Ridge appreciated Eddie distracting Kendall so he could pull himself together, though. As soon as the two men left him alone, Ridge opened the door enough to look at the canvases one last time, knowing he'd take the memories into the shower with him later.

Todd answered the door wearing a crop top and a pair of barely there shorts. It was something Ridge had gone wild for when they'd first started dating, but after seeing Kendall stretched out and wearing nothing but lace, Todd's attempt didn't budge Ridge's desire meter.

"Hey, stranger," his ex said playfully. "I—" His words died when he saw the expression on Ridge's face.

Eddie muscled around Ridge and smiled at Todd, who gaped at him in shock. "Hello, Todd."

"Eddie," Todd said with barely contained disdain before turning his scowl on Ridge. "You didn't say anything about bringing your friend with you."

"Is Sammy packed and ready to go?" Ridge asked.

Todd looked at him with wounded eyes. "Don't you want to come in and talk for a minute?"

"We have nothing to discuss, but I do want to come in for a minute. I brought a contract for you to sign."

"And a notary and witness to make it legal," Kendall said from behind Ridge.

"Who the hell is that?" Todd asked angrily.

Ridge stepped aside so Todd could see Kendall. "This is Kendall."

"And you are?" Todd asked.

"Um, he just said my name is Kendall."

Todd raked his gaze over Kendall's lithe body, and Ridge could see the storm building in his eyes. "No, I mean, what's your stake in all this?"

Kendall batted his lashes innocently. "I'm just the notary public."

"And I'm the witness," Eddie said. "I have lots to do today, so can we get on with it."

"Fine," Todd said, stepping aside so the three of them could enter.

Sammy loudly meowed when he saw Ridge. The miniature lion jumped down off the couch and made a beeline straight for him. Ridge bent down and scooped the cat up, loving the way his purrs rumbled through his body. Sammy butted his head against Ridge's chin. He'd always loved it when Ridge's facial hair grew out a little on the weekends. Todd might have manipulated most of the situation, but Sammy was deliriously happy to see him.

Todd sighed unhappily. "Fine. Let's get this over with."

Kendall handed him the contract, and Todd took his time reading it. In the end, Ridge was doing exactly what Todd's very own text messages had said he wanted. Ridge had found a place to live that would accept the cat. The document simply stated Todd was surrendering both his rights to the cat and any financial responsibility. Todd retrieved a pen from his desk and signed the agreement, then handed both items to Ridge. After he finished, Eddie took his turn as a witness before Kendall signed and stamped the agreement.

"I'm out of here," Eddie said. "It wasn't nice seeing you, Todd."

"Ah, we finally agree on something," Todd replied.

"Too little, too late," Eddie said before he exited the apartment. He'd driven separately since his plans with Jess took him in the opposite direction of Kendall's house.

Ridge gently placed Sammy in his carrier while Kendall grabbed the things Todd had packed up for him. "Goodbye, Todd." Ridge had almost made it to the door when his ex called out.

"Can we talk privately for a few minutes?" Todd asked.

Ridge stopped but didn't turn around. "There's nothing to discuss."

"I don't agree."

Ridge turned around to face him. "Fine. But Kendall stays."

Todd rolled his eyes. "I just wanted to say I'm sorry."

"For cheating or for gaslighting me?"

Todd sighed. "Because your dad's heart attack left you in a vulnerable place, and I exploited it to get a marriage proposal from you. I knew our relationship was doomed, and I clung harder when I should've let you go. And I'm sorry about the other things too."

In shock, Ridge stared at Todd. "So, this deal with Sammy wasn't a con to win me back?"

Todd's cheeks turned pink. "It might've started out as a ploy, but the cat really does love you more, and he hasn't been the same since our breakup."

Nodding, Ridge said, "Take care, Todd."

"You too."

He left the apartment without a backward glance.

"I'm sorry about your dad," Kendall said softly when they reached the elevator.

Ridge had the strongest urge to pull the man to him for a hug and bury his nose in Kendall's neck, but he managed to resist. "Thanks. He's much better now."

"Good. What about you?"

Sammy meowed in his carrier, making Ridge smile like a lunatic. "I'm better now too, aren't I, Sammy?" Feeling Kendall's eyes on him, Ridge glanced up. "What?"

"Nothing." His lips quirked into a wry smile.

"Not nothing. What are you thinking?"

"You're so damn cute with your cat."

"Am not. Sexy, maybe. Never cute."

"Right now, you're both."

Ridge would've replied, but the elevator arrived. Once inside, he lifted the carrier to look into Sammy's worried eyes. "It's just a short ride, buddy. I promise. No vet. No snip snip."

Kendall grimaced. "I could hold him on my lap or sit with him in the back if it helps."

"Would you like that?" Ridge asked the cat.

Meow.

Sammy made his discontent known with incessant yowling the moment Ridge started the SUV.

"Maybe I should drive, and you hold the cat," Kendall suggested.

"Hell no. Your driving would traumatize Sammy even more."

Kendall laughed but didn't argue. He did slide a hand inside the carrier to stroke Sammy's fur. Ridge was insanely jealous and utterly charmed at the same time. The cat still meowed, but his protests became fewer as Kendall cooed to him and told him what a beautiful boy he was. His voice was so hypnotic Ridge nearly ran a four-way stop.

"Close call," Kendall said, tightening his hold on the carrier.

"Sorry. I got a little distracted."

Their eyes met and held while Ridge waited his turn to go. The zing of lust he'd felt earlier was tempered by something more profound and far scarier.

He was good and fucked.

Chapter Ten

THE FIRST PROBLEM WITH SHARING A SMALL HOME WITH THE man Kendall couldn't seem to stop craving presented itself on Monday morning. He was confident it would've occurred sooner if they'd spent more than a few minutes together over the weekend. Kendall had envisioned a bonding scene where they got to know each other over wings and pizza, but Ridge had been called into work not long after they returned home with Sammy.

"I'm so sorry," Ridge had said.

"Why? It's the nature of your job, and you warned me it would happen."

Ridge had rubbed the back of his neck and continued to look unconvinced. "Yeah, but I didn't expect it to happen on the first day I moved in." He took a deep breath. "I can't even say how long I'll be gone."

Kendall had lifted the cat into his arms and felt his insides go gooey when the big beast started purring and rubbing his head against him. "This is no hardship," he'd told Ridge. "Go take care of business, and we'll be here when you get back." Kendall turned the cat to face Ridge and said, "Give Daddy kisses."

Ridge had maintained eye contact with Kendall when he lowered his face to kiss Sammy on top of his broad head. Kendall's heart fluttered like butterfly wings, and it took all his control not to launch himself into Ridge's arms. His absence became a welcome relief, especially when he remembered the photographs he'd accidentally left in the spare closet. Had Ridge seen them? God, he hoped not. Kendall had hauled ass to Ridge's room and was relieved to see his suits still laid out on the bed instead of hanging in the closet. He quickly transferred the canvases to his own room and made sure they were hidden behind seasonal wardrobe items.

Kendall didn't want to be reminded of past bad decisions every time he opened the door, but he'd been unable to throw the canvases away when he'd moved. Kendall hoped one day he could view the images without recalling how stupid he'd been to believe the sexy photographer had actually wanted him, not just sex. The photos had been Kendall's birthday gift to him. What had followed was a weeklong sexfest Kendall had mistaken for love until said sexy photographer ghosted him.

Ridge returned sometime on Sunday evening. He hadn't been there when Kendall left for work, but his SUV was in the driveway when he'd come home around two. Kendall had found it hard to fall asleep knowing Ridge was across the hall, especially since Sammy's side of the bed was also empty. Kendall had finally turned on his go-to show for falling asleep and drifted off sometime around four, only to be woken a few hours later when Ridge turned on the shower.

He was surprisingly quiet for such a big man, but the old pipes…not so much. Of course Kendall's brain immediately scrolled through all the things Ridge might be doing in the bathroom, and none involved him washing behind his ears. The longer Ridge remained in the shower, the lewder Kendall's fantasies became until he faced two problems: a hard-on and a persistent bladder.

Kendall couldn't barge into the bathroom while Ridge was showering, but his only other option was to piss off the porch, which was so not his style. Huffing a breath of frustration, Kendall threw back the covers and left his bedroom. Gravity turned his uncomfortable situation into an urgent one, so he burst through the bathroom door without knocking.

"So sorry," he called out on his way to the toilet.

"What are you doing?" Ridge asked.

"Relieving myself." Kendall released his dick from his boxers and aimed it at the toilet, only nothing happened. Peeing while fully aroused was no easy task, and he willed his mind away from the sexy man on the other side of the shower curtain. "What about you?"

Ridge choked. "Are you asking me if I'm relieving myself?"

Kendall bounced on the balls of his feet, hoping to jiggle something loose. "No."

"Because otherwise, it should be pretty obvious what I'm doing in the shower."

"You've been in there a long time," Kendall said without thinking. He couldn't take it back, so he continued full steam ahead. "I mean, I'm sure it takes a long time to wash all those yummy muscles…" Christ. He wasn't helping his situation any.

The metal curtain rings rattled when Ridge jerked the panel to the side. Kendall looked over his shoulder and saw Ridge had poked his head out to look at him. He caught the big man staring at his ass before their eyes met and held. Ridge's nostrils flared, and Kendall knew he wasn't the only one battling attraction. Ridge's hands weren't anywhere in sight. Where were they? What were they doing?

"Problem?" Ridge asked, wearing a knowing smirk.

"Was about to ask you the same." Finally, Kendall's erection ebbed enough he could piss. He turned his attention back to the toilet to make sure he didn't embarrass himself by making a mess.

Ridge chuckled, and the curtain rattled closed once more.

"I think *it's* clean now," Kendall called out as he flushed the toilet.

Ridge's laughter meant no further explanation was needed. "Concerned about water usage?" Did Ridge's voice sound thicker, or was that just Kendall's dirty imagination?

"Nope."

"Did you want to inspect my handiwork?" Ridge asked. That time there was no mistaking the desire in his voice.

"And wreck my streak of good behavior?" He knew without a doubt being bad would never feel so good. "Not today, friend."

Ridge's laugh bounced off the tiled shower walls. "And just how long is this *streak*?" Kendall knew exactly what he was asking.

Instead of exiting the bathroom like a sane person would, Kendall walked over to the sink and prepped his toothbrush. The shower was directly behind him, but the mirror was so fogged up he couldn't see anything. Kendall wiped a small circle with his fist, but he couldn't even make out a shadow through the opaque shower curtain. Bummer.

"Kendall?"

"Yeah, I'm still here," he said, then shoved the toothbrush in his mouth and got to work.

"So this streak of good behavior," Ridge prodded. "What am I up against?"

Kendall pulled his toothbrush free and spit into the sink. "I don't follow."

"Friends help each other out, yeah?"

"Uh-huh," Kendall said. "Do you want to help continue the *streak* or break it?" The only sound in the room was the running water and their breathing. "Don't answer that."

Kendall didn't need to hear Ridge's answer to know. He could pull back the curtain and climb into the shower with Ridge, who'd both welcome and cherish the opportunity to end his streak. Ridge didn't plan to stick around, so getting involved with him would be a big mistake. It was best to yank off the man's blinders.

"I haven't had sex with anyone in over a year after ending an affair with my stepbrother," Kendall said. There, that ought to do it.

"Sounds messy," Ridge said, but Kendall didn't detect a single ounce of censure in his voice.

"Very, but that's what I do best. I fall fast and hard and always for the wrong men. This time will be different."

"This time?" Ridge asked. "Sounds like maybe you have someone in mind."

"No," Kendall said. "I'm no good to anyone else until I can learn to love myself. Maybe that's why I keep picking losers. A part of me thinks it's what I deserve. And this conversation is too heavy without coffee." Kendall stuck his toothbrush in his mouth and finished scrubbing his teeth.

"Kendall."

He looked up and locked eyes with Ridge, who'd stuck his head out from behind the curtain again.

"I'm ready to get out of the shower now. I don't have a shy bone in my body, but maybe you're not ready to put your streak to the test."

Kendall turned and leaned against the counter, putting the entire length of his body on display. "You think I find you irresistible?" Ridge raked his gorgeous eyes over him, zeroing in on Kendall's crotch before meeting his gaze once more.

"I think I'm going to annihilate your streak right there on the bathroom counter if you're still here when I get out."

Kendall wanted to hook his thumbs under his waistband and shove his briefs down his legs. That's precisely what he would've done before deciding he deserved better from the men he took to his bed. Instead, he rinsed his mouth and replaced his toothbrush in the holder.

"Have a wonderful day, friend," he said on his way out.

Kendall returned to his bed and fucked his fist with a ferocity that stunned him and left him boneless, replete, and so damn lonely.

Chapter Eleven

RIDGE PROPPED HIS ELBOW ON HIS DESK AND CHECKED THE TIME on his computer. Eddie had texted him thirty minutes ago, saying he was dropping off lunch since Ridge was stuck in the office. Usually, Ridge would be grumpy about answering calls and running warrants, even though they all took turns, but getting caught jacking off to fantasies of Kendall in the shower had left him shaken. And Kendall's bathroom confession had left him reeling. His stepbrother? Really? Consenting adults had a right to choose their partners, but...no good could come out of a situation like that, and it must've knocked Kendall for a loop if he'd gone over a year without sex.

Ridge was starting to care way more than he should. He'd spent every quiet moment over the weekend thinking about the sexy canvases tucked away in his closet. Ridge had tried to convince himself they had been nothing more than a figment of his imagination when he'd arrived home Sunday evening to find them gone. He'd ordered carryout, set up his room, and spoiled Sammy, but he couldn't ignore the urge to prove the photos had been real. Though he knew it was wrong, Ridge began searching the house, and since he'd started in Kendall's closet, his mission ended quickly and satisfyingly. At least he'd had the decency not to jack off on Kendall's bed after he'd invaded the man's privacy. Ridge's growing obsession was a big red flag he planned to ignore.

An entire year since anyone else had touched Kendall? Ridge was starting to like that part a little too much for comfort, so he shifted his focus to his most pressing urge of the moment. His stomach.

Where the hell was Eddie? Ridge looked at his phone to see if he'd missed a message. Nope. Nada. The morning hours had dragged on, and he was looking forward to Eddie's visit to break up the tedium.

Ridge called his friend to get an ETA on the delivery. "I'm dying here," he said when his best friend answered.

"Calm your teats. I'm coming up in the elevator now." Eddie disconnected the call before Ridge could respond, and he cleared his desk to make room for food, then headed to the breakroom for two bottles of water. His partner strolled into the room a minute later but stopped suddenly after crossing the threshold.

"What the hell happened to you, Ridgey?"

"What do you mean?" He scanned his body and grimaced when his gaze landed on his feet. He'd put on two different boots. One was two shades darker than the other. Christ, Kendall had really rattled him.

Eddie came forward with a smug grin on his face.

"Don't start."

Ignoring him, Eddie said, "Distracted much?" He set the carryout bag on the desk and assessed Ridge again. "Or did you just not get much sleep?"

Ridge notched his chin higher and crossed his arms over his chest, knowing his defensive posture would only spur Eddie on even more. "I got a solid eight. How about you?"

"Barely three."

"Asshole," Ridge grumbled as he pulled the bag to him and peered inside. "Chinese food. I'll lapse into a food coma before this shift ends. You'll probably still find me here when you report for duty in the morning."

"Doubtful," Eddie said. "Pretty sure you have plenty of incentive to return to the cute little house."

"You can stop pushing so hard," Ridge said as he unpacked a container of General Tso's chicken. "Neither of us is looking for a relationship right now."

Eddie rolled a chair over from the desk in front of Ridge's, then flopped down on it. "Who said anything about a relationship? Why can't you guys just give in to the energy arcing between you and see where things go?"

"Because someone will end up hurt."

Eddie sighed. "Well, I'm the last person who should give relationship advice."

"But that won't stop you."

"True," Eddie agreed.

"Look, I just ended a relationship with my boyfriend—"

"*Fiancé.*"

Ridge bit back a growl. "I just ended a relationship with Todd, and I'm not looking to jump back into another. Kendall isn't someone I just want to work out my frustrations with, okay? He deserves better."

"I can't disagree."

"You could," Ridge said, "but we both know I'm right."

Eddie pulled out a container of sweet-and-sour chicken and fried rice before nodding to the file folders on Ridge's desk. "What are you working on?" he asked, changing the subject. Unfortunately, it was even touchier than chatting about his attraction to Kendall.

"You know damn well."

"Sheldon Harris?"

Rage simmered in Ridge's gut just hearing the ruthless killer's name. Sheldon Harris had worked his way up through the Cardoza cartel as their ace enforcer, leaving a trail of bodies in his wake. Ridge glanced over at the picture frame he kept on his desk. Seven-year-old Rashanda Knight smiled back at him. Her dark eyes glittered with promise that was cut short when a hail of bullets ended her life as she walked home from the bus stop. Her mother, Asia, had given the photo to him when he'd vowed to bring Rashanda's killer to justice. They'd been close to apprehending Harris twice, but the slick fucker had managed to evade them by escaping to countries that wouldn't extradite him.

"None other," Ridge admitted.

"We'll get him. It's only a matter of time before he fucks up and returns. We'll be ready."

"Hell yes, we will." Ridge had to believe Harris's days of freedom were limited. It had been a few months since he'd cycled through all the information in the file. A lot could change in eight weeks when you were dealing with a criminal. All Ridge needed was one associate to roll on Harris. It was a long shot, but he refused to give up.

"Get anywhere?" Eddie asked.

"I'd just started digging through the file when you texted me about lunch. The phones were busy this morning, but things seem to have slowed down. I'm planning to comb through everything we know about Harris to see if something jumps out at me." Ridge glanced at Rashanda's smiling face once more. "Recommitting myself to finding Harris is exactly what I need right now."

Eddie didn't linger after they finished lunch. Ridge threw away the trash, reopened Harris's file, and continued typing the names of his aliases and associates into the system until he got a surprising hit. Willis Morrison, also known as one-eyed Willie after he lost his left one in a bar fight, was in county lockup after a domestic dispute sent his girlfriend, Carmen Elliot, to the hospital. Would she be pissed enough to tell Ridge what she knew about the cartel?

There was only one way to find out. He ran her details through the system and saw she worked at a strip joint called Tit for Tat. It wasn't likely Carmen had returned to work already based on the injuries detailed in the police report, so he planned to swing by her place on his way home.

Chapter Twelve

KENDALL SMOOTHED THE WHITE CLOTH NAPKIN OVER HIS LAP. The fabric was pristine and expensive, not unlike the person sitting across the table from him. He'd been to Fernando's more times than he could count but never with this man.

Chet closed the red leather menu and caught Kendall watching him. "You haven't even looked at the menu."

"Why am I here?"

Chet sighed. "I want you back."

Kendall stiffened. His pitch sounded oddly personal. "You've never had me."

Chet coughed, then took another sip of water. "On my law team, Kendall. I should've been clearer. Sorry."

"Why would you want me to come back to the firm? I never got the impression you liked working with me."

A rueful smile tugged at the lawyer's lips. "I never got the impression you cared what I thought one way or the other."

"It's probably true that I didn't give you a chance. You were the lawyer they'd hired to replace Vivian. And you came in—"

"Like a wrecking ball," Chet said.

Kendall smiled for the first time since his former boss had called to invite him to lunch. Invited was a stretch. Chet had given him a time and location before requesting Kendall arrive promptly since he had a court appearance afterward. "Maybe a little."

"I regret that now, and I'm sorry."

Kendall cocked his head to the side and studied the contrite expression on the handsome man's face. Oddly, Chet appeared sincere, and Kendall wasn't sure what to think about it.

"Apology accepted," he said.

"Does that mean you'll come back?"

Kendall chuckled. "No. My departure has nothing to do with you." Chet aimed a dubious glance at him. "Okay, it had a little to do with you."

"I appreciate your honesty, Kendall. The firm misses you. *I* miss you. We want you back."

Kendall's chest swelled with pride, but he wouldn't let the compliments go to his head. "The firm is the problem, Chet. I don't want to spend my life helping dickbag clients get away with crimes or watch as they get a little slap on the wrist." He'd felt that way for a long time, but Bobby Jack Dennison had been the nail in the proverbial coffin.

"Okay, what do you want?"

All the joy Kendall had felt went *poof*. He dropped his gaze to his lap, not wanting to see disappointment or irritation in Chet's eyes. "I honestly don't know."

"Kendall, I'm not trying to lecture you. I'm just trying to help." Kendall raised his chin and met Chet's dark gaze. "Do you like managing the club?"

Kendall shrugged. "I think I have the potential to be good at it."

"That's not what I asked you, though." Kendall had heard Chet use this kind, brotherly voice when questioning defense-friendly witnesses on the stand. He just hoped he wasn't subjected to the hostile interrogation style the Bull Shark reserved for cross examinations. "What would make you happy?"

"I'm not sure anyone has ever asked me that before." Kendall was ashamed to admit it. "I've been programmed to focus on what would honor my family." And where had that gotten him?

Stanton had nearly had a stroke when Kendall had worn lip gloss to one of his dinner parties. His stepfather had taken Kendall into the study and lectured him about his obligations.

It's one thing to be queer, but can't you at least dress and act like a man and stop embarrassing your family? Try my tolerance, and you'll live to regret it.

Those words had been seared into his mind. The warning had been crystal clear. His time living under Stanton Burkhart's rule was coming to an end. So he'd applied for a job at the one place sure to piss off his step-father the most. Then he'd crashed another dinner party wearing his sexy aviator uniform.

"What is the meaning of this?" Stan had demanded.

Kendall had twirled around, letting him get the full effect of the booty shorts and mesh top. "You don't like my uniform?"

"How dare you humiliate our family in front of our guests."

"What?" Kendall asked with mock innocence. "I didn't put on the hat and aviator glasses in deference to your dress code. That would be too gauche, even for me."

Stanton had demanded he quit the job or move out. Kendall had chosen homelessness. A decision he hadn't regretted in the three years since.

"A career in law isn't in my future. That much I do know. I'll always be grateful I answered the firm's classified ad because it brought Vivian into my life, even if only for a few years. I completed my paralegal courses because it's what she wanted and because I needed to prove to myself that I could see something through to the end."

"Which leads me back to my question. What do *you* want?"

Kendall took a deep breath. "Do I need to have an answer right now?"

Chet's smile was kind. "Nope. You have plenty of time."

The waiter returned to the table and took their orders. Chet started to order salmon until Kendall reminded him about his court appearance. Chewing gum wasn't an option and brushing his teeth might not be enough. Kendall ordered a grilled chicken salad, and Chet said he'd have the same.

"See?" Chet said when they were alone again. "You're invaluable. I would've gone into court with salmon breath."

Kendall laughed. "You're welcome."

"The firm is donating the Dennison's retainer fee to The Trevor Project. I thought you might like to know."

"Wow," Kendall said. "I'm impressed."

Chet smiled. "Would you be more so if I vowed to donate my billable hours too?"

"Not enough to come back."

Snapping his fingers, Chet said, "Damn."

Kendall propped an elbow on the table and rested his chin on his palm. "What made the firm decide to donate the money?"

"I asked them nicely." Lunch with Chet had been one surprise after another, but this was the biggest one yet. "And now you want to know why."

"Obviously."

"Because a war is raging inside me. I believe everyone is entitled to a defense, but this is personal for me."

What was Chet telling him? Was he gay? Had he been bullied or known someone who had? Had someone he cared about harmed themself? "Meaning…" Kendall prompted.

"I'm gay too."

Kendall tried his best not to look or sound shocked. "Are you…out?"

Chet nodded. "I am, but I prefer to keep my relationships private. And before you ask, yes, I'd still attend the company functions solo if I were attracted to women."

Kendall smiled sheepishly. "I had no idea whether you attended the firm events with or without a date. Only the lawyers and senior management are invited to the country club."

"Oh," Chet said. "I didn't realize."

"Didn't you ever wonder why I never attended?"

"I just assumed you had cooler things to do."

Kendall chuckled. "You're not wrong there, but the environment at the firm isn't exactly inclusive. It's more of an us-versus-them vibe."

"I see," Chet said. "I never knew you felt that way."

"Well, our conversations centered around business."

"I know your favorite coffee creamer," Chet said. *He did?* "It's peppermint mocha. And you love plants. The office is drab since you've taken the greenery with you." *What the hell was happening here?*

Kendall was just about to ask when he became aware of someone approaching their table in his periphery. He turned his head and met the icy blue gaze of his mother. *As if this day couldn't get any stranger.*

"Hello, Kendall," Rebecca Burkhart said. Her voice was modulated and cool, but the expression in her eyes was warm. She wore a yellow sheath dress that showed off her lovely figure and tan. Her nude heels made her look much taller than her diminutive height. As always, his mother's hair was immaculately styled, and her makeup was artfully applied to enhance her lovely features.

Kendall stood up and set his napkin on the table. "Rebecca," he said coolly. Once, he would've called her mother and embraced her, but that was a long time ago. "It's good to see you."

Her wry smile called his bluff. "And you also." She glanced over at Chet and smiled. "Are you going to introduce me to your friend?"

"Oh, I'm sorry."

Chet rose to his feet and extended a hand. "Chet Dawson, ma'am."

"Mr. Dawson," she said as they shook. "I'm Kendall's mother, Rebecca Burkhart."

"It's lovely to meet you," Chet told her.

"Likewise. Would you mind if I steal my son away for a few moments?"

"Of course not."

"Kendall," she said, looping her arm through his so he couldn't refuse without making a scene. When they were a few feet away, she leaned closer and said, "He's so handsome."

"We're not on a date, Rebecca."

She sighed. "A mother can hope."

They continued to the valet station in awkward silence. She didn't speak again until the attendant left to retrieve her Mercedes.

"I want to reconcile."

Kendall sighed. "Rebecca, Stan wants me to be someone I'm not. I can't—"

"I'm not talking about you and Stan," she said. "I'm talking about us. You and me. And stop calling me Rebecca. I miss you so much, and I hope it's not too late for us."

Clearly, Kendall was still dreaming. Had he imagined the scene with Ridge in the bathroom too? And Chet asking him to come back? He briefly closed his eyes. When he reopened them, his mother was still standing in front of him.

"Kendall," she said, blue eyes searching his.

"Three years, Rebecca."

She swallowed hard and hung her head for a few seconds before meeting his gaze again. "I'm so sorry."

"For what part? Standing by silently as Stan cut me out of the family like I was a cancer? For continuing to choose him over me? Exactly what crime against your only son are you apologizing for?"

"All of them, Kendall."

"What did I do to deserve it?" he whispered. "For some stupid reason,

I looked to you after Stan issued his ultimatum. I foolishly expected you to stand up for me. You just stared mutely at the ground."

Rebecca took a shaky breath. "I'd just found Stan having sex with my best friend. I'd taken some anxiety meds and mixed them with alcohol. I don't even remember that night. I'm not trying to make excuses, though."

So that's what had happened to her friendship with Charlotte. Kendall ran his hand through his hair and muttered, "Jesus, Rebecca." He paced a few feet away before returning to her. "You could've died."

"I'm sober now."

"For how long? A week? A month?"

"A year," she replied. "Kendall, there is no excuse for my behavior." She reached forward and took his hands in hers. "I want to make things right. Will you let me?"

The attendant zoomed up before he could reply. He wanted to believe her; he truly did. She was his mother after all. But Kendall had learned the hard way not to trust her commitment to putting his feelings and needs before Stanton's. How many times had she turned to Kendall when Stan hurt her, only to pull away again when his stepfather came to heel? Each time, the knife carved bigger chunks from Kendall's heart until it resembled swiss cheese.

"That was fast," Rebecca told the kid.

"I could drive her around the block for you if you need another minute," he offered.

"That's quite all right." Rebecca turned to face Kendall. "I'll call you soon. Maybe we can have dinner? Perhaps you can bring your handsome new friend." He couldn't imagine introducing Ridge to Rebecca.

Kendall nodded because he didn't think the call would ever come. She gave him a little finger wave before climbing behind the wheel. Once Rebecca drove off, it dawned on Kendall she'd been referring to Chet. She'd thought they were on a date.

"Do you have your ticket?" the attendant asked Kendall.

"Uh, yeah, but I'm not leaving yet. I was just walking my mother out."

"Cool," the kid said in a bored voice.

Kendall headed back inside the restaurant to finish lunch with Chet. His former boss widened his dark eyes when he saw him.

"Are you okay? You look a little shell-shocked."

Kendall dropped into his chair and returned the napkin to his lap.

"More than a little. Ever have a day so strange you know you must be dreaming?"

Chet studied him for a few moments before replying. "More than once. Is that the situation for you today?"

"Yeah," Kendall said. "I feel off-balance."

"Is there anything I can do?"

Kendall shook his head, then let loose a bark of laughter that jolted Chet. "Rebecca thinks we're on a date."

Chet's scowl only made Kendall laugh harder. "And you find this humorous?"

Sobering, Kendall said, "Come on. You could do better."

"I don't agree."

Kendall snapped his gaze up to Chet's and froze.

"And I've just compounded your tumultuous day," Chet said. "I can see my second proposal will need to wait."

"Second proposal?" he asked weakly.

"Not an indecent one." Chet winked. "But now you've got me thinking I need to change my approach next time."

"Next time?"

"That we meet. Perhaps for dinner." It was the second dinner invite he'd received in a matter of minutes. The waiter arrived with their salads and ensured everything looked good before leaving them to their own devices.

Kendall picked up his fork and speared a piece of seared chicken. "Dinner, huh?"

"A guy can hope."

Yes, a guy could. Too bad Kendall wasn't thinking about the handsome man sitting across from him. "We'll see."

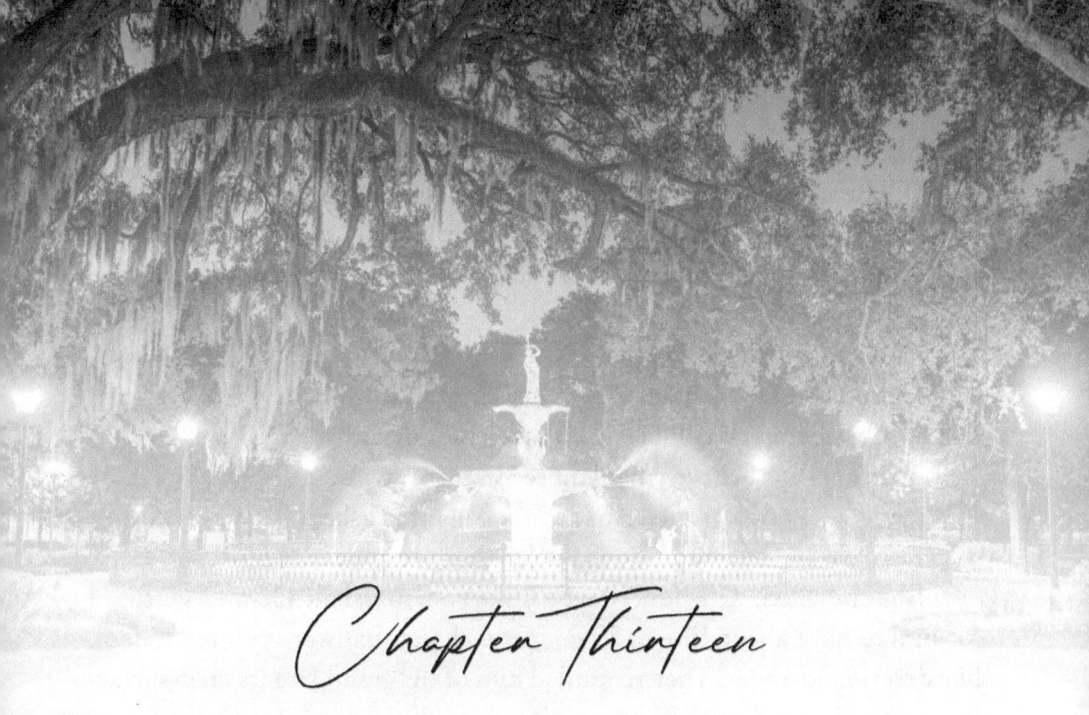

Chapter Thirteen

AT THE END OF HIS SHIFT, RIDGE SHUT DOWN HIS COMPUTER and headed out. Carmen Elliot's house was only a few blocks from the marshals' field office, which meant he arrived at her door around dinner time. Carmen's house was similar to the one he shared with Kendall from the size and architectural style to the flower beds overflowing with colorful blooms. *Not sharing, dumbass. You're renting a room.* Unlike *Kendall's* house, a fence surrounded the backyard. A children's pool, tricycles, and a swing set were visible from the sidewalk, but none were in use.

"Can I help you?" a woman asked as soon as Ridge took one step toward Carmen's house.

He turned and smiled at the neighbor, who was rocking on her front porch. She wore a strapless purple dress, a matching hair wrap, and a don't-mess-with-me expression. "Good evening, ma'am. I'm here to talk to Carmen."

"Uh-huh," she replied, sounding bored.

"Is she home?"

"The woman has three kids. Does it sound like she's home to you?" Carmen's house was quiet, so Ridge shook his head. The neighbor lady tilted her head and studied Ridge for a moment. "Come here. I'd like to speak to you, and I don't feel like yelling across the yard."

Ridge chuckled and walked to her house. "May I?" he gestured to the porch.

She nodded. "I do like your manners."

"I'll be sure to tell my mother." He extended his hand, which she reluctantly accepted. "My name is Kurt Dandridge, but my friends call me Ridge."

"Gemma," she replied. "Which branch of law enforcement do you work for?"

"I'm a marshal, ma'am."

Gemma crossed her arms over her chest. "I don't believe I've ever met one of those before, but I have seen some in movies."

"Can't always believe what you see in the movies."

"So you're not a group of badasses?" Gemma asked.

"No, we are, but we're much cooler than we appear in films."

She chuckled. "Uh-huh. Maybe I like you, marshal." Gemma gestured for him to have a seat. She had two metal chairs that were painted to look like desert landscapes. They reminded him of his grandparents' chairs when he was a kid, but those had been painted a dull shade of gray.

"I'm honored, ma'am." He lowered himself into the chair, expecting it to protest his bulk, but it held steady. "These chairs are beautiful."

She gave him a dazzling smile. "Thank you. They are my latest creations."

"You painted these?" he asked.

"I find them cheap at yard sales and repair the metal. Then it's only a matter of elbow grease and getting lost in my art."

"Do you sell them?"

Gemma nodded. "I go to craft fairs and have an online Etsy shop. I also take custom orders if you know someone who might be interested."

Ridge had no need for them, but he knew someone who'd love them. "I'd like to commission a set."

"Doesn't mean I'm going to talk about Carmen or her loser boyfriend."

"I respect that, and I still want to order a set." He spent the next few minutes describing the landscapes back home and his mother's personality. Gemma told him she'd google pictures of the area for inspiration.

"So, why does a marshal want to talk to Carmen?" Gemma asked. "She's just a hardworking woman with horrible taste in men. Surely that's not a federal crime."

Ridge laughed. "No, ma'am. And if we think prisons are overcrowded now, can you imagine if bad taste in partners becomes a chargeable offense?" He would definitely be incarcerated over Todd.

"Why are you here?"

"With all due respect, I'm not at liberty to discuss my reasons with you."

Gemma sighed and shook her head. "I had high hopes for you." She slapped her palms on her thighs before standing up. Ridge rose too. "I charge two hundred for a custom set of chairs. Then there will be the shipping costs. Still interested?"

"Absolutely." Ridge retrieved his wallet and pulled out five twenties and one of his business cards. "Here's half up front. You can call me when they're ready. I'll take care of shipping them to my mom."

Gemma took the money and his card, then searched his eyes again. "Don't get her killed. Those babies need their mama."

A lump formed in Ridge's throat. "I don't want any harm to come to Carmen."

"They watch her, you know."

"Is that why she left?"

"Left?" Gemma asked. "Carmen hasn't run away. She's simply at work."

"But she's injured."

"Her kids still need to eat."

Ridge could see her point. "Willie has guys watching her?" He subtly repositioned his body so he could scan the street. Nothing looked out of place.

"They're not going to hang out here when they could keep an eye on her at the club," Gemma said. "They're dedicated to Willie but not that much."

Ridge chuckled. "Thanks for your help."

Gemma shook her head. "All I did was sell you a set of chairs. I'll be in touch soon."

"Looking forward to it."

Ridge felt Gemma's eyes on him as he strode to his SUV. He waved as he drove off, then paid attention to make sure no one was following him. He took a circuitous route to the strip joint where Carmen Elliot worked.

Tit for Tat may have been on the same strip as The Cockpit, but that was where the similarities ended. The exterior sign had a neon, busty woman gyrating so her ample breasts bounced. Her nipples were covered with smiley faces, and Ridge had used thicker dental floss to clean his teeth than the G-string she wore. Once inside, the only difference between the neon lady and the ones serving up drinks and lap dances was the lack of smiley faces. The only thing on the servers' chests was body glitter to draw attention to their assets. Ridge had spent enough time with his mom in her craft room to know that shit went everywhere. How did anyone explain away the glitter stuck to their clothes and bodies after a night of debauchery?

"Hey, baby," said a sultry female voice. The stunning brunette was almost as tall as Ridge in her high heels. She raked her gaze over him from head to toe. "I'm Destiny. Welcome to Tit for Tat. Would you like a booth, a table, or a private room?"

Ridge quirked his brow. "Private room?" he asked. That didn't sound the slightest bit sketchy.

"For lap dances and peep shows," Destiny explained. She sauntered closer and raked a fingernail over his chest. "What's your poison tonight, baby?"

An enigmatic platinum-blond man with mesmerizing blue eyes and the softest pink lips Ridge had ever kissed. But that wasn't what Destiny had asked. He pulled his badge out and showed it to her. "None of the above."

Destiny huffed a frustrated sigh on her way back to the podium. "Well, damn. What can I do for you, then?"

"I'd like to speak to Carmen Elliot."

Destiny stiffened and scowled. "What do you want with Carmen? Life has knocked her around enough already, so you leave her alone."

"Did life knock her around, or was it Willie?" Ridge countered.

The hostess softened slightly, but her eyes still glittered with suspicion. "What do you want with her?"

"I just want to help," Ridge said. And he meant it. If he could offer Carmen a way out, he'd gladly do it.

"Yeah, I bet. You'll help yourself to her—"

"I'm gay," Ridge said.

"Oh." Destiny bit her lip and cast a glance toward the interior of the club. He saw the internal war raging behind the woman's eyes.

"I just want to help her," he reiterated.

"Men don't do anything for free, especially cops. You always want something in return. Maybe you don't want a blow job, but you're after something. You'll get her killed in the process."

"I'll do everything in my power to keep her safe," Ridge said. "Having this debate with you right now will only call unwanted attention to me. Just tell me where I can find Carmen."

Destiny arched a brow. "And just how do you plan to help her, law man?"

"Those are options I'll need to discuss with her," Ridge said. "I'm not leaving until I speak to her, so save us both the hassle and tell me where I can find her."

Destiny's shoulders slumped forward. "Benny said she could work in the kitchen until her bruises heal. Carmen can't afford to go weeks without a check, and this shithole doesn't offer any kind of benefits. Shake your tits, sway your ass, or go broke."

"Benny sounds like a great guy."

She shrugged. "He's worse than some but better than most."

"A ringing endorsement if ever I heard one," Ridge said. "Carmen is lucky to have a friend like you." *And Gemma too.*

Destiny smiled, then told him how to find the entrance to the kitchen. Since it was in a dark hallway, he saw and heard things that made his skin crawl. He'd never been happier to step into a kitchen in his life. Everyone glanced up and stared at the newcomer, but Ridge's eyes narrowed in on the petite woman washing dishes. Her bruises were now a greenish yellow, and Ridge could tell her jaw was still swollen. She was stunning despite her injuries. Carmen Elliot's eyes widened in fear when Ridge headed her direction.

He held up his hands to show he meant her no harm. "Carmen Elliot?"

A Hispanic man stepped in front of Ridge to block his path. "Who the hell wants to know?" Ridge showed the man his badge. "A marshal?"

Carmen approached them and rested her hand on the man's shoulder, patting it twice. "It's okay, José." Her voice was soft but confident. "I know why he's here. You're Dandridge, aren't you?"

"You've heard of me?" he asked.

"Willie and Sheldon have spoken of you often."

Ridge raised a brow. "All glowing things, I'm sure."

She didn't so much as smile. "I can't help you."

"Can't or won't?"

Carmen took a deep breath. "Can't. I know you're trying to get justice for that little girl, and I commend you. I have kids too, and I won't risk their lives. Not even for her."

"What if I could help you?" Ridge asked.

"Help me? How?"

Ridge lifted his hand and gestured to the room. "Is this the life you want to live?"

She stiffened, and anger simmered behind her eyes. *Good. Get mad.* It meant she had a fighting spirit. Maybe Willie's abuse had made her temporarily forget the steel in her spine, but Ridge could see Carmen's re-silience shimmering in her dark eyes. "Now you're an expert on my life?" she asked. "If I don't help you, you're going to do what? Turn me in so the county takes my kids away?"

"Nope. If you know something that can help bring down the Cardoza cartel, I'll help you and your kids find a fresh start somewhere else. New identities so Willie and the cartel won't be able to find you."

A dark brow shot up, and a spark of hope softened her jaded gaze. "Witness protection?"

Ridge nodded. "I will do my best to ensure you and your children are safe."

"You talk a big game. Where's the proof?" Carmen asked.

"I can't make you promises until I know what kind of information you have."

"Well, isn't that fucking rich?" Carmen crossed her arms over her chest. "Let me get this straight. I'm supposed to tell you everything I know, and you'll run it up the ladder to see if the information is worth saving my life." She took a step back and waved both her hands. "Hell no. Get on outta here."

He wasn't the type to give up so quickly, but Carmen already knew that if Willie and Sheldon had talked about Ridge in front of her. The hope he'd briefly witnessed in her eyes fizzled out. "You and I both know Willie is going to get out of jail. Then what?"

"Nope," she said, shaking her head. "I'm not dropping the charges this time."

"His men are watching you."

"So? They haven't made a move on me."

"Only because you haven't given them a reason to. That all changes when Willie realizes you're going to testify against him in the domestic abuse trial. He isn't stupid—"

"Willie's the dumbest fucker to draw breath," Carmen said.

"Maybe his IQ isn't anything to brag about, but he makes up for it in street smarts. If you're willing to sit in a courtroom and talk about his abuse, he's going to wonder who else you're talking to and what you're saying to them. He's not going to take the chance, Carmen. Even if Willie hesitates because of his affection for you, his associates won't be as forgiving."

Carmen looked around the kitchen as if she were assessing the danger right then and there. Her dark eyes met Ridge's again, and they crackled with rage. "You've put my life at risk just by coming here."

"You'd be in protective custody before and during the trial. We'd set you up with a completely new identity afterward. I know you're scared—"

"Fuck you. I'm a survivor." Carmen closed her eyes and trembled as she inhaled deeply. Tears trickled down her face as she continued mulling over her options. After a few moments, Carmen reopened her eyes, and Ridge felt like he was looking at a different person. "But my babies shouldn't have to live in constant fear. Do you really want to help me?"

"I do. I can't promise you this will go the way we want it to, but I assure you that I'm committed to seeing it through. I need your help, Carmen."

The woman swallowed hard and held out her hand. "Give me your card. Let me sleep on it."

Ridge pulled a card from his wallet and gave it to her. "Call me anytime. I mean it." He looked around the kitchen and was surprised no one seemed to be paying attention to them.

"These are my people. I'm safe here." She smiled at Ridge then. "He calls you Pat Garrett, you know?"

"Willie?"

She shook her head. "Harris. He's obsessed with the Old West and gunslingers. And not just the movies. He's a walking encyclopedia of facts. He believes in settling disputes in the streets."

"Guess that makes him Billy the Kid, and we all know how that turned out. Call me, Carmen. Day or night."

He stepped out of the kitchen and back into the darkened hallway. Left would take him to an emergency exit, probably to the back of the building, and right would take him down the hall of horrors. The emergency exit probably opened to a back parking lot, and he had no way of knowing what dangers could be lurking there. Ridge chose the wisest route and kept his eyes straight ahead as he passed the writhing and groaning couples.

Destiny gave him a finger wave as he reached her. "You get what you came for?"

Ridge shrugged. "Time will tell."

Grateful to escape the cloying smell of perfume and desperation, Ridge took a big gulp of fresh air and nearly choked on the humidity. Christ, he hated summer in Savannah. Ridge cranked up the air conditioning and steered his SUV toward home. *Kendall's home.* He was both excited and anxious to see Kendall again but worried he wouldn't be able to keep his guilt over that morning's jerkfest off his face. He didn't want Kendall to know he'd shot his load while staring at his ass in those too-tight boxers. Just recalling the moment made his head spin and his dick throb.

Ridge parked in the driveway and forced himself to whistle as he strolled toward the house. As he neared the porch, he heard music coming from inside. Ridge immediately thought of the bodies pressed together on the dance floor at The Cockpit. Then his mind shifted to Kendall dancing for him in a pair of lacy black underwear. His brain stuttered to a stop when he opened the door and saw his fantasy was on the verge of becoming a reality.

Kendall stood at the stove wearing only a tiny pair of shorts. His hips swayed to a song about dancing with a stranger. It was the most hypnotic thing Ridge had ever seen and was far hotter than the temperature outside. He shut the front door harder than he intended, and his tormentor spun around, clutching his bare chest.

Ridge raked his gaze over Kendall's dewy skin and said, "Honey, I'm home."

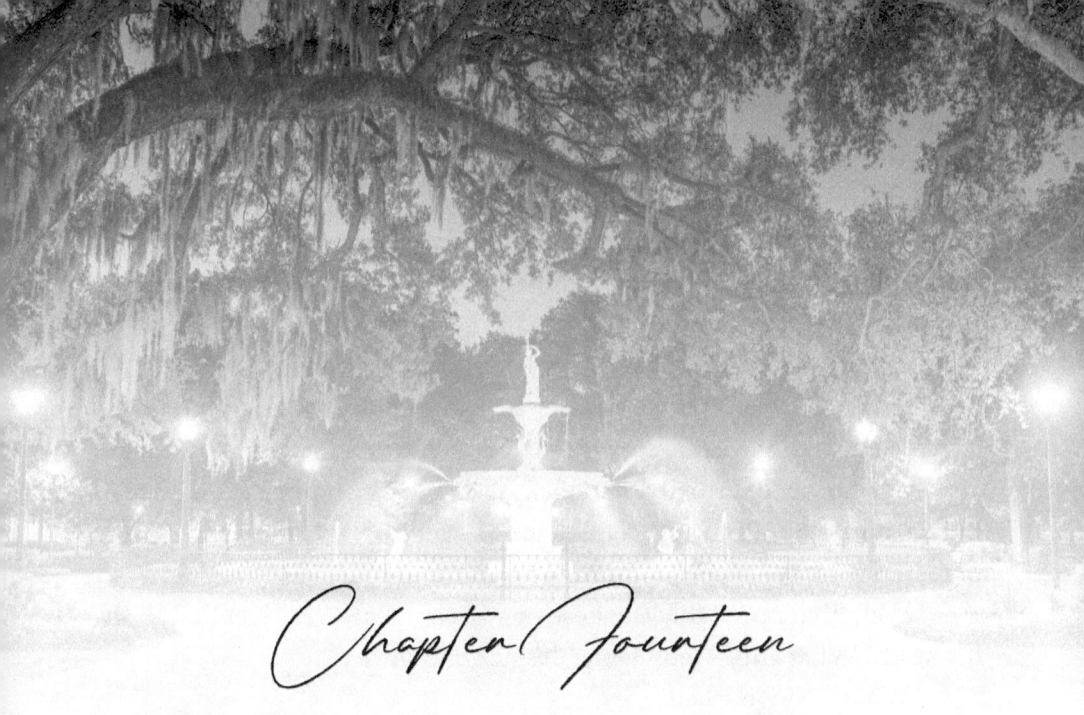

Chapter Fourteen

KENDALL CONTINUED TO STARE AT RIDGE FOR A FEW MOMENTS before snapping out of his trance. He crossed to the table and fumbled with his phone until he stopped the music. "Sam Smith has this effect on me," he said sheepishly. "Probably should've warned you, huh?"

Ridge dropped his duffle bag on the floor and strode silently across the room. "I don't know who that is, but if this is the view I can expect nightly…"

Kendall smiled sheepishly. "Then you want a rent reduction?"

Ridge took a deep breath, making his shoulders look even broader. "I'll pay double."

Heat rushed to Kendall's cheeks, making him want to stick his head in the freezer. Ridge stepped closer and placed his hands on Kendall's hips. That's when Kendall noticed a dusting of glitter on Ridge's shirt and a smattering of rogue shimmer on his face. Ridge smelled like sweat, perfume, and sin. Kendall stifled a sigh and took a step back, breaking the loose hold Ridge had on his hips. Too bad his heart wasn't as eager to part ways.

"Strip club?" he asked.

"Huh?" Ridge's voice was thick. Was it from desire or confusion? Perhaps a little of both.

"The glitter on your shirt and face." Kendall reached up and swiped a fleck off Ridge's cheek and showed it to him.

"Fuck. I'd hoped to get in and out without getting that shit on me." Kendall's stomach pitched, and all he wanted to do was curl into a ball. Ridge's eyes widened, and he shook his head vigorously. "Not like that. Nothing happened."

"Says every man who visits that type of establishment." Kendall had injected sass and sarcasm into every word to disguise his disappointment.

Ridge growled, turned his back on Kendall, and began to pace. "I didn't go to the club to get a lap dance or *whatever*. I went to interview a potential witness."

"Well, that's probably the best excuse I've heard yet." Kendall shook his head. "What am I even saying? It's not like we're..."

"What?" Ridge asked.

"A couple. Dating. You're free to get lap dances and *whatever*, and I'm free to date my boss."

Ridge's expression turned thunderous as he stepped into Kendall's personal space again. "That Drew guy?"

"Former boss, I should say." Kendall wrinkled his nose and waved his hand in front of his face. "I don't mean to be hateful, but you reek. That perfume doesn't work well on you."

Ridge turned his head and took a whiff of his sleeve. He scrunched up his nose and looked adorably irate. "It's probably a combination of several perfumes."

"A real popular guy at Tit for Tat, huh?" When Ridge raised a brow, Kendall said. "It's the only strip club after The Alley Cat burned down."

"For the record," Ridge said in a growly voice, "I'm gay as fuck. While I think women are beautiful, I have zero desire to sleep with them." Kendall resented the hope blossoming in his heart. He tried to speak but could only nod. "And I'm going to take a quick shower to wash off the glitter and *whatever* is sticking to me after walking through the club." Kendall was curious to know what a quick shower was for Ridge. Fifteen minutes? "Then I want to hear about this former boss as potential boyfriend material situation." He sounded less pissed about the idea, and Kendall's hope deflated like a balloon.

Kendall wasn't interested in dating Chet, and he was even less keen on discussing why, especially not with Ridge. But his day had been weird, and Ridge was an objective party without skin in the game.

"Okay, but you'll have to let me repay you in wings and pizza."

"Can we do takeout? I'm pretty tired after this weekend."

"I'm planning to treat you to my homemade wings and pizza," Kendall said, then made a shooing motion to get Ridge going. He needed a moment to regain his composure. Once his sexy tenant had shut himself in the bathroom, Kendall ran to his room and pulled a tank top on over his head. Changing his booty shorts would've been too obvious, so he kept them on. Besides, he liked the look in Ridge's eyes whenever he caught him staring. All those squats and lunges were finally paying off.

When Ridge returned to the kitchen, he smelled delicious and looked even better. Kendall had been swaying to the song from earlier, even though it was only playing in his head, and adding the finishing touches to the sauce in the pan.

"You can turn your song back on," Ridge said. "I don't mind." The wolfish smile on his handsome face made Kendall want to tempt fate. But then Ridge said, "About this potential boyfriend."

"Chet Dawson is not boyfriend material."

Ridge squinted. "Chet Dawson. Why do I recognize that name?" His eyes widened when his memory kicked in. "You're going to date the Bull Shark?"

Kendall groaned and rolled his eyes. "I just said I wasn't interested."

"No, you said he wasn't boyfriend material. That's not the same thing," Ridge pointed out.

"Semantics." Kendall waved away further protest. "Anyway, when I accepted Chet's lunch invitation, I didn't expect him to say he wanted me back." Ridge stared at him unblinkingly until Kendall took a deep breath. "To *work* for him."

"You told him no?" Kendall nodded. "So he pursued you personally?"

"Not right away. Chet asked what would make me happy." Kendall dipped a clean spoon into the pan, coating it in the wing sauce. He trailed his finger through the green liquid, then licked it clean before setting the spoon in the sink. Ridge made a whimpering sound beside him, but Kendall was too focused on perfecting the flavor profile to pay him any attention. He shook some chili pepper flakes into the pot and gave it a stir.

Ridge cleared his throat. "What did you say?"

Kendall looked over at him and shrugged. "I told him no one had ever asked me that before, so I wasn't really sure how to answer."

"I see. Then your boss asked you out."

"*Former boss*. And I think so."

Ridge crossed his arms over his chest. "You think so?"

Kendall chewed on his bottom lip for a moment before recalling the conversation. "It was a pretty low-key dinner invitation and not the first of the day."

"Popular guy," Ridge said dryly.

Kendall chuckled. "The first came from my mother." He picked up another clean spoon and stuck it into the sauce. He repeated the process of swiping the sauce and tasting it. "Almost there."

"Yeah, I am," Ridge said huskily.

Kendall elbowed him but otherwise ignored his comment. "Acid is right. Heat is right. It needs a little something sweet." A light bulb went off, and the solution came to him. He turned to look at Ridge, who was still staring at his lips. "Do you mind retrieving the maple syrup from the refrigerator?"

Ridge didn't acknowledge his request right away but blinked a few seconds later and nodded. "Maple syrup." He pulled open the refrigerator and stared at the interior for far longer than necessary.

"It's the tall bottle in the door with a log cabin on the label."

"What in the hell is all this?" Ridge asked. He looked over at Kendall and gestured to the numerous plastic containers filled with colorful liquids.

"It's what makes me happy."

"Strange liquids?" Ridge asked before reaching for the syrup and handing it to Kendall. "Is it a diet thing?"

Kendall laughed. "Not for me, but I think I could convince you with minimal effort."

Ridge aimed a horrified look at the closed refrigerator door. "Doubt it. And I'm starting to have second thoughts about you cooking our dinner."

"These are potential sauces for the wings at the club."

"The chef sends them home for you to test?" Ridge asked.

"Not exactly," Kendall said as he added a little syrup to the sauce. "I'm the one who creates them."

"You're responsible for the sauces?" Ridge asked.

Kendall cocked his head to the side and narrowed his eyes. "I can't tell if your astonishment is a good or bad thing."

"Definitely good. Where do you come up with all your ideas?"

"I watch a lot of random cooking shows featuring cuisine from all around the world," Kendall said. "Sometimes I get ideas from social media."

"And? Because I can tell there's more."

"It's embarrassing," Kendall mumbled.

Ridge placed his big hand on Kendall's neck and massaged the tense muscles there. "I won't judge you."

"Do you know how Taylor Swift writes songs about people who broke her heart?"

"Um, no."

"Well, I'm the culinary Taylor Swift. Many of my sauces are inspired by life events and heartbreak."

"Oh."

"You must think I'm an immature idiot."

Ridge released his neck and trailed his hand down Kendall's spine, pulling away when he reached his waistband. "I think you're a genius. Can I be your taste tester?"

Kendall turned and looked into Ridge's warm brown eyes. "Really?"

Ridge nodded. "I'm not so sure about this green sauce, though."

"It's the hottest one I've made yet. I'm not sure it will go over well with the chef either. Not sure the patrons will want to eat green chicken wings. Maybe I can offer it as a dipping sauce on the side." Ridge didn't say anything; he just studied Kendall. "What?"

Ridge grazed the back of his hand over Kendall's cheek. "I'm curious what or whom you regret."

Kendall took a shaky breath. "So many things." Currently topping the list was not knowing what it felt like to lie in Ridge's arms.

"What about this green sauce? What name will go on the menu should it make the cut?"

"Envy."

Ridge quirked a brow. "I'm dying to hear the story behind this."

Kendall smiled and stepped back from him. "I'm not telling you all my secrets tonight. It's bad enough I told you about my stepbrother this morning."

"Please tell me the relationship was consensual."

"Of course. We were both adults before we had sex. Travis is only two years older than I am, so he hadn't groomed me or anything. I was the aggressor in the relationship, not him."

"Did your parents know?"

"No, and I want to keep it that way."

"Are you in love with him?" Ridge asked.

"Hell no." And for the first time, Kendall realized he meant it. He'd always love Travis, but he had never been *in love* with him.

Ridge narrowed his eyes, and it was obvious he had more questions, but he let them drop when Kendall dipped a clean spoon into the green liquid to test the newest tweak to the recipe. Like before, Kendall trailed his finger through the sauce, but Ridge reached out and snagged Kendall's wrist, bringing the finger to his own mouth instead. Firm lips wrapped around Kendall's digit and sucked it into wet heat.

"Oh," Kendall said breathlessly. But Ridge wasn't done yet. He swirled his tongue around the tip of Kendall's finger until his knees threatened to buckle. "Is it good?"

Ridge allowed Kendall's finger to slide from his mouth. "You tell me." He cupped Kendall's neck and pulled him in for a kiss. Kendall parted his lips, and Ridge slid home, teasing and twirling his tongue around Kendall's. He was too focused on the man and noticing the wet glide and rasp of tongues to scrutinize the sauce's flavor until the heat came on late, tickling his throat.

Kendall whimpered and clutched at Ridge's T-shirt to keep himself upright. He pulled his mouth free and stared up into Ridge's eyes. "Best sauce I've ever made."

Ridge dropped his hands to Kendall's waist, digging his thumbs into his hips. "You must be very envious." Kendall nodded. "Of whom?"

He took a steadying breath, prepared to confess all, but Ridge's phone rang.

"No. No. No," Ridge snarled as he pulled the cockblocking device from his pocket. He checked the display and added a terse "Fuck" to the mix. He cleared his throat and put some distance between himself and Kendall before jabbing a finger at the screen. "What's up, Eddie?" Ridge listened for a few seconds before saying, "I'll be there in fifteen." Ridge disconnected and blew out an impatient breath. "I'm so sorry."

Kendall shook his head, wondering if the disruption had been divine intervention. "It's your job. And besides, you don't owe me an explanation."

Ridge nodded abruptly. "Right," he agreed. "Can I get a rain check on green chicken wings, pizza, and…"

"A night of trashy reality television." They both knew that hadn't been the direction their evening was heading before Eddie called.

"Right. Television."

Ridge walked over to the living room where Sammy was supervising them from the back of the couch. He fussed over the feline for a few seconds before giving Kendall one last regretful look on his way out the door.

Kendall turned his music back on and tried to dance away his disappointment. He made the homemade pizza as planned because it was something Ridge could reheat whenever he returned. Afterward, he curled up on the couch with Sammy and fell asleep watching *90 Day Fiancé*.

He woke sometime later to find Ridge sitting at the end of the couch, mowing his way through pizza and wings. The horrified expression on the man's face caused Kendall to panic.

"Is it the Envy sauce or the pizza that's making you pucker?"

Ridge flinched, then smiled. "Which end? Pretty sure they're both puckering but for different reasons."

Kendall sat up and dipped his finger into the Envy sauce. It was much hotter than when it had been fresh on the stove. Some peppers got hotter the longer they sat. "That accounts for the puckered lips." Kendall took a bite of Ridge's pizza but couldn't find fault with it.

"This is the best pizza I've ever had," Ridge said.

"Thanks. So why the secondary puckering?"

"This show," Ridge said, gesturing to the television with another slice. "What am I watching?"

"Reality television at its finest." Kendall launched into a detailed explanation of the concept, smiling at the faces Ridge made.

"This can't be real," he said.

Kendall shrugged. "The producers claim it is. I'm just here for the entertainment."

"Huh." Ridge sat back and continued eating until the only thing left on his plate was chicken bones. "You watch this kind of thing every night?"

"Nah," Kendall said. "*Forensic Files* is my go-to. Helps me sleep."

Ridge snapped his head around to stare at Kendall. "Watching a show about criminals helps you sleep at night?"

"It's a show about catching criminals," Kendall corrected. "And the narrator's voice is so soothing."

Ridge shook his head and stood up. "And with that, I'm tapping out. Sweet dreams, Kendall."

Ridge walked his plate into the kitchen, rinsed it, and placed it inside the dishwasher. Another facet of his personality for Kendall to admire.

"Sweet dreams."

Sammy followed Ridge down the hall, his fluffy tail swishing dramatically from side to side. Envy, or perhaps it was the aptly named sauce, simmered in his belly. What he wouldn't give to be that cat for the night.

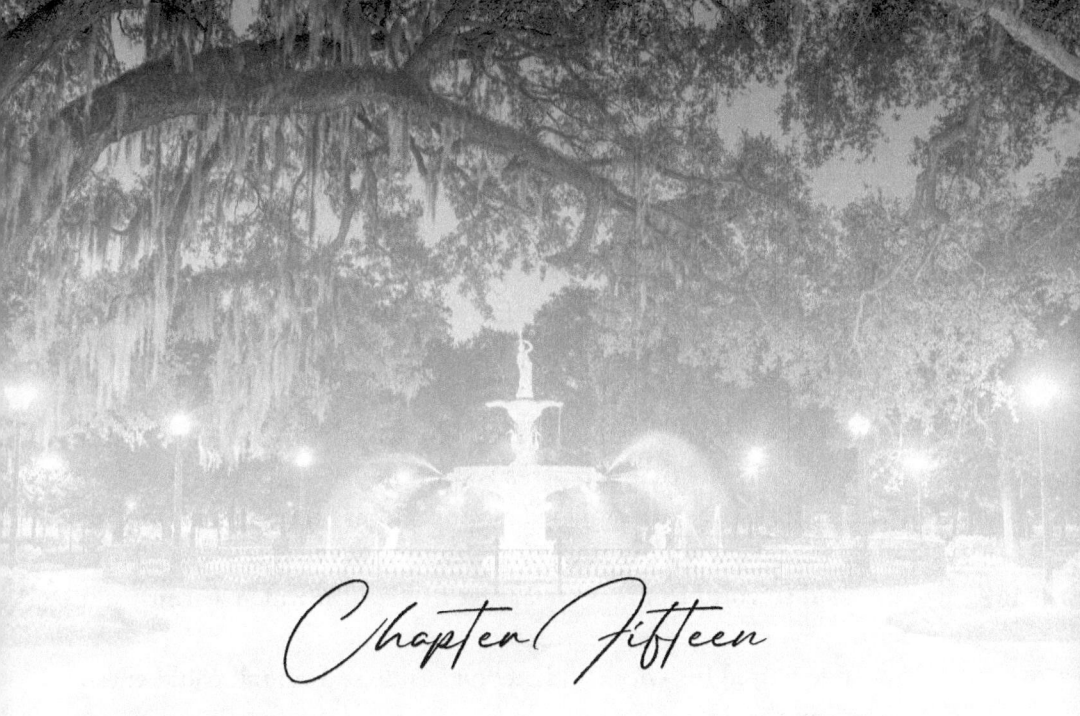

Chapter Fifteen

BY SATURDAY, KENDALL'S WEEK HADN'T SETTLED DOWN. IF anything, it had amped up even more because someone leaked security camera footage of the Rodney James takedown to Sassy in Savannah, a social media site popular in the LGTBQ+ community. The video clip of Kendall bringing the fugitive to his knees and knocking him unconscious started out as a local story but quickly went viral. He had received and rejected interview requests from all over the world. Kendall wasn't sure who was behind the leaked video, but he didn't appreciate having his life turned upside down. Drew had addressed the situation with the employees and said further instances would result in immediate termination.

If that wasn't bad enough, Rebecca had followed up on her dinner invite. When Kendall had ignored her, hoping she'd give up, Stan had sent him a brusque text message. *Saturday at 7:00. No excuses.* Kendall didn't owe the asshole a damn thing, but Rebecca had reached out three additional times. She was trying, and though he could think of a hundred things he'd rather do on a Saturday night, Kendall jogged up the steps of the Burkhart mansion and rang the doorbell. Moments later, a petite, dark-haired woman opened the door. Her cool, professional smile morphed into one of pure delight when she saw him.

"My boy," she cried, opening her arms wide for him. "I've missed you so much."

Kendall stepped into the housekeeper's embrace and held on tightly. She always smelled like vanilla and cinnamon, two fragrances that always brought him comfort. "Hi, Adelaide. I've missed you too."

She dropped her arms and stepped back, assessing him with a shrewd gaze. When their eyes met again, Adelaide's worry was evident. "You look too skinny. Are you eating?"

"Yes, ma'am."

Adelaide swatted his arm playfully. "None of that *ma'am* stuff. And why are you ringing the doorbell? This is your home."

Stanton Burkhart's mansion had never been his home. It was a prison Kendall had escaped. "It just felt like the right thing to do." After all, the summons he'd received from his stepfather had held as much warmth as a subpoena.

Adelaide patted his cheek and stepped aside so Kendall could enter. "Everyone is in the drawing room."

"Everyone?"

"Your parents, Travis, and his new girlfriend," Adelaide said. "Poor girl. Your mother thinks she could be 'the one,' but I think the nice young lady should run." Yet another clueless woman Travis had trotted out in front of his father. "There are a few more guests yet to arrive. I thought you were them when you rang the doorbell."

"What other guests?"

Stan's text was the first communication he'd had from his stepfather since he'd moved out. He thought the summons would result in a stern lecture in Stan's study. His stepfather couldn't be happy about Kendall's name being tied to the club, even though no one had connected Kendall to Stanton. Yet. It was only a matter of time until somebody discovered his mother was married to the wealthy CEO of an investment firm. Stan would be livid because that "trashy club" was the hill Kendall had chosen to die on.

"William Everly and his family," Adelaide said. "He's a potential client your father is trying to impress," Adelaide said.

"Stepfather."

"Yes, dear. I'm sorry."

"So why am I here?" Kendall asked her.

Stiletto heels echoed against the marble floors, and Kendall looked up to see his mother approaching. She looked stunning in an icy blue dress and matching heels. Rebecca had pulled her hair up into a classy bun and left a few wispy strands free to frame her face. In a surprising move, she opened her arms and embraced him. This wasn't the cold hug he'd grown accustomed to receiving from her but the warm, lingering embrace from her pre-Stan days. Right then, she wasn't Rebecca Burkhart, trophy wife of Stanton Burkhart; she was Becca Blakemore, Kendall's mother.

She pressed her lips to his cheek and kissed him before pulling back to look into his eyes. "You're the guest of honor tonight, and I don't want to hog all your time, but do you think we could have a private word before you leave?"

"Why am I the guest of honor?"

"To celebrate your bravery, of course." When Kendall continued to stare, she added, "When you helped capture the fugitive in the club. So, will you make time to have a private chat with me?"

Kendall nodded and walked beside her to the drawing room. This had to be a weird dream.

"I made all your favorites," Adelaide said as she followed behind them.

Rebecca looped her arm through Kendall's. "Adelaide, I just received a text from Amber Everly. They've run into a bit of traffic and are running late," she said over her shoulder.

"No problem, ma'am," Adelaide said as she veered off toward the kitchen.

"You don't seem very happy about your celebration dinner," Rebecca told him.

"I'm not. You could've warned me about the other guests. I thought I was here to get lectured."

She stopped and looked up at him. "Stan said he'd taken care of it, so I assumed he had."

Kendall repeated Stan's text verbatim. "Was I to surmise a celebration dinner from that?"

"You know how Stan is. He's too busy to waste time on pleasantries. He cuts straight to the chase."

His stepfather found plenty of time to fuck around behind his mother's back but couldn't find an additional few seconds to word his text messages better? Bullshit.

Rebecca sighed. "This is our first family dinner together in three years. Can we try to get along?" Of course it would be his fault when everything went to shit.

Kendall tightened his jaw to keep his thoughts to himself and to keep from asking the question burning hottest in his mind. What the fuck was going on here? It was morbid curiosity alone that caused him to nod and say, "As you wish, Rebecca."

She blew out a frustrated breath and continued to the drawing room. Stan glanced up when they crossed the threshold. "Ah, there he is."

Kendall wasn't surprised Stan was wearing a three-piece suit to a family dinner, but the smile on his stepfather's face gave him pause. When was the last time Stanton Burkhart had smiled at him? Maybe the night Rebecca had introduced them when they'd first started dating. The millionaire would've wanted to make a good impression on the leggy blonde he'd hired as his secretary, at least until he'd gotten her into bed.

Just like that fateful night nearly two decades ago, Stan strode across the room and clapped both of Kendall's shoulders in a firm grip. He had to give Stan credit. His stepfather had aged well, still spending his free time in the gym and thwarting the middle-age spread. Stan's steel-gray eyes hadn't softened either. Kendall knew all too well how quickly his gaze could cut a person to the bone. The man was a predator—in and out of the board-room. Firm lips parted, showing off a brilliant white smile. *My, what sharp teeth you have.*

But Kendall wasn't a gullible eight-year-old any longer. He'd bled enough for this man and wasn't willing to give him so much as another nibble.

"It's good to see you," Stan said, the lie rolling off his tongue as smooth and silky as Adelaide's chocolate pudding.

Stanton Burkhart resented the very air Kendall breathed and viewed him as an embarrassment. Kendall took immense joy in living up to the man's low opinion of him. What was it costing Stan to pretend to care about his stepson? And what was behind the farce?

"Hi, Stan," Kendall said, knowing how it grated on his stepfather's nerves.

Stanton narrowed his eyes but managed a dry chuckle. Then he raked his shrewd gaze over Kendall's outfit. The tan chinos, white shirt, blue and gold striped tie, and navy blazer earned a rare approving nod. "It's good of you to dress for dinner."

Rather than respond to Stanton's dig, Kendall said, "I didn't know I was dressing for dinner at the time. I'm dressed for work."

"An improvement over those skimpy boy shorts, huh, Dad?" Travis said. His voice was slow and thick, and Kendall knew without looking that his stepbrother had already been hitting the liquor hard.

Kendall forced himself to face Travis, and his stepbrother's lips curled into a sneer as he lifted his tumbler of whiskey in a mock salute. "To Kendall, our hero."

"Hello, Travis," Kendall said coolly. He glanced at the woman sitting next to his stepbrother and introduced himself when it became apparent no one else was going to do the honors.

She was a petite woman with platinum-blonde hair and icy blue eyes named Sandra. Boy, did Travis have a type. Kendall would bet a month's salary that she was from a prominent family, well educated, soft spoken, and had no clue what she'd signed up for when she'd accepted a date from Travis. He'd also guess they hadn't made it past first base. "It's nice to meet you," Sandra said sweetly.

"Likewise." He wanted to tack on "run for your life" but kept his mouth shut.

"Have a seat," Stan said, returning to the leather loveseat he'd vacated. "Rebecca, get Kendall something to drink."

"Nothing for me, thanks." Kendall lowered himself into a club chair facing Stan and Rebecca. The other options placed him across from Travis, and he'd rather avoid that at all costs since his stepbrother wasn't always the nicest when he was drunk. Kendall had no desire to be his target.

Rebecca lowered herself onto the loveseat beside Stan. She crossed her legs primly and placed her hand on her husband's knee. Stan scowled at the gesture as if his wife touching him was wholly unexpected and inappropriate. He turned and stared at Rebecca until she cowered and withdrew her hand, placing it on her lap. Kendall should've felt a pang in his heart for his mother and spoken up in her defense, but it had always blown up in his face. *You made your bed, Rebecca. Too bad your husband isn't sleeping in it.*

"So," his stepfather said, then aimed a round of rapid-fire questions at him. Stan didn't do small talk; he conducted interrogations. Kendall preferred being ignored over Stan's sudden interest in his life.

Most of Stan's curiosity seemed aimed at Kendall's job at The Cockpit, which was an abrupt change in attitude. The club's name alone had made Stan's face red with fury, and the uniforms had caused the veins to bulge in his forehead and ultimatums to spew from his mouth. Kendall noted

Stan refrained from using the club's name when posing his questions. Since Kendall's heroics—the media's terminology, not his—Stan seemed almost approving of his choices. There had to be a catch. Kendall knew it was only a matter of time before his stepfather revealed his hand. And since he had a few hours to kill before his shift started, why not settle in and let the game play out.

"Where'd you learn to fight like that?" Stan asked when he ran out of questions about the club.

Before Kendall could reply, Travis let loose an obnoxious snort. "From fighting off dirty old men," he said. "You've seen the indecent uniforms they wear around there."

Kendall turned his head to look at his stepbrother, who was too busy knocking back another drink to look at him. Travis had loved peeling him out of those shorts, but no matter how angry Kendall was, he'd never redirect Stan's wrath toward his only son.

"Travis," Stan said sternly, "don't be crude."

Travis smiled at his father. "Yes, sir." Travis lifted his left hand off the back of the sofa and flipped Kendall off behind Sandra's lovely head. Travis craned his neck and leaned forward to meet Kendall's gaze.

"Whatever happened to paralegal school, anyway? Was it just another thing you couldn't see through?"

"Travis," Sandra said softly, "what's the matter with you?"

Kendall could answer her question, but no one would like his answer, so he saved his breath. Instead, Kendall said, "I did finish school and graduated with honors."

"Then why aren't you pursuing that career?" Travis pressed.

It was a legitimate question but not one he wanted to get into with any of the people gathered, especially not Travis. The doorbell rang, saving Kendall from having to answer.

Stan rubbed his hands together. "The Everlys are here."

Kendall figured his stepfather was about to reveal his hand, so he rose with everyone else and turned to face the door. Stan and Rebecca were halfway across the room when Adelaide ushered an elegantly dressed couple into the space.

"Bill. Amber," Stan said jovially. "We're so happy you could join us."

"Welcome to our home," his mom said. Kendall bit the inside of his cheek to keep from grinning when Rebecca sized Amber up. The brunette woman was svelte, leggy, and buxom, three traits Stan loved in a woman.

"I thought Graeme was joining us," Stan said.

"He is," Bill assured him. "He had to take a call from the hospital. He's not on call tonight, but he never turns his patients away."

"Sounds like father found a real lively one for you," Travis said.

Kendall was too busy observing the power play between his mother and Amber to notice Travis approaching. He turned and looked up at his stepbrother. "What are you talking about?"

Travis snorted and shook his head. "Oh, did you think Stan invited you to dinner because he missed you? Ha. This is just the first time your queerness has come in handy. He'd already been planning this coup with Bill Everly, but your heroic little stunt was the icing on the cake. Or should I say you're the carrot father wants to dangle in front of Bill and Amber's gay son?"

Kendall looked at the two couples who'd moved over to the wet bar. Bill was attempting to talk to Rebecca, but she was too busy glaring at his wife. Amber's hand had lingered longer than necessary on Stan's when she accepted the drink he passed her, and his stepfather aimed a predatory smile the brunette's way. "Is Stan trying to seal a deal with Bill's company or his wife?"

"Both," Travis said.

"Gross," Kendall and Sandra said at the same time. The two exchanged a smile before returning their attention to the tableau unfolding across the room.

Rebecca hadn't missed the exchange between her husband and Amber and had moved to stand between them. *Yeah, like that would stop Stan.* For all he knew, Amber and Stan were already intimately acquainted. Kendall caught the faint echo of footsteps on marble and turned his head toward the door in time to see a tall man with dark hair and alluring hazel eyes enter the room. Graeme Everly had worn dark denim jeans and a light blue button-up instead of a bespoke suit like his father. His hair was on the long side, shaggy even, but the soft strands framed his face, accentuating his masculine bone structure.

"Oh, he's handsome," Sandra said.

"Very," Kendall agreed. Travis had intimated Stan wanted to fix Kendall up with Graeme Everly, but that couldn't be right.

"There's my boy," Amber said, waving Graeme over. "Come meet Stanton and Rebecca."

Bill made the introductions, and Graeme shook each of their hands. They exchanged pleasantries for a few moments before Stan brought the tall gentleman over to meet Kendall, Sandra, and Travis. Stan introduced his son first, and Travis was smart enough to drop the sneering jerk act to welcome their guest. Stan made a dismissive introduction of Sandra, but Graeme stopped and made small talk with her. Then he finally joined Stan in front of Kendall.

"Hello," Graeme said, his voice deep and rich like a decadent brownie.

"Hi," Kendall returned.

"The two of you have a lot in common," Stan said.

"Oh?" Kendall asked. Based on what? Their assumed sexuality? Kendall was curious to find out how much, or how little, Stan knew about him.

"And how would you know that?" Graeme asked. His voice sounded more curious than annoyed.

Neither Stan's smile nor his arrogance faltered. "I feel like I've gotten to know you through the many conversations I've had with your parents."

"Interesting," Graeme said in a voice that expressed the opposite.

Just then, Adelaide stepped into the drawing room and told them dinner was ready. Usually, he would've been grateful for her interruption, but Kendall wanted to see Stan squirm like a worm on a hook.

Unsurprisingly, Kendall found himself seated beside Graeme and opposite Travis and Sandra. The staff moved in to fill soup and salad bowls as soon as they were seated.

"Would you like a glass of wine?" Stan asked Graeme. "Or a cocktail?"

"I don't drink," the dark-haired man said, "but thank you."

"Another thing you and Kendall have in common," Stan said.

Graeme held up his glass of water to Kendall. "Cheers."

Smiling, Kendall clinked his glass against Graeme's.

The conversation began in earnest with most of the questions and comments being aimed at Kendall and Graeme. The attention was weird and unwelcome, making him long for the days of being ignored. Stan beamed with false pride at Kendall while his mother glared at Amber. Sandra kept her eyes in front of her while Travis oscillated between staring daggers at Graeme and making passive-aggressive remarks to Kendall. Neither Bill nor Amber said much, but maybe it was because the former was too busy knocking back the liquor to stay engaged while the latter was doing her best to catch Stan's eye. Of course, Rebecca saw it all too. She tried to interject herself into the conversation only for Stan to offer her a not-now-dear pat on the hand.

The tension thickened in the room until Kendall felt like he couldn't breathe let alone eat. He felt horribly guilty Adelaide had gone to the trouble of making boeuf bourguignon for him. Kendall had taken tiny bites, but it felt like the meat and vegetables kept getting stuck in his throat. He excused himself to use the restroom when the staff cleared the main course dishes.

"Is everything okay?" Adelaide asked him in the hall outside the formal dining room. "Didn't you enjoy your dinner?"

"Oh, Adelaide, it was delicious as always. Stan didn't tell me we would be having dinner, so I ate before I left the house."

She narrowed her eyes, and Kendall could tell she didn't believe him. Instead of pushing, she patted his cheek again. "Would you like me to pack up some leftovers?"

"There's nothing I'd love to eat more after a long night at the club." Kendall hugged the housekeeper and breathed in her comforting fragrance once more. Adelaide had been the best part of living under Stan Burkhart's roof.

"Swing by the kitchen before you leave."

Kendall nodded, kissed her cheek, then headed to the bathroom. He didn't really need to use the facilities. He just wanted a few moments of peace and quiet to pull himself together. Kendall didn't care about pissing off Stan or his mother, but Graeme seemed like a nice guy. Unfortunately for Stan, there was absolutely no spark between them. His stepfather would need to close the deal and bag the babe on his own merit. *Christ. What has my life become?*

Kendall eased the door shut behind him and braced his hands on the marble vanity. Taking a deep breath, Kendall allowed his head to fall forward, and he peered into the sink for a few moments to clear his mind. When that didn't work, he turned on the cold water tap and splashed his face. With the shock came clarity. It didn't matter how kind Graeme seemed. Staying in this house for another minute wasn't healthy for him.

He'd just turned off the water and reached for a towel when the door opened behind him, and Travis stepped in. Kendall's stomach soured and threatened to reject the little food he'd managed to swallow.

"What are you doing in here?" Kendall whispered. His stepbrother's lustful gaze and sneering lips projected his thoughts before his liquor-addled brain could convince his limbs to act on them. Kendall stepped to the right just as Travis lunged for him. The bigger man tipped forward and braced his hands on the marble, catching himself before his forehead smashed into the mirror. "No, Travis."

"Are you pissed because I brought a date?"

"Nope," Kendall said emphatically. "I'm outraged on her behalf, though. What's the matter with you? I understand why you don't want to tell Stan the truth. Your father didn't exile me for being gay. I just wasn't the kind of gay he approved of. It could've been you he introduced to Graeme."

Travis barked a dry laugh. "You say that because you weren't privy to the things my father said behind your back. He used to laugh at you in front of his friends." Travis's lips quivered. "I used to join in because it was expected. God, I fucking hate myself."

Travis's words were like a knife to his heart. Not the part about Stan making fun of him behind his back. On some level he knew it. It shattered Kendall that Travis thought so badly of himself.

"It's okay, Trav," he said softly. "I know you didn't mean anything you said. And I understand why you don't want to come out to Stan, but surely you don't want to hurt innocent people with your deception."

"Hurt her? I haven't touched Sandra." Travis collapsed into himself and fell against the wall. He looked at Kendall with a crestfallen expression that would've crushed him in the past. "I've tried. I wish I could want her, but I…"

Kendall shook his head vigorously. "Please don't."

"I love you."

Kendall forced himself to harden his heart. Travis didn't know the first thing about love. And yeah, he might not know what love was either, but he sure as hell knew what it wasn't. "You're horny and confusing lust with love."

"Two sides of the same coin," Travis slurred.

Kendall shook his head. "That's love and hate, Trav. You don't feel either of those for me. I was nothing but fun and games for you."

Travis shook his head vigorously, which made him sway a little. "Not at first. You were everything to me. But there—"

"Was no future for us," Kendall finished. Travis hadn't been willing to sever his relationship with his only living parent. "I understand that better now. But you started turning to me whenever you wanted to spite Stan."

Travis flinched like Kendall had slapped him. "That's not true. You were my safe place. You're the only person who truly knows me, Kendall."

"I deserve better." For the first time in his life, Kendall meant it. "I don't want to be only a safe place. I want to be somebody a guy is willing to risk it all for."

Travis straightened to his full height and snorted. "Love like that doesn't exist anymore. Probably never did."

"Yes, it does. I'm not going to settle for anything less."

Travis slowly raised his hand and cupped Kendall's cheek. "Take me back. I'm sorry I hurt you."

Kendall shook his head. "There's no future for us. You were right about that, and I never should've—"

Travis suddenly pushed off the wall and boxed Kendall in against the vanity. Tears filled his eyes. "Please don't say you regret me."

Kendall shook his head. "Never that. Growing up, you were the only person who ever really saw and understood me."

"I've loved you since you moved in here," he admitted. "You had such sad eyes, and I wanted to take on the world for you." Travis closed his eyes and tears spilled down his cheeks. "And I hurt you just like the others did."

Travis's rejection had hurt him more than anyone else's, including Rebecca's, but it would serve no purpose to air their grievances. They weren't innocent little boys or hormonal young adults anymore. They were grownups, and it was time they acted like it.

"I want you to be happy, Travis," Kendall said. "You'll never find it in lies and pretense. Come find me when you're ready to live your truth. I'll repay the kindness you showed to a little boy with no champion in the world."

Travis took a deep, shaky breath, fisted Kendall's navy blazer, and leaned his forehead against Kendall's. "I don't think I can ever be as brave as you."

"You can. Step one is breaking off this awful farce with Sandra. She seems like a really nice woman."

Travis sighed. "She is. I want to love her."

"You can't wish it to be true. You'll figure that out eventually."

"It's too late. I've already lost you."

Kendall didn't want to rehash parts of their conversation. Travis wouldn't likely recall their bathroom chat anyway, and if he did, he'd be pissed Kendall saw him in a vulnerable state. "We need to get back, Trav. They'll get suspicious if we stay in here much longer."

"Just one last kiss?" Travis tried to smoosh his lips into a pucker, but it looked more like a childish pout. Either way, it wasn't the least bit attractive.

Kendall shook his head and stepped out from between him and the sink. "I said no, and I meant it. Go back to the dining room."

"Or what?"

"I'll do to you what I did to the fugitive. Maybe worse."

Travis threw up his hands in surrender, then wobbled on his feet. "Fine. You win."

Kendall held his breath until Travis left the room, then he lunged forward and locked the door in case his stepbrother changed his mind. He wanted to pat himself on the back for saying no to Travis for the first time in…ever, but his reckless streak was a caged beast thrashing against the metal bars holding him in captivity. The unresolved sexual tension with Ridge was only compounding his problem. It was only a matter of time before Reckless bent the metal or tricked Kendall into setting him free so he could join his twin, Impulsive. He could battle inevitability or ensure he made the safest of dumb choices. Kendall wanted to fight the good fight, but his resistance was waning and dangling the key to the cage in front of the ferocious beast.

Reckless and Impulsive. They would make exceptional names for future sauces.

Kendall took a few deep breaths and exited the bathroom. Instead of returning to the dining room as expected, he took a detour to the kitchen where the staff was busy preparing dessert plates. Kendall nearly whimpered when he saw the poached pears dripping chocolate sauce with a scoop of vanilla bean ice cream on the side.

He heaved a sigh and said, "Pears Belle Helene."

Adelaide looked up and smiled. "I told you I made all your favorites." Then she opened the lid on a plastic storage container and showed off the cookies inside. "Palmier cookies too."

Kendall could almost taste the crisp, buttery cookies. "Could I get a few of those to go?"

Adelaide's smile fell from her face. "You're leaving so soon?"

"There's an issue at work that needs my attention." He hated lying to Adelaide, but he wasn't willing to divulge the truth and risk losing her affection.

She replaced the lid and carried the cookies around the long work island. "Take them all," Adelaide said as she shoved the plastic container into Kendall's hands.

"No, I couldn't."

"I made them just for you," Adelaide said. "Mrs. Burkhart is only expecting me to serve Pears Belle Helene to her guests."

"I shouldn't." His crumbling resolve made Adelaide smile. "But I will."

She rose onto her tiptoes and kissed his cheek. "That's my boy. Give me a few minutes to pack up your leftovers."

Kendall didn't bother protesting because they both knew it was as worthless as Monopoly money. Instead, he took the time to catch up on what was going on with her family. She'd been blessed with a beautiful grandson since the last time Kendall had seen her.

"He's adorable," Kendall said when she showed him photos on her phone. "Congratulations."

"Thank you." Adelaide leaned closer and lowered her voice. "I haven't spoken to your mother about this, but I plan to resign at the end of the month. My son and daughter-in-law could use my help."

"And they're more deserving of your love and devotion," Kendall said. "Promise me one thing."

"Name it," Adelaide said without hesitation.

"Keep in touch."

Adelaide folded her arms over her stomach. "As you've done with me?"

"Touché." Kendall took a deep breath. "I didn't mean to include you in my clean break from this household."

She patted his cheek. "I know, love. I know. I should've called to make sure you were okay, but I didn't know if it was my place."

Kendall pulled the woman in for another hug. "I can't imagine what my childhood would've been like if not for you and the refuge I found in your kitchen. You will always have a special place in my heart."

Adelaide sniffled and pulled back after a few moments. "We'll both do better this time."

Kendall nodded.

"But give me your address so I can at least send you a Christmas card in case you forget this conversation."

"I won't," he said, but he wrote his new address down for her anyway.

She packed up a large tote with enough leftovers to feed a battalion before adding the cookies on top. Adelaide handed him the bag and said, "I'll make your excuses to your mother."

"Still running interference for me, I see." Kendall doubted Rebecca would notice or even care, but he appreciated Adelaide's gesture.

"Some things never change." Her dark eyes took on a somber expression. "Others take time, but they're worth the effort."

Her words reminded him of the internal war waging inside him, and he metaphorically tucked the keys to the cage away for the time being. "I love you."

"I love you too."

Kendall exited the house through the kitchen, choosing to walk around the mansion rather than risk running into Stan before he escaped. When he rounded the side of the house, he saw Graeme leaning against the wall near the front door. He held a phone to his ear and appeared to be in the middle of a serious conversation. Graeme glanced up as he approached and offered a friendly wave.

"Nice meeting you," Kendall whispered as he walked by.

"You too," Graeme mouthed.

Kendall didn't release the breath he'd been holding until he'd driven away from the Burkhart mansion.

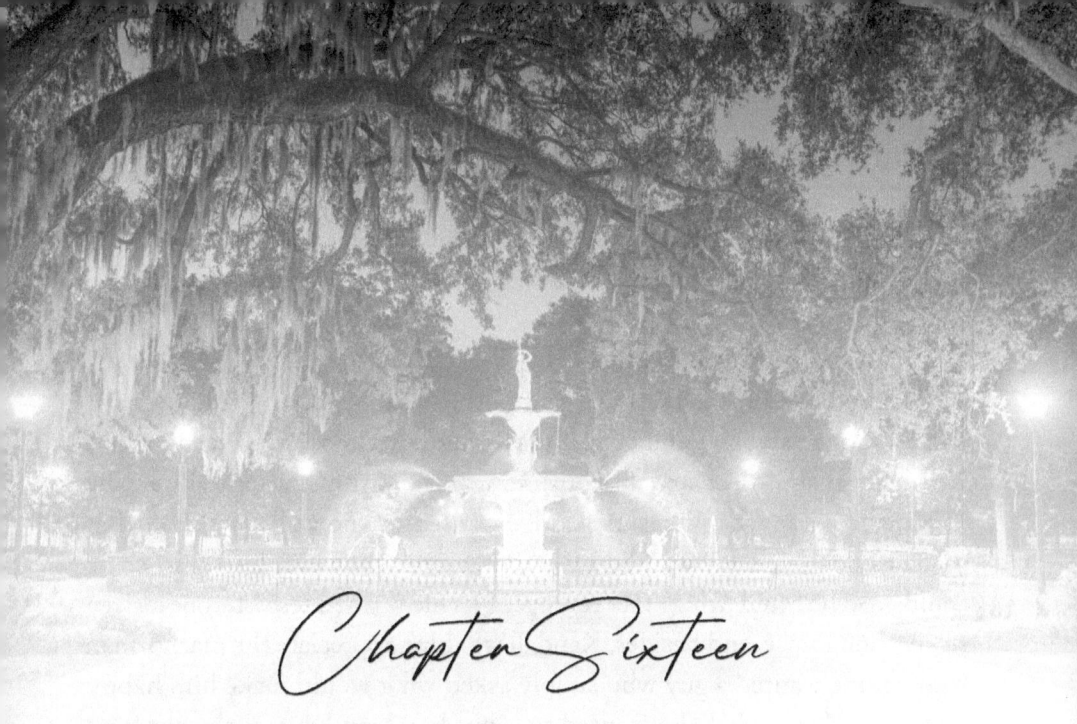

Chapter Sixteen

EDDIE STOPPED BY HIS DESK AND PERCHED HIS ASS ON THE CORNER. "Saturday night plans foiled again," he said on a sigh. "Lieutenant said the warrants will come through any minute now. You ready?"

"Yeah." They were about to serve arrest and property seizure warrants to two of Savannah's wealthiest citizens, so it was all hands on deck, including the SPD officers and Chatham County officers deputized to work on their multiagency task force. Frenetic energy buzzed around the room like a swarm of wasps. "Why do you ask?"

Eddie shrugged, and a wry smile tilted the left corner of his mouth. "You seem a little distracted. Seems like I'm not the only one with wrecked plans tonight."

"I didn't have plans unless you count a quiet night at home with Sammy."

"Watching that awful show you can't stop talking to Jess about? What's it called again?"

"*90 Day Fiancé*," Ridge grumbled. "And you're just jealous because Jess likes me better."

"Unquestionably," Eddie agreed. "But I'm having serious doubts about the longevity of our relationship based on her television choices." His best friend angled his head and studied Ridge closer. "If I didn't know better, I'd say you were moping."

"Moping? Why? I have everything I wanted after my breakup with Todd."

Eddie raised his hand and stroked his jaw. "Moping isn't the right word."

"Pining," Zack said as he joined them. "Maybe he's jonesing for something."

"Or someone," Eddie added.

Ridge rolled his eyes. "Fuck you both." Moping, pining, and even jonesing weren't strong enough verbs. His desire to know everything about Kendall was soul-deep and all-consuming. He didn't just want to know the sounds he made when he came; Ridge wanted to know all the things that made Kendall tick. He wanted a list of everyone who'd ever hurt him, so he could…So he could, what? Get revenge? His life wasn't a testosterone-driven retribution movie, and besides, Kendall wouldn't appreciate the macho-man routine. He wanted a guy who simply asked what would make him happy. Ridge could ask—hell, he wanted to—but he'd kept his mouth shut for a simple reason. If he knew the answers, Ridge would move heaven and earth to see Kendall's hopes come to fruition, and that scared the bejesus out of him. No roots. No entanglements. His growing feelings for Kendall were the antithesis of free and loose.

"Holy crap," Zack said. "Do you see the panic in his eyes, Eduardo?"

"Hard to miss. Our Ridgey's got it bad."

Ridge would've commented, but their assistant chief deputy, Jayne Marks, and their inspector, Asher Dunleavy, stepped into the operations room. Marks was a petite, Black woman who took a minimalist approach in both her fashion sense and demeanor. She had no time for frills or bullshit, and they all respected her deeply. Standing beside Asher, who resembled a brawny lumberjack, she seemed even smaller, but Ridge would rather tussle with the lumberjack in a dark alley than the assistant chief deputy any day. Marks practiced several martial arts, and her size made her fast and deadly.

Asher held up a stack of papers in his hand. "We're serving arrest and seizure warrants at the homes of Jenner Jones and Stanton Burkhart as well as at their corporate office. The two men are accused of using their investment company to bilk billions of assets from their investors and defraud the IRS in the process. We need to split into three teams and hit their locations simultaneously so one location doesn't tip off the other."

For the next ten minutes, Asher went over a detailed plan before dividing them into three teams. Asher went with the crew heading to the corporate office, Zack went with the Jenner Jones unit, and Eddie and Ridge had Stanton Burkhart duties.

The Burkhart team was in position first but waited down the street until the other two units were in place. When Asher gave the signal, the convoys switched on their lights and sirens and moved in on their targets.

Eddie, Ridge, and Tiffany Janey took the front door while the others took the sides and rear of the property. Eddie rang the doorbell repeatedly while Ridge banged on the ornate wooden door and identified them as federal marshals. Seconds later, a woman wearing a drab gray uniform answered the door.

"We have an arrest warrant for Stanton Burkhart," Ridge told her. "Where can we find him?"

Before she could respond, a blonde woman joined her at the door. "Mrs. Burkhart, these men are here to arrest Mr. Burkhart."

The blonde woman's pale blue eyes widened. "What? There has to be some mistake."

"Afraid not. Step aside, ma'am," Janey said.

"Rebecca," a man said from deeper inside the residence. "What's going on? I was giving Amber a tour of the house when I heard all the commotion."

Rebecca Burkhart snorted, then stood aside and gestured to the trio. "They're here to arrest you."

All the color leached out of the man's face. "What? There must be a mistake."

They stepped past Mrs. Burkhart and entered the grand foyer. Eddie politely showed the warrant to Stanton Burkhart, who snatched the document out of his hand.

"I don't fucking believe this," the investment banker said. "It says you're to seize all my assets."

"What?" Mrs. Burkhart screeched.

A younger version of Stanton Burkhart staggered drunkenly down the hallway. "Dad? What's going on?"

"Not now, Travis," Burkhart sneered. "You better return to the drawing room and drink what little liquor you've left untouched before these assholes seize it."

"That's US Deputy Marshal Asshole to you," Eddie said. "Hands behind your back, sir."

"Call our lawyer, Rebecca," Stanton said as he obeyed Eddie's command.

Ridge let their team know they were inside and had Burkhart in custody. "Move in and make sure all the residents, guests, and staff are rounded
up and placed in one location. We want to make sure nothing is removed
from the house and no documents or evidence are shredded or otherwise
destroyed."

"You're not taking a damn thing from this house," Mrs. Burkhart said
as she held her phone to her ear. "Our attorney, Roger Carmichael, won't
let you."

"I don't answer to Roger, ma'am," Ridge said. "He's entitled to supervise
the cataloging and removal of property, but he can't stop us."

"And we'll arrest him and anyone else who tries to interfere with us
executing a federal warrant," Janey said.

The woman glared daggers at them until her lawyer answered. She
stepped away and spoke to him in hushed tones, but Ridge could hear most
of what she said. None of it was flattering toward the marshals who'd interrupted her dinner party.

Once Ridge had Stanton secured, he led him to a sitting area off the
foyer. "Have a seat."

"I want to talk to my attorney," Stanton said.

"Mrs. Burkhart can hold the phone to your ear," Eddie told him.

"Rebecca," Burkhart called out. "Bring the phone over here. I don't want
you to fuck this up."

The woman spun around and glared at Stanton. "Me? I'm not the one
in handcuffs."

"Do as I say, woman. Then I want you to find Amber. I don't want the
Everlys to get the wrong impression."

Rebecca Burkhart stomped across the marble floor looking angry
enough to slug him. "Shouldn't you be worried about what Bill thinks since
he's the one you're trying to do business with? Just what were you and his
wife getting up to on this *tour*?"

Mr. Burkhart glowered at her for a few seconds. "Hold up the phone
so I can talk to Roger."

"Tell me the truth," Rebecca demanded. "Are you screwing Amber
Everly?"

"This isn't the time for this conversation. I need Roger here now."

"Not until you tell me the truth," his wife shouted. "Are you fucking
her?"

Ridge rubbed the bridge of his nose and wondered what the hell horror they'd stepped into. This was better than the trashy reality television Kendall loved so much, and Ridge hated that he couldn't share the details with him.

"Yes!" Stanton shouted. "Are you happier now that you know the truth? Give me the phone."

"You son of a bitch," Rebecca yelled. She cocked her arm back, but Eddie blocked her attempt to strike the man.

"Ma'am," Eddie said kindly. "Your name isn't on the arrest warrant. As bad as this night is, you get to walk away from it."

"With nothing," she cried. "After I've given him *everything*."

"Darling, we'll fix this," Stanton said. "I'm sorry I couldn't resist her seduction."

"Jesus," Ridge muttered. He hadn't meant to respond, but was this guy for real? And how many times had a similar scene played out? He'd bet Eddie's right nut it wasn't the first time Stanton had cheated.

Mrs. Burkhart must've believed it because she held her phone up to her husband's ear.

After a terse exchange with his attorney, Stanton nodded at his wife, who withdrew the phone and disconnected the call. "Roger will be here in twenty minutes."

"Gives us plenty of time to clear the residence to make sure no one is sneaking out the back with the silverware, jewelry, or artwork," Eddie said.

"You can't be serious," Mrs. Burkhart said.

"I once had a woman try to hide diamonds under her tongue," Eddie replied.

"That isn't what I meant," she said. "You can't possibly take jewelry that belongs to me if I'm not included in the warrant."

"We can, and we will," Ridge said.

"The items you claim are yours were bought with illicit gains and are now the property of the United States," Eddie said.

Mrs. Burkhart whirled around and faced her husband once more. "Stanton, what have you done?" She sounded more outraged over losing her jewelry than hearing her husband admit he'd had an affair.

Roger Carmichael arrived faster than the lawyer had predicted, and that's when the real fun began. The man looked over the warrant and shook his head. "I'd hoped to get an emergency injunction from Judge Temple, but she didn't answer my calls."

"Try again," Mr. Burkhart groused.

The lawyer ran a hand over his forehead. "She's the one who signed the warrant, Stanton. They're seizing your personal assets—Jenner's too—as well as everything the company owns. There's nothing I can do about this until Monday. I can try to get you out on bail then."

Burkhart bristled in his chair. "Fuck."

"I can't stop them from taking anything, but I can photograph and catalog each item." The lawyer grimaced for a second.

"What's wrong?" Stanton asked.

"Besides the fact that we'll be homeless and penniless?" Rebecca asked her husband.

The attorney cleared his throat. "We'll need to discuss how you plan to pay for my legal services."

"Christ," Burkhart said. "I would've thought forty years of doing business together meant something to you, Roger."

"I'll cover it," the drunk man named Travis said. He snorted and hiccupped. "Guess I should be glad you refused to hire me as the CFO of your company, Dad."

"Excuse me," an attractive brunette woman said. "Is my family free to go?" She gestured to two men Ridge assumed were her husband and son. "We're not involved in Mr. Burkhart's business, and none of the possessions in this home belong to us."

"Bet you're sorry you wasted your time sleeping with my husband," Rebecca Burkhart blurted out. "Better find out if Stan gifted her expensive jewelry like he did with his other mistresses." Mrs. Burkhart tipped her head to the side. "Oh, wait. That comes after the newness wears off and he breaks up with them. A parting gift, if you will. I could tell by Stanton's demeanor your affair had just begun. He could barely wait to finish dinner before whisking you off on a *tour*."

Amber gasped, Bill flinched, and their son, Graeme, buried his head in his hands.

"Jesus, Rebecca," Stanton said. "Read the room. This isn't the time or place." Burkhart looked at Ridge. "Can they leave?"

Eddie and Ridge stepped to the side and quickly conversed. They decided there was no reason to keep the Burkharts' dinner guests. The gentlemen emptied their pockets, and Mrs. Everly opened her handbag to prove she wasn't aiding and abetting the Burkharts.

"You're free to go," Eddie told them.

The trio hastily retreated to the door. Bill Everly halted at the threshold of the sitting room and glared at Stanton.

"Needless to say, I'm not interested in doing business with you, Stanton. And you'll regret the day you were born if you come anywhere near my wife again."

Burkhart looked at Ridge. "Are you going to let him threaten me?"

"An ass whipping is the last thing you should be worried about, Mr. Burkhart," Ridge said.

Asset forfeitures were tedious, highly emotional, and drawn-out events. A few deputies supervised the staff as they retrieved their personal belongings and then escorted them to their vehicles. Travis Burkhart and his dinner date, Sandra, were also cleared to leave.

"Ma'am, please tell me you're driving," Eddie said.

"I'd walk home otherwise," she replied.

Travis staggered to his feet. "I'm fine to drive."

"Come on, Travis," Sandra said in an exasperated tone.

"And then there were two," Ridge said to Stanton and Rebecca, who just glared at him.

"Let's get this over with," the attorney groused.

Ridge, Janey, and Eddie did a quick cycle through rock-paper-scissors to see who got stuck babysitting the Burkharts while the other two joined the forfeiture teams. Janey went paper while Ridge and Eddie went scissors.

"Damn it," she murmured.

Eddie went upstairs to the bedrooms while Ridge stayed on the first floor to help gather artwork, collectibles, and other items of value. A few hours later, Eddie met Ridge in Stanton Burkhart's office where he was documenting and boxing up Burkhart's impressive collection of baseball memorabilia.

There was a display of photos on the bookshelves that grabbed Ridge's attention. The largest frame in the center featured a picture of Rebecca and Stanton dancing at their wedding. They were smiling and gazing into each other's eyes like it was the happiest day of their lives. Maybe it was, but they'd fallen a long way since then.

There were a few more smaller photos of Stanton with his son. Most of the images were taken during big moments like graduations and proms. There was only one recent photo of them together, and it looked like it was taken on a golf course. Neither man looked happy to be in the other's company. The rest of the pictures were all framed newspaper or magazine articles touting the brilliance of Burkhart and Jones.

"Nice office," Eddie said when he walked into the room, "but where's the safe?"

"That's what I'm trying to figure out. We subpoenaed their personal and commercial bank records, and there are no safe deposit boxes registered at their institutions—personally or commercially. I expected to find one or two safes hidden behind paintings on the first floor, especially in Burkhart's home office, but nada. Did you find any upstairs?"

"Nada," Eddie echoed. He put his hands on his hips and surveyed the room. "I don't know jack about jewelry, but one of the deputies said what we found was nothing more than costume stuff." Eddie met Ridge's gaze. "Does the diamond and blue stone set Mrs. Burkhart is wearing look like costume jewelry to you?"

"Diamond and sapphire, Eduardo. And no, it looks very much like the real deal."

"There must be hidden doors and safes. We probably shouldn't have released the domestic staff so hastily."

Nodding, Ridge said, "I'd just come to the same conclusion. Let's check the studs."

Eddie shrugged. "Okay. I may not play for your team, but I know a hunk when I see one."

Ridge laughed. "Your enlightenment astounds me, but I was referring to the support beams behind the walls."

"Oh," Eddie replied, his eyes twinkling with humor.

Ridge rapped his knuckles against the smooth mahogany paneling. The solid *thunk* indicated he'd found a stud behind the wall. He moved over a few inches and knocked again, receiving the hollow sound he expected to find in a gap between studs.

Eddie walked over to the wall on the opposite side of the room. "How far apart should the studs be?"

"Sixteen inches." He'd helped his father build their ranch in Montana and would never forget the meticulous way Mitchell Dandridge had laid out their home. Ridge glanced over at his friend. "Unless there's a restraining order, then it's five hundred feet."

Eddie shook his head and kept knocking on the wall. The guys continued testing their theory until Ridge came across a large section of wood paneling with a solid structure behind it.

"That's at least five to six feet wide," Ridge estimated. "Now we just need to find out how we can access it." He ran his finger along the seams of the paneling, looking for a hidden latch or button.

"How about a crowbar?" Eddie suggested.

Ridge snorted. "Let's try other methods first. Maybe the attorney will be helpful. Sure, he wants to protect his clients but not at the risk of being charged with obstruction or getting disbarred."

He continued looking around the room for any type of hidden device that might open the secret panel. The desk was locked, something they'd rectify before the seizure was over, but Ridge did find a remote control on top of it. Unfortunately, it only turned on an electric fireplace. Eddie returned with Carmichael a few minutes later.

"We need access to the safes, counselor," Ridge said.

Good ole Roger looked around the room with a bewildered expression on his face. "I don't see a safe."

"Cut the bullshit," Eddie said. "Burkhart said you've been doing business together for decades. Do you expect us to believe you've never been in this office when he's had to open his safe?"

A deep flush crept up the man's neck and face as he glowered at Eddie. "That's exactly what I want you to believe. I have known and represented Stanton for a long time, but my only invitations to his home were for social events until this evening. We've always conducted our business dealings in my office or his."

"Convenient," Ridge said, his voice sounding as flat as the pancakes Eddie had made him for breakfast once.

The attorney notched his chin higher and stiffened his shoulders. "I don't appreciate your nasty attitude and disdain. I've done nothing to deserve it."

They could argue with the lawyer all night or take up their suspicions with his client. Ridge's gut said Roger was telling the truth, so the latter would be more prudent. He gestured to the door and said, "After you."

The three of them returned to the room where the Burkharts were being held. Ridge could hear them arguing from the opposite side of the mansion, and the annoyed look on Janey's face told him the pair hadn't let up since the seizure had begun.

Ridge glanced over at the couple and noticed their antagonistic body language. They were sitting beside one another, but they were angled away from each other. "Did their hostility loosen their tongues?"

Janey shook her head. "Not beyond what we'd already deduced about Mr. Burkhart. She's spent all this time berating him for his affairs and listing all the things she's sacrificed for his happiness. And he countered with the cars, vacations, and jewelry he's given her."

Ridge took a deep breath. So, the jewelry was likely somewhere in the house or possibly in a safe at the corporate office. He'd call Asher for an update if they struck out with the Burkharts. "Okay."

Ridge joined Eddie and Roger. The unhappy couple glared at him with matching malice.

"We need you to unlock the safes," Eddie said.

"We don't have safes," Stanton replied.

Ridge glared at the dumbass. "The hell you don't. We will search every inch of this house until we find every hidden safe, room, and hidey-hole."

"What good will it do without the combinations?" Burkhart asked.

Their attorney heaved a sigh. "Stanton, they will subpoena an override code from the manufacturer. These are federal marshals, not some clueless, local yokels."

"Or we'll take a crowbar to the wood paneling in the office and drill a hole through the safe once we uncover it," Ridge said.

"Tell them how to access the safes and give them the codes, Stanton," the attorney said.

Burkhart bristled. "Kiss my ass, Roger."

Rebecca pivoted on the loveseat and faced them. "I'll show you to each of the safes and provide the combinations."

That set off a harsh verbal exchange between husband and wife. Ridge could tell a lot about a couple by the insults they hurled at one another. There wasn't a shred of love between them.

"Enough," Eddie shouted after a few minutes. The Burkharts snapped their mouths shut and aimed their ire at him instead of each other. "Save the petty fighting for later. I want access to the safes, and I want it now."

Rebecca rose to her feet. "Let's go."

Burkhart sprang to his feet. "I'm going too. I want to see what you remove."

"To be clear, we're taking everything," Ridge replied.

The pissed-off investment banker glared at his attorney. "Are you just going to let them walk all over you?"

"I'm doing what the law requires of me," Roger replied. "I'm not going down for you."

Rebecca snorted and headed toward the door. "That makes two of us," she tossed over her shoulder.

Once inside the study, the bickering and blaming continued until Eddie whistled sharply through his teeth. "You have ten seconds to reveal the safe before I go out to my truck and get the crowbar and drill," he warned them.

"Unlock the desk, Stanton," Rebecca said.

"Fuck you," he sneered.

Before anyone could predict her next move, Rebecca swung her fist and tagged Burkhart in the balls. Her husband doubled over while Ridge fought the urge to cover his crotch with his hands. "Maybe that will take you out of commission for a few days," she said. Then Rebecca grabbed his bicep and dragged him over to the desk. Burkhart was too busy howling in pain to fight her off. She wrenched the arms cuffed behind his back into the air until his hand was under the middle drawer. An audible click came from the desk, then the middle drawer opened.

"Hand scanner?" Eddie asked.

Rebecca released her husband's arm, and he collapsed onto the floor, writhing in pain. "Nothing but the best for Stan," she said. "The best homes, food, wine, and whores."

Burkhart paused his bitching and moaning long enough to lift his head and sneer at his wife. "Takes one to recognize one."

Rebecca started to kick her prone husband, but Roger stepped between them. "Right now, you're not being held responsible for Stanton's actions. Keep it up, and you'll end up in a holding cell next to him," the attorney cautioned.

Rebecca took a deep breath and nodded. Then she pulled open the middle drawer and hit a button on a tiny remote. Seconds later, the hidden panel opened to reveal a large walk-in safe.

"She doesn't know the combi—"

"Twelve. Sixty-nine. Twenty-one," Rebecca said.

Burkhart slowly staggered to his feet and faced his wife. His attempt at a glower was diminished by his hunched shoulders. "This is the last straw. We're through, and you won't get a penny of my money."

Rebecca barked a dry laugh and crossed her arms over her chest. "What money, Stan?"

"*Do not* call me that." He straightened marginally and looked at Ridge. "Her good jewelry is hidden in two safes in her walk-in closet."

"Shut up, *Stan*."

"Can you be more specific, sir?" Eddie asked. "The closet is bigger than my apartment."

Mr. Burkhart's laughter was sharp enough to cut. Then he told Eddie precisely where the safes were located and how to open them.

"You son of a bitch," Rebecca roared, charging at him with her fist held high. She cocked her arm back and let it fly before Ridge could intervene. Eddie was closer and leaped into the fray. Burkhart ducked at the last minute, so Rebecca's right hook caught Eddie in the jaw. She must've packed a wallop because Eddie's head snapped back with a *crunch*. "Oh shit."

"Indeed," Ridge said, stepping forward and securing her hands behind her back. He removed his handcuffs and snapped them onto her slender wrists. "And now you become our guest for the night."

Her shoulders shook as tears streamed down her face. She aimed her forlorn gaze at Eddie and whispered, "I'm so sorry."

Eddie was a hard-ass, but even he was susceptible to a woman's tears, so Ridge shoved him toward the door. "Tell the team upstairs about the jewelry safes. I'll take care of the office." Ridge looked at the lawyer. "Are you going upstairs or staying here?"

The lawyer looked between his clients and the door. Ridge firmly expected the man to use any excuse to leave the room, but instead, Roger sighed and gestured for Ridge to open the safe.

By the time they locked down the estate, the marshals had seized millions of dollars in assets from the home, including half a million in cash and several luxury vehicles. Rebecca's jewelry collection alone had to be worth a small fortune. They wouldn't know the total value until their assessors cataloged and appraised everything.

"I can't imagine having this kind of money and being so fucking greedy," Eddie said after they'd locked the Burkharts in separate cells. They could've put them in the same cell and sold tickets for the ass whooping Rebecca would give Stan, but that was as unethical as Stanton Burkhart bilking billions of dollars from people.

"Ready to go home?" Eddie asked.

Ridge checked his phone for the first time in hours. It was almost two in the morning. Kendall would be getting off soon. Ridge cringed at his phrasing. He'd be leaving work soon. Not getting off. Or would he? The tension between them had continued to grow until it had become almost unbearable. Rubbing one out in the shower wasn't enough. And what about Kendall? Was he letting off a little solo steam? Had Ridge moving in eased his loneliness or had it made his reckless impulses stronger? How much longer before Kendall gave in to being bad with someone who wasn't Ridge? The thought enraged him.

"Whoa," Eddie said. "You should see your face right now."

Ridge flipped him off, then headed out. "See you on Monday, Eddie."

Instead of heading to bed, Ridge drove to the club to make sure Kendall's good streak was still intact. *Yeah, that was it.*

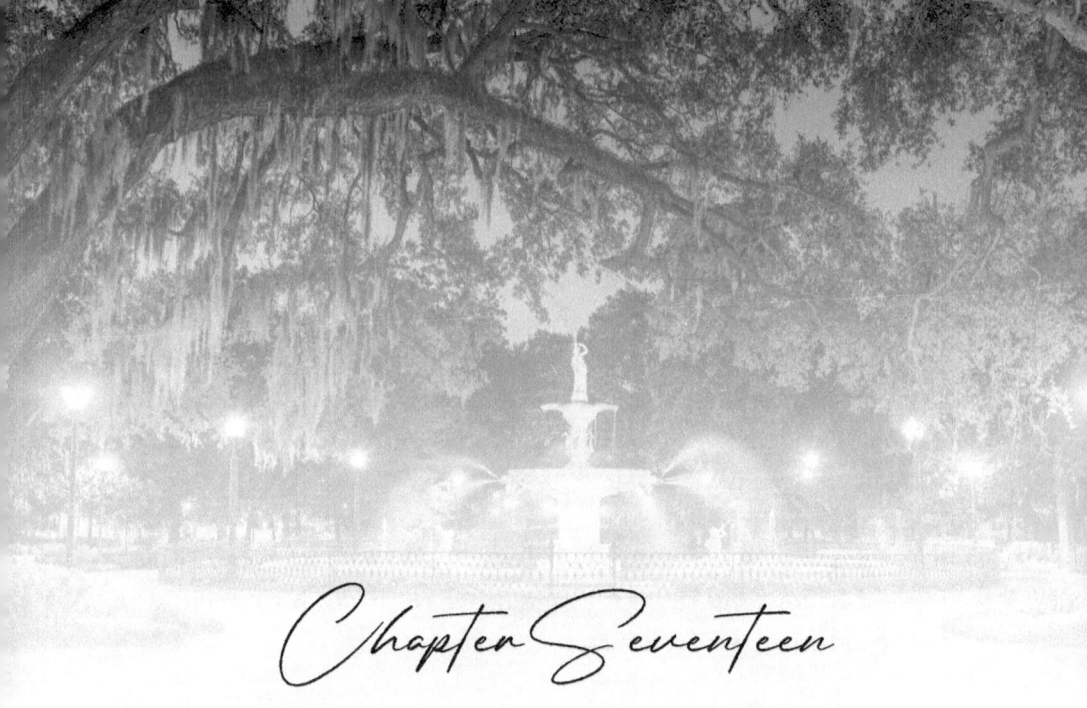

Chapter Seventeen

KENDALL PLACED THE FINAL PACKAGE OF NAPKINS ON THE SHELF, then stood back and surveyed his handiwork. There'd been dozens of boxes of inventory when he'd started his project, and he'd unloaded each of them. It was better to stay busy so he wouldn't fixate on everything that had transpired at dinner. Stanton Burkhart had lived rent-free in his head long enough, and Kendall wasn't giving the man any more space, especially when he had someone wonderful who needed the room. He chuckled dryly and shook his head. Kendall had been *fixating* a lot since Ridge had moved in.

"Hey."

Kendall jolted and turned around. Emmett was leaning against the doorjamb, his dark blond brows slanted in a frown. "Is everything okay?"

"Yeah, why?"

Emmett straightened, crossed the room, and leaned against the shelving unit. The bartender stood a little too close for comfort, so Kendall discreetly eased over and pretended to straighten the boxes of cocktail stirrers. Emmett's light chuckle made Kendall think he hadn't been as subtle as he'd hoped. "You just seem distracted tonight."

Kendall turned to face him again. "Just a lot on my mind."

"Like trying to figure out if I'm straight or just taken? Seems to be the talk of the club since I started working here."

"Don't forget alien," Kendall said.

Emmett laughed and crossed his arms over his chest. "Seriously?"

Kendall nodded. "A recent suggestion by someone who thinks you're too perfect to be human."

"Huh," Emmett said. "I'm not sure if I should be happy or insulted."

"He didn't mean it as an insult if that helps."

A hint of a smile played on Emmett's lips. "Why couldn't I be all those things at once?"

"A straight, monogamous alien?"

Emmett's hint of a grin turned into a full-blown, boxer-scorching smile. "On Earth to save my lover and planet."

Kendall snorted. "I like you."

Emmett threw his head back and laughed. It was dark and throaty and only added to the total package. "Well," the bartender said, "I guess I'll let you live. The rest of the earthlings will not earn a stay of execution."

"Gee, thanks," Kendall said drolly. "I'm doomed to live out the rest of my existence in total solitude." Some might like the notion, but it sounded like a fate much worse than death to Kendall. He was a people person who craved connections. He just couldn't be trusted to make the right ones.

Emmett sighed deeply. "Fine. I'll take you back to my planet with me."

Kendall laughed. "I'd probably stand a better chance of finding love with an alien race."

"Nothing ever happened between you and the marshal?"

"What's your definition of nothing?" Kendall asked. Technically, a lot had happened between him and Ridge, but he doubted Emmett was referring to Kendall getting Ridge hooked on reality television.

"Are you dating?"

"Nope."

Emmett eased closer. "So, you're available, then?"

"Uh…" Old Kendall would've taken Emmett up on the blatant offer he saw in the bartender's eyes. But it would be a mistake, both professionally and personally. Screwing up his personal relationships was nothing new to him, but Kendall had never allowed his mistakes to screw with his professional prospects.

The management position had been a golden opportunity. Not only was Kendall receiving a handsome salary, but he would also earn a percentage of the profits the club made. It was in his best interest to make sure everything ran smoothly and with as few complications as possible. Sleeping with his employees would be the worst kind of trouble, and Kendall wanted no part of it. Besides, the only reason the management position had been open in the first place was because his predecessor had the morals of an alley cat.

Kendall would not make the same mistakes. A knock sounded on the open door before he could clear the air with Emmett. Seth grinned at him as if he'd just won the lottery. "What's up?"

"You have a visitor." The adorable host waggled his brows. "A certain delicious deputy marshal."

"And there's my answer," Emmett said.

Not really, but it was better to let him think Ridge and Kendall were together than to give Emmett false hope over something that wouldn't happen. "Thanks for checking on me."

"Anytime."

"Did I interrupt something?" Seth asked when they were alone in the hallway.

"Not at all," Kendall managed to say, even though his heart was in his throat. "What section did you seat Ridge in?"

"I didn't. He said he needed a private word with you, so I showed the hottie to your office."

A private word at two in the morning? That couldn't be good. "Did he say something was wrong?"

Seth chuckled. "I don't think he's here to arrest you if that's what you're worried about."

"I'm not."

"But," Seth said, "I don't think handcuffs are off the table."

One could only hope.

He and Seth parted ways a few moments later. Kendall came to an abrupt halt when he saw Ridge leaning against the wall outside his office, his head tilted back and eyes closed. Ridge must've sensed him, or maybe Kendall let out a lovesick sigh because Ridge lowered his head and met his gaze. When Kendall just continued to stare, Ridge shoved off the wall and strode toward him. Damn, his long legs gobbled up the distance in no time at all.

"Hi," they both said at once.

"Is everything okay?" Kendall asked.

"I…um…" Ridge rubbed the back of his neck and glanced at Kendall's closed office door. "Can we talk in there?"

Kendall nodded. "Of course. You could've waited inside for me."

"Seth said as much, but I didn't feel right doing it."

Once in his office, Kendall shut the door, but he hadn't retreated too far into the room before Ridge snagged his wrist, halting him. Heat and electricity crackled from their connection and spread up Kendall's arm. He glanced down at his limb, expecting his white dress shirt to look scorched, but the material remained pristine.

Ridge stepped up behind Kendall, wrapped his free arm around his waist, and pulled until Kendall's back met a solid wall of muscle. Ridge splayed his hand over Kendall's abdomen, placed his lips against Kendall's ear, and whispered, "What would make you happy?"

A hard shiver rolled through Kendall, and he turned in Ridge's embrace, resting his hands on broad shoulders. Kendall used his momentum to push the bigger man up against the closed door. Ridge's mouth fell slack for a second before parting into a delighted smile.

"Kiss me," Kendall said as he slid one hand into Ridge's hair. "That would make me really fucking happy."

Kendall wasn't one to wait for someone else to make their move, but it seemed essential to hang back and make sure Ridge knew what he wanted. The man didn't keep him waiting. He swooped down and captured Kendall's mouth, keeping his touch light and tentative at first before tracing his tongue along Kendall's bottom lip. The teasing felt good but made Kendall ache for more, so he raked his nails over Ridge's scalp.

Ridge released Kendall's wrist and cupped the back of his head, then sank his teeth into Kendall's bottom lip. The move shot electricity straight to his groin, and he gasped. Ridge pressed his advantage and plunged his tongue into Kendall's mouth, sending the wait-and-see approach up in smoke.

Kendall became the aggressor, sucking Ridge's tongue into his mouth and trailing his hand over Ridge's chest, eliciting tremors in its wake. Pulling back from the kiss, Kendall smirked at the taller man. "So, this is how you move a mountain, huh?" Said mountain swooped down for another kiss, but Kendall evaded him by stepping free of his embrace. "Not so fast." Ridge stared back at him with a slack expression, and his arms hovered awkwardly in the air. Cursing himself for making a mess of the situation, Kendall stepped back into the space he'd vacated and cupped Ridge's face. "I mean, not here. I want you in my bed."

Ridge smiled. "I just want to shower off my night first."

"A rough one, huh?"

"Some people just make my skin itch," Ridge said.

Kendall leaned forward and kissed him. "I have an idea. How about you hang out here and let me feed you, then we can shower together like we've both been fantasizing about this week." Ridge's head thumped against the door, and his eyes glazed over. Kendall knew the kinds of dirty things he was imagining. "Yes, we can do each and every one of those things."

"I didn't tell you what I was thinking."

Kendall nipped Ridge's lower lip, then ran his tongue over the mark he left behind. "Doesn't matter. The answer is yes."

Ridge sucked in a shaky breath. "You really are trouble."

Kendall nodded and stepped back. "Which is why I won't blame you if you do change your mind. I'm hell on the heart."

Ridge snagged him before he could go too far. "I'll take my chances."

Kendall wanted to kiss him again, but his self-control was slipping. "Make yourself comfortable. We ran out of wings right before you showed up. Do you want to look at a menu, or would you like me to surprise you?"

Ridge pushed off the door and sauntered over to a chair. "I trust you."

Kendall took a deep breath to gather himself before exiting his office. He received a few catcalls when he strolled into the kitchen. "Word travels fast around here."

Matt, one of the line cooks, glanced up from wiping down his station and hooked his thumb toward the cook beside him. "About as fast as Hector handing out his phone number to the pretty boys."

Hector paused his cleaning to flip Matt off, then launched into a rapid stream of Spanish. Kendall wasn't fluent, but he recognized enough to know Hector had accused Matt of being jealous.

Matt laughed and resumed his wiping. "You wish, papí."

Kendall retrieved his dinner leftovers from one of the commercial refrigerators and deflected curious questions while plating and reheating food for his visitor. When he returned to his office, Ridge was sprawled in a chair, looking at his phone. All semblance of nonchalance disappeared when he got a whiff of the food. Ridge bolted upright and relegated his device to the table. "Christ, that smells good. What is it?"

"Boeuf bourguignon. It's a fancy beef stew."

Ridge accepted the plate. "You made that here?"

Kendall snorted. "Heavens no. I had dinner at my mother's house tonight and took more leftovers than I could possibly eat."

"So, you're saying I'm doing you a favor."

"In more ways than one," Kendall replied with a lurid wink.

Ridge looked at his plate with so much longing it was almost comical.

"I'll leave you to it while I finish up my shift. I won't be long. Maybe an hour."

"Okay." Ridge forked a bite of beef and potato stew into his mouth and moaned.

Kendall beat it out of there while he still had the willpower to do so. For the next hour, he made a mental list of all the ways he could make Ridge moan louder than he had over Adelaide's stew.

But Kendall's confidence floundered when he stood outside his office after his shift ended. The man he couldn't stop thinking about was waiting for him on the other side of the door, so why was he hesitating? They were both unattached, consenting adults. So what if Ridge had only been single for a month?

The door swung open suddenly, making Kendall yelp and jump back. "You scared the hell out of me." He clutched his chest and leaned against the wall across from his office.

"Are you done?"

"Yes, we can go now," Kendall said.

Ridge strode from the office and pinned him against the wall. "I meant, are you done talking yourself out of taking me to your bed?"

"I wasn't. I—" Kendall narrowed his eyes. "How'd you even know I was out here?"

"The same way I know you're lying in bed stroking your cock every time I take a shower."

Kendall's body went up in flames, but he didn't bother trying to deny it. "Are we going to pretend you're not fucking your fist at the same time?"

"Hell no," Ridge said gruffly. "Let's get out of here."

He nodded and led Ridge out through the back exit. Just like after the James takedown, Kendall drove Ridge around to his SUV. But the similarities ended there. Ridge didn't just shove open the door and climb out. He cupped Kendall's neck and pulled him into a long, searing kiss.

After they parted, Ridge winked and said, "And now I'm happy."

Ridge got stuck at a red light, which gave Kendall extra time to wipe his sweaty hands on his pants and pull himself together. He didn't fumble the keys, and they didn't engage in awkward chitchat when they entered the house. Ridge and Kendall reached for each other simultaneously, a tangle of limbs, greedy hands, and eager mouths. They toed out of their shoes by the door and left a trail of discarded clothes on their way to the bathroom, stopping every few feet to explore newly revealed skin.

Kendall ran the back of his fingers over the erection straining Ridge's underwear while they waited for the water to heat up. "You could have a successful career modeling briefs if this marshal gig doesn't work for you."

"I'll take that into consideration," Ridge said, then captured Kendall's mouth in another heated kiss.

When steam filled the bathroom, Kendall pushed Ridge's underwear down his thick thighs before reaching for his own.

"Let me," Ridge growled. He made a big seduction out of it, dipping his fingers under the waistband and slowly pushing the fabric down to free Kendall's cock.

Their lips met once more beneath the spray as their soapy hands roamed freely over each other's bodies. When they finished, Ridge hoisted Kendall into the air and pinned him against the shower wall. The shock of the cold tile was tempered by the wall of hot muscle pressing against his chest. Kendall wrapped his legs around Ridge's waist and held on for dear life when the taller man snapped his hips forward, grinding their erections together. Kendall cried out and raked his nails over Ridge's back.

He shuddered hard, hitched Kendall higher, and pinned Kendall's hands to the cold tile above his head.

"You play dirty," Kendall said.

Ridge thrust harder against him, their guttural moans echoing throughout the steamy room. Ridge's head rolled forward, landing on Kendall's shoulder. "You feel so damn incredible." He turned his head and sucked on Kendall's neck before kissing a path upward. "I don't want to be a selfish lover. I want to make this good for you," Ridge whispered against Kendall's lips.

With his hands and body pinned to the shower wall, Kendall had limited weapons available in his arsenal. He tightened his thighs around Ridge and rocked his pelvis. Ridge sucked in a sharp breath and jerked his head up to lock eyes with him, letting Kendall see his doubt and vulnerability.

"There isn't enough room for him in this shower." Kendall wouldn't say Todd's name, and after tonight, he hoped Ridge would forget his ex's existence. "There's only you and me. No bullshit. No doubts. No lies others want us to believe. Just us." Ridge's brown eyes softened, and Kendall could tell the man wanted to believe him. He wasn't quite there yet, but he would be by the end of the night. "Your hands are around my wrists. Feel how my pulse is racing for you and how my body trembles in your embrace. *You* make me happy. Don't let him win."

Ridge stared into his eyes for a few heartbeats before crashing his mouth against Kendall's.

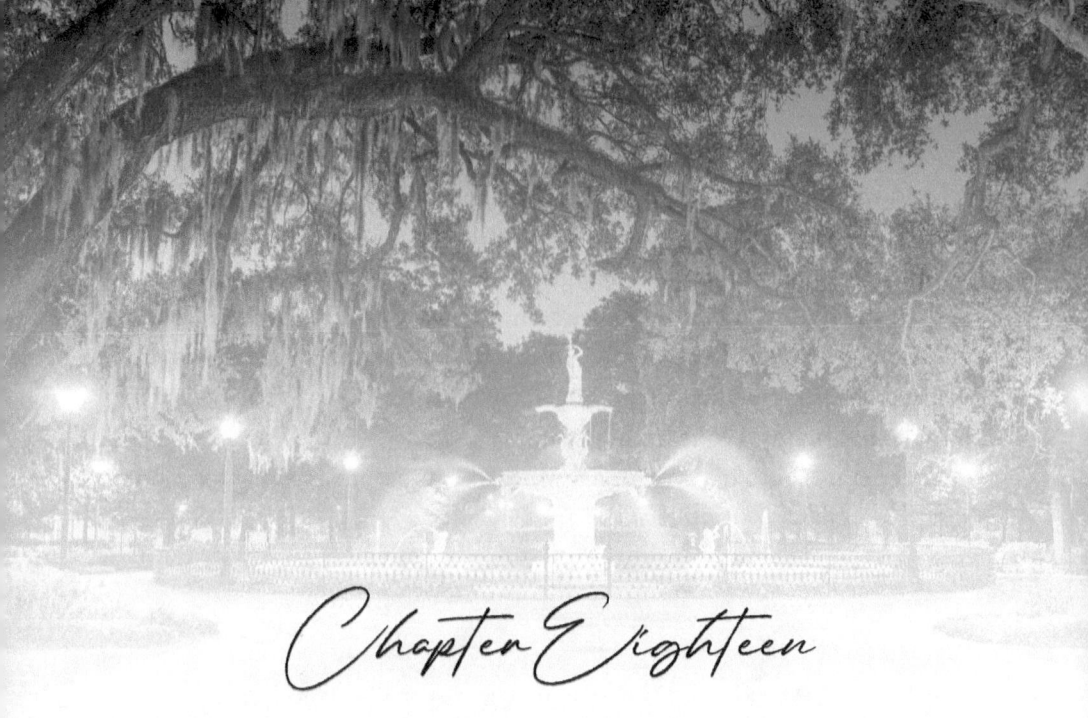

Chapter Eighteen

D*ON'T LET HIM WIN.* IT SHOULD'VE WORRIED RIDGE HOW EASILY Kendall saw beyond the obvious. Then again, it was no weirder than him knowing Kendall had been on the other side of the door without hearing him approach. They just clicked.

"I need to touch you. Please," Kendall pleaded.

The lust flowing through his bloodstream was hotter than lava. "But you beg so prettily."

Fire sparked behind Kendall's icy blue gaze. He stuck out his tongue and slowly wet his lips in the most lascivious way. "Just wait until your cock is in my mouth and I beg you with my eyes."

Kendall knew exactly what he was doing to Ridge and the dirty images he'd spawned. Ridge crossed Kendall's wrists over his head and pinned them there with one hand, freeing the other so he could swipe his thumb over Kendall's wet lips. Just in case Ridge was obtuse, Kendall sucked the digit into his mouth and rolled his tongue around the tip. There was no doubt in either of their minds as to who was really in command. Kendall could bring Ridge to his knees with a few wicked words or a flick of his tongue.

Ridge pulled his thumb free of Kendall's mouth and released his hands. Kendall immediately returned to clawing his back and driving him mad with lust.

"You like that?" the sexy imp asked. "Imagine what we could do spread out in my bed. I could mark every inch of your hot body."

If Ridge gave it too much thought, he'd come right there on the spot. He lowered his hands to Kendall's ass and sped up his thrusts. Kendall slid one hand into Ridge's hair, gripping the strands hard enough to make him cry out. The doubts he'd shoved aside washed down the drain when Kendall made a mewling sound against his lips. Had he turned the tide in his favor?

"I don't want to come yet," Kendall moaned.

Ridge immediately stilled but kept Kendall's lithe body pinned against the tile, spreading his ass cheeks and circling his puckered rim. Kendall's eyes rolled back in his head, so Ridge applied more pressure until the tip of his finger eased through the tight ring.

"So responsive," Ridge murmured against Kendall's neck. "I can't wait to have your cock in my mouth."

"Oh god." Kendall wriggled and bucked his hips to take Ridge's finger deeper into his ass. "Wait," he said suddenly. "I don't want to come yet."

Ridge chuckled against his neck. "Stop squirming, then."

"Can't help it."

Ridge eased back and carefully lowered Kendall's legs to the floor before he turned off the faucet and grabbed the towels off the rack. He barely skimmed the terry cloth over his wet skin before reaching for Kendall again. They replayed the scene from earlier where they couldn't go very far without kissing and touching.

They fell onto Kendall's bed together, and Ridge rolled Kendall to his back, pinning him beneath his weight and kissing him until they were both breathless. Kendall panted against his lips and smiled up at him. The perfection of this man rendered Ridge motionless long enough for Kendall to gain the upper hand and roll him onto his back. Instead of straddling Ridge's thighs, Kendall repositioned his body to straddle his head. Kendall leaned over Ridge's torso, and his taut balls swung over Ridge's mouth. Kendall's precum dribbled onto Ridge's lips. The little minx's hot breath ghosted over Ridge's erection, making him moan and buck up. Knowing what was to come still didn't prepare him for the feel of Kendall's mouth sucking on his cock's flared head. The sensation short-circuited his brain and momentarily delayed him from returning the favor.

Ridge lifted his head and swiped his tongue over Kendall's drooling dick before drawing it deeper into his mouth. Doubt started to creep back in like a dense fog until Kendall's moans of pleasure dispersed it. The vibrations bounced along Ridge's cock, prompting the same verbal cues from him. Ridge tightened his mouth around Kendall's erection and drew it deeper until the fullness bordered on uncomfortable. Breathing through his nose, Ridge focused on the way Kendall's cock pulsed against his tongue. Then he raised his hands to grip the firm ass above his head. Spreading the cheeks wide, Ridge rubbed his middle finger over Kendall's puckered rim.

Kendall groaned again and took Ridge down to the base of his cock. The move was so surprising that Ridge grunted and bucked his hips up. Kendall reached down and fondled Ridge's balls with the perfect amount of pressure and pull. They continued sucking each other off and eventually synchronized their rhythm. Ridge's control was tenuous at best, and he knew he couldn't hold back much longer, so he let Kendall's cock slide from his mouth and patted Kendall's ass cheek.

Ridge breathed a sigh of relief when Kendall suspended his oral ministrations, but his reprieve ended when the sexy devil looked at him. Kendall's pink lips were puffy and slick with saliva and precum. He licked them just as dirtily as he'd done in the shower, and Ridge was dying for a taste. He crooked his finger, and Kendall pivoted and began a slow crawl up Ridge's body. Kendall's sexual energy crackled through the room and set Ridge's nerve endings on fire.

He straddled Ridge's hips and leaned over him, bracing his hands on Ridge's chest. "You beckoned?"

So many words reverberated in Ridge's skull but none of them formed a coherent thought. Instead of saying what he wanted, Ridge showed Kendall by cupping his face and pulling him down for a wet, filthy kiss to combine their essence.

Ridge pulled back after several minutes. "What will make you happy?"

Kendall's gaze softened and grew damp. Then his pouty lips stretched into a devastating smile. "Condoms and lube."

Kendall reached over and opened his nightstand drawer to retrieve the supplies. He resumed his position, tore open the condom wrapper, and rolled it onto Ridge's erection. The intense expression in Kendall's eyes said the time for foreplay was over. Grabbing Ridge's hand, Kendall drizzled lube over two of Ridge's fingers before positioning them between his spread legs. With one hand on Ridge's chest and the other around his wrist, Kendall lowered himself onto the fingers.

Staring into Ridge's eyes, Kendall began riding his digits. "Fuck, this feels good." He tilted his head back, and his mouth went slack. Soft whimpers escaped Kendall's lips, and he tightened his hold on Ridge's wrist and dug his fingers into his pectoral muscles as if he feared Ridge would try to escape. Fucking fat chance of that. He'd sooner die than miss out on seeing Kendall orgasm around his dick. "It's been too long, and I'm about to make a shameless slut out of myself."

"Use me," Ridge said.

Kendall rolled his head forward and met his gaze. He released Ridge's wrist and eased off his fingers. Kendall gripped Ridge's erection and positioned it against his pucker. "You asked for it, big guy," he warned an instant before he sank all the way down onto his shaft.

"Fuck," Ridge roared as he gripped Kendall's hips to still him. The heat and clench were almost enough to make him shoot. Ridge clamped his jaws shut and gritted his teeth, willing his body not to fail him.

Kendall leaned forward, using his hands to brace himself on Ridge's chest, and stared into his eyes. "Want me to stop?"

Ridge forced his jaw to relax. "Hell no. I just needed a minute. I didn't want to—"

Kendall cut him off with a deep kiss that made Ridge's world spin on its axis. Fuck, this man could pack a wallop with such little effort. Would he even survive the night? If not, he'd go out with one hell of a bang. Kendall kissed him until Ridge relaxed and let go of his fears. Then he began to move, a slow, rolling gyration of hips that had to be illegal in most states. Kendall used his thumbs to tease Ridge's nipples, catching his gasps of ecstasy with his mouth.

Ridge's body quaked as the pleasure in his core built and tightened. As hot and horny as he was, Ridge couldn't banish the voice of doubt from his mind. It pointed out that he was just lying there and letting Kendall do all the work. *Lazy. Selfish.*

In a sudden move that surprised them both, Ridge rolled Kendall onto his back. He pinned Kendall's wrists over his head with one hand and gripped Kendall's cock with the other. Ridge snapped his hips forward hard, driving deep inside the tight heat, making the man beneath him cry out in ecstasy. Ridge buried his head in the crook of Kendall's neck, kissing the tender flesh while he pounded his ass and jerked him off.

Kendall dug his heels into Ridge's ass, driving him deeper and encouraging him to go faster and harder. Ridge didn't let up his pace until Kendall stiffened beneath him and shot hot cum all over his hand.

"Want to touch you," Kendall mewled between pants.

Ridge released his wrists, knowing the hellcat would sink his claws into his flesh as soon as he was free. Kendall didn't disappoint, raking his nails up and down Ridge's back and digging them into Ridge's ass. The onslaught of sensation sent Ridge right over the edge to where Kendall waited with open arms.

Knowing he weighed a fuckton, Ridge eased out of Kendall's tight clench and tried to roll off to the side, but his partner in lust wouldn't have it.

Kendall tightened his thighs around Ridge's hips and pressed a kiss to his temple. "I want you right here."

"I weigh too much." His protest was as limp-noodled as his legs.

Kendall chuckled. "I won't break."

Ridge lifted his head and stared into heavy-lidded eyes. Kendall's contentment and satisfaction shone in his brilliant gaze. Though Ridge urged his brain not to, he couldn't help but make comparisons, not between the performances of his two most recent lovers or even their responses to him but the way Ridge felt in their arms afterward. The peacefulness washing over him was new, wholly unexpected, and so very welcome.

Kendall lifted his hand and brushed wet strands of hair from Ridge's face. "What are your thoughts on postcoital cuddling?"

Ridge smiled. "I'll give it my best shot, but I might not be any good at it."

Kendall ran his hands over Ridge's biceps and halted at his shoulders. "These big, strong arms belong to a man born to cuddle. You're like a giant teddy bear."

They kissed lazily for a long time before Ridge persisted in peeling himself out of Kendall's arms. "I'm just going to clean up and get you a washcloth."

"Hurry back."

Ridge stumbled into the bathroom on limp legs. He removed and discarded the condom before washing up in the sink, then wetted another washcloth for Kendall. The delicious tempter remained sprawled in the center of Kendall's bed. His eyes sparkled like diamonds in the dimly lit room. Ridge climbed back on the bed and wiped the semen from Kendall's chest and abdomen.

"This is a first," Kendall said.

Ridge jerked his head up to meet his gaze. "What is?"

"No one has ever pampered me like this after sex." Kendall sat up and reached for him. "You're fucking adorable."

Heat crawled up Ridge's neck. "Am not."

"You are so going to cuddle the hell out of me tonight. I'll have to start calling you Ridgey Bear."

Ridge grimaced and shook his head. "Hard pass."

Kendall broke into his rendition of Elvis's "Teddy Bear," replacing the words with Ridgey Bear.

"Fuck no," Ridge said and slid off the bed.

Kendall immediately stopped singing. "Where are you going?"

Ridge held up the washcloth. "I'm going to toss this in the bathroom and get us something to drink."

Kendall slid from the bed. "I'll come with you. If you're nice, I'll let you eat some of my Palmier cookies."

"Never heard of them."

Kendall pecked a kiss on his lips. "They're made of flaky, buttery pastry crust. You're in for a real treat."

Ridge tossed the washcloth into the sink, then they made their way to the kitchen. Kendall pulled open the refrigerator door and peered inside.

"What do you feel like drinking? There's a variety of flavored water, some Gatorade, and—"

Ridge cut him off by swatting his ass. "Water is fine. Now, about those cookies."

Kendall removed two bottles of water and grabbed the plastic container he'd brought home with him from Stanton's. On the way back to the bedroom, Ridge got so caught up in staring at Kendall's ass he nearly slammed into the back of him when Kendall slowed to turn into his room.

"Distracted much?" Kendall tossed over his shoulder.

"I'm just regretting the little time I spent getting to know your ass."

Kendall pivoted and walked backward. The only thing separating them was the container of cookies in his hands. "I seem to remember straddling your face not too long ago."

"And there's more I wish I'd done to you when I had the chance," Ridge countered.

Kendall set the cookies on the nightstand, turned on the bedside lamp, and turned off the overhead light. Then he crossed the room and placed his hands on Ridge's shoulders. Kendall worked his bottom lip between his teeth until Ridge reached up and freed the tormented flesh.

Ridge brushed back the damp hair from his forehead. "What are you thinking?"

Kendall took a shaky breath. "That I'm going to wake up and discover this has all been a dream."

Ridge shook his head. "I'm not a dream." He smiled wickedly. "Possibly a nightmare, though."

"No way."

"Time will tell." Ridge pulled back the bedding and gestured for Kendall to slide in.

"This is my side of the bed," Kendall protested.

"I sleep closest to the door. No exceptions."

Kendall searched his eyes for a few seconds before nodding. "Fine. But don't complain when I crowd you in your sleep."

Ridge reached around and cupped one of Kendall's firm ass cheeks. "I think I'll manage."

"Mind if we watch some TV?" Kendall asked.

"I don't mind a little television before bed to wind down." Ridge chuckled. "The family we served warrants to tonight could definitely have their own reality show."

"Fucked up, huh?"

"You wouldn't believe me if I could tell you about them."

Kendall snorted. "I wouldn't count on it."

He grabbed the remote from the nightstand, then slid between the sheets to sit on the far side. Ridge handed him the box of cookies before joining him in bed. Kendall's mattress was a lot more comfortable than his. The memory foam cradled his body like a loving hug.

Kendall aimed the remote at the television and pushed a button. "Kill the lights, please."

Ridge leaned over and turned off the lamp. Kendall scrolled through the menu on a streaming service and stopped on *Forensic Files*.

"This is seriously your idea of light television before bed?"

Kendall shrugged and handed him a cookie. "Don't knock it until you try it."

Ridge scoffed but had to admit six cookies later that he was feeling pretty relaxed. Maybe it was the cloudlike bed or the carbs making his eyelids droopy. Perhaps it was the narrator's monotone voice that made his eyelids heavy. More than likely, it was the man partially draped across his body.

One minute, Kendall was calling a burglar a fucking amateur for leaving his fingerprints behind, and the next, he lay utterly slack in Ridge's arms. He fumbled for the remote, intending to turn the television off and join Kendall in dreamland, but the unfolding case on the screen took an unusual twist. He dropped the remote back down and settled in to watch the rest of the show, but he didn't even stay awake until the next commercial break.

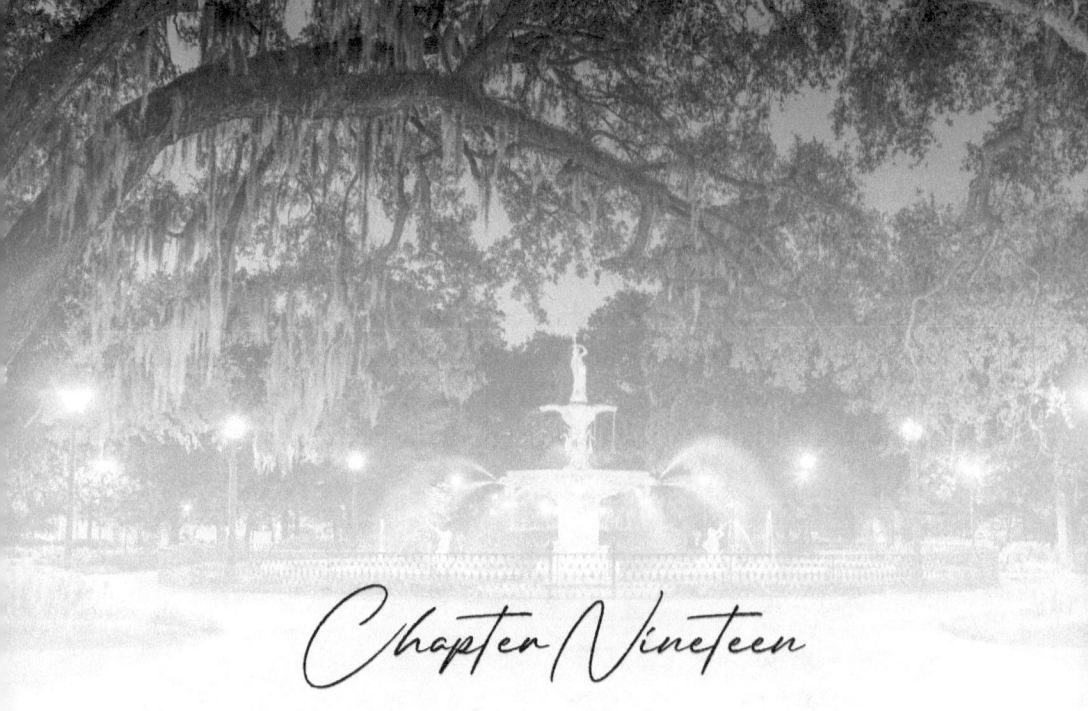

Chapter Nineteen

KENDALL WOKE SUDDENLY FROM A DEEP SLEEP. SUNLIGHT
filtered through the blinds, giving the room a dreamlike quality.
His heart pounded in his chest, but he didn't know why. Had it
been a bad dream? If so, he couldn't remember. Slowly, he became more
aware of his surroundings. He'd slept on the wrong side of the bed, and he'd
fallen asleep with *Forensic Files* playing again. Then his body became aware
of the mountain-sized man curled protectively around him.

I knew he'd be a teddy bear.

Ridge slept peacefully behind him, and Kendall took comfort in feeling
the man's chest rise and fall against his back. He located the remote without
waking Ridge and turned off the television. He'd just closed his eyes again
when he heard someone pounding on his front door. That must've been
what had woken him up. Somehow Ridge had slept through it, so Kendall
eased out from beneath his strong arm to ensure he stayed that way.

He stopped long enough to slip on a pair of shorts before dashing to
the front of the house where the banging had gotten louder and more persistent. Kendall yanked open the door without checking to see who his visitor was. He stared in disbelief at the sight before him.

"Mom?" In his shock, he'd forgotten to address her as Rebecca. Kendall
raked his gaze over her baggy T-shirt, black leggings, and flip-flops. "What
are you wearing?" He hadn't seen her dressed so casually since the summer

they'd gone to Myrtle Beach for a long weekend. That had been before she'd met Stan, so…a lifetime ago. He looked over her head to see if his step-father was loitering somewhere on his lawn, but he wasn't there. A faded silver Oldsmobile was parked behind his in the driveway, though. "Are you driving Adelaide's car?"

"Yes," Rebecca said. "And what took you so long to answer the door? And why haven't you taken my calls? I've been trying to reach you for hours."

Kendall grimaced. "I was exhausted when I got home from work and forgot to put it on the charger last night." Exhausted sounded better than extremely horny. "What's wrong?"

"For starters," she said dryly, "my only son has chosen to interrogate me on his front porch instead of inviting me into his home."

"Sorry," Kendall said. "I'm just so surprised you're here. I wasn't aware you had my new address."

"Adelaide gave it to me after she let me borrow some clothes and her car. May I please come in now?" She stepped through the door and chuckled before gesturing to the clothes and shoes strewn on the floor. It was blatantly obvious the items belonged to more than one person. "Exhausted, huh?"

Ridge had worn Kendall out, but he wasn't going there with his mother. "What's going on?"

Rebecca turned and met Kendall's gaze once more. Her usually vibrant eyes were devoid of any spark. The cloak of aloofness she wrapped around herself was fraying at the edges, giving Kendall a glimpse of the insecure woman she used to be. Her bottom lip trembled for a second before she stiffened it along with her posture.

"And how does this involve Adelaide?" he asked when she remained silent.

"She picked me up from jail this morning," Rebecca replied, sounding as cool as a cucumber. "I tried calling you first, but you already know how that went."

"Jail?" Kendall screeched.

Rebecca flinched and lifted her hands to her temples. "Please dial it down a notch or two. I've had a headache since the feds showed up at our house last night."

A snippet of his early morning conversation with Ridge replayed in his mind. He'd mentioned a freak-show family worthy of a reality television show. *Oh fuck.* "Feds?" he asked weakly.

"Yes," she repeated. "Would it be too much to ask you to make a pot of coffee?"

"Oh, um, sure." Kendall walked to the kitchen and filled the reservoir with water, then removed his coffee grounds from the freezer and scooped enough into the filter to make a whole pot. He retrieved a bottle of ibuprofen and a bottle of water and set them in front of Rebecca.

"Thanks. Adelaide taught you to store the coffee in the freezer," she said softly.

"She's taught me many things over the years." Kendall regretted the remark as soon as it left his mouth, even though his mother had it coming. He switched on the coffee pot and turned to face her. Rebecca's shoulders slumped forward as she stared down at the ground. "Sorry."

She lifted her chin and met his gaze. "Why? I'm very aware of my shortcomings regarding you, Kendall. I meant what I said at Fernando's the other day. I want to repair the damage I've done to our relationship." She took a deep breath. "For now, let's stick to the most pressing issue at hand."

"The feds kicking down the door and arresting Stan?" Kendall asked, not bothering to hide his hopefulness.

Rebecca's mouth quirked and humor added a glimmer of life to her eyes. "You'll be disappointed to hear they didn't kick down the door." Before he could follow up, she lifted her hand to stop him. "But they did arrest him."

"Wow," Kendall said. "I missed all the fun."

"Well, it's been all over the news this morning, but…" She gestured to the clothes on the floor. "Anyway, there was absolutely nothing fun about the marshals seizing every asset we'd ever acquired."

And was one of those marshals sleeping in his bed as they spoke? Kendall crossed his arms over his chest as acid churned in his gut. "They must've had a damn good reason."

Rebecca sighed. "He's accused of tax evasion, embezzlement, and defrauding their investors and the federal government. Roger also said something about a Fonzie scheme."

"Ponzi," Kendall said. "Jesus, that's bad stuff. Really bad." He leaned against the counter and stared at the carafe as it slowly filled with coffee. Once there was enough for two cups, he pulled the pot out and filled two mugs. He added almond milk to both and added a squirt of sugar substitute to his. Kendall handed Rebecca her cup and said, "What will you do next?"

Rebecca dropped her gaze to the mug in her hand. "I'm not sure. I meet with Roger in a few hours to go over my—"

Kendall was too busy studying his mother's forlorn body language to notice she'd stopped talking until he registered the heavy footsteps approaching from the hallway. *Fuck. Oh fuck.* Kendall only made it two steps before Ridge stepped into the open living room and kitchen area. At least he'd thought to pull his underwear on. The thickly muscled man rubbed his eyes with both fists and yawned.

"Do I smell coffee?" he asked. "And what would it take for you to bring me a cup in bed?"

Rebecca stared at Ridge, and her mouth fell open in a silent gasp. Kendall wasn't sure if it was because she recognized Ridge from last night or because of the way his morning wood strained his underwear. "Well, we meet again, Deputy Marshal Dandridge," she said.

Ridge dropped his hands to cover his crotch as he assessed the situation with a shrewd gaze. "What's going on here?"

"Ridge, meet my mother, Rebecca Burkhart."

His mother saluted Ridge with her coffee cup before taking a sip. "Soon to be Rebecca Blakemore again," she announced.

Ridge blew out a harsh breath and shook his head before fixing his gaze on Rebecca once more. "How's the hand? Did you bust any knuckles?"

"What?" Kendall screeched.

Rebecca cringed and glared at him. "Son, not so shrill, please," she said, then lifted her right hand to inspect it. "A little swollen. How's your partner's lip?"

"Oh fuck," Kendall said.

Rebecca shot him a disapproving glance. "Language."

Kendall placed his mug on the counter. "Wait a damn minute. You show up unannounced and drop an atomic bomb worth of information at my feet. I find out the guy I…um, know, was one of the arresting officers during a raid at your home and that you punched his partner, but I can't curse. Give it a break, Rebecca. Jesus."

"In her defense," Ridge said, "she meant to hit your father."

"Stepfather," Kendall and Rebecca said at once.

"I'd raise my hands to surrender, but…" Ridge said. His underwear clung to every magnificent inch of his bulge, enhancing rather than disguising it.

Kendall turned to Rebecca. "Why'd you take a swing at Stan?"

"Because I'd had enough," she said.

"I can't wrap my head around any of this."

"Drink more coffee," she suggested.

Remembering Ridge had zombie shuffled out to the kitchen looking for caffeine, Kendall looked in his direction. Ridge was picking up his discarded clothes as discreetly as one could while trying to keep his goods covered.

"Do you want a cup?" Kendall asked.

Ridge straightened and looked at him. "Nah. I'll just get dressed and head out so you can have some privacy. It's obvious the two of you have a lot to discuss."

Kendall and his mother quietly sipped their coffee until Ridge reappeared a few minutes later, his duffle bag in hand. "I'll walk you out," he told Ridge.

Neither said anything until they reached the SUV. Kendall placed his hand on Ridge's shoulder, uncertain if he'd ever get another chance to do so. "I was right about you."

Ridge settled his hands on Kendall's hips and pulled him closer. "Yeah? About what?"

"You make an excellent teddy bear."

Ridge laughed and glanced back toward the house. Kendall followed his gaze and chuckled when the curtain fluttered back into place.

"There's an extra blow job in it for you if you can locate footage of the asshole being led from his mansion in handcuffs," Kendall said.

Ridge's eyes darkened, and he took a shaky breath. "I'm sure that can be arranged." He took a deep breath. "The situation with Burkhart complicates things for us."

Kendall closed his eyes, resigning himself to saying goodbye to Ridge and Sammy quicker than he'd hoped. He swallowed his disappointment and met Ridge's earnest gaze. "I understand."

"No," Ridge said, shaking his head. "I don't think you do." Then he pressed a gentle kiss to Kendall's lips. "We'll figure this out, okay? Text me after your mom leaves."

Kendall nodded, refusing to allow hope to take root and blossom. He remained there until Ridge drove away, then returned to the house.

Rebecca was sitting at the small table tucked away in the kitchen. She glanced up when he stepped inside. "So, this thing with the marshal…"

"You want to play the concerned mommy now, Rebecca?" he asked. She stiffened, and Kendall wanted to kick himself harder than he'd just booted her. He blew out a breath and said, "It's new, and that's all I'm willing to say right now." He walked to the bedroom and returned a moment later with what remained of the Palmier cookies. Ridge had done some significant damage to the stockpile after he'd fallen asleep. Kendall set them on the table, then pulled out the chair across from her. "What can I do to help?"

She snapped her head up, and tears filled her eyes. "I don't deserve you."

Kendall chewed a cookie while he considered how to proceed. He'd been down this road with her in the past. Stan would break her heart, and she'd inevitably turn to her first-but-forgotten love for comfort. Kendall would soften and let down his walls, only to get shunned again when Stan asked Rebecca for forgiveness. It was a toxic cycle they both needed to break. Correction: one he would break. The question remained if Rebecca would be joining him on the healthier journey.

"Maybe not," he finally said, "but you also don't deserve a bastard husband. I'm not sure there's a future for us until you're ready to acknowledge that much."

Rebecca took a long, shaky breath. "I don't deserve a bastard husband."

Kendall scooted the container of cookies toward her. "You'll even believe it one day."

Her expression was a mixture of hope and hesitation, much like Kendall felt about their tenuous reunion. Rebecca helped herself to a cookie and nibbled on one end. She briefly closed her eyes, and a look of appreciation washed over her. "Lord, I think Adelaide's cookies can fix anything." She dunked her cookie in her coffee and took another bite. A move he hadn't seen from her since she'd given up Oreos and milk nearly two decades ago. "You're usually stingy with her baked goods, so I'm shocked you're sharing them with me."

Kendall had eagerly shared them with Ridge just hours before, but again, he wasn't going there with Rebecca. "These are extreme times," he said after polishing off a second cookie. "Speaking of which, what are you going to do? Where will you stay? I have some money—"

She waved off his offer before Kendall could make it. "Adelaide has offered to let me stay in her spare room, and I've accepted. Other than that…" Rebecca shrugged. "I'll get a job and find a good attorney. Do you have a recommendation?"

"For which?" he asked.

Rebecca chuckled. "Both, but I think the lawyer is top priority."

"I don't think you should trust Roger Carmichael's counsel. He'll have Stan's best interest at heart, which is at cross-purposes with yours."

"What do you suggest?"

Kendall smiled. "I know a shark who disguises himself as a lawyer. Would you be willing to meet with him if I could get you an appointment?"

"Yes," she said. "Would you consider going with me?"

"Of course." He lifted his coffee mug. "To the end of an awful era."

Rebecca clanked her cup to his. "I'll toast to that."

It was a good start.

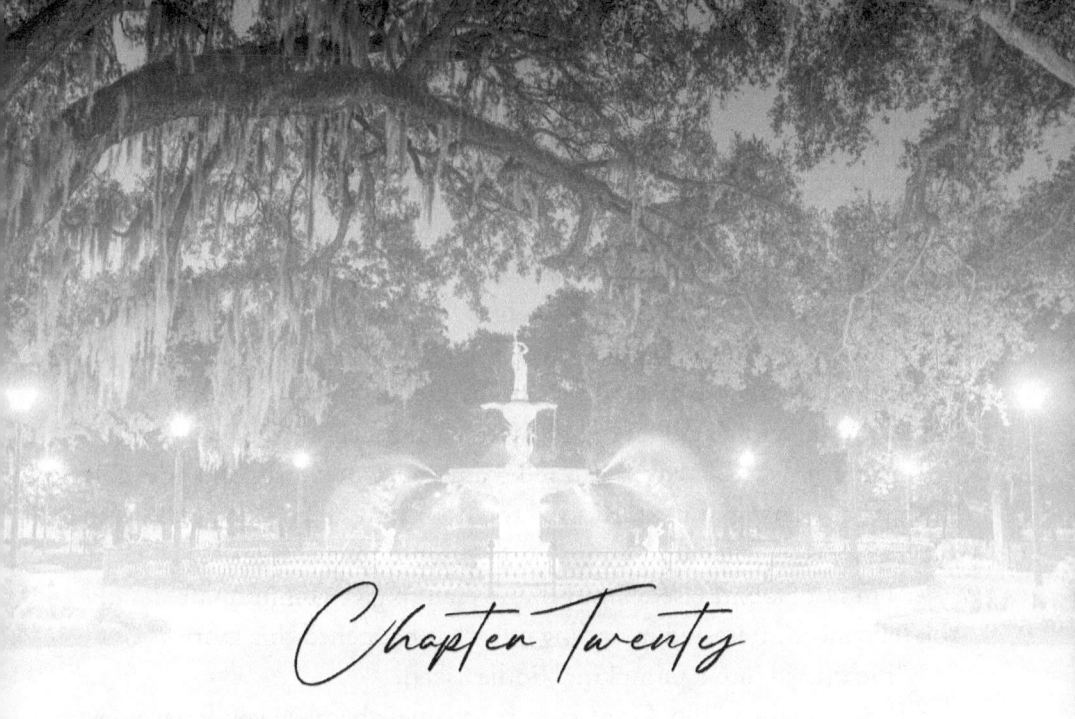

Chapter Twenty

RIDGE UNLOCKED THE DOOR TO EDDIE'S APARTMENT WITH THE key he hadn't returned. Jess's car hadn't been parked beside Eddie's, so he figured it was safe to enter the apartment. Somehow Ridge felt both weary and juiced up at the same time and wasn't sure how to process his thoughts.

"Hey ho," Eddie said as he stepped from the hallway leading to the bedrooms. His friend wore a dark blue suit and a crisp white shirt and was in the middle of securing a lavender-and-navy paisley tie around his neck.

Ridge whistled. "Sunday brunch?"

"Jess's cousin is getting baptized. I told you this at least three times, and you were the one who suggested this suit and tie combo."

"Sorry," Ridge said absently on the way to the coffee pot. Caffeine would help to alleviate his weariness but would also add fuel to the fire burning in the pit of his stomach. He poured himself a generous mug and took a sip of black coffee because peculiar circumstances called for undiluted octane. "You won't believe what happened last night."

Eddie looked up from smoothing his tie. "Oh, I have a pretty good idea. And you better have saved me some coffee." His friend strode into the kitchen and snagged a travel mug from the carousel and emptied the rest of the pot into it. Eddie turned and studied him through narrowed eyes. "You look too rested and sated to still be relying on hand-to-gland combat."

"Gross, Eddie."

His friend laughed. "Look at you blush. You're such a Boy Scout. So, you finally surrendered to Kendall's charms, huh?"

Boy had he ever. He couldn't wait to surrender again as soon as possible.

A hand appeared in front of Ridge's face and fingers snapped. "Hey. Come back to me, buddy," Eddie said.

Ridge gave himself a mental shake and met his friend's concerned gaze. "So, yeah, you and Zack were right. Kendall and I click." *So fucking well.*

Eddie smirked. "Yeah, I can tell from your goofy grin and adorable blush what transpired next, Ridgey. You don't have to go into great detail if it embarrasses you."

"I'm not embarrassed, and I didn't plan to give you intimate details. You'll be more interested in finding out what happened this morning."

"He turned into a pumpkin?" Eddie asked.

Ridge laughed. "No. Don't even try to guess because you'll never get it right."

Eddie couldn't resist a blatant challenge and spent the next three minutes tossing out every wild idea that crossed his mind. The list was both impressive and a little worrisome. When his friend gave up, Ridge enjoyed drawing out his suspense as he wove the tale.

"Get the fuck out of here," Eddie said once he'd finished.

Ridge took a deep breath and gave his friend a hangdog expression. "Okay."

Eddie slapped his chest and held him in place. "You know what the fuck I meant. Rebecca Burkhart is Kendall's mother?"

"Yep. You could've knocked me over with a feather."

"I bet," Eddie said, staring off into space and rubbing a hand over his chin. There was no outward bruising from the blow Rebecca had landed, but Ridge was certain Eddie still felt its effect. "He seems so normal."

"I don't think it's a great relationship," Ridge said. The thought made him pine for his mother's warmth.

Eddie met his gaze again. "What are you going to do?"

Ridge rubbed the back of his neck. "I honestly don't know."

"Listen, I know you like this guy," Eddie said, "and you know I do too."

"But…"

"You can't be associating with Stanton Burkhart's stepson. It's career suicide, Ridgey." *Fuck.* Eddie was right. "I know it's not fair. Kendall probably has nothing to do with Burkhart's activities, but the press would have a field day if it got leaked, and the brass would be furious. There's no way in hell a judge is going to let these guys out on bail. They're too big a flight risk. The likelihood these assholes don't have a contingency plan with false identities is slim to none."

"Yeah, I don't see our judge taking that gamble."

"So that means we'll be responsible for transporting Burkhart and Jones to and from court. Someone will accuse you of passing information or showing them preferential treatment."

Ridge puffed out a breath. "Yeah, I get it."

Eddie cupped his shoulder. "I'm sorry, man. You need to make peace with saying goodbye."

Ridge had never hesitated to utter the word before, but now…it felt like someone had put his heart in a vise and slowly tightened it.

"It doesn't have to be for good," Eddie said kindly. "Maybe just so long for now."

Ridge nodded. He wasn't sure what to say. Ridge had taken his breakup with Todd much easier, which was stupid. He'd only known Kendall for a month. "Do I text him and explain?"

Eddie shook his head. "No. You don't want to leave a digital trail. Go back to his house and talk to him. Kendall deserves that much. Just don't wind up in his bed again," Eddie cautioned. "You can explain away the first incident as not knowing, but now you do. You're welcome to stay here until you figure something else out. We'll chat more after the baptism." Eddie squeezed Ridge's shoulder, picked up his travel mug, and headed out.

Once alone, Ridge didn't know what the fuck to do with himself. He poured the coffee down the drain to show mercy on his angry stomach. Sleep was out of the question, that much Ridge knew. He padded down the hall to the guest room and grabbed a change of clothes out of his duffle bag before heading into the bathroom. Ridge turned on the shower, pushing the handle all the way over to hot. He'd only paused long enough to brush his teeth before leaving Kendall's. It would've been too awkward to take a shower there, knowing Rebecca Burkhart was in the kitchen. And Ridge hadn't been eager to wash Kendall's scent off his skin. He still wasn't, but he stepped into the enclosure and shut the door.

Hot water pelted his face and chest, easing the tension gripping him by the balls. Ridge let his head fall forward so the water could cascade over his neck and shoulders. Rivulets streamed down his back like tears, and his flesh tingled and burned as if it were acid rain. *What the fuck?* Then he remembered the way Kendall had clawed at his back when he couldn't get enough of Ridge.

He turned so the water hit the scratches, and the stinging sensation caused him to hiss. The pain didn't last long, but the memories of his night with Kendall continued to play through his mind on an endless loop, stirring desire in his gut and hardening his dick. Fantasizing about fucking Kendall felt as dangerous as seeking him out in person, but Ridge wouldn't deny himself the pleasure. It didn't take too many strokes to give him the relief needed to clear his mind.

Ridge hurried through the rest of his shower, then dried off. He wiped off the condensation on the mirror, then positioned his body to get a good look at his back. Red slashes crisscrossed over his flesh, and his chest swelled with pride. Ridge smiled as he dressed in a pair of shabby sweats and a raggedy T-shirt. He didn't feel like watching television where his options would be political talk shows or trashy TV. He didn't need the high blood pressure or brain rot. Ridge checked the time on his phone and dialed his mom. Even with the time zone difference, he knew she'd be awake. Cheryl Dandridge woke before the roosters and hit the ground running.

His mom answered on the second ring. "I was just thinking my morning couldn't get any better," she said instead of a traditional greeting. "I was so wrong. How's my boy?"

"I'm good, Mom. How are you?" As he expected, she'd already exercised, meditated, fed the animals, and made his dad's breakfast. "How's Dad doing?"

"More stubborn than Speedy."

Ridge pictured his dad's favorite mule and laughed. "Was the donkey ever fast?"

"Have you ever met one that's in a hurry?" she countered. "Slow, steady, and stubborn."

"So, not an ideal patient?"

She chuckled. "Every day, I catch him in the act of getting dressed so he can sneak down to the barn."

"It's a good sign Dad's stamina and strength are returning, right?" he asked.

"Yes, but it makes it harder to convince him to rest. I threatened to tie him to the bed this morning." She huffed a breath. "He's grumpy, pissed at the world, and doesn't want to listen." His mom sniffled. "But I'm so damn grateful to have this daily fight with him."

Ridge's heart ached. "I'm sorry, Mom. I wish I could be there to help you."

"Honey, please don't feel guilty. I have your sister and our ranch hands to help with the daily operations. The neighboring ranchers have also offered to pitch in. I'm not alone, okay?"

While it was great to hear she had so much support, it wasn't coming from him. "I want you to call if things get to be too much. I can be on the next flight out."

"I know, and I love you."

"Love you too, Mom."

"Enough about me," she said. "How's the new living arrangement? Has my grand cat settled in nicely with your new roommate?" *Roommate* was such an inadequate way to define Kendall's role in Ridge's life, or it would've been before the revelation that had rocked their newly formed foundation.

"It's the perfect setup since I don't plan to stay in Savannah."

"Ridge, you've been saying that for five years already. Maybe it's time to consider you've already planted your roots there."

He sighed. "That wasn't the plan."

"Plans change, my love. Your father and I want you to be happy." Shuffling sounds came from her end of the connection. "Oh, I need to get off here. Your father has taken advantage of my distraction to try to sneak out. I'll call you back later."

"Good luck. I love you."

"Love you too." She blew him a kiss through the phone before disconnecting.

Their brief conversation had left him feeling even more restless, so Ridge retrieved his sketchbook and charcoal pencils from his bag. He flipped on the television and scrolled through the channels, looking for something to play in the background. Ridge smiled when he saw a *Forensic Files* marathon and turned it on. Opening to an empty page, he turned off his brain and began to sketch. Ridge had planned to draw one of his favorite Montana mountain peaks from memory, but a different image burned brighter, begging to be immortalized. He worked until the rough outline of Kendall's face became a detailed rendering of the way he looked after orgasming. Ridge traced his thumb over the pouty lips, softening the harsh charcoal line.

The tug in his chest was a warning; one he didn't heed when Kendall texted him.

The coast is clear.

Eddie's voice echoed in his head, but the racing blood in his ears drowned him out. *Be there in fifteen.*

Kendall met him at the door, and they lunged for each other as soon as he closed them inside the house.

"This is the morning I wanted," Kendall said between kisses as he made quick work of removing Ridge's shirt. He placed his mouth on the flesh he bared and peppered kisses across Ridge's collarbone. "There's so much of you I didn't get to explore."

"And flesh you left on my bones," Ridge said before turning around.

Kendall gasped and traced his fingers over Ridge's back. "I'm so sorry."

Ridge spun around and pulled Kendall into his arms. "I'm not. It was a pleasant little reminder of our night when I got in the shower."

Kendall looped his arms around Ridge's shoulders and cocked his head to the side. "How pleasant?" Ridge let his smile answer for him, and Kendall inhaled sharply before reaching into his pocket and removing a condom and small tube of lube. "So, we won't need these—"

Ridge shoved Kendall's shorts down his hips and cupped his half-hard erection. "Hell yes, we will."

He proceeded to prove just how *up* he was for the task by bending Kendall over the couch and taking him hard and fast, driving the man up on his toes with the force of his thrusts. Ridge couldn't be sure which version of Kendall he liked most: the seductive minx who owned him with a single glance or the one who was too lost in his pleasure to string coherent words together. Both were beautiful and made Ridge feel like a god.

Afterward, they cleaned up in the kitchen and collapsed together on the couch. Kendall draped himself across Ridge's chest and tucked his head under Ridge's chin.

Stroking a hand over Kendall's smooth back, Ridge said, "Are you going to start purring now?"

"Was thinking about it," Kendall replied, his voice as thick and slow as molasses.

Ridge chuckled and tightened his embrace. Moments later, Kendall's breathing evened out as he drifted off to sleep. Ridge didn't mean to follow him, but the aftermath of two powerful orgasms and the lure of the man in his arms was too much to resist.

He awoke sometime later when Kendall shifted his weight to nestle between Ridge and the back of the couch. Ridge rolled onto his side to make more room and noticed Kendall was wide awake. His expression was the same serene one he'd captured in charcoal that morning.

"Hi," Kendall whispered.

"Hi."

Kendall worried his bottom lip until Ridge rescued it.

"What's wrong?" Ridge asked.

"I keep waiting for you to tell me goodbye."

Eddie's advice replayed on repeat until Kendall brushed his hand over Ridge's forehead.

"You'll get premature wrinkles if you don't stop doing that," Kendall said.

"Doing what?"

"Frowning." Kendall tucked his hand under his cheek and smiled softly. "It's okay to tell me what's on your mind. I won't be mad at you."

Ridge rested his hand on Kendall's hip. The need to anchor this man to him was so strong it stole his breath away. "I should move back to Eddie's."

Kendall narrowed his eyes. "But…"

Ridge heaved a deep sigh and stroked a finger down Kendall's nose. "I don't want to."

"But…" Kendall nudged again.

"This will be a high-profile case, and the US Marshals Service will be responsible for transporting Stanton to the courthouse for hearings and trial. If people find out that I'm involved with his stepson…"

Kendall sat up so fast he nearly rolled Ridge onto the floor. "You need to go. I can't be responsible for destroying your career."

After steadying himself, Ridge sat up too. He reached for Kendall's hands and tugged. The minx resisted for a few minutes before sliding onto Ridge's lap. "I like you a lot, and damn it, I haven't asked the universe for much. Maybe I can talk to the assistant chief deputy and explain the situation. Will your mom be a problem for us?" *Us.* Ridge hadn't even planned on there being an *us* when he'd acted on impulse the previous night. He couldn't deny how right the word tasted on his tongue.

Kendall huffed a short breath. "I wish I could assure you Rebecca won't be an issue, but I can't. If she can use this to her advantage, she most likely will." Ridge's heart ached at the sadness and shame he witnessed in Kendall's eyes. "I want to trust her, but I can't…yet."

"Marks can make sure I'm not on Stanton's detail. Maybe then—"

Kendall shook his head. "I'm not worth the risk."

Ridge gripped the back of his head. "I think you are."

Kendall closed his eyes and took a deep breath. When their gazes met again, Ridge could see the resolve firmly in place. "If I hadn't left Stanton's house early, what we shared last night wouldn't have happened."

"I'm not so sure about that," Ridge admitted.

"I am. You're a wonderful, moral man who always does the right thing. I will not be the reason you lose the job you love so much."

Ridge gathered Kendall closer and kissed him long and hard, pouring every ounce of emotion into his kiss. The minx melted against his chest, and trouble had never felt so damned good.

"I can't say it," Ridge said after they pulled apart for air. Tears pooled in Kendall's eyes, and he started to speak until Ridge placed his finger over his lips to silence him. "I want just one more day with you. Maybe it's stupid or selfish, but I don't care."

Kendall looked like he was going to protest, but after a few moments, he nipped Ridge's finger and smiled wickedly. "If all we have is today, let's make the best of it."

Chapter Twenty-One

WHISTLES GREETED RIDGE WHEN HE STEPPED INTO THE bullpen the following day.

Zack leaned his ass against Eddie's desk and raked his gaze over Ridge. "Why are you so dressed up?"

"It's a shirt, tie, and dress pants," Ridge replied. "Why are you acting like I turned up in a tuxedo?"

Ridge locked eyes with Eddie, who just shook his head. He knew Ridge hadn't returned to the apartment as they'd discussed. "What gives?" Eddie asked. "Are you attending a funeral today?" His best friend's scowl made it clear he thought Ridge's career was dead in the water.

Christ, Eddie. I get it. I fucked up. But he didn't regret his decision. Maybe a little when he'd been forced to put on a high-collared shirt to hide the freaking hickey Kendall had left on his neck at some point the previous day or when their farewell tour had rolled over to Monday morning. They'd barely separated long enough to take care of the most basic functions, so he hadn't noticed the problem until he'd gone into the bathroom to start getting ready for work.

"Got my days turned around and thought I had court duty," Ridge tossed out as he set his coffee cup and keys on his desk. "Have you seen Marks? I need to run something by her."

Eddie's expression begged him to reconsider ruining his career, but he said, "Yeah."

He took a sip of coffee to shore up his nerves and headed out of the bullpen. Ridge knocked on Assistant Chief Deputy Marks's open door. "Do you have a minute, Chief?"

She paused her typing to wave him in before resuming her task. Ridge sat down in a chair opposite her desk and patiently waited while she finished. Adrenaline raced through his blood, and he squelched the urge to bounce his knees and fidget while trying to figure out how much to say about his involvement with Kendall. He noticed she'd added another photo of her twin sons to the collection on her credenza. This time they posed in baseball uniforms but for opposing teams.

"You have my undivided attention now, Dandridge."

He met her gaze head-on. This is it. Time to come clean. "Having two kids playing sports all year round must be tough. Juggling separate teams must be brutal." *Nice going, chickenshit.*

Marks was impervious to his internal struggle and laughed. "Keeps things interesting for sure."

Ridge smiled and relaxed a little. "What's the competition like in your house?"

Marks shook her head. "It's not as bad as it looks. Both my boys love playing sports, but Eric is just naturally better at it than Ethan. Eric had the opportunity to play for a select team, and we had some tough decisions to make. He had outgrown the rec league he'd been playing for since he was big enough to hold a bat. Ethan is a better athlete than most kids but is only an average baseball player. Did we hold Eric back from pursuing opportunities to spare Ethan's feelings? No. Ethan is Eric's biggest fan and wants the best for his brother."

"Sounds like you have great kids," Ridge said.

She held up her hand and rocked it from side to side. "They'll do in a pinch." Smiling, she dropped her hand back to the desk. "But you didn't come in here for parenting tips, did you?"

"Not yet, but maybe someday."

Marks laughed. "I'll be ready. What can I do for you right now?"

Ridge decided to broach the easiest topic first. He handed her the information he'd found on Willie Morrison. "This is the best chance I've had in five years to capture Sheldon Harris. I'm close. I can feel it."

"What do you need from me?"

Ridge recounted his conversation with Carmen Elliot and his belief she could be the key to unraveling the whole thing. "I think she really wants to talk but needs some assurances. I've given her some time to think it over and would like to approach her again."

Marks narrowed her eyes and drummed her fingers on her desk. "I'm not sure," she said after a long pause, then lifted her hand before Ridge could speak again. "Hear me out for a minute. The fact that she's alive tells me she doesn't know anything of value to us."

"Or has the cartel underestimated her?" Ridge countered. "It's entirely feasible she has all the dirt on them without their knowledge."

"It's possible," Marks said.

"And I know for a fact they've talked about me in front of her. Their nickname for me is Pat Garrett."

Marks tilted her head. "She could've made that up to flatter you."

"Yes, she could have."

"But you believe her?" Marks asked.

"I do. I believe Carmen wants to do the right thing, but protecting her kids is her primary concern. Carmen isn't convinced she can trust us."

"What do you propose?"

Ridge breathed a sigh of relief. He hadn't expected Marks to shoot him down outright, but asking her to rely on his hunches was a pretty giant leap of faith. "I told Carmen we can't make her any guarantees until she tells us what she knows. She doesn't want to tell us anything until she hears what we can offer in return for information and testimony."

"The chief director and I could sit down with Carmen and give her an idea of what her future could look like, but we can't help the woman if she's not willing to meet us halfway. The other option is to go straight to Willie and offer him the same opportunity."

The thought made Ridge sick to his stomach. "It's a sucky alternative."

"Agreed," Marks said. "What if we just make her think that's what we'll do if she doesn't help us?"

Ridge didn't like that any better, but he couldn't think of another option, so he nodded. "I'll leave going to Willie as a last resort. Thanks, Chief."

"No problem. Keep me updated." She called out his name when he reached the door. He turned and met her curious expression. "What's going on there?" she asked, gesturing to his clothes.

Ridge looked down the length of his body, worrying he'd mismatched his shoes again or something. Nope. She was smirking when he made eye contact. "What do you mean? It's just a simple shirt and tie."

Marks narrowed her eyes. "You're not on courthouse detail this week, and you never dress up voluntarily." Her lips tilted into a teasing smile. "Reminds me of the time our oldest son dressed in a suit for church without being told to. It *never* happened. Andre had been attending services every Sunday without fail for nearly eighteen years. I'd reminded him every week during breakfast that he needed to wear a suit, except for the morning after senior prom. The silly fool thought he could hide a hickey under his shirt collar without me noticing."

Busted. Ridge chuckled to cover his embarrassment. "Did he forget what you do for a living?"

"Right? I asked Andre if he planned to wear a suit every day until the hickey went away. You should've seen the look on his face."

Ridge figured his looked pretty much the same. "A bit shortsighted, huh?"

Marks nodded. "Turns out Andre hadn't thought that far ahead. Hormones and such. So we swung by the drugstore on the way to church to find a concealer that matched his skin tone."

"That's good information to have…*if* I should ever need it."

"Uh-huh. Keep me posted about Carmen."

"Yes, ma'am."

She tilted her head and studied him. "Is there something else on your mind, Dandridge?"

It was his opportunity to come clean. Instead, he said, "No, ma'am."

"Our real estate assessors will be assessing the property values for Burkhart's and Jones's commercial and personal real estate. Since you're dressed for the part, I'd like you to supervise. They're starting at the corporate office in thirty minutes."

Ridge didn't budge from the threshold. This was the time to explain his predicament or at least find a legitimate reason to recuse himself. To remain silent was inexcusable and would be damning if it blew up in his face. Then he remembered Kendall snuggling in his arms in the predawn hours. Telling Marks would force Ridge to make a choice he wasn't ready to make.

"Dandridge? Is there a problem?"

"No, ma'am." Only that he was a fucking idiot. He mentally kicked his ass all the way back to his desk. What the fuck was wrong with him? He ended his internal ranting when he noted his keys were missing. He knew damn well he'd left them on his desk before going to speak to Marks. He opened each drawer and even checked the trash can. His keys weren't anywhere to be found. The office was suspiciously empty, and Ridge got the impression he was the butt of another stupid prank. "Not now, guys," he muttered as he moved over to Eddie's desk.

Footsteps echoed on the tile floor, and Ridge jerked his head up when Zack entered the room. He had a cup of coffee in one hand and a file in the other. "What's going on?"

"I stupidly left my keys on my desk while meeting with Marks." It was never wise to leave shit unattended around these animals.

Zack set his drink and file down. "And someone took them. We're immature assholes sometimes, huh?"

"Sometimes?"

Zack snorted and helped Ridge look. They made quick work of searching all the desks, trash cans, and even the supply closet. No keys.

"I don't have time for this shit. I have to meet the appraisers at Burkhart and Jones in"—Ridge checked his watch—"fifteen minutes."

"Sign out a car from the impound lot," Zack said.

Oh, sure. Debauch Burkhart's stepson, supervise his asset forfeiture, and drive the bastard's car. That wouldn't reek of impropriety.

Zack slapped his arm to get his attention, then pulled a set of keys from his pocket. "Take mine. I'll sign something out before I leave. I've never driven a Bentley before."

Ridge accepted the keys. "Thanks, man. You're a lifesaver."

He headed out to the parking lot and pushed the remote to see what Zack was driving. The responding beep came from the far-right corner. Ridge turned his head and groaned when he saw the bright pink Volkswagen Beetle with yellow flowers and ladybugs painted on it. Someone had even added what appeared to be long eyelashes over the headlights. Ridge turned and looked up to the floor where their offices were located. He couldn't see Zack through the tinted windows but knew the asshole was up there, laughing his ass off. Ridge shot him the double bird and headed for the Beetle.

He wanted to be pissed but figured the universe was calling him out on his recent sketchy behavior. It didn't mean Ridge wouldn't pay those fuckers back, though. He'd just have to get really creative and bide his time to ensure it was as epic as this prank. When he started the car, the radio blared "Barbie Girl" from the speakers so loudly he nearly pissed himself.

Ridge reached over and turned the volume down, and that's when he heard the hooting and hollering. Every single one of the assholes had come outside to enjoy their joke. Some of them were doubled over while others were filming the incident on their phones.

He'd give them something to record. Ridge rolled down the windows and cranked the radio up. He backed out of the parking spot and drove a big loop around the lot, holding out his middle finger as he passed his so-called friends. It was hard to tell who was laughing harder—them or him—by the time he exited the lot and turned onto the main street. Ridge forgot to turn the music down until he reached the next intersection and got a dirty look from an elderly woman.

Fuck. She probably thought he was a pervert trying to lure kids into his car. Ridge rolled his windows up, blasted the air conditioning, and tried his best to forget what he was driving. He'd nearly accomplished the feat until he pulled into the lot at Burkhart and Jones and found their appraisers, Emma and Jess, speaking with the Burkharts' attorney, Roger Carmichael, and another suited gentleman.

The group gawked at him when he exited the hot-pink mess and headed in their direction.

Emma's ruby red lips trembled, but she was the first to recover. "Good to see you again, Dandridge."

"Always good to see you, Ms. Hampton," he replied warmly. Emma had pulled her sleek black hair into a ponytail, showing off her delicate bone structure that always reminded Ridge of fairies. He knew from sparring with Emma that her lavender suit jacket hid a colorful dragon tattoo sleeve on her left arm. It was every bit as fierce as the woman who wore it, and it was no mystery why Zack was so crazy about her. Ridge's friends had excellent taste in partners, and he wished he could introduce Emma and Jess to Kendall.

Jess gestured to the car's eyelashes. "I've heard about the pranks you marshals pull on one another, but this is the first time I've witnessed one. Wow."

"You don't like Bessie?" he asked. "She drives like a champ."

The man Ridge didn't recognize stepped over and jabbed his finger toward Ridge's chest. Luckily the asshole stopped just short of touching him.

"Can we get started, or do the three of you want to exchange recipes first?" he asked in a snide tone. "I want to get this over with."

Ridge glanced over at Roger Carmichael. He held up his hands and shook his head, signaling he didn't want to be lumped in with the acerbic jerkwad. Ridge turned to the stranger and said, "And you are?"

"Maximillian Ambrose," he replied.

"Don't forget 'the fourth,'" Emma said, earning an arctic glare from the man.

"I'm representing the Jones family," Ambrose said.

"Deputy Kurt Dandridge." Ridge didn't bother extending his hand. The lawyer wasn't interested in exchanging pleasantries, and Ridge didn't want any of his smarminess to rub off on him. Instead, he gestured to the front of the building. "After you."

Emma, Jess, and Ridge fell in behind the two lawyers, who'd started to bicker quietly.

"Seems like someone is in a hurry," Ridge said. "He does know this will take most of the day, right?"

Emma smirked. "If not, he'll find out quickly. This is one of the largest forfeitures I've worked on, and I'll be damned if I do a rush job because The Fourth is in a snit." She smiled apologetically at Ridge. "Sorry. I'm sure you'd rather be doing anything else than asset forfeiture."

"I'd choose this over prisoner transport," Ridge quipped. "I'm totally cool if you want to drag your feet to draw out The Fourth's suffering."

She held out her fist, and he bumped it.

Emma hadn't been exaggerating when she declared it would take all day. Their last stop for the day was the Burkhart estate where Ridge was reminded of two crucial things: the con man had more money than sense, and there was no trace of Kendall anywhere in the house. The realization had left him feeling as cold and hollow as a forgotten log in a forest. Is that how Kendall felt in his own mother's home? Forgotten and unseen? It wasn't fair of Ridge to make assumptions, but he drew a direct correlation between Kendall's ridiculous notion he was bad at love and the erasure of his presence at the Burkhart residence.

While the lack of photos provided Ridge with plausible deniability, it made him deeply sad and weighed heavily on his mind as he drove back to the field office to retrieve the keys for his SUV. His fellow marshals were assholes, but they weren't psychopaths who'd force him to drive the pink monstrosity for more than one day.

In the dark hours before dawn, Ridge and Kendall had agreed to continue their living arrangement as roommates only. He'd held Kendall tightly against his chest and kissed him long and deep before easing from his bed and walking away. In light of everything he'd discovered, Ridge couldn't be just another person who'd erased Kendall from the picture. He needed the man to know he was seen, wanted, and cherished—all emotions so fucking foreign to Ridge they stole his breath. He smiled to himself as he headed out to retrieve his vehicle. No, Ridge hadn't accounted for Kendall Blakemore in his grand scheme, but he was damned grateful for waylaid plans.

Ridge hit the fob to unlock the door and did something else completely uncharacteristic of him: he swung by the grocery store to buy a bouquet from the floral department. He'd only purchased flowers for his mother and sister before and wasn't sure what Kendall would like. A bouquet of pink, yellow, and orange blooms caught his eye. He had no idea what the flowers were called, but they reminded him of a glorious sunrise over his beloved mountains and of Kendall's smile. Standing in the middle of the supermarket, Ridge imagined the warmth of both things. He closed his eyes and felt the phantom sun on his face, and joy swelled in his heart, chasing away the chill and filling the hollowness he'd felt at the Burkhart estate. Ridge snatched up the bouquet and paid for it before he could talk himself out of the gesture.

Kendall was dancing in the kitchen once more when he arrived home, and Ridge took a few moments to observe his grace. How could anyone want to erase this beautiful man from existence? How was it no one had cared about his happiness until now? The realization hit him with the intensity of getting clubbed in the head. Ridge felt a little woozy but couldn't deny it was true. He cared. He cared a fucking lot.

When Kendall turned from the stove and spotted the blooms, a radiant smile lit up his face. Ridge didn't need to ask what would make him happy because he was witnessing it firsthand.

Chapter Twenty-Two

KENDALL PULLED HIS EARBUDS OUT AND SHOVED THEM INTO HIS pocket. "Hi," he said. His gaze fell to the bouquet in Ridge's big hand, and his joy soared to a higher level. No one had ever given him flowers before.

"Hi." Ridge awkwardly extended the bouquet toward him, making Kendall wonder if it was a new experience for him too. "Um, these are for you."

Kendall accepted the gift and lowered his head to inhale the gorgeous fragrance. "These are beautiful. Thank you." He rose on his tiptoes to peck a kiss on Ridge's lips. Oh shit. Kissing wasn't part of their agreement, and neither was Kendall lingering to inhale Ridge's scent. "Christ, you smell even better than I remembered." He took a step back, but Ridge's arm snaked out and hooked his waist, hauling Kendall back in for another kiss, longer and with tongue. Kendall swayed on his feet a little after Ridge released him. He wanted to be confused about the abrupt departure from their early morning agreement, but he couldn't rustle up enough resources to combat his euphoria.

"Whatever you're cooking smells delicious," Ridge said. His stomach growled in emphasis as if cued by a director. He grimaced and said, "Sorry. My lunch was a bag of chips from a vending machine, and that was like five years ago."

"Long day, huh?"

"You can say that again." A dark emotion washed over Ridge's face but disappeared when he blinked. Kendall wanted to ask questions but knew better, so he nodded toward the kitchen. "Come on. Dinner will be ready in a few minutes. I have just enough time to put these beautiful flowers in a vase."

Ridge followed so closely Kendall could feel the heat rolling off his body. "I feel underdressed," he tossed over his shoulder. "You're wearing a nice suit, and I have on my old, faded, holey jeans, a tank top, and no shoes." But they weren't on a date, so it didn't matter, and he needed to stop rambling. Kendall set the bouquet on the counter and opened a cabinet to assess his options for the flowers. He didn't have a vase, but he had several different sizes of mason jars and a few pitchers. He picked the largest mason jar, set it beside the flowers, and shut the cabinet.

"You look perfect," Ridge said, stepping up behind Kendall and sliding both arms around his waist. Ridge ran his nose along Kendall's neck, eliciting a full-body shiver. They probably should address the boundaries they were blowing through, but Kendall didn't want to spoil the moment. "You smell perfect." Ridge slipped a hand under Kendall's tank top and circled a finger over the ticklish skin around his navel. Talking could wait. "You feel perfect." Strong fingers gripped Kendall's hips and turned him around. Ridge lowered his head, his lips hovering over Kendall's. "You taste perfect too. I can't get enough of you."

Ridge captured Kendall's lips and stole his breath. Their kiss was long and languid as if neither of them had anything else to do with the rest of their lives. Ridge's fingers snuck back under the hem of his tank and traced the waistband of his jeans while Kendall stroked his hand over Ridge's silk tie. He wrapped the fabric around his wrist and gave it a nice tug. Ridge gasped and broke their kiss.

"I want to tie you to my bed with this," Kendall told him.

Ridge's mouth fell open, and his eyes glazed over. "Okay." But then his stomach rumbled again.

Kendall released the tie and stepped free from his embrace. "After I feed you." He filled the mason jar halfway with water and sprinkled in the packet of plant food that had come with the bouquet. "I know much of your job is classified, but I want to hear about your day." Kendall pulled a pair of scissors from his knife block and began snipping the ends off the flower stems.

He'd seen Adelaide do it many times over the years when she put together centerpieces for their formal dining room. "What's something you can share?"

A rumbling chuckle pulled Kendall's attention away from his task. A dark flush stained Ridge's cheeks and his eyes glittered with humor. He looked both embarrassed and tickled at the same time.

"Must've been a real doozy," Kendall said.

Ridge picked up the next flower and handed it to Kendall, who trimmed the stem and arranged it in the jar. "It was one for the records."

They worked together like that as Ridge recounted his morning at work, starting with his lieutenant giving him advice on covering hickeys to the Barbie Beetle stunt the other deputy marshals had pulled off. Kendall better understood the juxtaposition of Ridge's blushing cheeks and laughing eyes.

"You should've seen the looks I got when…Hey, what's wrong?"

Kendall glanced up from his task. "Hmmm?"

Ridge eased the flower from Kendall's fingers and held it up. He'd gripped the stem tight enough to bend it. "What did I say that upset you?"

"I didn't mean to mark your skin and invite speculation," Kendall whispered. He reached up and loosened Ridge's tie so he could see the damage for himself. The red spot was small but definitely recognizable as what it was.

"It's nothing. I like wearing your marks." He dropped a quick kiss on Kendall's lips. "Maybe just put them someplace where no one else will see them."

"But we said—"

"It won't work. And I don't want it to. I'll figure something out."

"*We*. We're in this together," Kendall said, then raked his gaze over Ridge's body to map out all the places he wanted to lick and suck and leave his mark. The timer on the stove went off. "You're saved by the buzzer."

Ridge snorted. "I'm not feeling very grateful at the moment." But he changed his tune when Kendall pulled baked rigatoni from the oven. "Holy shit, that looks delicious."

"I hope it turned out well. This is my second favorite dish of Adelaide's. I asked her for the recipe, and she emailed it to me." Kendall laughed. "I had to call her several times since I've never made marinara sauce from scratch. She also helped me make her infamous chocolate bourbon pecan pie."

"Wow," Ridge said. "You didn't need to go to so much trouble."

"On the contrary," Kendall countered. "Staying busy quiets my anxious mind."

"You're anxious about me living here?" Ridge asked.

Kendall set the casserole dish on top of the stove and shut the oven door. He tossed his mitts onto the counter and faced Ridge. "I'm anxious in general, but today I was hyperfocused on keeping my hands to myself." They both glanced down to where Kendall's hand rested on Ridge's chest. "As it turns out, I had reason to be concerned."

Ridge cupped his face. "Not anymore. I want your hands on me. Let me worry about my job, okay?"

"I'll try."

Ridge searched his eyes for several seconds before letting go. "Can I help set the table?"

Kendall nodded. Ridge laid out the dishes and cutlery while Kendall carried the pan of baked pasta over, then retrieved the salad and a loaf of Italian bread. He quickly sorted their drinks and joined Ridge at the table.

"You're one of those people who can do anything, right?" Ridge asked.

Kendall chuckled. "I don't know about that." He scooped up a large portion of baked rigatoni and put it on Ridge's plate before taking a smaller amount for himself. He'd have to take little bites until he overcame his nervous stomach. "I'm one of those people who puts in a hundred percent effort when I decide to do something. It doesn't always turn out the way I want it to, though."

Ridge grabbed the salad tongs and filled their bowls. Kendall liked that he hadn't skimped on the greens. The baked rigatoni smelled like Adelaide's, but would it taste as good? Kendall held his breath while he waited for Ridge to take his first bite but released it on a sigh when a euphoric expression washed over Ridge's face as he chewed.

"Good?" he asked.

Ridge made Kendall wait through another bite before answering. "It's the best thing I've ever eaten." Kendall must've worn a doubtful expression because Ridge chuckled and pointed at his uneaten food. "Try it for yourself."

Kendall cut a small piece and blew on it until the steam dissipated. Ridge made an inarticulate noise that sounded like a combination of a growl and a whimper. Kendall glanced at Ridge and caught him staring at his mouth, so he licked his bottom lip to see if he could entice the same guttural reaction. Ridge's nostrils flared, and he snapped his gaze up to lock with Kendall's. Ridge's smoldering intensity left him breathless.

"Eat your food," he said huskily. "I have plans for your wicked mouth."

Kendall intended to make a big seduction out of eating his tiny bite. He slowly parted his lips and lifted the fork to his mouth but forgot all about his plan when the flavors burst on his tongue. "Holy fuck."

Ridge chuckled. "It's pretty awesome when the chef manages to impress himself."

"This is good," Kendall said, digging in for a second bite.

"Damn good."

They quietly ate for a few minutes, exchanging goofy grins instead of words between bites. There was no awkward pressure to fill the silence; they were content to simply eat and be together. Ridge finished off his water, and Kendall pushed his seat back to retrieve the pitcher.

"I'll get it," Ridge said. "Eat."

Ridge returned a moment later and refilled Kendall's glass before resuming his seat and serving himself. "So, how else did you stay busy today?"

"I finished unpacking the last few boxes from the garage, did my laundry, and cleaned the house."

"All while making marinara sauce from scratch?" Ridge asked.

Kendall shrugged. "Oh, and I reorganized my closet and fine-tuned the Envy sauce."

"Your closet, huh?" Something in Ridge's tone snagged his attention. The smoldering expression Kendall had witnessed before was now a five-alarm fire. What in the world could've revved him up? Then it hit him. Ridge had seen those damn canvases before he'd moved them. Apparently, Ridge was reliving the moment and getting hot under the collar because he loosened his tie and the top few buttons on his shirt.

"You liked those pictures, didn't you?" Kendall asked, crossing his legs to hold on tighter to the thrill building in his groin.

Ridge swallowed hard and nodded. "I see them every time I close my eyes." A wide smile spread across his handsome face. "Or step into the shower."

Knowing he affected Ridge so strongly was the strongest aphrodisiac he'd ever experienced. "Are you assuming I put the canvases in my closet, or did you go looking for them?"

Ridge's grin grew wicked. "What do you think?"

Kendall imagined him digging through the closet until he found them. And then what? "Did you—"

Ridge shook his head. "Searching your closet was bad enough. I might've thought about it, though."

Kendall let his mind conjure up an image of Ridge stretched out across his bed, taking himself in hand while staring at the pictures.

"Why'd you tuck those beautiful photos away?" Ridge asked. "Why not hang them in your bedroom?"

Kendall took a deep breath. "They're a reminder of the person I used to be, not the person I want to be."

Ridge cocked his head to the side. "And you can't merge the two versions together?"

"Not yet."

Kendall saw the questions burning in Ridge's warm eyes, but he didn't press. "Will you tell me about the inspiration behind the mysterious green sauce now?"

"You are."

"I'm what?" Ridge asked. "Annoying? Nosy?"

Kendall laughed. "You're the inspiration for the sauce."

"You're envious of me?"

Kendall held Ridge's gaze and took a deep breath. "I'm envious of the man who'll eventually win your heart."

"When?" Ridge asked.

"Are you asking me when you'll fall in love? I'm not clairvoyant."

Ridge laughed. "No, when did you start creating Envy?"

Once the truth was out, Kendall wouldn't be able to take it back. Playing it safe might save him from getting hurt when Ridge eventually left town, but Kendall would never know if Ridge could love him. "I made it the night we met. I was still amped up and jealous of Todd, a man I'd never met, when I got home."

Ridge's brows shot up. "But you didn't know anything about me."

"I knew I liked what I saw. I knew I resented all the hands that had ever touched you, especially the ones that had betrayed you. I started the base for the sauce the same night and added to it the night we toured the apartments. By then, I knew what it felt like to have your body and mouth pressed to mine. Envy is a burning emotion, so I decided to use a much hotter pepper."

Ridge leaned forward, cupped his neck, and pulled him closer for a brief kiss. "I'm incredibly turned on by your confession, but I've consumed so much pasta I'm doubting my ability to act on the emotion."

Kendall waggled his brows and forced a diabolical laugh through his lips. "All part of my evil plan."

"To render me impotent?"

"Hardly. I just loaded you down with heavy carbs to slow your escape."

Ridge laughed. "Is that why you're eating more salad than pasta?"

Kendall replied with a wink as he chewed.

They kept the conversation light going forward, sticking to pop culture topics like music and movies. Kendall was surprised to discover Ridge loved sci-fi movies and black-and-white classics.

"They don't make movies like *The Maltese Falcon* anymore," he said.

Ridge seemed just as stunned when Kendall confessed his love of hockey.

"I'm in it for the hot dudes," Kendall admitted. "That stamina. Whew." He fanned his face. "Same reason I've seen every *Fast and Furious* movie a dozen times."

"I love those too," Ridge said. "The guys aren't really my type, but I love the over-the-top action."

Most surprisingly was that they both loved the movie *Twister*.

"A classic," Kendall said.

"Timeless."

"Would you like to watch it after dinner?"

"After I clean the kitchen," Ridge said.

Kendall shook his head emphatically. "No way. I'll get it tomorrow."

"My mother would never forgive me."

Kendall took in Ridge's firm jaw and tense posture and knew he wasn't going to give in. Did he really want to waste his energy arguing when he could use his powers of persuasion for much more memorable purposes later? Kendall allowed his gaze to drift lower to the tie and imagined it securing Ridge's wrists to his headboard, allowing Kendall free rein of his body. *Oh, the places he could mark.* "Fine. You win." *This time.*

It didn't take Ridge long to restore Kendall's kitchen to pristine condition so they could retire to the living room. Ridge sprawled on the couch while Kendall pulled up his Amazon Prime account. He dropped onto the sofa in front of Ridge when the opening credits began, and Ridge spooned in behind him. Kendall had probably watched the movie fifty times, but seeing it with someone who loved it as much as he did was an entirely unique experience. Both men spoke their favorite lines along with the characters and often found themselves quoting the same parts. Ridge laughed when Kendall tensed and flinched in certain scenes, even though he knew the outcome.

"I can't help it," Kendall said. "I still act like I don't know the ending of *Friday Night Lights* too."

Ridge laughed. "Yeah, same."

When the closing credits started to roll, Kendall did too so that he was facing Ridge instead of the television. "I can't believe you're still wearing your tie." He'd loosened it, but it still hung around Ridge's neck. "Aren't you uncomfortable?"

Ridge nipped Kendall's bottom lip and settled his hand on Kendall's waist. "Guess not since I'd forgotten all about it."

Kendall trailed his fingers over the silky-smooth fabric, and his earlier fantasies rushed to the forefront of his mind. "You know, this is usually the part where I seduce you."

Fingers flexed against Kendall's body, and Ridge's eyes darkened with a wicked promise. "Do I sense a *but* coming?"

"I still want to tie you to my bed and do delicious and dirty things to you," Kendall said.

"Okay."

Kendall kissed Ridge's smiling lips as he unknotted the tie. Instead of pulling the silk free, he left it looped around Ridge's neck, then started on the buttons down the front of his shirt. Kendall took his time, angling his head and deepening the kiss in between stops. Ridge slid his hand under Kendall's tank top and traced a finger above his waistband, stopping to explore the places that elicited a shiver.

Kendall threw his leg over Ridge's outer thigh, and the bigger man bent his leg and pushed it through the gap, tucking it under Kendall's balls. The friction pulled a slutty moan from Kendall's throat, and he couldn't resist rocking against the thick muscles. Ridge grunted and gripped Kendall's ass with both hands like he was worried Kendall would vanish.

They kept kissing and touching until the need for air took precedence and forced them apart.

Ridge swiped his thumb over Kendall's lips. "You have the prettiest mouth I've ever seen."

Kendall released a deep sigh and nipped Ridge's finger until he pulled it away. "You haven't seen a fraction of what it can do to you."

Ridge smiled and trailed his hand down Kendall's chest until he reached his jeans. Then he hooked his finger through a belt loop. "Why do I get the impression I won't be seeing these other tricks tonight?"

"Because for once, sex isn't the most pressing urge I have where you're concerned."

Ridge smiled. "This sounds like a backhanded compliment, but I'll bite. What feels more important than having me at your mercy?"

Kendall's pulse hammered at his throat. "I'm handling this all wrong."

"I don't need to be handled," Ridge replied. "And you don't need to sugar coat your feelings on my behalf."

Kendall cupped Ridge's face and kissed him. "I just…I need this thing between us to be different. I want to get to know you." Snuggling deeper, Kendall tucked his head into the curve of Ridge's neck. "Where did you grow up? Where does your family live?"

"My family owns a ranch in Montana. It's situated in the valley between the Bitterroot Mountains and Sapphire Range."

"Montana? I never pictured you as a cowboy."

Ridge laughed. "I'm not." He lowered his voice to a husky pitch and said, "I could pretend to be, though, if it turns you on."

Kendall lifted his head. "You're from Montana? You ride horses and stuff?"

"Technically, I was born in Germany where my dad was stationed. He was in the army. We moved back to the states when I was a few months old and kept moving until my dad retired to Montana at the end of his career."

"You bounced around a lot, huh?"

"I think I attended eight different high schools before my dad made his final transition to Corvallis, Montana."

Kendall cringed. "Yikes. Eight high schools? One was bad enough." He ran his hand up and down Ridge's arm. "Did you hate the constant moving?"

"I loved it. Mom said it's responsible for my wanderlust. Montana was the first place to feel like home, though. Those mountains just call to me."

"I bet you fit in pretty well there."

Ridge snorted. "Not really. I was a scrawny, awkward kid who'd rather draw pictures of the mountains than interact with people my age."

"An artist, huh?" Kendall asked. "How romantic."

"No one would call me either of those things."

Kendall thought about the gorgeous flowers Ridge had brought home but didn't argue. Ridge's lips were loose and spilling details, and he wanted to keep it that way. "Just so you know, I would've been your friend," Kendall said, nestling closer. "You would've tried to shake me, but it wouldn't have worked."

Ridge slid his hand into Kendall's hair and massaged his scalp. "I wouldn't have appreciated you the way I do now. I wasn't ready to admit my attraction to the same sex back then, and I would've resented the feelings you stirred inside me."

"I'm no stranger to resentment," Kendall said. "But I'm glad we're meeting now."

"Me too." Ridge moved in and resumed their kiss for several languid moments.

The intense emotions Kendall felt earlier still simmered beneath the surface, but he lusted for knowledge over sex, so he broke the kiss. "I want to see some of your art."

"Fuck no."

Kendall smiled at his vehemence. "Okay, tell me more about your family."

"Now?"

Kendall nodded. "I want to know about the people who produced a man like you. What are your parents like? Do you have siblings?"

"I have a twin sister," Ridge said. "Her name is Sierra."

Kendall pulled back and narrowed his eyes.

"What?" Ridge asked. "You don't believe me?"

Kendall smiled. "Of course I believe you. I'm just trying to picture what a feminine version of you looks like, and I keep seeing you in drag." He buried his face in Ridge's neck and laughed again. "Does your sister have shoulders like a linebacker too?"

Ridge laughed. "No, she's the exact opposite of me. Petite and blonde like my mom where I look like a carbon copy of my dad. Only I'm taller and broader now," he said with no small amount of pleasure. "I might be bigger and stronger than Sierra, but I wouldn't want to tangle with my sister for any amount of money."

"Who was born first?" Kendall asked.

"Sierra by thirty minutes."

"Thirty minutes?" Kendall knew a few sets of twins, and their births were much closer together. "What the hell took you so long? Did they have to coax you out with a cheeseburger or something?"

Ridge's shoulders shook with laughter. "Mom said I was just grateful for some damn peace and quiet after being bossed around and jabbed by Sierra's bony elbows for thirty-eight weeks. She likes to say my sister entered this world raising hell and hasn't stopped since. It's no wonder she's a kickass attorney." The smile on his face was one of pure pride.

"What's your family ranch like? It's obvious those mountains speak to something deep inside you."

"Heaven," Ridge said. "Mom swears the mountains have healing powers. I feel the stress wash out of my body just by staring at them."

He went on to tell Kendall about the organic bison and beef they raised as well as the different vegetables and grains they grew, taking full advantage of each growing season.

"You grow chickpeas in Montana?"

"Parts of the state, yes," Ridge said.

"I love to experiment with hummus flavors almost as much as my sauces for chicken wings."

"You'd get along great with my mom. One of her dreams is to produce her own line of health foods, including hummus. In fact, she's on the verge of realizing that dream." Something in Ridge's voice was off. Instead of sounding excited, his words came out heavy and hung in the air.

"What's wrong?"

"I still can't believe my impenetrable father had a heart attack. Seeing him lying in a hospital bed and hooked up to all those monitors…" Ridge shuddered in Kendall's embrace, so Kendall held on tighter, hoping to give him comfort. "Dad was pretty out of it one night at the hospital, and he mentioned wanting to see me settled and happy before he died. He wanted me to have what he'd found with Mom." Ridge blew out a breath. "A world without my dad in it is something I'm not ready for, and letting him down wasn't an option either. So I tried to make something out of nothing."

Kendall kept his opinion of Todd to himself. "But your dad is doing better now, right?"

Ridge nodded and tightened his hold on Kendall. "Yeah, he's going to make a full recovery, but it landed a mighty blow to his ego. He's worried about the impact it will have on Mom's business endeavors. He's afraid of losing consumer trust if people find out he's human."

"Are you going to be as stubborn as your dad when you're older?" Kendall asked.

"Probably. Some would say I already am."

"I'll make a note."

Ridge's laughter was music to Kendall's ears. "You still plan on know-ing me thirty years from now?"

Heat infused Kendall's cheeks as he struggled to find the right words. Christ. Could he run a guy off any faster? "Well, I don't have grand designs on your future if that's worrying you."

"Oddly, I feel more charmed than scared."

"Okay, good. Brace yourself for my next declaration," Kendall teased.

Ridge snickered before making a big show of anchoring himself to the couch. "Ready."

"I, um…I will always want to know you, Kurt Dandridge. We might become best friends who talk all the time, or we might drift apart and only check in with each other occasionally, but if I'm breathing, I'll still want to know you."

Ridge's eyes softened like melted chocolate. "That's the sweetest thing anyone has ever said to me." And the bravest words Kendall had ever dared to speak. Ridge cupped his face, stroking a thumb over Kendall's cheek. "And I feel the same way about you."

"Even after meeting my family?"

Ridge nodded. "I can't help but wonder…"

Dread pooled in his gut. "What?"

"How'd you end up so amazing?"

Kendall laughed and pressed his cheek into Ridge's palm. "My mom wasn't always cold and distant," he said. "Before she met Stanton, Rebecca was the best mother a kid could ask for. We grew up together. She was so damn excited when she landed the secretary position at Stanton's company. They were a startup back then, but the money was still better than her old job. The higher salary got us a nicer apartment with access to a pool until we moved in with Stan and Travis."

Ridge let out a cute little growl, and his hand stilled. "Travis is the stepbrother that you…"

Kendall nodded. "I only have one."

"You really tensed up there," Ridge said, resuming his caress. He shifted his hand lower, working on the muscles in Kendall's neck. "I didn't mean to get you all knotted up."

Kendall had been unaware of his tension until Ridge drew his attention to it. He took a deep breath and allowed Ridge's tender ministrations to ease it away. "Sorry."

"Don't be. I don't want to stir up pain and misery, and I'm not judging you, okay?" Kendall nodded. "We don't have to talk about it."

Kendall allowed himself to get lost in Ridge's warm gaze. It felt as if something genuine and unique was blooming between them, and he needed to build it on a solid foundation. It was better to show Ridge all the worst parts of him now rather than wait until later when the rejection would hurt so much more. He resolved to have an honest conversation with Ridge and to let the chips fall where they may. "I think we do."

"Don't do that," Ridge whispered.

"Do what?"

"You're bracing yourself for goodbye. Knock it off. Let's get something straight right now. I will always want to know you too, Kendall Blakemore. I promise to listen without judgment now or whenever you're ready. Okay?"

Kendall took a deep breath and nodded. "Stan Burkhart was the worst thing to ever happen to us. The asshole was nice to me until he put a ring on my mom's finger, then he resented the very air I breathed. I tried hard to please him, but I failed to meet his expectations. Stan made it his personal mission to drive a wedge between my mother and me. It happened gradually, but she became a person I no longer recognized. My warm, loving mother became cold and aloof. I eventually stopped turning to her when I had something exciting to share or when I wanted her to nurse my broken heart." Kendall smirked up at Ridge. "I was always a sensitive, dramatic little thing, so it was a daily occurrence." Kendall chewed on his bottom lip as he thought about the right way to transition to more challenging topics.

"Stop doing that too," Ridge said, rubbing his thumb over the abused flesh.

"I was ten when I started to wish I could just disappear."

Ridge sucked in a sharp breath and tightened his grip on Kendall's hip but didn't say anything.

"Stan sent Travis to a boarding school in London. He told Travis it was to open up doors for him, but I think Stan wanted to punish his son for showing kindness to me. Without Travis there to deflect some of the verbal abuse, Stan's attacks grew more intense until I just wanted to fade away. Those thoughts manifested as a nasty eating disorder."

"Fuck," Ridge growled and resumed his massage.

"It wasn't intentional," Kendall said. "I didn't make a conscientious decision to stop eating or to harm myself. My stomach just got tied up in knots from the stress, and it became too painful to eat."

"Where the fuck was your mother?"

"Stan kept her busy with all kinds of committees and social engagements. Most of them happened in the evenings, so I was in bed before she came home."

"And the mornings? You didn't see her before school?"

Kendall shook his head. "She was sleeping off the effects of self-medicating with booze and pills. Stan took advantage of my mother's absence in more ways than one."

Ridge stiffened, and Kendall worked quickly to assure him Stan had never physically or sexually abused him. "I was referring to his many affairs."

"So Stan's affair with Amber Everly wasn't the first time he strayed?" Ridge asked.

Kendall's eyes widened. "That came out during the raid?"

Ridge nodded and bit his bottom lip to keep from laughing. "I'll tell you about it someday."

Kendall smiled. "Amber was probably his hundredth affair."

"I just need five minutes alone with Stan in a room with no cameras. I can make this right," Ridge said.

Kendall's heart melted. "Five minutes couldn't possibly undo the damage, but I appreciate the thought."

Ridge dropped a soft kiss on his forehead. "When did your mom figure out you were starving yourself?"

"She didn't," Kendall replied. "Travis came home for a school holiday and flipped out. He made an anonymous call to children's services. God, it was a fucking mess. I don't know whose pocket Stan greased to make it all go away, but he must have paid someone off. He would've punished us harshly if my mom hadn't caught him with the housekeeper around the same time."

"Adelaide?" Ridge asked.

Kendall snorted. "God no. She would've cut Stan's dick off and forced him to eat it. Mom hired Adelaide to replace the woman she fired."

"So, did the power dynamic change once your mom had irrefutable proof Stan was a cheating asshole?"

"Briefly," Kendall replied. "Stan played the remorseful husband who wanted to do better. My mom fell for it. Hell, even I did. It didn't take long for the power to shift back to the asshole. But in the interim, my mom made three life-changing ultimatums that Stan never reneged on."

"And they were?"

"She hired Adelaide, who became my surrogate mom and biggest ally in the house. Rebecca arranged for Travis to return home and attend his regular school. She also sent me to therapy for my eating disorder. And boy, did Stan hate paying for that."

"Therapy helped?"

"Yes, but I'm going to battle this disorder for the rest of my life. It gets better but never fully goes away. When I get really stressed, my stomach still knots up. I have to use the techniques my therapist taught me to override the instinct that tells me to skip meals."

Ridge stroked a broad hand up and down Kendall's back. "Something about you stirs my protective instincts. No, *stirs* is too tame a word. It's more like poking a bear."

"Because you don't think I can take care of myself?"

Ridge rolled his eyes. "You can't be serious. I saw you take down a hardened criminal with your fist and a serving tray. You're more than capable of taking care of yourself, but I still want to shield you from ugly things."

"But you can't."

Ridge smoothed Kendall's hair off his forehead and pressed a kiss there. "I want to."

Kendall stretched and yawned. "My evil-genius plan to bog you down with carbs has backfired. I don't know what was heavier: the food or the conversation I insisted we have. I really know how to bring down the tone of an evening."

"You did no such thing," Ridge assured him.

Kendall rolled over, grabbed the remote off the coffee table, and switched the television over to cable. He turned on *Forensic Files* and scooted until there wasn't even an inch of space between his back and Ridge's chest. "You know what to do," he said over his shoulder.

Ridge looped his arm around Kendall's waist, resting his hand on Kendall's stomach. "We're both going to be asleep in minutes."

Kendall yawned. "Seconds."

Chapter Twenty-Three

RIDGE STOOD OVER KENDALL'S BED EARLY THE FOLLOWING morning as the beautiful blond man lay sleeping. They'd woken at some point in the middle of the night and stumbled down the hallway toward the bedrooms. Ridge hadn't even considered veering off to his own room, and Kendall sure hadn't protested his presence between his sheets. Kendall had thrown a possessive arm and leg over Ridge like he was terrified Ridge might sneak off at the first available opportunity. The thought hadn't so much as flitted across his mind.

Unable to resist, Ridge ran a hand over Kendall's silky hair, earning a soft whimper from the slumbering man. He arched his back like he was trying to get closer, and Ridge would've made it a reality if he hadn't wanted to arrive at work early to talk with Marks. Sammy, who'd been curled up on Kendall's lower back, raised his head and glared at Ridge.

He chuckled and scratched the little lion's chin. "Mind your own business," he whispered to the cat. Ridge leaned over and kissed Kendall's cheek, inhaling the intoxicating scent of sexy and sweet that was uniquely his. He stepped back from the bed and noticed his silk tie on the floor. They'd undressed hastily in the middle of the night, and it had still been pitch black when Ridge had forced himself from Kendall's bed to get ready for work. He'd managed to pick up all his dirty clothes except the tie. Promises from last night echoed in his ear.

I want to tie you to my bed with this.

Ridge leaned over, picked it up, and looped it around Kendall's bedpost so he'd see it and remember too.

Ridge stepped into the kitchen and made a single cup of coffee to go before heading out. He had to make one stop before he could meet with Marks. There was a Walgreens on the way to the field office, and Ridge knew they were open twenty-four hours. The store looked lit for Jesus at the predawn hour, and the three walls of windows made him feel like he was swimming in a fishbowl. He headed straight to the cosmetics section, thinking it would only take him a few seconds to find the concealer. What. The. Fuck? There had to be a hundred different shades between a few dozen companies. Some he could rule out right away. The point of concealer was to hide something, not to draw attention to it by using a shade too light or dark. But there were too many variations of what looked like the same color, and it irritated him. Ridge bit the bullet and asked the clerk for her opinion.

"I don't wear makeup, so I probably won't be much help." She held the packages up to his face and shrugged. "They all look the same to me."

Ridge let out a little growl. Then an idea hit him. Emma and Jess would be able to help. "Can I buy these and return the ones I don't need?"

"As long as the packaging and seals aren't broken."

"Deal."

He pulled into the parking lot at work a few minutes later and was dismayed to see so many people had arrived already. Damn workaholics. Ridge spotted Jess's and Emma's vehicles but wasn't surprised since they were working overtime on Burkhart's and Jones's assets. Just thinking Burkhart's name made Ridge want to punch something. He hadn't been joking when he'd said he only needed five minutes with Stanton. Ridge could tell Kendall saw his mother as another of Burkhart's casualties, and she was, but it was tough for him to give the woman a pass.

Ridge headed straight for the asset forfeiture department, or the dungeon as Jess and Emma referred to their basement offices. He stopped at Emma's first and knocked on the glass wall.

"Have a minute? I need some help."

Emma snapped her head up. Her hair was so inky black it appeared blue in the fluorescent overhead lights. "Of course. What's up?"

"Can you come with me to Jess's office?"

Emma scooted her chair back and stretched until Ridge heard her vertebrae pop.

"You did go home last night, right?"

"For a little bit," Emma replied as she fell into step with him.

"What time did you come back?"

"Too damn early," Jess said around a yawn when they stepped into her office. "What's going on?"

Ridge upended the pharmacy bag and the array of concealers fell into the middle of Jess's desk.

"Yeah, we'll be needing some of that later," she said.

"It's for me." Ridge tugged down the collar of his polo shirt.

"Whoa," Emma said. "Someone burn their neck while curling their hair?"

Ridge bit back a laugh. "It's razor burn."

Jess snorted. "Who is he?"

Ridge grinned because he was eager to tell his friends all about Kendall but knew he had to get his ass in gear if he wanted a shot at talking to Marks before he lost his nerve. "I want to tell you all about him, but I need you to help me cover this up before Eddie sees it."

"Too damn late," Ridge's best friend said from behind him.

Ridge dropped his collar into place and turned to greet his friend with a smile, but Eddie just scowled. He held a drink carrier with three coffees in one hand and a pastry bag in the other.

"You fucking moron. I knew you were hiding something under that dress shirt yesterday."

"Eddie!" Jess and Emma exclaimed.

"Don't feel sorry for him," Eddie said as he strode forward and set the drinks and food down. "Let me see it."

Ridge peeled back his collar again.

"You and I are going to have a serious talk," Eddie said.

"Not until I speak to Marks first."

Ridge and Eddie continued staring at one another for several moments.

"What the hell is going on?" Emma asked.

"Don't know, and I'm oddly okay with it," Jess replied.

"Do you know what you're getting yourself into?" Eddie asked.

Ridge grinned and winked at his friend. "Trouble."

Eddie raised both hands and stepped away from the desk. "I won't get in the way of the ladies giving you a makeover."

"Don't be jealous, baby," Jess said. "There's a shade in here that will work on you."

Ridge snorted. "You're a real smartass, Jess. I like you a lot."

She slapped his bicep. "I like you too, big guy. That's why I'm going to save your ass. None of these concealers will give you the coverage you need."

"Damn," he grumbled.

Jess held up a finger before he could spew other curses. "Fear not. I have a solution." She patted her vacated desk chair. "Make this easier on a girl and have a seat."

He looked at the chair and calculated the likelihood it would break under his weight.

"I better sit over here," Ridge said, pointing to the visitor's chair in the corner.

"The lighting isn't as good over there," Jess countered.

"Babe," Eddie said, "you're not contouring his face or giving him a smoky eye. Just dab the crap on his love bite."

Jess giggled and shook her head as she rooted around in her purse. "Aha," she said, raising a small tube in the air like it was a trophy. "This is what you need to apply first before the concealer will work."

"But it's green," Ridge said.

"Green cancels out the red," Emma explained.

Jess nodded. "It's what you use to cover acne or rosacea or just a ruddy complexion. Then you go over it with a concealer or foundation that matches your skin tone."

"Marks didn't say anything about green concealer," Ridge said.

Eddie groaned and started pacing. "Dude, Marks gave you advice on how to cover your hickey? Assistant Chief Deputy Jayne Marks? Our boss?"

"Yes," Ridge said. "It's not quite the bonding moment you're envisioning. She basically compared me to her horny teenager." Ridge told them about their conversation, and the three of them had a great laugh at his expense.

Jess dabbed the green stuff on first while Emma scrutinized the concealers, murmuring something about undertones he didn't understand. "You did a great job choosing shades. I think this one will work best," Emma said, showing him the lightest one he'd picked.

"I want to hear about this guy," Jess said as she fanned her hand in front of Ridge's neck.

"Me too," Emma said.

"I'll introduce you to him soon. I promise. Maybe we could—"

"No," Eddie said. "You're not dragging us all down with you."

Jess swatted her boyfriend hard on the arm. "Eddie, you're not in charge of me. I want to meet…" She looked at Ridge.

"Kendall," he supplied.

"And I—" She snapped her head back in Eddie's direction. "Wait a damn minute. That's the name of that cute guy we met at the barbecue. The one you said would be perfect for Ridge."

"Oh," Emma said. "I remember Kendall. Why don't you like him now?"

"I do like him," Eddie said, softening his voice. "Kendall's a great guy, and he makes this big lug smile like I've never seen before."

"But?" Jess and Emma asked.

"It's complicated," Ridge said. "Eddie is right, though. I need to have a conversation with Marks before I drag anyone else into my situation."

"Fine." Jess dabbed on a second layer of concealer with a light touch before stepping back to survey her handiwork. "Not bad at all." She pulled a compact mirror from her purse and handed it to Ridge.

He closely inspected Jess's work and handed it back to her. "You did good," he said, just as she came at him with a spray bottle.

"Tip your head back."

He immediately obliged, and she hit the spot with a couple of squirts. "What's that?"

"Setting spray," Eddie said.

Ridge looked over at his friend. "How do you know this?"

"I pay attention to the things that are important to my lady."

Ridge kissed Jess's cheek, then Emma's. "You're lifesavers." He took a deep breath to settle his jitters as he tossed the cosmetics back in the bag. "Wish me luck, yeah?"

"Good luck," his three friends said.

"You're going to need it," Eddie added.

Ridge heard the ladies chastising his friend on his walk to the elevator. Served him right. Ridge's phone rang just as he stepped onto his floor. The number was local but didn't belong to anyone he had programmed into his contact list.

He accepted the call and said, "Deputy Marshal Dandridge."

"Hello, Pat Garrett."

Carmen Elliot. There was only one reason she'd be calling him. "You ready to do the right thing?"

"You ready to fulfill your promises?" she countered.

"Yes, ma'am."

"Good. Be in Hinesville at one o'clock." She rattled off a restaurant and address. "I'll have a small sample of the information I can give you on Willie and Sheldon Harris."

"I'll be bringing the assistant chief deputy and chief deputy. They're the ones you need to convince for WITSEC placement."

She chuckled. "That should take me all of twenty seconds."

"Carmen, are you someplace safe right now?"

"Yeah, I'm good. Just be there at one. Bring your appetite and your credit card. Lunch is on you."

"Yes, ma'am."

Ridge ended the call and headed straight for Marks's office. This was the break he'd been waiting for.

Chapter Twenty-Four

KENDALL RAISED HIS FIST TO KNOCK ON THE BLUE DOOR BUT froze before his hand could connect with the wood. The paint color reminded him of the silk tie he'd found looped around his bedpost; the same one he'd trailed over his morning wood and used to masturbate while thinking about Ridge. He rapped his knuckles against the smooth panel and forced his mind to pick a subject that wouldn't cause a reaction that would shock his mother.

The breakfast invitation from Rebecca had been a pleasant surprise, and he'd readily accepted. It felt like the second chance he'd longed for but never dreamed would come. Hope and fear were the kissing cousins of emotions wreaking havoc on his heart. Individually, the reactions were necessary for survival, but together…they didn't mesh. *Afraid to hope.* Who wanted that? Certainly not Kendall, but it was the latest quagmire he found himself in.

The boldly painted door suddenly swung open, giving him his most significant surprise of the day. "I feel like I've stepped through time," he said, raking his gaze over Rebecca. She wore white, wide-leg beachcombers, a turquoise tank top, and a pair of flip-flops. She'd pulled her hair into a high ponytail and greeted him sans makeup. And her smile…Kendall couldn't recall the last time he'd seen a genuine expression of joy on her face.

"What I wouldn't give for a time machine about now," she replied, standing up on her tiptoes to kiss his cheek. "I would change so much." Rebecca stepped aside so he could come inside.

Adelaide's home was as warm as he'd expected. Kendall noted the earthy tones in the furniture fabrics and wall treatments, which she'd accented with jewel tones in her decorations and area rugs. Kendall sniffed the air appreciatively, breathing in the cinnamon and vanilla he always associated with Adelaide.

"This must be what heaven smells like," he said. "Is Adelaide making French toast?"

"Of course. It's your favorite. Adelaide has it in the warmer while we finish cooking the rest of the food." *We?* His mother hadn't cooked in ages.

Another welcome aroma greeted Kendall's nose and his mouth watered. "Bacon?"

Rebecca nodded. "Extra crispy, just like you like it." She smiled again, and Kendall could no longer keep his thoughts to himself.

"It's been nearly two decades since I've seen you smile so effortlessly, and suddenly I see it twice in two minutes."

"Odd, isn't it?" she asked. "My world has turned completely upside down. I have no money, home, or even clothes to call my own, but I've never been happier. I feel like I've escaped a prison, even though it was one of my own choosing."

Kendall shook his head. "No one chooses to be brainwashed, bullied, and abused. You didn't sign up for any of that when you agreed to marry Stan."

"No, but I should've been wiser. I can't even claim I was blindsided." She snorted. "Did I really expect Stan to be faithful to his clients and honest with the IRS when he couldn't show me the same courtesy?" Her glow dimmed before his eyes.

Eager to get it back, Kendall forced down his shields and reached for her hands. "What-ifs won't get you anywhere. Let's start asking what next instead, okay?"

She took a deep breath and nodded. "What next. I like it."

"Good."

"Breakfast seems like a good starting point, right?" she asked.

Kendall sniffed the air appreciatively again. "The best."

He followed his mom into the kitchen where Adelaide was busy creating culinary magic. She glanced up when they entered and beckoned Kendall to her for a hug.

"My boy," she said, patting his back.

"Hi, Adelaide."

Rebecca's cell phone rang, and she excused herself and stepped out of the room to take the call. He stared after her for a few seconds, wondering who was calling her.

"She was waiting on a call from your lawyer friend," Adelaide said, reading his mind. "She's much stronger this time."

Kendall met Adelaide's sincere gaze. "Thank you so much for taking such good care of my mom. We'll never be able to thank you for your kindness."

"You guys can thank me by socking it to Stanton Burkhart," Adelaide said, flipping the bacon.

"We'll give it our best shot." Kendall walked over to the counter where an open carton of eggs sat next to a bowl. "Want me to crack some eggs?"

"Nope."

"Why not? You taught me how to do it without getting shells in the bowl."

Adelaide laughed. "Yes, and now I'm teaching your mother. She wants to make the scrambled eggs."

"I'm back," Rebecca said as she breezed through the door. She shooed Kendall away from the bowl and lifted an egg. "Chet sends his best, by the way."

Unsure how to respond, Kendall said, "That's nice."

"Give it a good whack against the edge of the bowl," Adelaide said when Rebecca was in position. "You want a nice clean break to prevent the shell from falling in."

Rebecca tapped the egg against the edge, barely producing a crack. She gave Kendall a sheepish grin.

"Pretend it's Stan's face," he said.

On her second attempt, she cracked the egg so hard the shell split in two, and most of the egg landed on the counter and not in the bowl. "Oops. Looks like I have a lot of rage."

"Justifiably so," Kendall said, then pointed to the bowl. "But no shells."

Rebecca laughed and tried again. The third time was a charm, and she whooped in celebration when the egg landed cleanly in the bowl. "Two down and…" She looked to Adelaide.

"Four to go."

Kendall helped himself to a cup of coffee while Adelaide and Rebecca worked together. His mom was surprised to hear Adelaide whisked in a splash of heavy cream.

Kendall sipped from his mug. "Makes them extra fluffy."

A few minutes later, they made their plates and carried them over to the small dinette tucked into the corner. The tabletop was a mosaic of bold red, blue, green, and yellow tiles. The four wooden chairs surrounding the table were painted in matching hues. Sunlight filtered in through the windows, making the space even cozier.

As always, the French toast was perfection, but Kendall stopped noticing the flavors after the first bite or two. He couldn't take his eyes off his mother as she chatted over the shared meal. Rebecca seemed too composed and calm about her situation. Decades of being Stanton Burkhart's wife had indeed taught her to suppress her feelings, but she wasn't in his home anymore. She was with her son and…What exactly was her relationship with Adelaide?

Kendall shifted his attention to the housekeeper he loved like family. His mother and Adelaide had always had a positive working relationship, but opening up her home to her former boss? That seemed above and beyond even for someone as kind as Adelaide. Were they friends? Were they…more?

A soft snort pulled him from his reverie. Kendall glanced over and caught Rebecca smiling. She gently elbowed Adelaide to get her attention. "He thinks we're lovers."

Adelaide's eyes widened seconds before she lapsed into girlish giggles.

Rebecca joined her and said, "You're not doing anything to disabuse him of the notion."

"A woman like your mother attracted to someone like me?" Adelaide said. "That's preposterous."

Rebecca sobered immediately. "Why wouldn't I be? You're a beautiful woman with a kind heart and loving nature. I'd be lucky to win your affection."

Adelaide placed her hand on Rebecca's shoulder and said, "You're too kind." Then she looked at Kendall. "There's nothing but friendship between us, sweetheart."

"Damn," Kendall said.

Rebecca forked another bite of fluffy eggs into her mouth and chewed. "I can see we need to build up Adelaide's self-confidence."

"I'm in," he said.

Adelaide dismissed them with a wave of her dainty hand. "I'm too old for any kind of makeover."

"Nonsense," Rebecca said at the same time Kendall blurted out, "Bullshit."

Adelaide giggled harder and shook her head.

"You're helping me to become more self-sufficient. I think it's only fair I help boost your self-esteem." Rebecca chuckled. "But maybe my current circumstances nullify that ability."

Adelaide patted her hand. "You're fiercer than you realize. I'm proud of you."

His mother nodded and turned her hand to squeeze Adelaide's. A beat later, her gaze swung back to him. "Kendall has romance on the brain, so he's projecting it onto everyone else."

Adelaide lowered her fork and narrowed her eyes. "Is that so? Who is he, and when do I get to meet him?"

Kendall dropped his head as heat infused his cheeks. He forked a bite of eggs into his mouth as an excuse not to answer. The ladies saw his tactic for what it was and laughed.

"It's a bit *complicated* right now," Rebecca said. "I think Kendall's trying to get a feel for where things are going."

Kendall raised his head and smiled to show his appreciation. Rebecca reached across the table and patted his hand.

"You're still young," Adelaide said. "Take all the time you need."

Time. How much longer before Ridge's urge to roam kicked in? Kendall should slow things down instead of hurtling himself toward heartbreak at breakneck speed.

"Kendall," his mom said, her voice as soft as a kitten.

He looked up and caught her watching him closely.

"I know it's hard to believe right now, but sometimes you just need to have faith things will work out as they're intended," she said.

Kendall inhaled a deep, shaky breath and released it slowly. "You're right. The world doesn't revolve around my every whim and fancy." *Could it revolve around just one, though?*

After breakfast, Kendall and his mom insisted on cleaning up. Adelaide argued with them until she realized she was wasting her breath.

"Fine. I'll just go read my new book."

Once alone, Kendall bumped his hip against Rebecca's at the kitchen sink. "What was the call from Chet about?" He shoved his hand beneath the suds and scrubbed the egg skillet. Rebecca had forgotten to hit it with cooking spray, so it was a bit of a mess.

"There was a scheduling conflict, and he wanted to personally apologize for the inconvenience and work out a new time for us to meet." She nudged Kendall with her elbow. "He speaks very highly of you, and it sounds like the office isn't running as smoothly with you gone."

Kendall pulled the skillet from the soapy water and closely inspected his work. Satisfied, he rinsed the pan and handed it to his mother to dry before moving on to a platter. "He'll adjust. Chet isn't used to someone telling him no." Kendall had declined one of Chet's offers outright and avoided the other. "When's your appointment?"

Rebecca glanced up from her task. "Friday at one."

"I'll be there."

She heaved a sigh. "Oh, good."

"What are your plans for the day?" he asked.

"Well, I was hoping I could talk you into helping me look through the classifieds for a suitable job and maybe help me pick out an interview outfit. There's a great consignment shop in the neighborhood." She chuckled. "I bet they still have some of the pieces I donated last month."

"Let me buy you something new."

Rebecca stored the dried dish before facing him once more. "I appreciate your offer more than you'll ever realize. I don't want to be Rebecca Burkhart anymore, so I'm trying to do the exact opposite of what she'd choose."

"Who do you want to be?"

His mother's eyes filled with tears. "Becca Blakemore. Do you remember her?"

A lump of emotion lodged in Kendall's throat, making it impossible to respond at first. He nodded until the tightness dissipated. "She was the best. I really miss her."

Rebecca patted his cheek. "Me too. I say we coax her out of hiding."

"Definitely."

"Becca loved consignment shop bargains, so I thought it would be a great place to start."

"I remember going to the Goodwill stores in the wealthier cities," Kendall said, smiling at the memory.

"I dressed you like a little prince for a few dollars."

They returned to the dinette when they finished cleaning the kitchen and looked through the job postings. Kendall's gaze landed on an ad for a receptionist at a thriving private investigator's office.

He circled the ad, then tapped it with the pen. "Baxter and Jacobs. I know one of the partners, Rocky Jacobs. I could get you—"

His mom covered his hand to cut him off. "I need to do this on my own. I'll apply just like everyone else. Think you can help me jazz up my résumé?"

"Of course."

They spent an hour on Adelaide's laptop creating a résumé before sending it to Baxter and Jacobs as well as a few other promising listings they'd found. Afterward, the pair headed out on foot to the consignment shop Rebecca wanted to check out.

"A portion of the proceeds goes to the women's shelter," she told him. "And since I sat on the board for the shelter, I know the shop's claim isn't just window dressing."

"That's good to know."

Rebecca stopped suddenly half a block away from the shop. "Do you think anyone will recognize me?"

The Burkhart-Jones bust had topped the headlines ever since the raid, but the photo of his mother the media was splashing around looked nothing like the woman standing in front of him.

"No way."

She sighed in relief, and they continued down the sidewalk. The boutique had just opened when they arrived, so they had the entire place to themselves. Kendall helped her pick out a few suits for interviews and a few other casual pieces.

"So Adelaide can have her clothes back," Kendall said, then winked.

They argued briefly about who should pay when they reached the cash register. Kendall was shocked to hear Travis had stopped by to check on her and had given her some cash to cover essentials. She wanted to use the money to buy clothes, but Kendall refused. The salesclerk's attention volleyed between them, her lips quirked in amusement, but she didn't recognize Rebecca.

Kendall looked out the big picture window and widened his eyes. "Ohmygawd is that Patsy Hanover?"

"What? Where?" Rebecca asked as she spun around to look for her country club nemesis. If there was one person who'd recognize his mom, it was that she-devil.

Kendall took advantage of her distraction and handed his debit card to the clerk, who winked at him.

Rebecca spun back around. "You little shit."

"I believe the words you're looking for are *thank you.*"

She laughed as the clerk handed her the bag. "Thank you, Kendall."

"You're welcome."

Rebecca looped her arm through his, and they exited the store. Her flip-flop got caught on something, and she stumbled a bit. After glancing down at her feet, she met Kendall's gaze with a sheepish expression. "I'm going to need some shoes. A nice pair of ballet flats would go with these outfits."

"There's a shoe store down the street," he said, gesturing in that direction.

This time, Kendall kept quiet and allowed her to pay for her purchase. It was painful to watch her count out her money, knowing it was all she had to her name. His mother didn't seem fazed, though. She smiled and thanked the salesclerk when he handed her the shopping bag.

Back out on the sidewalk, Kendall looped his arm around her shoulder. "I'm proud of you."

She tucked her head against his chest. "That means more to me than I can say. There are moments like this when I just feel so happy to have survived being married to Stan. Others, I'm terrified of what my future holds."

Kendall squeezed her shoulder. "You're fiercer *and* smarter than you give yourself credit for."

She sighed heavily. "Fierce, I can believe. But smart? A wise woman would've planned better before she decided to call in an anonymous tip and turn her husband into the Federal Trade Commission."

Kendall stopped suddenly and stared down at his mother in shock. A slow smile spread across his face as the gravity of her words sank in. "Attagirl, Becca."

Chapter Twenty-Five

RIDGE BOUNCED HIS LEG AND CHECKED HIS WATCH AGAIN.

"Relax, Dandridge," Marks said. "Chief McKinley is never late."

He blew out a breath and stood. Outward displays of anxiousness were unlike him, but the meeting in Hinesville was too important to blow. Carmen might be able to give him the first solid lead he'd had on Sheldon Harris in three freaking years, and the responsibility he felt toward Carmen and her kids pressed heavily on his shoulders. And that wasn't all.

Marks was someone he admired, and earning her respect hadn't come easily. The trust she'd placed in him and her regard for his character would crumble if he continued to keep his relationship with Kendall a secret. And if she found out through other channels or if his decisions reflected poorly on her...he would be toast.

"Something else on your mind, Dandridge?"

He snapped his head up and met her shrewd gaze. Of course she hadn't missed his uncharacteristic behavior. It was on the tip of his tongue to come clean, but Chief McKinley strode into Marks's office before he could respond.

"Sorry to keep you waiting," she said, extending a hand to Ridge. Nell McKinley's grip was as firm and no-nonsense as her demeanor. She was nearly as tall as Ridge, and her Nordic heritage had given her glacial eyes and cheekbones, both sharp enough to slice cheese. "It's good to see you, Dandridge."

"Ma'am," he said with a nod.

Marks stood up and joined them. McKinley towered over her, but Marks reminded Ridge of a stick of dynamite—small but deadly. "Let's get on the road before Dandridge wears a hole in my floor."

"Nervous?" McKinley asked as they filed out into the hallway.

Yes, ma'am," he replied honestly. "A lot rides on the success of this interview." He longed for the day when he could call Rashanda's parents and tell them Harris was in custody.

McKinley fell into step with him. "We'll have an hour to come up with a strategy."

"I'll drive," Marks said. "No offense, Dandridge, but I don't want to get caught up in the prank war going on with your team."

"I was an innocent victim," he said. *This time.* Ridge had instigated his fair share of trouble over the past five years. He'd miss the team like crazy when he moved on.

Marks snorted. "Save it for someone who'll fall for that puppy dog expression."

"Yes, ma'am."

During the hour-long drive, the trio discussed various strategies based on what little Ridge knew about Carmen's personality. Then they explored the different outcomes they faced, ranging from walking away empty-handed to moving Carmen and her family into protective custody. As extreme as the options sounded, there wasn't a whole lot of middle ground to give. Carmen either had the information they needed to crack the cartel's organization, or she didn't. If she possessed proof, would she use it.

They arrived at the diner fifteen minutes early, but Carmen was already there and seated in a rear corner booth with three children and an older woman Ridge assumed was her mother. Carmen held up a finger, and Ridge acknowledged her with a nod.

Ridge, Marks, and McKinley sat down at a table in the opposite corner of the restaurant. In the car, he'd been too nervous to even think about eating, but the tantalizing aromas wafting through the dining room had him rethinking his plans to skip lunch. It also reminded him of the night he'd just shared with Kendall, which stirred reactions he didn't want to encourage.

Ridge sat where he could keep an eye on Carmen until their waitress swung by to take their drink orders. After she moved on, Ridge noticed Carmen appeared to be having an intense conversation with the other woman. He couldn't hear them over the din of the lunch crowd, but both women wore pinched expressions and gestured with their hands. If Ridge had to guess, Carmen's mother was trying to talk her out of meeting with them. He couldn't blame her. Ridge hoped Carmen would allow them to address her fears.

The waitress returned with their drinks, cutting off his view of the two women once more. "Do you know what you want to eat, or do you need another minute?"

Ridge hadn't so much as glanced at the menu yet. "We'll need a few minutes."

"Sure thing."

The waitress moved on to the next table, allowing Ridge to check in on Carmen. His heart stalled when she wasn't in the booth but relaxed when he saw her mother and children were still there. Carmen's mother pinned him with a hard stare, then pointed to the hallway at the back of the diner. Above the archway was a restroom sign. Ridge nodded at the woman and took a sip of his too-sweet tea.

"Whoa," he said, reaching for a glass of water to wash away the sugary residue clinging to his mouth.

"Mmhmm," Marks said. "I didn't ask for a glass of sugar with a splash of tea."

A moment later, Carmen exited the bathroom and made her way to their table. She pulled out the chair next to Ridge then blew a kiss to her kids across the room. Her mother pulled out some coloring books and crayons from a large purse. The kids forgot all about their mother as they argued over the items.

"Cute kids," Ridge said.

"Thanks. I think so too."

Ridge introduced Carmen to Marks and McKinley."

"I wish I could say it was nice to meet you," Carmen said.

McKinley cracked a smile. "I'm used to it."

Ridge wondered if he should warm Carmen up with small talk or cut right to the chase. This wasn't a date, and he didn't want to insult her intelligence.

Carmen reached into her tote and removed a flash drive, proving she had no misconception about who was truly in the driver's seat. "I have audio files on this. Do you have anything you can plug it into?"

McKinley retrieved a laptop from the messenger bag she'd stowed beneath the table and inserted a pair of earbuds before accepting the flash drive. The deputy chief averted her eyes as she listened but snapped her gaze up to meet Carmen's within a few seconds. Ridge's pulse hammered as his imagination kicked in. McKinley showed him mercy by not making him wait for long, handing the laptop and earbuds to him.

The noise-canceling headphones blocked out eighty percent of the noise around him, making Ridge feel like he was locked in a tunnel where the only sound he heard was his own pounding heart. He forced himself to calm down and push play.

"Did you have anything to do with shooting the little girl, Willie?" Carmen asked on the recording. A muffled sound came in response, and it took Ridge a second to realize it was an anguished sob.

"She wasn't supposed to get hurt," Willie replied. "Harris got careless."

Carmen burst into tears. "Rashanda was in our daughter's class. How are you going to look her mother in the eye, knowing what you did?"

"Melodee's not my daughter. Stop calling her that."

"You're the only daddy she's ever known," Carmen argued.

"Not my fault you fucked nothing but losers before we met," Willie snarled. "And I didn't shoot the girl. I don't harm no kids. I just drove the vehicle. Harris pulled the trigger."

Ridge listened raptly, wanting to hear Willie say Rashanda's name. Without it, this recording was probably worthless.

"You gotta turn him in, Willie."

"Fuck you, bitch," Willie snarled. "I'm not spending the rest of my life in prison. I already told you I didn't shoot Rashanda. Harris did. What're you asking all these questions for? You fucking crazy all of a sudden? Just shut up about it." And there it was. Proof Willie had been driving the vehicle when Harris shot Rashanda.

"You didn't just drive the car, Willie. You took care of the cleanup, didn't you?" Carmen pressed. "Harris doesn't wipe his own ass at this point, so there's no fucking way he got rid of the gun. Turn it over to the police. They can trace it—"

A loud slap echoed through the earbuds, and Ridge flinched as Carmen could be heard crying on the recording.

"Shut your whore mouth before I do it for you. Is that what you want? Keep causing trouble, and I'll make sure it stays closed for good." A gagging sound came from the recording, and Ridge suspected Willie had wrapped his hands around her throat. Ridge suddenly found it hard to breathe until the recording stopped abruptly.

He met Carmen's gaze. "You're very brave."

Tears filled her eyes. "Not yet, but I will be." She took a deep breath and looked at the women sitting across from them. "That's just the tip of the iceberg. I have hours of recordings." Carmen met Ridge's gaze. "This one is for you. I can tell how much getting justice for Rashanda means to you." She looked at Marks and McKinley. "I need some promises if you want the rest."

This was the part of the negotiation that could go sideways. Most of the people in WITSEC were connected to unsavory people or circumstances. Yes, there were a few who had unfortunate luck and wound up in the wrong place at the wrong time, but usually, they were scratching the feds' backs to save their own asses or the asses of someone they loved. They'd been asked to overturn convictions and other things beyond their scope and reach. Ridge didn't know enough about Carmen to even guess what her stipulations were.

"I just want a fresh start in a new city," she said. "I want to go to nursing school, I want to live in a safe neighborhood, and I want my kids to have opportunities."

"That's it?" Marks asked.

Carmen nodded. "It would be everything I've ever dreamed of."

"Why did Willie tell you these things?" McKinley asked.

"He's not the badass he wants everyone to believe. Sure, he can rough me up, but killing kids isn't something he'd ever willingly do." Ridge could point out that pedaling drugs and guns did, in fact, kill plenty of children, but he didn't want to piss her off. "As you heard, my daughter went to school with Rashanda. Willie and I attended the little girl's funeral and comforted Melodee when she had nightmares." Carmen took a deep breath. "And she wasn't the only one suffering restless nights. I thought Willie's restlessness was because he wanted to be a good parent until I caught him sobbing in the dark one night after we'd gotten Mel back to sleep. I knew he was involved, and it would only be a matter of time before he wanted to talk. I was ready to capture that conversation and every one since."

"Were any of these confessions coerced through alcohol, drugs, or any other means?" McKinley asked.

Carmen snorted. "Other means? Like sex?"

Of course the waitress chose that moment to arrive. She blinked a few times and offered to leave again, but the group ordered. After the heavy meal he'd consumed with Kendall, Ridge ordered the same grilled chicken and strawberry salad Marks ordered.

"I didn't coerce any of the confessions from Willie," Carmen said once they were alone again. "You'll be able to tell that when you listen to them." She ran through the highlight reel of confessions, which was enough to impress his stoic bosses. According to Carmen, Willie wasn't shy about discussing the names of cartel associates he worked with or their processes for moving their product into and around the US. "Plus the dirty cops and politicians on their payroll." The last part made Ridge sick to his stomach, even though it was expected.

"We'll have to authenticate the recordings and make sure they weren't altered," McKinley said.

Carmen didn't flinch. "I wouldn't expect anything less, ma'am." She glanced across the diner and gave her mother a thumbs up. "Saying goodbye to my mama is going to hurt so bad."

Marks leaned across the table. "She can come with you."

Carmen sat up straighter and stared at Marks. "Are you for real right now?"

"As real as the sugar in this damn tea."

Carmen smiled. "Thank you."

Marks nodded at her before turning her attention to Ridge. "Get your partner down here to help you relocate the witnesses."

"Now?" Carmen asked. "I wasn't followed."

"That you know of," McKinley said. "You were smart to pick a public meeting place, but there's no guarantee Willie's guys aren't outside watching the place. We'll tuck your family away in a safehouse for now and will move you to a permanent location once we get a plan in place."

"Oh god," Carmen said. "This is really happening."

"You've got this," Ridge assured her. "And we've got you."

Chapter Twenty-Six

KENDALL SET HIS GRILLED CHEESE SANDWICH DOWN AND LOOKED across the table in the employee breakroom. "What do you think of the Envy sauce?"

Emmett wiped his mouth and took a long drink of water. Kendall had passed the first hurdle, which was impressing Chef Mike and the line cooks. The next phase was testing it out on a few volunteers. Some of the staff had been suspicious of the green sauce, but not Emmett. Chef Mike had given the fearless bartender two different options to test: wings tossed in the sauce and naked wings with the sauce on the side.

"Or do you want me to address you by the name given to you on your planet?" They'd had some good laughs over the alien suggestion, but Emmett hadn't flirted with him since the night Ridge had shown up at the club.

"Your human ears wouldn't comprehend the sounds, and you certainly wouldn't be able to pronounce it."

Laughing, Kendall rolled his eyes. "Try me."

Emmett looked left and right as if making sure no one was too close to overhear his secret. Then he opened his mouth and released a sequence of the most ridiculous noises Kendall had ever heard in his life. Before Emmett finished, Kendall leaned against his chair and hoped he wouldn't fall off from laughing so hard.

Straightening, Kendall wiped at the tears sliding down his face and stuck out his hand. "Nice to meet you, Steve."

Emmett widened his eyes dramatically as he shook Kendall's proffered hand. "You *are* one of us."

Kendall held a finger to his lips. "Don't tell."

The bartender crossed his heart theatrically, then resumed eating the wings. After two more of each—coated and naked but dipped—Emmett sat back in his chair. He cleaned his hands carefully and mopped the sweat dotting his forehead.

"Fucking fantastic," he finally said. "That's what you should call them."

"Mike insists on keeping it classy," Kendall said. He asked Emmett a series of questions and made notes. By the time he finished, he was confident the flavor profile was what he was looking for but worried the sauce was too hot and the color made it unpalatable. Those were things he could work out with Mike. The color was probably easier to work around than the heat level. "Thanks for being brave enough to eat them and provide feedback."

Emmett winked. "Anytime." *Okay. So he flirted a little.*

Seth burst into the breakroom. "Kendall! There you are. I've been looking all over for you."

"I told Colt I was taking my break a little early."

"Yeah, but a break for you consists of five minutes alone in your office, which is where I dropped your handsome visitor," Seth told him.

Kendall stood up, his heart racing as he picked up his notebook and pen. He forced himself to finish the partially eaten triangle of grilled cheese and offered the uneaten one to Emmett, who'd devoured it before he cleared the breakroom.

"Handsome visitor?" he asked.

Seth fell into step with him. "You're having a banner week, my friend."

"Who is it?"

Shrugging, Seth said, "Never seen him before. Very handsome, though."

Kendall racked his brain for the possible identity of his visitor but remained clueless. "But you thought it was okay to leave him alone in my office?"

Seth grimaced. "Okay. Maybe that wasn't the smartest idea. He's very, very handsome. Oh! He claimed to be a personal friend."

"Well, in the future, keep any personal friends at the host station until I come out or seat them in the dining room," Kendall said.

"Even your favorite marshal?"

"I don't think he'll be a frequent visitor."

Seth smirked. "But if he is?"

"The rule doesn't apply to him."

"I knew it."

Kendall looped his arm around Seth's neck when they reached his office and rubbed his knuckles over the host's hair. "You know nothing of the sort."

Seth landed a few light punches to Kendall's middle before he managed to pull free. "Keep telling yourself that. And until the marshal shows up, enjoy this hottie for me."

Kendall waited until Seth disappeared around the corner before he opened his door. His visitor rose from a chair, and Kendall came to a sudden halt as if he'd smashed into an invisible wall.

Travis rushed toward him. "Are you okay?"

Kendall pulled himself out of his stupor when Travis reached for him. He automatically took a step back to avoid the contact. Travis stilled his hand midair, and a deep V formed between his brows. He took a deep breath, lowered his hand, and gave Kendall the space his body language demanded.

Steeling himself for something unpleasant, Kendall stepped inside the office and closed the door. "I'm sorry about Stanton," he said, breaking the awkward silence.

Travis laughed, and Kendall was pleased it sounded genuine. And sober.

"No, you're not," Travis said as he dropped into a chair.

Kendall shrugged. "Maybe I'm not sorry on his behalf, but I am worried about the impact this will have on my mom. And you," he added.

Travis smiled, but it didn't reach his eyes. "Thanks. How is Rebecca doing?"

"As good as can be expected, I guess. She submitted her résumé for a couple jobs, and we went shopping for a few interview outfits. Thanks for checking on her and making sure she had some cash."

"Of course." Travis blew out a harsh breath, then sprang to his feet. Kendall silently watched him pace around the office. Travis ran a hand through his hair and mumbled something incoherent, but his words weren't meant for Kendall's ears. He'd seen Travis in a similar state before and knew he'd eventually get his thoughts off his chest. He stopped suddenly and faced Kendall. "How do you do it?"

"I'm afraid you'll need to be more specific," Kendall replied, even though he had a pretty good idea what Travis meant.

"Live authentically or whatever the head shrinkers are calling it these days."

"Well, absolutely no one refers to therapy as head shrinking anymore," Kendall said. Travis arched a brow. They knew plenty of people who would refer to it as such; Stanton Burkhart being the primary offender. "Okay, so no one who would actually benefit from the sessions calls it that." A person had to believe in the process and want to change before it could happen. "Therapy, Travis. Say it with me." Kendall repeated the word slowly, and though Travis didn't join in, a genuine smile briefly tugged at his lips. Kendall cocked a brow, and he threw his hands in the air.

"Therapy," Travis said, drawing the word out so it was obnoxiously long. "Are you happy now?"

Kendall snorted. "I'll be happier if you give it an honest try. Stan has really done a number on you, Trav. You can't undo his kind of influence through drinking, drugs, or wishful thinking. Do you really want to live an authentic life?"

Travis slowly crossed the room and lowered himself into the chair. "Yeah."

"It starts with honesty, and I'm talking the brutal kind. You have to be willing to take responsibility for your actions and deeds."

"You mean I can't just bitch about how my mother dared to die in a freak accident and left me alone with a heartless bastard of a father?"

"Therapy isn't about passing all the blame onto others, but it will help you see why you made some of your decisions. You can't heal if you don't acknowledge your mistakes."

Travis shot to his feet and resumed his pacing. Unlike the first time, Travis wasn't searching for a way to get things off his chest. He was fighting the urge to unleash his feelings.

Kendall had seen this before too. "Don't hold back."

Travis stopped suddenly and pinned Kendall with a sharp stare. "I'm so angry, Kendall. I don't even know how to process it all. I've spent my entire life trying to live up to my father's impossible standards, and he…" Travis's voice broke, and his lips formed silent words as if they were too incomprehensible to speak.

"Your father has been accused of many things right now, but he hasn't been convicted of any of them," Kendall reminded him. He didn't dare mention that his mother had been the whistleblower. It would probably come out eventually, and he'd deal with the fallout then. "Things look very damning, but maybe…I can't believe I'm about to say this." He took a deep breath. "Maybe you give him the benefit of the doubt until you can talk to him or see the evidence they have against him. You're an accountant, and you'll be able to make sense of the numbers."

Travis huffed a heavy sigh. "I'm an accountant my father refused to bring on board at his company. That alone makes me extremely suspicious of his actions."

"Nepotism," Kendall pointed out. "Maybe there were company rules in place to avoid it."

"His business partner's kids worked for the company. He was stealing even back then, Kendall. It's the only explanation. All this time, I've been kicking myself in the ass for not being good enough."

"You're more than good enough," Kendall said. "You landed a job as CFO for a global corporation before your thirtieth birthday. They don't just hand a title like that to any ole bean counter."

Travis chuckled. "God, I want to believe you. I don't want my worth to be tied to Stanton Burkhart anymore. What do I do?"

"You go on and live your best life. What better revenge will there be when your dad spends the rest of his days in prison? Maybe he'll see pictures of your big gay wedding in the society pages."

"Oh, that's devious. I like it," Travis said.

"Well, you can't exist solely on revenge unless you want to become a vigilante. The first step is healing. It will make your revenge even sweeter because your happiness will be genuine and fulfilling. Anger and hatred will just leave you cold and brittle."

Travis shivered. "Like Stanton."

"Yes," Kendall agreed.

Travis cocked his head. "How'd you get so smart?"

His situation with Ridge was the opposite of clever, but Kendall was having difficulty finding remorse over it. "I'm not always, but you asked how I live an authentic life. This is me keeping it real."

Nodding, Travis said. "You think therapy will help me?"

"If you meet your therapist halfway. They can't do the work for you."

Kendall opened his desk drawer and pulled out a pad of sticky notes.

He scribbled a name and number on the top sheet, pulled it off, and handed it to Travis. "Karen is a wonderful therapist, and I think she'd be a good fit for you. She instinctively knows when to push and when to pull back." Kendall grinned as Travis scowled at the note. "She also knows when you're trying to bullshit her, so don't bother trying."

Travis's chin notched upward, and their eyes locked. "Sounds like you've tried to pull one over on her a time or two."

Kendall laughed as he recalled her gentle but firm rebukes. "Yep."

"Well," Travis said softly, "therapy seems to have worked wonders for you."

Kendall chuckled. "For the most part, but the temptation to fall back on bad habits is hard to overcome." Like falling for another guy whose heart he could never win.

Travis nodded. "I imagine apologizing to people you've hurt is a good start."

"Yeah, and it's as difficult as you're imagining right now. You put yourself out there and hope the person forgives you. The harsh reality is they may still want to cling to their anger, and that's their choice. You just try to forgive yourself. Can I be brutally honest with you?"

"Of course," Travis said.

"It's easier to receive grace from other people than it is to offer it to yourself."

Travis tilted his head. "Yeah, I can see that. Do you mind if I give it a practice run?"

"Here? Like role-playing?"

"Not exactly," Travis said. He stepped forward but didn't round the desk or reach for Kendall. "Of all the people I've hurt, I regret none of them more than you." Travis took a shaky breath. "You quickly became a beacon of light and goodness in my life, and I betrayed that. First by pursuing you romantically, and later by making you feel unworthy." Travis closed his eyes. "If I could go back and do things over…"

"You wouldn't have been my first love?"

Travis snapped his eyes open, and Kendall saw a bevy of emotion he hadn't expected. "I'll never apologize for or regret our connection. Just the awful way I behaved afterward. All I ever wanted was to be with you, but I would've had to forgo everything else. I didn't think the sacrifice was worth it."

He'd always known Travis would never belong to him, but hearing him admit the reasons why cut Kendall to the quick. "Because you didn't really love me. It was just infatuation."

Travis shook his head. "I was wrong then, and you're wrong now. Can you forgive me?"

Kendall's heart stuttered to a stop. "I already have."

Travis sighed, and tension melted from his tall frame. "I understand it's too late for us to be more than friends, and I respect that. I hope to have your friendship someday." Travis shook his head. "No. I'm going to work hard to earn it. You can't be doling it out willy-nilly like with your lemonade stand."

"Willy-nilly? My booth made a killing. Remind me how many cookies you sold when you set up a competing stand? Five dollars for a single cookie was too steep, even in our overpriced neighborhood."

"Cheap bastards drove right by me in their Bentleys and Mercedes," Travis groused. "And I'll have you know, I still made more money, even though you moved more product, because my sales covered the cost of production, whereas your cheap-ass lemonade barely broke even."

Kendall was laughing so hard by the time Travis finished that he had to lean on his desk. "We're going to be okay, Trav. We really are."

"What about you and your mom?"

"Time will tell, but I have a good feeling," Kendall said.

"Good." Travis rubbed the back of his neck. "Think we could have lunch soon?"

"Yeah. That sounds nice."

Travis smiled ruefully. "And maybe you could properly introduce me to Seth."

"Prove you deserve an introduction, and I will."

Travis nodded. "Take care, Kendall."

"You too."

After an awkward lull, Travis took a few steps back. He lifted the sticky note with Karen's name and number. "I'll call her in the morning."

"You won't regret it."

Travis crossed his fingers and exited Kendall's office, leaving him alone with his swirling thoughts. Sitting around and mulling things over was the absolute last thing Kendall needed at the moment, so he got up and headed out to the club. He greeted patrons and stepped in to assist the staff wherever he was needed.

He stayed so busy that it was closing time before he knew it. After the patrons left, the lights went up, and the music went down, even though the DJ still entertained them as they closed. His new favorite song, "Dancing with a Stranger," came on, and it reminded Kendall of the time Ridge had caught him dancing to it. Kendall stopped wiping down a table, closed his eyes, and swayed to the music. When he reopened them, he found his favorite marshal leaning against the table next to his. It was like he'd conjured him out of nowhere.

I want to see him naked. Kendall closed his eyes and spun around, but Ridge was still dressed when he tested his newfound powers. "Damn. You still have clothes on."

Ridge walked to him, placed his hands on his, and pulled Kendall flush against his body. "For now." Ridge dropped a kiss on his lips, then said, "Teach me to dance."

"Here? Now?"

"It's clear you love this song."

Kendall didn't question it; he just started moving. Ridge was stiff at first, but he loosened up a little more with each beat. "Move your body with mine. Mirror what I'm doing."

Ridge tightened his grip on Kendall's hips and swayed with him. It felt as intimate as having sex, and Kendall was equally as turned on. He saw the answering lust sparking in Ridge's eyes. He released Kendall's hips to cup his head. Ridge captured his lips in a deep, devouring kiss while continuing to sway to the music.

The music stopped abruptly, and a booming voice said, "I'm thinking you two should take that on home."

Ridge and Kendall jerked apart. Kendall looked over at the DJ booth, and Curtis blew him kisses. Catcalls erupted all around them, so Kendall took Ridge by the hand and led him out of the club. They started kissing again as soon as they exited through the door. Kendall took advantage of the shadows out back to drop his hand and squeeze Ridge's cock through his pants.

Ridge sucked in a sharp breath. "Fuck, I need you."

His lust only encouraged Kendall. He pushed Ridge against the hood of his car, then dropped to his knees. Ridge groaned and tightened his hands in Kendall's hair as he made quick work of his belt and pants.

"We shouldn't." Ridge whispered. Kendall smiled at the sheer lack of conviction in Ridge's voice, then wrapped his lips around his cockhead. "Baby, someone—" Ridge's protest became a guttural groan when Kendall swallowed him down to the base. Ridge tightened his hand in Kendall's hair, working his dick in and out of Kendall's eager mouth.

He continued sucking Ridge off until his big thighs trembled. Kendall pulled back suddenly, letting Ridge's erection slide from his mouth.

"What?" Ridge asked when Kendall stood up. "You're just going to leave me like this?"

"I figured I'd drive you around to your SUV so we could finish this at home. I seem to recall a blue silk tie hanging around my bedpost and an unfulfilled promise."

"You little minx," Ridge growled as he tucked his cock away. "You're going to pay for this."

Kendall blew him a kiss as he unlocked his car. "Here's hoping."

Ridge was all hands and lips during the short drive to the front lot, and Kendall barely managed to avoid crashing into a parked car. The dome light felt especially bright when Ridge shoved the passenger door open.

"Drive carefully," Ridge said, pinning him with a dark look before shutting the door.

Kendall rolled the window down and called out Ridge's name. He turned around, and Kendall said, "I hope you don't mind, but I stained your tie this morning."

"With what?"

Kendall laughed and hit the accelerator, nearly jumping the curb when he turned to exit the parking lot. Ridge caught up to him quickly, his headlights looking big and menacing in Kendall's rearview mirror. His phone rang, and he knew who was calling without looking.

"Hello."

"What kind of stain did you get on my tie?"

"Oh, I think you know exactly what I leaked onto it."

Ridge growled, and Kendall laughed as he approached the next intersection. The traffic light turned yellow, and instead of stopping, Kendall pushed down harder on the gas. He glanced up, expecting Ridge to stop, and was shocked to see his front grill looming even closer.

Kendall gasped in mock outrage. "You just disobeyed a traffic law, deputy."

"I need you," Ridge growled.

Thank fuck the rest of the traffic lights were in their favor, and no innocent bystanders were harmed in their horny pursuit of each other. Kendall didn't bother waiting for Ridge; he headed straight for the front door, knowing two-hundred-plus pounds of muscle would be right behind him.

They fell into the house, all roaming hands and hungry lips.

Ridge gripped Kendall's cock through his dress pants, setting off fireworks behind his closed eyelids. Ridge dropped to his knees and released Kendall's cock, licking and sucking until Kendall was an incoherent mess of thrusting hips and snarly growls.

Ridge released him as quickly as Kendall had done to him back in the dark parking lot. Glaring, Kendall said, "Finish me off."

"Make me," Ridge said as he backed toward the hallway. He peeled his polo shirt over his head and tossed it to the ground.

Sammy released a low growl and ran for cover behind the couch.

Kendall pushed off the door and caught up to Ridge halfway down the hall. He pressed his bare chest against the wall of muscle and practically purred at the heat and energy radiating off Ridge. They were entirely naked by the time they reached Kendall's bedroom, both their cocks erect and shiny with precum.

Ridge grabbed the tie off his bed and inspected it closely. When he saw the dried cum, he snapped his head up to meet Kendall's gaze. Ridge's nostrils flared, and he lifted the fabric to his nose, inhaling deeply.

"Next time, I want to watch," Ridge said.

"Now?"

Ridge shook his head. "Now, I want you to come on my cock."

He slid onto the bed and positioned himself so Kendall could secure his hands over his head. Kendall climbed onto the bed and straddled Ridge's chest, letting his dick drool on the handsome face beneath it while he secured one end of the tie around Ridge's hands and the other around a curlicue scroll cut into the headboard.

He gave the tie a sharp tug to make sure it was secure before checking on his prisoner. Wicked brown eyes met his as Ridge jutted his tongue out to lick Kendall's precum off his lips.

"Like that, do you?"

Ridge lifted his head and licked the underside of Kendall's dick. He rocked his hips forward so he could feel the wet friction from base to tip. Then Kendall pushed the weeping head inside Ridge's mouth, feeding him his shaft until he met resistance. Ridge breathed deeply through his nose and swallowed around Kendall's cock. Fuck, he wouldn't last long if Ridge kept this up.

Kendall pulled back, rocking his erection against Ridge's tongue again and repeating the deep penetration until his balls pulled tight. He knew it was time to move on and leaned over to retrieve a condom and lube from his nightstand. He dropped them on the bed beside Ridge before kissing a path down Ridge's delicious body, stopping to savor, explore, and entice.

"Bring your cock back up here," Ridge said. "I didn't get enough."

"Huh-uh." Kendall dipped his tongue inside Ridge's navel before sucking the sensitive skin above it. "I'm calling the shots." Kendall looked up the length of Ridge's body and locked in on his dark, hot gaze. "I decide who shoots, where, and when."

"I think you're liking this a little too much."

"I think so too." Having Ridge under his control had gone to his head, but Kendall wouldn't leave the other man wanting for anything, especially not pleasure.

Kendall continued his exploration, dragging his nose through the trimmed curls at the base of Ridge's cock. Fuck. He smelled so good.

"Your mouth," Ridge whined. "Give me your mouth."

Kendall chuckled, then kissed and licked everything but Ridge's cock, taking plenty of time to suck and lick his balls and taint. Every moan and groan only amped Kendall's pleasure to a higher peak. He kept his gaze locked on Ridge's when he finally licked a path up his cock, circled the head, and sucked it deep inside his mouth. Ridge arched his hips, going deeper than Kendall had expected. He gagged a little but didn't panic. Kendall worked him until Ridge was on the edge but pulled back before he could climax.

"Evil. Pure evil. We'll both end up on the ID Channel. They'll call our episode 'Fucked to Death.' Suck me or fuck me, but please put me out of my misery."

Kendall let loose a wicked laugh. "So soon?" he asked even as he reached for the condom.

"Some of us didn't rub one out this morning."

"Bet you won't make that mistake again," Kendall said. Ridge stiffened and bowed off the bed when Kendall rolled the condom down the length of his cock. Of course, it might've been because he used his mouth and tongue.

"Get on my cock."

Kendall bit his lip to keep from laughing at the desperation in Ridge's eyes. His body looked tight enough to snap, and they couldn't have that. There was so much pleasure to be shared. Kendall straddled Ridge's thighs, facing away from him.

"What are you doing?"

Kendall poured some lube onto his fingers and rubbed them together to smear the moisture. He looked over his shoulder and caught Ridge staring hungrily at his ass. "Reverse cowboy for my cowboy." Ridge snapped his gaze up, but it didn't stay there long because Kendall eased his hand between his spread cheeks and began teasing his own hole with slick fingers.

Ridge tugged at his restraints and growled. "I can't believe I agreed to this."

If Ridge was stressed or uncomfortable, Kendall would've untied him. He was neither of those things—just extremely horny. So Kendall made a big show of stretching himself open before smearing additional lube on Ridge's cock.

"Christ, Kendall, you're killing me."

"With kindness, baby." Kendall sank all the way down onto Ridge's erection. Kendall's groan mingled with Ridge's euphoric cries. Indeed, he didn't think Kendall would get him off that quickly. He rested his ass against Ridge's pelvis and pressed his feet flat on the bed so he could rock and swivel on the cock buried deep in his ass. Kendall relished the sensation of being stuffed by this man, and he wouldn't be rushed, despite the begging and snarling going on behind him.

"Fuck me, please," Ridge begged hoarsely. "I want to come in your ass."

Kendall stilled his hips and looked over his shoulder. "Not until you need it more than oxygen."

Ridge bucked his hips upward, trying to get Kendall to bounce on his cock, but Kendall pushed the center of gravity into his ass to make it harder for Ridge to buck him off. Ridge surrendered with a growl and relaxed on the bed. But then he switched tactics. "Please, baby. I need you." Now they were getting somewhere.

Kendall took pity on him by using his thighs to slowly lift up and lower himself onto Ridge's erection.

"Fuck," Ridge snarled. "I can see your greedy ass taking every inch."

"I came up with this idea when I was jerking off this morning," Kendall said. His breath hitched, and he saw stars when Ridge's cockhead brushed against his prostate. "It's even better than I imagined." Kendall worked out a lot and practiced a ton of yoga, but his thighs screamed for mercy along with the sexy man beneath him. He leaned forward, pushing his fists into the mattress between Ridge's spread legs and using the leverage to ride his cock harder and faster.

"Baby, I need to come," Ridge said, his voice sounding guttural and desperate.

Kendall took pity on him, reaching between his splayed thighs to cup and massage his taut balls. Ridge shouted and bucked up, flooding the condom. He kept riding him until the big man melted into the mattress. Only then did he ease off Ridge's spent cock and crawl his way toward the head of the bed.

Ridge's dark eyes glittered with delirious delight, daring Kendall to be bad. He straddled Ridge's head and painted his lips with his dripping cock.

"Finish me off," Kendall instructed as he pushed his throbbing erection between Ridge's lips.

He knew it wouldn't take much, a few short thrusts in a hot, wet mouth, and Kendall's balls drew up tight. He pulled back at the last second and painted Ridge's lips, tongue, and chin with his release. Ridge moaned and licked it up, and Kendall had to taste himself on Ridge's tongue.

They kissed for several moments before Kendall eased up enough to release Ridge, who then rolled Kendall to his back, made himself at home between his legs, and they kissed and touched until they worked themselves up again.

The second time was slower and more intimate than anything Kendall had ever experienced. Ridge didn't just worship him with his body; his warm gaze promised things Kendall was afraid to believe in. Ridge's eyes silently searched his as if asking what would make Kendall happy. *This. You.* But he wasn't brave enough to speak the words out loud. Not yet.

Afterward, they lay together in a heap of sweaty, tangled limbs. Kendall pressed tighter into Ridge's embrace, burrowing into his heat as sleep pressed in on him.

"Please don't break my heart," he whispered. He thought Ridge might've already fallen asleep until he tightened his embrace and pressed a kiss to Kendall's forehead.

"I won't."

Chapter Twenty-Seven

"**S**O, CAN WE TALK ABOUT OUR GAME PLAN, OR ARE WE GOING to pretend we don't need one?"

"About Willie?"

It was a perfectly legitimate question since they were on their way to the county jail to meet with Willis "One-Eyed Willie" Morrison, his attorney, and the federal prosecutor overseeing the cartel investigation. For three days, they'd spent endless hours listening to recordings and had just peeled back the surface layers of the cartel's organization and reach. It would take a lot more investigating and a special grand jury to issue the sheer number of indictments they needed to make a dent in the evil empire, but Ridge was excited to serve the one that meant the most to him until he stood face-to-face with Sheldon Harris.

"Hardly, but nice try," Eddie said. "You know damn well I'm talking about Kendall and possibly the reason why you're wearing long-sleeved dress shirts during summer in Savannah."

Ridge fought the urge to rub the fabric burns beneath his shirt cuffs. It had been his first experience with any form of bondage, and he'd been unprepared for the marks it left behind. Kendall, also a novice, had felt awful and expressed remorse for binding his wrists so tightly. Ridge wasn't sorry. Wearing a lightweight dress shirt was a small price to pay for the most incredible experience of his life. Just thinking about it made him want to squirm.

"Stop thinking about sex with your man," Eddie griped from the passenger seat.

"I'm not." But now he was. "My fashion choices aren't your concern, buddy."

"They are when they're hiding something that could get you in big trouble."

Ridge glanced over at his best friend. "The worst Marks will do is fire me. How does that impact you?"

Eddie slugged him in the shoulder. "Stop being an idiot. I'd lose the best partner I've ever had, and I could get swept up in the tide that drags your ass out to sea."

Ridge hadn't really thought about how his deceptive behavior could affect his best friend. "I'm sorry."

"About which part? Falling for the guy or not having the conversation with Marks you agreed to have days ago?" Ridge had promised Eddie, but that was before the case against Willie and Harris had heated up. "Your tunnel vision will cause you to get blindsided. Makes me think of a few quarterbacks I played against. Brilliant athletes until you blitzed them."

"Blindsided by who? No one knows about my living situation," Ridge said.

"Kendall's mother knows. Do you really think she won't use the knowledge to her advantage?"

Kendall hadn't said much about the situation with his mom, but he had told Ridge Rebecca was the one who'd tipped off the FTC. Stan had gotten careless and left falsified documents on his desk, and Rebecca had overheard a few phone conversations between Stanton and his business partner. The news bumped her up in his esteem but only slightly. Ridge couldn't get past his thoughts of Kendall practically starving himself as a kid because he wanted to disappear.

Ridge tightened his grip on the steering wheel and forced his thoughts back to the conversation with Eddie. "I don't know."

And it was true. One good deed didn't make Rebecca Burkhart someone Ridge could trust. He'd seen firsthand what a damn good actress she was. No one involved in the raid would've known the blindsided, cheated wife was the person who'd triggered the avalanche.

Ridge and Kendall had spent very little time together since the cartel investigation had kicked into high gear, and the time they did steal wasn't spent discussing topics that might dampen the mood. Ridge had learned a lot about the kind of entertainment Kendall liked and got to witness the creative genius develop a new sauce for the club. It was delicious, and Ridge's praise made Kendall blush. Seducing the sauce's name from Kendall had left them both in a sticky, sweaty, and satiated mess. Ridge had volunteered to be Kendall's taste tester whenever he liked but regretted it when a look of sadness washed over Kendall's face.

Ridge's previous assertion that he would leave Savannah as soon as the case wrapped up still hovered over them like a depressing pall. He could dispel the gloomy cloud with just a few words but didn't. His relationship with Kendall was so new and right on the heels of a breakup. He'd promised not to break Kendall's heart and giving him false hope and flimsy promises would surely do just that because Ridge's urge to leave was still there. It wasn't as strong, and Ridge would be the first to admit it, but he also couldn't deny his reasoning might not be sound.

Kendall wasn't asking him for a commitment on any level, and Ridge wasn't going to volunteer one until he knew his affection for Kendall and the urge to stay weren't just fleeting emotions.

Eddie snapped his fingers. "Come back to me, buddy."

Ridge glanced over at him. "What?"

"I said, 'I don't know' isn't a good enough answer." Eddie chuckled and shook his head. "I know you've got it bad for the guy, and I'm overjoyed for you."

"You're just glad you can say *I told you so*."

"No, that's Zack. He's the smug bastard in this friendship."

Ridge laughed, but it didn't linger. "Eddie, I do care about Kendall a lot, but I'm not sure the relationship is serious enough to lay it all out there for Marks." The words felt all wrong, almost like a lie, which only ratcheted up Ridge's anxiety.

"You're an idiot," his friend said. "It may not be serious enough to keep you in Savannah, but I promise you the relationship is damaging enough to ruin your career in any city. That's where your brain needs to be right now, but you're so hyperfocused on—"

"Do not say sex or anything else that belittles Kendall," Ridge warned.

Eddie was silent for so long that Ridge glanced over at him again.

Eddie's smile was brilliant and rare, the one usually saved for talking to Jess or about her.

"Not that serious, huh? You're an idiot," Eddie finally said. "I wasn't going to say anything about Kendall. I was accusing you of being so hyperfocused on capturing Sheldon Harris that you weren't using your best judgment. See, right now, you're worried Marks will pull you off the cartel investigation if she finds out about your relationship with Stanton Burkhart's stepson."

Eddie wasn't wrong. Ridge had thought the exact thing too many times to count, though he'd never spoken his fear out loud. "Estranged stepson," he said, which was the closest he'd get to admitting his friend was right.

"Estranged? Didn't you tell me Kendall had been there that night for dinner?"

"And the staff can confirm he left abruptly," Ridge said.

"It won't be good enough for Marks, and we both know it." Eddie sighed. "Look, I don't want to see my best friend unhappy, whether you're only here for a few more weeks or you retire to Tybee Island at the end of a long career. Burkhart's lawyers will drag this out forever, and it will hang over your head until you come clean."

"I know."

"I have your back, Ridgey. No matter what happens. Just do me one favor."

"Name it."

"Stay away from Burkhart and his codefendant. Don't give the brass more ammunition to use against you."

Ridge took a deep breath, relieved to have Eddie on his side. The tension between them had been weighing heavily on his heart. "And what do you propose?"

"I don't care how you do it," Eddie said firmly. "Call in sick if you get assigned to transfer them or volunteer for more desk duty."

Ridge snorted. "Like that's not suspicious."

"No worse than you wearing long-sleeved shirts." Eddie quieted as they pulled up to the guard shack at the jail. Once they showed their credentials and drove through the gate, he started back up again. "So, handcuffs? Zip ties?"

"Shut the hell up, Eddie."

He continued guessing every outlandish thing he could think of until they entered the jail. Then their demeanor and conversation matched the tone of the upcoming meeting as they navigated the various security checkpoints. An undercurrent of euphoria spiked Ridge's bloodstream, making him feel a little buzzed when they greeted federal prosecutor Francesca Baro. The woman's sleek hair was pulled into a tight bun, displaying a face with delicate cheekbones and a vivid scar across her right cheek that made her look like a warrior ballerina.

"Gentlemen," she said as she shook their hands. "The accused is already in the interview room, but we're still waiting for his attorney to arrive."

Knowing Willie was on the other side of the steel door amped up Ridge's energy. A jovial laugh echoed down the hallway, and he turned to watch a tall, roguish man wearing an expensive suit and a wicked grin approach. Ridge had seen him before, of course, and couldn't help but notice Vincent Bianchi had more gray hair at his temples than the last time they'd met.

"Well, if it isn't my cousin Vinnie," Francesca said drolly.

"Seriously?" Eddie asked. "Are you really related, or are you spoofing on the movie?"

Bianchi laughed when he reached them. "Cousins by marriage." He leaned forward and kissed her offered cheek.

"Enemies by choice," she said, patting the taller man on the arm.

Their tones and demeanors were far too friendly to mark them as enemies, but that all changed when they entered the interrogation room. The pair immediately started arguing as soon as everyone was seated at the table. Ridge would've wondered what their family functions were like if he hadn't been focusing all his energy on staring Willie down.

The asshole had the nerve to look smug and unconcerned about the reason for their visit. The look never wavered as Willie refused to answer any of the questions Francesca asked him, and Bianchi silenced him on the few occasions it looked like Willie might break.

"My client knows nothing about the allegations you've just made," he said after the first hour passed. "And if you have any proof at all, you would've charged him by now."

That's when Francesca opened her laptop and hit play. Ridge had never been so grateful to sit in during an interview as he was the moment Willie realized they had him by the nuts. It didn't happen quickly; it was a slow awareness dawning over his features until his face became mottled with red splotches.

"That bitch!" Willie roared as he tried to lunge to his feet, but the ankle cuffs attached to a ring in the concrete prevented him from getting far. "I'll kill—"

"Enough, Willie," Bianchi growled angrily. "You're not helping. Let me handle this." He settled his client back down in his chair, then straightened his suit jacket. "You expect us to fall for this doctored recording?"

"I'll take my chances with a jury," Francesca said. "And this is just the tip of the iceberg, which you'll find out during discovery." Ridge held his breath while he waited for the next part. Francesca pulled the federal warrant out of her briefcase and handed it to Bianchi. She glanced at Ridge. "Will you do the honors?"

It would be his pleasure. Ridge smiled at her before meeting Willie's scowl. "Willis Morrison," Ridge began, then stated his formal charges before reading his rights. "The US Marshals Service is taking you into custody and transferring you to FCI in Jesup." Away from his local thugs and where they could isolate him to minimize Willie getting word out to his crew.

"Your plan won't work," Willie said when Ridge rose from his chair and came around the table to begin transportation. "I will never betray my brothers."

"Maybe so, but your days of breathing air as a free man are over, Willie. You're going to die in prison," Ridge said.

The drive to Jesup took over an hour. Willie didn't utter a single word, not that they attempted to interrogate him after he'd invoked his right to counsel. Just escorting Willie to federal prison was enough for now. The rest of the chips would fall into place soon enough. He didn't look so brave when the federal prison guards met them at the facility and looked even less so when he'd been remanded behind bars.

"Give Sheldon my love, Huckleberry," Willie bravely said once he was out of reach.

Ridge didn't know what the hell the huckleberry reference was all about. "Will do when I find him."

"Or he'll find you first." Willie's laughter echoed ominously as the guards dragged him deeper into the prison.

"Huckleberry?" Eddie asked as they stepped into the sunlight.

Regardless of the weather, the air was always fresher once he exited the prison. "I have no idea, but it sounds vaguely familiar."

"Me too. It's going to bug me until I remember," Eddie said.

It might drive Ridge crazy later, but not until after his euphoric buzz faded.

"Congratulations, Ridgey," Eddie said and clapped him on the shoulder. "I know we don't have Sheldon yet, but this is the next best thing."

It was, and Ridge knew precisely who he wanted to celebrate the victory with.

Chapter Twenty-Eight

"**P**ink, huh?" Chef Mike asked as they watched the timer for the fryer count down the last few seconds. "I'm not sure I like it better than the green."

"Kinda reminds me of sweet-and-sour sauce," Emmett said from Kendall's other side. "What's this one called?"

Ecstasy. But Kendall wasn't ready to share the name yet. It was just too personal. "I want to get your impressions first."

The kitchen doors swung open and Drew rushed in. "Am I too late?" he asked, loosening his tie. "I had a meeting with my banker, and he was especially chatty. Wouldn't stop talking about Burkhart and Jones." Kendall averted his eyes to the timer so no one would see his reaction to hearing Stan's name in one of his safe spaces. "I get why he wanted to assure me his firm wasn't robbing me blind, but geez."

The timer went off, silencing the conversation for the small group gathered in the kitchen. Kendall had chosen the slowest period of the day to do a test run of his latest creation, which meant several staff members had time to spare.

"Pink, huh?" Drew asked. "Guessing what the next color will be is almost as fun as tasting the sauce."

"I think someone is in his feels," Emmett said, nudging Kendall with his elbow.

"Love is a wonderful inspiration for food and art," Mike said as he coated the wings in the sauce.

When he finished, everyone took a wing and sank their teeth into the crisp skin. Kendall grinned as the collective group reacted to the flavor profile.

"Oh, it is sweet," Emmett said.

Mike nodded, then his eyes widened. "Oh, there it is."

Drew smiled as he chewed another bite. "The heat starts slow and toys with you a little before building to a big finish."

Like sex with Ridge. *Ecstasy.*

Emmett reached for the last wing and got his hand smacked by Mike. "What?"

"Go find something to do," the chef said.

Drew snagged the last wing and held it up in victory. "I'll just take this off your hands and end any fighting before it can start."

Emmett leaned in close. "If he weren't the boss, I'd sucker punch him and take the wing." He winked at Kendall. "You did damn good. That sauce could become addictive." *Like sex with Ridge.*

"Thanks," Kendall replied. He always loved pleasing his coworkers and club patrons, but their praise had a more profound effect when his creations were spawned by something so deeply personal.

The group disbanded once the chicken was gone, leaving Kendall, Drew, and Mike alone to chat.

"I don't care if it's pink," Mike said. "That's your best sauce yet."

Drew licked the tips of two fingers before Mike tossed a damp towel at him. "I agree. What's the name?"

Kendall averted his gaze and used the tip of his shoe to trace the grout line between floor tiles. "It's a little embarrassing. Not sure I want to put the name I came up with on the menu."

"No problem," Mike said, scanning the ingredient list. "I'll come up with a name based on a single ingredient and the flavor profile."

"Thanks, Mike."

Drew scanned the recipe too and looked at Kendall with a raised brow. "Pineapple juice?"

Kendall smiled and nodded. He thought it was quite possibly the most underrated fruit of them all.

"I know you're not on the clock right now, but do you have a few minutes to chat?" Drew asked.

"Sure."

They chatted about trivial things until they were alone in Drew's office. "I want to hear how you feel about the job. It was a pretty big change for you all of a sudden."

"I've learned I'm better at some things than I realized and need to step up my game in areas I thought would come more naturally to my personality."

"From where I sit, you're doing a wonderful job. I'm very pleased you accepted my offer," Drew said.

"Thank you. I appreciate the opportunity so much and didn't want you to regret your decision."

Drew leaned back in his chair and studied him closely. "I sense you're still not comfortable in the new role. Is there anything I can do to help you?"

"I just don't think managing people is in my wheelhouse. It doesn't come naturally to me."

"We'll agree to disagree on that one," Drew replied. "I think you might be judging yourself too harshly."

"Possibly. I'm just not convinced this is what I want to still be doing in ten years."

"Fair enough. What would you like to do?"

Kendall laughed dryly. "What I wouldn't give to know that answer."

"What are you passionate about?"

A man who's trying to solve a case so he can leave Savannah with a clear conscience. Kendall sighed because that wasn't what they were discussing. "Creating sauces for wings, but it's not a career."

"Says who?" Drew asked.

"It's a hobby at best."

"I disagree. Specialty restaurants are all the rage now. And what about food trucks? They used to just pop up at fairs and festivals. Not anymore."

"Me? Owning and operating a food truck? Can you imagine?"

"Absolutely. I think you'll succeed at whatever you put your mind to."

Kendall bit his bottom lip. "I wouldn't even know where to begin. I don't know anything about cooking commercially or running a business."

"I do," Drew said as he pulled a notebook and pen from a desk drawer. "Well, the business part, anyway. It just so happens I live with a

Michelin-starred chef." He did? "And Mike would also take you under his wing if Pierre isn't looking for an apprentice." Kendall just blinked as Drew steamrolled on. "Money is always the first consideration." He wrote the word and underlined it. "There's the cost of buying a used truck and refurbishing it." He wrote that down, then added the other things Kendall would want to research. "You'll also want to get quotes for business insurance and find out how much licensing fees will cost you."

Trucks, insurance, and licenses, oh my. Kendall's head started to spin, but he couldn't deny the picture forming in his head thrilled him.

"And once you're working with some solid figures, you'll decide how much of it you can do on your own and how much financial assistance you'll need. That's when you create a proposal. Your two obvious choices for assistance are a small business loan or finding investors who believe in your dream."

"Find investors, huh? You make it sound so simple."

"It can be if you know the right people." Drew set his pen down and gave Kendall his full attention. "And I think you know the right people."

Kendall was momentarily confused. Had Drew made the connection between Kendall and Stan? If so, he had to know his stepfather wasn't going to have enough money to buy a pack of gum when the feds got done with him.

"I can tell your mind has gone somewhere dark," Drew said. "I was talking about myself, and I wasn't proposing anything more than a business venture."

"Oh my god," Kendall said, dropping his face into his hands. After a few seconds, he met Drew's gaze once more. "Stanton Burkhart is my stepfather, so I initially thought you were talking about him."

"God no," Drew said. "Like he'll have any money left."

"Right?"

"And I already knew Burkhart was your stepfather." Drew winced. "I guess it slipped my mind when I was running my mouth in the kitchen a few minutes ago. Sorry about that."

"It's no problem, but how'd you know."

"The asshole offered me money to fire you when you first started working here. I told him to go fuck himself."

Kendall's mouth fell open, and he stared at Drew in shock. "Stan came here?" he asked once he recovered.

"God no. He sent some pompous asshole to do his dirty work."

Kendall covered his face once more. "This can't be my life."

"Oh, knock it off," Drew said. "I wouldn't have held his actions against you—then or now."

"But to get in business with me, knowing what you do about him…"

"You're not anything like Stan Burkhart. You'd go hungry before you'd steal from someone else."

Kendall sighed and nodded. "I have to give this idea some thought. I feel like I've been floundering without an anchor lately."

"Take all the time you need. This doesn't have to be a move you make right now. It's something you can plan ahead for and save some capital."

"Thanks, Drew."

His brain churned out the thoughts like an ice cream maker, but instead of a delicious frozen treat, Kendall ended up with a headache. He curled up with Sammy on the couch, closed his eyes, and willed his brain to settle down. The next thing he knew, warm lips pressed a greeting to his forehead. Kendall jerked awake and looked into the most beautiful brown eyes he'd ever seen.

The room wasn't quite dark, but the sun had shifted enough to cast the living room in shadow.

"I see you're trying to steal my guy," Ridge said warmly.

"Nah," Kendall said as he rubbed the sleep from his eyes. "I was just holding your spot until you got home. Sammy still loves you most."

Ridge cupped Kendall's face and kissed his lips. "I was talking about Sammy trying to steal you away from me."

Steal my guy. Oh, the way his heart bucked and leaped at the thought. But his hopes were dashed the next instant when Ridge updated him on the progress of his case. He couldn't say much, but Kendall saw Ridge's joy and pride in his beaming smile. He wouldn't begrudge Ridge his victory, and he was happy they were one step closer to justice for Rashanda Knight's family, so he replied with the enthusiastic embrace expected of him. Kendall held on a little tighter, inhaled Ridge's scent a little deeper, and lifted his shields a little higher.

Chapter Twenty-Nine

RIDGE'S LIFE BECAME AN ENDLESS STREAM OF SIXTEEN-HOUR workdays. Two dozen local, state, and federal investigators combed through everything Carmen had given them and cross-referenced the recordings to known cases both solved and unsolved. The task force combined old techniques, such as boots on the ground and surveillance, with new ones, like feeding the data into a supercomputer built by Kendall's friend, Jonah St. John, who worked for the Georgia Bureau of Investigations. The results of their tireless work resulted in Francesca presenting the case to a federal grand jury. The fate of their investigation was in the hands of twenty-three strangers.

It wasn't just the case hanging in the balance. Ridge was on the verge of gaining the freedom to leave with a clear conscience, so why did the mere thought of going make his stomach churn as if he'd overindulged in spicy food? Where had the sense of suffocation gone?

"That's a cute one," Eddie said, nudging him from his thoughts. "Did you know our Ridgey was an artist?"

"No," Zack said, "but I knew he met Todd at an art gallery. Makes more sense now."

Ridge focused his attention on the napkin he'd been absently doodling on. The rough sketch of a food truck wasn't what he'd call art, and Ridge had never thought of himself as an artist. He hadn't consciously set out to draw a symbol of the dream slowly taking root in Kendall's beautiful soul. Ridge started to crumple the napkin but thought better of it and smoothed out the paper before folding and tucking it away. To do what with it? Pretend Kendall hadn't been pulling away the past three weeks and present it to him? Pretend their kisses and intimate moments weren't tinged with desperation because their time together was slipping away? Had Kendall picked up extra hours shadowing a chef named Pierre because he was working toward ful-filling a dream, or was he avoiding Ridge? Was he eating?

The churning magnified, and Ridge pushed the plate with his half-eaten sandwich farther away from him.

"Are you sick?" Zack asked him. "You never leave food on your plate, and the Reuben is your favorite sandwich in this joint."

The *joint* was a café close to the courthouse, and they'd gathered there to eat while the grand jury deliberated on the cartel member's fate. And on Ridge's fate.

"Moping," Eddie replied. "Or maybe there's a battle waging deep within, huh? Busting Harris and moving on has lost its allure a little, yeah?"

Ridge glared at his friend but didn't comment. His look said it all.

"It's okay to admit defeat," Zack said.

"Or stop acting like a stubborn mule and acknowledge your plans have changed," Eddie added.

Ridge's phone rang before he could reply to his friends' harassment. Besides, what could he say that wasn't an outright lie? He was acting as stubborn as his father and his father's favorite mule. Ridge forgot all about his problems when he saw the identity of the caller.

"Dandridge," he said into the phone.

"I just received word the jury will be returning their verdicts in thirty minutes," Francesca said.

He only needed ten to hoof it back to the courthouse. "We're on our way."

"Go," Eddie said, pushing him from the booth. "We'll settle the bill and meet you there."

Adrenaline pumped through Ridge's veins like gasoline, feeding the fire burning in his gut. He wanted to run to the courthouse, but he would need to save his energy for what would follow because he refused to believe the indictments weren't coming.

He found Francesca and her co-counsel, Rafael Baez, standing outside the courtroom talking to Marks. All three wore confident expressions on their faces. He'd heard most lawyers were rarely surprised by an outcome in court, so Ridge took their assurance as a positive sign.

"I'll give the greenlight as soon as we have the indictments in hand," Marks said. "Are you ready?"

"Yes, ma'am." Truer words had never been spoken. Ridge might not know what lay ahead for his future, but he was certain busting Harris was part of the bigger scheme.

They'd planned for all contingencies before the hearing, and dozens of team members were on standby waiting to hear the results. It was ridiculous to think they'd isolated all the people Harris had on the inside, so waiting until after the indictments came down to plan the takedown mission was a recipe for disaster. They were not going to allow these scumbags to run.

Eddie and Zack arrived a few minutes later, and the group huddled together, talking quietly until the bailiff informed the prosecutors the jury would be seated momentarily. Since Marks had been the one to testify on the marshals' behalf, she was permitted to sit in during the session if the jury had additional questions. Since Ridge, Eddie, and Zack weren't there in an official capacity—transporting or providing judicial protection—they waited in the hallway. Ridge paced back and forth, working out the excess energy buzzing through him.

They only needed twelve out of twenty-three jurors to side with them. He reminded himself of how confident Francesca and Rafael looked. Eddie and Zack didn't tease him for once, which Ridge greatly appreciated. It seemed like an eternity before Marks rushed out through the double doors with her phone held to her ear in one hand and a stack of indictments in the other.

"Operation Karma is a go," she said, then disconnected.

"All of them?" Ridge asked hopefully.

"Every single one," she replied, slapping the indictments into Ridge's hand. "Gentlemen, you have work to do."

Eddie and Zack clapped Ridge on the back, and the trio set off for the exit. The papers would later describe Operation Karma as "shock and awe" and a "sweeping stance on organized crime." And it was just that. The task force had done their homework and knew the schedules of everyone involved. They knew where they'd be at any given time, making the arrests for nearly three dozen people swifter and easier. Shock and awe, indeed. The hard part was processing and questioning them all, which stretched on for days. Some lawyered up right away, while others seemed to enjoy cat-and-mouse games. None of the detainees gave a single clue until the fourth day when a runner who went by Skinny Pete, though he was neither skinny nor named Pete, referred to Ridge as Johnny Ringo instead of Pat Garrett and said Ridge looked like someone had just pissed on his grave.

And that's when the huckleberry reference clicked into place. Both he and Willie had loosely quoted lines from *Tombstone*. Doc Holliday had said similar lines in the movie, although Skinny Pete should've said he looked like someone had walked over his grave, not pissed on it. First the Pat Garrett reference and now Johnny Ringo? Was Sheldon Harris just a fan of westerns, or was there some hidden message there? Did Harris view himself as a modern-day Doc Holliday? And why the hell would they refer to Ridge as the outlaw in the scenario? Pat Garrett made sense but Johnny Ringo? And what did that make Willie? Wyatt Earp? No fucking way.

Ridge didn't let on he recognized the line, the movie, or the reference. He sat silently while Rafael Baez conducted the interviews. The prosecutors were the ones in the driver's seat after the marshals had made the arrests. Ridge just liked being an intimidating, scowling presence. He sat in as many interviews as possible, hoping word got to Harris that he wasn't backing down.

Desmond Bobbitt, a.k.a. Skinny Pete, made one other fortuitous slip by referencing Tiggy Barnes during questioning. Bobbitt didn't say Barnes's name, but the vague mention of a chubby, balding gunrunner with a Tigger tattoo was all Ridge needed to make the connection. Tiggy had never been directly connected to their cartel investigation, although it made sense. He'd deal with anyone who had the cash to pay for his services.

Tiggy looked genuinely surprised to see Ridge when he paid the man a visit. "Still having guy problems?" he asked.

Ridge didn't respond but was certainly glad they'd kept the conversation vague in Tiggy's presence. He wouldn't be able to live with himself if something terrible befell Kendall or even Todd.

"You're not dealing with Deputy Dandridge," Francesca said. "You're dealing with me."

Tiggy waggled his brows and raked a lewd gaze over her. "Now we're talking. How about you and I have a *private* conversation?"

"Don't make me tell your granny about your disgusting behavior," Ridge said.

Tiggy's face turned bright red. "You leave my granny out of it."

"What's she going to think when she finds out you're in bed with the Cardoza cartel?" Francesca asked.

Tiggy stiffened and tried to school his features into a neutral mask, but Ridge saw a flash of fear in his eyes. He could tell Francesca hadn't missed it either because she dove in hard and didn't let up. Tiggy had been a fool to waive his right to have his attorney present because he was no match for her. And just like that, they had a new direction.

Ridge left a message for Marks on his way back to the field office, and she called just as he pulled into the lot.

"Chief, I got intel Harris plans to enter the US through El Paso in two days," Ridge said when he answered. "We need to mobilize quickly. Get border patrol and—"

"I want you in my office yesterday, Dandridge." She disconnected without letting him respond.

Fuck, that didn't bode well for him, and he knew in his gut the shit had hit the fan. He just didn't know how.

"Have a seat," Marks said when he entered. Ridge hated the disapproving look she gave him. "Are you familiar with a social media account called Sassy in Savannah?"

Ridge just blinked. This wasn't at all the direction he expected. "No, ma'am."

She spun her laptop around to display a photo of him kissing Kendall in the club. It had been taken the night he asked Kendall to teach him how to dance. It should've worried Ridge that his first thought was how beautiful they looked together.

"The video is even nicer," Marks said. "Who knew a big guy like you could move so smoothly? I want to know everything about your relationship with Stanton Burkhart's stepson. And don't even think about lying to me."

"No, ma'am," Ridge said.

"Not even through omission." Her voice sounded low and deadly.

"No, ma'am." Ridge told her everything, starting at the beginning with his initial trip to The Cockpit after his breakup with Todd. She at least looked a little sympathetic after learning he'd found him in bed with his boss, but it didn't last long because Ridge told her about moving in with Kendall before the bust.

"When did you discover that the man you were *living with* was Stanton Burkhart's stepson?"

Ridge blew out a breath and rubbed the back of his neck. "The day after the bust, ma'am. Rebecca Burkhart, Kendall's mother, showed up at the house after her release, and we obviously recognized each other."

Marks cleared her throat. "I really don't want to ask personal questions about your relationship with Mr. Blakemore, but…" She took a deep breath and shook her head. "At what point did your relationship become intimate?"

"The night of the bust. Until then, we'd just circled around the attraction."

She crossed her arms over her chest. "And you obviously continued to have a romantic relationship with him once you realized his affiliation with Burkhart."

"He's not affiliated with Stanton Burkhart," Ridge said. "They're estranged. He barely has a relationship with his mother, though they are trying to work through their differences."

"Their estrangement won't be enough to save your job, Dandridge. The mere idea you were in a position to pass information between Burkhart and someone on the outside is enough to destroy your reputation and mine. Did you stop to think about that? What about Beaumont and Chandler? Do you think the brass will believe they weren't covering for you?"

"Ma'am, Zack and Eddie—"

"Save it, Dandridge," she said tersely.

"Can I ask how you ended up with the video and photo?" he asked. Was this something that had gone viral?

"My son, Andre, follows Sassy in Savannah and saw it. Apparently, they shared the video of Kendall taking down Rodney James too."

"I believe so, yes."

"The first video went viral, so you need to assume it's only a matter of time before the attorneys for Burkhart and Jones get their hands on this one. I won't be able to save your job when that happens. I am so disappointed, Dandridge."

"Ma'am, I understand you're furious. I should've been forthright about the situation from the start and taken action to mitigate the damage. I should never have kept this from you, and I apologize. I will resign immediately, but Zack and Eddie—"

"Are busy packing for the trip to El Paso, which I suggest you do as well."

Ridge's heart galloped. Dare he hope? "Ma'am?"

"I'm many things, but heartless isn't one of them. Pack your bags and be ready for wheels up at oh four hundred. I want a transfer request or a resignation letter on my desk as soon as you return from Texas."

"Yes, ma'am."

Ridge should've called Eddie and Zack after leaving the chief's office with his tail tucked between his legs, but all he could think about was getting to Kendall. He found him lounging on the couch with Sammy. His eyes were red and puffy, and Ridge didn't need to rely on years of training to figure out he'd been crying.

"Hey," Ridge said softly as he knelt beside the sofa. "I guess you saw the video."

Kendall sat up and blinked away tears. "What video?"

"The one Sassy in Savannah posted of us."

"What?" he shrieked.

Ridge told him about his conversation with Marks and watched in awe as Kendall's expression morphed from shock to anger. Kendall grabbed his phone off the coffee table and looked up the video.

"I'm going to kill him."

"Him, who? Do you know who Sassy in Savannah is?"

"I have a pretty damn good idea based on the camera angle," Kendall said. "I'll take care of it." He closed his eyes and sadness washed over his features again. "But the damage is already done. Your job—"

"Let me worry about it." Ridge pressed a light kiss to Kendall's lips. "I want to hear why you've been crying."

Kendall attempted to smile but failed miserably. "I was just watching a sappy movie."

Ridge moved to sit beside Kendall on the couch. Sammy huffed off with his tail twitching, and Kendall tucked himself under Ridge's arm. "Which one?"

Kendall sniffed. "I'm not saying. It's too embarrassing."

Ridge knew then that Kendall was lying to protect his feelings. The little minx wasn't shy about what he liked, so there was no reason to be embarrassed. Kendall had been crying because his heart had been breaking over the past few weeks, which was something Ridge had promised not to do.

He cleared his throat because the next part was going to be so hard. "I got the break I've been waiting for and have to leave for Texas soon."

Kendall sat up and looked into his eyes. "Is this it? The big one?"

Ridge nodded. The euphoria he'd expected to feel wasn't there. How could he be happy when Kendall's beautiful blue eyes swam with unshed tears.

"So, this is goodbye?"

Chapter Thirty

O F COURSE IT WAS. KENDALL COULDN'T BELIEVE HE'D ASKED such a dumb question. Ridge had been honest about his intentions from the start. And Kendall thought what? That their connection and chemistry would change Ridge's outlook on the future?

"I'm sorry," Kendall said, moving to put some space between them. "I didn't mean to put you on the spot."

Ridge's hand snaked out and grabbed his wrist before he could scoot too far away. "Don't." His voice suddenly sounded thick and raw as if he'd been yelling for hours. "Come here."

Kendall went to him, his heart in his throat when he straddled Ridge's thick thighs. The tears he'd tried to stem spilled down his face. He wanted to beg but wouldn't. Kendall might not have a lot to offer, but he had pride, and he'd cling to it until the worst of his heartbreak faded.

Ridge cupped his face and kissed him long, deep, and with so much emotion it only made him cry harder. Their kiss was tinged with Kendall's salty misery, which only made the sweetness of their embrace all the more acute. Losing Ridge would hurt far worse than the others, but he was a survivor. Kendall didn't want to spend what little time they had wallowing in self-pity when he could be indulging himself in Ridge. He'd rather choke on the words he yearned to speak in favor of having one last night with this man.

Kendall slid from his lap and extended his hand to Ridge. They didn't tear each other's clothes off like they usually did as they stumbled to the bedroom. Instead, they waited until they reached Kendall's room to slowly undress one another in between passionate kisses and adoring touches. They didn't come together in frenzied desperation once they climbed onto the bed either.

They took their time as if trying to burn the memory of every kiss and touch into their brains. When Ridge finally slid inside him, Kendall's eyes filled with tears again. He tried to turn his head to hide them, but Ridge wouldn't have it. He cupped Kendall's face, forcing him to meet his gaze. Kendall blinked, and his tears slid down his cheeks, clearing his vision and allowing him to see matching tracks trailing from Ridge's eyes.

He wasn't sure if he felt better or worse that Ridge was as miserable as he was. Kendall wouldn't let himself think about it because he'd either get his hopes up or he'd get angry. Neither emotion would help him, so he pushed his thoughts away and focused on making love with Ridge for the first time.

Kendall wasn't alone in his emotions either. Everything was different about Ridge from the reverent look in his eyes to the way he cherished Kendall with his hands, mouth, and body. It was so much more than sex, so different from all the times they'd been together before. Kendall tightened his hold around Ridge, pressing tighter against his muscular frame. He felt the telltale signs when Ridge was on the verge of orgasm. Instead of giving in to his desire, Ridge stilled, closed his eyes, and leaned his forehead against Kendall's.

"I'm not ready for it to be over."

Kendall wasn't sure if Ridge meant sex or their brief relationship, but it didn't matter. Both endings were inescapable. Kendall teased Ridge's lips open, then slid his tongue into Ridge's mouth. The big man shuddered in his embrace, gasped, and took over, dominating the kiss as he surged deeply into Kendall's body. The tempo morphed into the fierceness Kendall had come to expect, but the tender look in Ridge's dark eyes remained, even through a savage climax.

Afterward, they lay in a tangle in the center of the bed. Ridge kissed Kendall repeatedly as he trailed his fingers up and down Kendall's spine. These weren't the actions of a man who was eager to pack his meager belongings and get on the road.

"Can you have dinner with me, or do you need to leave?" Kendall asked.

Ridge pressed a kiss to his forehead, making the damn tears well up again. "I can stay longer. I don't board the plane until four." He carded his fingers through Kendall's damp hair. "This is where I want to be."

Leaning into his touch, Kendall said, "What do you feel like eating?"

Ridge rolled Kendall onto his back and said, "Who said anything about food?"

Meow.

Kendall opened his eyes and turned his head to find Sammy sleeping on the vacant pillow beside him. Sunlight streamed through the window, making the cat's golden eyes glow. All the pain and misery he'd managed to stifle the previous night flooded to the forefront of his mind. He reached over and sank his hands into the cat's thick fur as the tears fell anew.

Meow.

Sammy stood up and stalked toward him, and that's when Kendall realized the furry beast had been lying on a stack of folded papers.

"What were you hiding, pretty boy?"

Kendall's breath seized in his throat when he unfolded the first sheet and saw a sketch of himself smiling dreamily. He didn't know when Ridge had drawn the image, but he was pretty certain he knew the source of joy behind the smile. He'd never felt so seen in all his life. How unfair was it that the person who saw him well enough to draw such a beautiful sketch would never belong to him?

He looked at one drawing after another—seven in all. Each sketch showed a variation of joy and humor on Kendall's features. It was in his eyes, the tilt of his head, or the quirk of a brow. It was all there on vivid display—the teasing, the laughing, and the loving. A part of Kendall wanted to ball them up and throw them across the room, but instead, he neatly folded the drawings and tucked them away in his nightstand. That's when he noticed a napkin left behind on the pillow. It had a crudely drawn food truck with the words Kendall's Kickin' Chicken written on the side. It looked like Ridge had started to add a chicken and chili peppers above the lettering but got interrupted before he could finish.

Kendall's Kickin' Chicken.

He hadn't allowed himself to think too far ahead but couldn't deny the name was damn catchy. Kendall sighed deeply and tucked the napkin away with the other drawings. One day, he'd take them out and look at them again when they didn't make him want to sob. When he stood up, sadness pressed heavily on his shoulders, making them stoop as he walked to the bathroom.

He flipped on the light and saw another sheet of paper taped to the mirror. It was a note instead of a drawing this time.

Kendall,
Never goodbye. You promised you'd always want to know me. I'm going to hold you to that.
Ridge

Kendall smiled through the tears. He had said he'd always want to know Ridge, and he'd meant it. He might just need a little time to get past his disappointment first. He had a better grip on his emotions by the time he showered and dressed for the day.

His first act was to deal with Sassy in Savannah, which meant watching the video again. Kendall sucked in a sharp breath when he saw him and Ridge dancing together. The urge to throw himself down and bemoan the unfairness of it all was strong, but he shoved it aside. Instead, he read other posts and picked out familiar quirky phrases his suspect commonly used. Then he sent a tersely worded text to Seth.

I don't know how you got security footage from the club, but that's going to be Drew's problem to fix. You've caused an epic shitstorm with your stunt, Sassy. Get the posts down now! Don't bother trying to deny it. Save your excuses for Drew.

He wasn't sure when Seth would see the text since he'd been scheduled to work the previous night. Kendall had given the guy a ride home before and knew where he lived but decided to give Seth a chance to make it right before driving over there. For insurance, Kendall texted his suspicions to Drew and washed his hands of the matter.

By the time Kendall made breakfast and coffee, he was even committed to not falling into his old self-destructive habits. Which meant he couldn't sit around the house and fixate on Ridge coming back to pack his things and pick up his cat.

Kendall grabbed his phone and called the person he'd been growing closer to, even as he'd pulled away from Ridge. They'd talked on the phone every day and met for lunch a few times a week.

She answered on the second ring. "Hello, love."

"Hi, Mom."

"What's wrong?" she asked.

"Ridge will be leaving soon, and I'm gutted."

"This calls for French toast and bacon."

Kendall chuckled. "I appreciate it, but—"

"I'm not making it, silly. Adelaide volunteered."

"I'll be there in fifteen minutes."

Chapter Thirty-One

THE SIZE OF THE TASK FORCE NEEDED TO HAVE EYES ON THE multiple US border-crossing stations in El Paso was staggering, and making sure they remained inconspicuous was nearly impossible. Their first line of defense was the border patrol agents, who were tasked with not only identifying Harris but letting him cross into the US without tipping the wily fugitive off. The information they had about his reentry, though credible, didn't include any aliases. Harris wouldn't be so bold as to attempt entry under his real name, and they could only guess what the name on his fake documentation would be. Ridge was convinced it would align with Doc Holliday or one of the other famed gunslingers, so they'd included possible aliases, including several variations of John Henry Holliday.

Their objective was to let Harris pass through the checkpoint and follow him until he pulled away from the crowd before moving in to avoid innocent bystanders getting caught in the crosshairs. El Paso was hosting a huge festival that brought tons of tourists and extra people into an already crowded city, adding further complications they didn't need.

"What's a Sky Lantern Festival?" Zack asked. As usual, he was behind the wheel of their borrowed stakeout SUV. The dude had serious control issues.

"It's just what it sounds like," Eddie said from the front passenger seat.

"People write messages about their hopes, dreams, or grief on paper lanterns. They'll celebrate with food and music during the day, then light the lanterns and release them into the air once it gets dark."

"What's the point, though?" Zack asked.

Ridge kept his eyes glued to his laptop, watching the camera feeds from multiple crossing stations. "It symbolizes giving wings to your hopes and dreams and releasing grief."

He heard Zack pivot around in his seat, but Ridge kept his eyes trained on his task. "How do you both know so much about this festival?"

"It was part of the mission brief," Eddie said, sounding disgusted. "Some of us actually read every page."

"Yeah?" Zack asked. "Well, some of us were still reeling from the ass-chewing they got over Ridge's illicit affair. Some of us weren't privy to this information until seconds before getting called into the chief's office."

Ridge glanced up but only for a second. "I said I was sorry. I was trying to avoid the very thing that happened."

"I'm more pissed about being left out of the loop than getting my ass chewed by Marks," Zack replied.

"I said I was sorry about that too. I've tried to make it up to you."

Zack huffed. "The amazing breakfast you bought me was a good start, but you're still not forgiven. I'm heartbroken."

"It's indigestion from all the hot sauce you poured on your breakfast skillet," Eddie said. "I hope you don't shit your pants while chasing after Harris."

"Ha!" Zack said. "I won't be the one on foot."

"Famous last words," Ridge said.

The banter and video-feed scanning continued for hours without triggering even the slightest buzz of recognition until just past midday. Ridge clicked on the feed so the image filled his entire screen. He narrowed his eyes and watched as a man swaggered toward the border patrol booth. Same height and similar gait. This man's hair was long and scraggly as was the beard covering the lower portion of his face. Harris had two unique characteristics—a distinctive scar and heterochromia. This man wore a white cowboy hat and a pair of aviator glasses, so Ridge could not confirm if he had a jagged slash on his right temple or sported one green eye and one brown eye beneath the shades.

"He's not breathing," Eddie said.

"You got something, Ridgey?" Zack asked.

Ridge's mouth had gone dry, and his pulse hammered loudly in his ears, but he managed a nod.

"Breathe," Eddie said. "You don't want to pass out before you get a chance to slap the cuffs on the slick fucker."

Ridge forced himself to calm down as he watched his target get closer and closer to the booth. He knew border patrol would insist he take off his hat and glasses while they checked the documentation presented, but Harris could angle his body to make recognition harder.

"Got eyes on a potential target getting ready to cross into the US at the station on Paisano Drive," Ridge said into the comms.

"How certain are you, Dandridge?" Asher asked.

If he made the wrong call, they'd pursue the man into the city and possibly miss their chance to catch Harris reentering the US. So much could be fabricated or impersonated to throw them off. Hell, even the heterochromia could be faked with contacts.

Ridge reported the issues back to his inspector. "He's at the far-right checkpoint. Three back from the agent."

"The guy wearing the white cowboy hat, wife-beater tank, and a pair of skinny jeans tucked into cowboy boots?" Asher asked.

"That's him."

"Sounds like Kid Rock," Eddie said.

"I don't think he tucks his jeans into his boots," Zack said.

"Can we focus, fellas?" Asher asked.

It felt like it took forever for the people in front of their target to get through the checkpoint. Ridge zoomed in and watched the man remove his glasses and hat. The scar was a match, but again, it could be faked.

"Turn your head for the camera, asshole," Ridge mumbled.

As if the target heard him, the man looked directly into the camera, showing off one green eye and one brown. Then he smiled arrogantly and lifted his hand, scratching his head with his middle finger.

"It's him!" Ridge said, his heart slamming against his rib cage like it was trying to escape.

"Documentation identifies him as Johnny Holliday," Asher said. "You were right, Dandridge."

"I've got him," Adriana Rodriguez, a marshal from El Paso, said. "Will follow on foot."

"Keep a safe distance," Asher told her. "This is one wily coyote."

Ridge wanted to throw open the door and run down the street but knew it would be a mistake. Harris would make him too quickly.

"Christ, why does everyone in Texas wear a cowboy hat?" Rodriguez grumbled a few moments later.

"Are you losing him?" Asher asked.

"No, sir, but he's approaching a white Ford F-150. A woman with strawberry-blonde hair just exited the driver's side and is coming around to greet him."

"Shit," Asher said. "Do we have an ID on this woman?"

"Negative, sir," Ridge said. "I've never found his soft spot. This could be her, and she's just managed to stay off the radar all this time."

"Or it's someone new he met online, and she has no idea of the danger she's inviting into her life," his inspector said. "Treat her as a hostile until we know otherwise."

Rodriquez reported that the couple embraced and shared a passionate kiss before getting into the truck. She rattled off the license plate as soon as it became available. "Dark tinted windows," she added. "I can't see into the vehicle, but it's heading east on Paisano toward the historic district."

"And the huge fucking crowds there," Ridge said.

Asher instructed one of the teams to pick Rodriguez up and wait for further instruction.

"We're up next," Zack said, then shifted their SUV into drive.

They waited for a visual on the truck, and Ridge growled when he saw three vehicles matching the description approaching their position. Only one had tint dark enough to match Rodriguez's description, so Zack waited to let it get a few car lengths ahead before easing into traffic. They stayed a lane over and a few cars back once they confirmed the license plate.

"Coming to you guys," Asher said. "We'll catch up to you the next block over. Hixon, what's your position?"

"I'm on Overland, sir," he replied.

Ridge checked the aerial maps and saw Hixon was two streets over, moving parallel. They agreed to rendezvous at the intersection of Paisano and Kansas and execute the takedown. But like with most operations, things went sideways.

"Fuck," Hixon yelled. "A trash truck just pulled into the intersection and got stuck when the light changed." Furious honking ensued, followed by more cursing. "There's no place for him to go. I won't make the rendezvous."

"No worries," Asher said. "The next intersection is Campbell and Paisano. We'll—" Loud metal crunching cut their inspector off. "Fuck me. Some asshole just rear-ended us."

What next? An asteroid?

"Do you still have Harris in sight?" Asher asked.

"Yes, sir," Ridge said.

"Do not try to take him down on your own," Asher commanded before ordering other teams to converge to take his position and offer additional backup to Hixon's and Ridge's team. "Wait for the other unit to arrive."

"Copy," Ridge said. Both the traffic and the street crowd became more congested the closer they got to the historic district. "Let a few more cars in between us, Zack. We can't see Harris, but I guarantee his head is on a swivel looking for trouble. If we're not careful, he'll burn us and bail out of the vehicle and try to disappear in the crowd."

Zack backed off and allowed two smaller cars to cut over in front of them. Ridge tore his gaze away from the back of Harris's truck and surveyed their surroundings. People were everywhere, many of them wearing white cowboy hats to shield their faces from the scorching Texas sun. Ridge caught a brief glimpse of a helicopter on the periphery and confirmed it was their eyes in the sky.

The white truck swerved into the right lane immediately before the next intersection. When the light turned red, the passenger door opened, and Harris stepped out.

"He's going on foot," Ridge said.

"Did he make you?" Asher asked.

"Not sure. Are there any other units in the area who can follow?" A rapid roll of negative responses came through his earbuds.

"It's me and you, Ridgey," Eddie said.

"Let's do it."

"Keep your comms on," Zack said. "I'll park and catch up as soon as possible."

"Negative," Asher said. "Follow the female driver. Once Harris is in custody, I want you to pull her over and arrest her."

"Yes, sir," Zack said.

They removed their vests and untucked their shirts to cover their badges and guns. It only took seconds but felt like hours. They threw open the door and stepped onto the sidewalk, doing their best to blend in with the crowd while keeping an eye on Harris.

"We stand out like a sore thumb," Eddie complained.

Up ahead, the foot traffic became denser as they approached the street festival. Craft vendors and food booths lined the sidewalks, congesting the area further. People stopped suddenly or gingerly bounced back and forth, blocking their progress and putting more distance between them and their target. On the flip side, there were a few times Harris got bogged down, and they were forced to back off and look busy shopping to avoid getting too close.

Ridge used the time to buy a couple cowboy hats to better blend in with the people filling the sidewalks.

"He's on the move again," Eddie said.

Hats firmly in place, they resumed following Harris without crowding him. The helicopter buzzed over again, and it was even closer than the last pass.

"Lose the helicopter," he said into comms.

"Relax," an unfamiliar voice said. Ridge presumed it was the pilot or someone on his crew. "Helicopter tours are buzzing over the city all hours of the day or night."

Ahead, Harris appeared to have picked up the pace a little. It wasn't so much that he was walking faster, but he was no longer stopping to look at the various booths.

"Are we burned?" Eddie asked.

"I don't think so." The energy buzzing through Ridge made it hard to stay calm and focused.

Ridge groaned when Harris got into line for the streetcar. "Fuck."

"What?" several voices asked.

"He's waiting to ride the streetcar," Ridge replied. "There's no way in hell we can get on it too. Zack, where's the woman going?"

"Just turned onto San Antonio Avenue," he replied. "I'm not sure what she's up to."

Ridge ducked into an alcove and checked his phone, zooming in on the map showing the streetcar route. "There are tons of streetcar stops along the loop. I bet she plans to pick him up at one of them."

"So this was just a test to see if he was being followed?" Zack asked.

"Possibly."

"Stay with the woman," Asher said. "I exchanged information with the person who hit us, and our vehicle is drivable, so we're coming to you."

"I'm in position," Hixon said. "Got lucky and found a parking spot. Let me know if you want me to mobilize someplace else."

"Intercept Zack so he doesn't spook the woman," Asher said.

"Copy, sir."

"Even in these dopey hats, Eddie and I stick out like a sore thumb."

"I got you," Rodriquez said. "I'm half a block behind you. Eddie, hang back and follow at a distance. We'll act like a couple out for a day of fun. Maybe it will be enough to throw Harris off."

Ridge kept his body angled to keep an eye on Harris while watching for Rodriguez as the streetcar chimed in the distance. She reached him a few moments later, throwing her arms around Ridge's neck and pulling him down like she was going to plant one on him.

"Harris is looking in this direction," she whispered.

Ridge kept his back toward Harris and watched Eddie fade into the street crowd, which was no easy feat for someone his size. The chimes grew louder as the streetcar drew nearer. The noise was taxing Ridge's nervous system even further.

"Hang in there," Rodriguez said, slipping her arms around his waist and burrowing into him as a lover would.

Ridge patted her back, then eased from her embrace. Arm in arm, they slowly made their way down the street. They stopped to check out the wares at various booths, and Ridge bought Rodriguez an ice cream cone. Harris remained in line and kept his back toward them as he waited for the streetcar to approach. Ridge briefly contemplated taking down Harris himself, but Rodriguez squeezed his hand.

"Don't do it," she said. "Wait for backup."

They were running out of sidewalk between them and Harris, forcing them to linger longer at a few booths. Ridge's gaze landed on a leather cord necklace with a heart-shaped gemstone the same color as Kendall's eyes. He picked it up and imagined it resting against Kendall's skin or binding his wrist to—"

"Oh, that's pretty," Rodriguez said, breaking into his poorly timed thoughts.

The vendor was an older man, whose long lifespan was etched in the many wrinkles on his tanned face. "You should buy your pretty lady a neck-lace, fella."

"Oh, no," Rodriguez said. "I don't wear much jewelry."

The vendor wasn't about to let a potential sale walk away and kept teasing Ridge, getting louder and louder. Ridge pulled out some cash and bought the necklace to shut the guy up before he drew unwanted attention to them. The vendor thanked him for his business when he and Rodriguez moved on.

A group of young ladies burst out of a café, laughing and giggling. One of them slammed into Ridge's chest and teetered on her sky-high heels. He reached out and took her arms to steady her.

"Hey there, cowboy," she said, patting his chest while batting her eye-lashes. The alcohol on her breath was strong enough to burn his nostrils. "My name's Madison."

"His name is Taken," Rodriguez growled. "Maybe you should step back."

Madison's friends formed a half circle behind her, and Ridge could see the trouble coming a mile away. Fuck. This was the last thing they needed.

"Looks like someone is afraid you'll steal her man, Maddie," one of the friends said.

Madison raked her scathing gaze over Rodriguez. "As she should be."

"Not now, not ever," Rodriguez said.

"This really isn't the time," Ridge said, trying to defuse the situation.

"Kick her ass, Maddie!" one of the women yelled.

Fuck. "Listen," Ridge said. "You'd be fighting the wrong person, but I can assure you my boyfriend is pretty scrappy." He said, thinking about Kendall taking down Rodney James.

Madison's eyes widened, and her friends snickered. She held her hands up in surrender and backed up. "My bad." On her next step, Madison's heel got stuck in a sidewalk crack, and she crashed into her friends, bowling two of them over. A mixture of screaming, crying, and even laughing rent the air, pulling everyone's attention—including Harris's—to the pile of women on the ground.

The literal and figurative crash happened so fast Ridge didn't have time to turn away. He locked eyes with his fugitive and saw recognition bloom. A sick grin spread across Harris's face in the next instant, and Ridge knew what the man was going to do as surely as if he'd announced it out loud.

The two men pulled their weapons at the same time. Ridge aimed his at Harris while the fugitive held his gun to the head of the woman who'd been standing in front of him. Her little girl screamed bloody murder as she watched the man drag her mother toward the streetcar that had just pulled to a stop.

Multiple people shouted, "Gun!"

Pandemonium ensued as the people on the sidewalks ran for cover, and the people on the streetcar tripped and stumbled over each other trying to climb out the emergency exit at the rear, including the conductor. Several people went down and were trampled, but Ridge couldn't tear his gaze away from the man who was backing onto the car with a hostage as a shield.

"Mommy," the little girl cried, trying to follow.

"Shut her up!" Harris yelled. "I have no problem putting a bullet in a little girl who stands between me and revenge. Ain't that right, Pat Garrett."

A bystander grabbed the little girl and pulled her to safety while Ridge and Rodriguez kept walking steadily toward Harris, guns steady while waiting for any opening.

"You might as well surrender," Ridge told him. "There's no place for you to go."

"Fuck you," Harris spat. "You won't take a shot at me as long as I have a hostage."

"Guess we'll find out. This ends today, Harris," Ridge said.

"Don't get on that streetcar," Rodriguez told him.

"I don't have a choice. Stay out here. If you see a shot, take it."

Ridge carefully entered the vehicle, his gun trained in front of him. "You're going to be okay, ma'am," he told the sobbing woman.

Harris laughed, sounding unhinged. "I should put a bullet in her brain right now and show her how little your words mean."

"Why don't you let her go, and we can handle this man-to-man." He just needed to buy them some time until someone from the task force crept up the emergency exit. Harris was so focused on Ridge he wasn't checking to see if anyone was coming up behind him. "Let her go. You and I can square off like old gunslingers at high noon. Doesn't that sound fun?"

Harris laughed harder and jammed the barrel of his gun into the woman's head. "Or why don't I—" He stopped and sniffed the air before looking down. A growing puddle of liquid pooled around their feet. "Did you just fucking piss yourself? I paid six hundred dollars for these alligator boots."

Ridge caught the woman's gaze and gestured for her to drop, knowing the sudden shift would catch Harris off-balance. Her eyes widened in fear, but she did as Ridge asked just as Harris was shifting his gaze back to Ridge. The woman lurched forward, pulling Harris off-balance. Ridge fired his weapon, hitting Harris in the shoulder of the arm holding his gun.

The fugitive let out an enraged scream as the gun clattered to the ground, and his hostage crawled away from him. Harris lunged for the gun at the same time Ridge hurdled over the woman. He was about to fire his weapon again, but Eddie rushed Harris as if he were a rookie running back and the big game was on the line. Harris landed face-first in the woman's piss.

He flailed and screamed about police brutality as Ridge leaned over his prone body and slapped handcuffs onto his wrists. The only sounds he loved more were the ones Kendall made deep in his throat when he curled into his arms after sex. Ridge hauled Harris to his feet while Eddie called for medical attention.

"Who's the huckleberry now?" Ridge asked. Harris's only response was more sniffling and whining. "It's a flesh wound. You'll live."

Asher signaled Zack and Hixon to take down the female companion, and they arrested her without incident moments later.

Ridge handcuffed Harris to a gurney and left him under supervision so he could check on the hostage who'd been reunited with her daughter. They clung to one another on the sidewalk.

"You both were so brave," he told them.

Rodriguez stayed with them while Ridge rode in the ambulance with Harris to the hospital. He wasn't nearly as brash and bold now that he was in custody. Ridge's bullet had gone clean through the meaty part of Harris's shoulder, and much to the fugitive's disappointment, only required a thorough cleaning and stitches. He wasn't getting a drug-induced escape; the asshole was getting some extra strength Tylenol and a one-way ticket to Georgia.

"Wow, would you look at that," Zack said a few hours later.

They were killing time back at the hotel while waiting to meet their transport plane at El Paso International. Witnesses were moved on commercial flights, but dangerous fugitives were moved on JPATS flights like the one made famous in *Con Air*.

Ridge looked out the hotel window and saw what looked like hundreds of giant fireflies floating through the sky. It took him a minute to realize he was looking at lanterns from the festival. Each one of the lights represented someone's hopes, dreams, or anguish. He'd thought the festival sounded like a neat idea when he'd read about it but seeing the lanterns floating in the sky was something you'd have to see to believe. Ridge tried to take a video, but it was impossible to decipher what the glowing lights were. He wished he was sharing the moment with Kendall. The thought reminded Ridge of the conversation he'd had with his dad while Harris was being processed.

"Congratulations, son. I'm proud of you," his father had said once Ridge told him his news.

"Thanks, Dad. That means a lot to me."

"What's next?"

Ridge blew out a short breath of frustration. "I'm not sure."

"Can I make a suggestion?" his dad had asked.

"Of course."

"Maybe it's time to admit you've planted roots in Savannah."

"You sound like Mom."

Dad chuckled. "Thank you for the lovely compliment."

"Savannah wasn't in my plans."

"Well, I hadn't planned for your mother either. You see how that turned out." They shared a laugh. "Son?"

"Yeah?"

"Bring Kendall home to meet your family. I want to meet the man who's responsible for the happiness I've heard in your voice."

"That's just it, Dad. We haven't known each other very long. How can this happiness be real?"

"You sound just like me after I met your mother. You can fight it, or you can embrace the light he brings to your life."

"I wasn't even aware I talked about him that much during our weekly chats."

"I could buy a new tractor if I had a penny for every time you said his name," Dad said. "Talking about Kendall comes so naturally to you that you don't know you're doing it. That's how I know it's the real thing. Mom knows it too, so she's knitting a Christmas stocking for him."

Ridge had been unable to think about anything else since the conversation ended. He knew Kendall would fall in love with his mountains and would soak up his mother's affection like a sponge. Ridge imagined Kendall curled up next to him by a roaring fireplace or riding on the back of his horse. The two of them could share a sleeping bag and camp beneath a starlit sky. Ridge turned his attention back out the window and watched the lights continue to drift upward.

Those little symbols of hope had left an indelible mark on him, not unlike the man he longed to make love to and hold in his arms. Everything Ridge thought he knew and wanted shifted like those paper lanterns in the breeze until a new dream started to emerge. Something clicked deep inside Ridge's chest, and a sense of peace he'd never experienced before washed over him. Gazing at his beloved mountains was close, but even they couldn't hold a paper lantern to the rightness he felt just then.

"What's with his dopey face?" Zack asked.

Eddie glanced over at Ridge and smiled. "He's a man who finally gets it."

Zack scratched his head. "Gets what?"

"The secret to life," Eddie replied.

They didn't land in Savannah until five the following morning. A small army of reporters and their cameramen waited at the airport, wanting sound bites for the morning shows. Ridge felt like he had sand trapped under his eyelids and wasn't in the mood to stop to piss, let alone grant an interview. The sun was starting to come up when they grabbed their gear and loaded into the SUVs to get Harris settled at lockup.

"I got this, Ridgey," Eddie said. "Go make your call."

Ridge blew out a shaky breath and nodded before hugging Eddie and Zack.

He strode as far as he could get from everyone and dialed the number stored in his contacts.

"I've seen the news. Is it true?" Asia Knight said in place of a typical greeting.

"Yes, ma'am. We arrested Sheldon Harris yesterday in El Paso and transported him back to Georgia to face charges."

Ridge heard her broken sobs, then her husband came on the phone and said, "Thank you for keeping your word."

"I hope it will bring your family peace of mind."

After their brief call, Ridge headed into the bullpen to clean out his desk and write his resignation letter. His possessions were few since he was a minimalist who liked to make moving easy and painless. Ridge stared at the photo of Rashanda for a few moments before tucking it away in the box. No matter where he went or what he did, Ridge would want her smiling face to brighten up his desk. Then he sat down and typed up his resignation.

Ridge wasn't surprised to find Marks at her desk. She was dressed to the nines for a media appearance and glanced up when he knocked on the doorframe.

"Congratulations, Dandridge. That was excellent work in El Paso."

"Thank you, ma'am." He strode to her desk and extended the sheet of paper toward her. "You asked me to have a decision ready."

She glanced at the paper before meeting his gaze. "And you're sure this is the right one for you?"

"Yes, ma'am. I'm sorry I let you down." He would not apologize for falling in love with Kendall Blakemore.

She sighed, rotated in her chair, and swiftly fed his resignation letter through her paper shredder.

"Ma'am?"

"Stop being so dramatic. I'm not giving up one of my best agents, so don't even think of transferring out of here."

Ridge managed to stifle his smile. "No, ma'am."

"I'm not so heartless I want to stand in the way of true love either." She grinned wickedly. "Though I will make you suffer mightily until I deem you worthy of my trust again." All the possible shit jobs she could foist on him rolled through his tired brain, but it didn't matter.

"What about the video of Kendall and me? Won't that still be a problem?"

"Not where you're going," she said ominously. "Besides, Francesca told me she'd handle it if the video or photo resurface."

"Resurface?"

"Sassy in Savannah took them down, but you and I both know that doesn't mean they're gone for good."

"No, ma'am."

"Francesca is confident the video won't be a problem. If she's not worried, neither am I."

Ridge felt boneless with relief.

"Get out of here, Dandridge. I don't want to see you for three days."

"Yes, ma'am."

Chapter Thirty-Two

SHELDON HARRIS'S CAPTURE AND RETURN TO SAVANNAH HAD been all over the media. Kendall's phone had chimed several times with Google alerts when the news hit the internet. He'd held out for an hour before he clicked on the links and read the articles. The photos that accompanied the stories triggered tears of pride and sorrow. One of the links included a video of Ridge escorting Harris in chains to a waiting vehicle. Ridge stood tall and walked proudly. His expression was one of peace and victory, though Kendall suspected he was exhausted. It wasn't likely he'd slept much before the apprehension and not at all afterward.

Where would he lay his head down to rest now that he was back? The images were captured before dawn, but Ridge hadn't returned to his house. How long would processing Harris take? Surely not hours? Had Ridge decided to crash at Eddie's place? Why? To avoid an emotional scene or to spare Kendall's feelings? Would Eddie be the one to show up and collect Ridge's things? He discounted that idea as soon as the thought registered. No way. It wasn't in Ridge's nature to back down from challenging situations, and he'd vowed not to break Kendall's heart. Sending Eddie to retrieve the cat and his belongings would shatter his promise.

Kendall stroked the cat's silky fur and braced himself for the goodbye he knew was coming. "Not sure how much longer we have, big fella." The miniature lion purred loudly and rubbed his face against Kendall's palm. "I'm going to miss you too."

Kendall's thoughts shifted to the ingredients he'd need for the new sauce brewing in his mind. He'd need Carolina Reapers for starters. What other pepper burned as hot as heartbreak? No, this was deeper than heartbreak. This sorrow sank into the marrow of his bones. "Devastation," he whispered. It completely described his feelings, and Reapers were the perfect pepper to express them. But what could he add to counterbalance the heat and avoid searing people's taste buds for life?

He cycled through ingredients, some sweet and some savory, discounting ones that were too common or not feasible for a large-scale recipe. Sammy leaped onto the back of the couch seconds before Kendall registered the familiar sound of Ridge's SUV pulling into the driveway. The powerful engine rumbled to a stop, and Kendall forced a smile to his face as he stood up from the couch. He would stifle his feelings, congratulate the man, and not make this harder for either of them. Kendall wouldn't beg or barter or grovel at Ridge's feet. He cared too much, and Ridge's happiness was paramount to his own.

His good intentions started to waver the moment he heard Ridge's key turning in the lock, and then, there he was—big, beautiful, and bursting with pride.

"Hi," Ridge said.

Kendall set down his coffee cup and strode forward. "Fuck the high road," he said, pulling Ridge into a no-holds-barred kiss. Rolling over and playing dead wasn't an option. No mercy. No surrender.

Ridge met his eagerness with a surge of passion that left Kendall breathless. He released a slight growl as he backed Kendall up against the small table. The jolt pulled Kendall out of his trance, and he experienced a moment of pure panic. What if this was Ridge just working through the adrenaline of his big arrest? All the doubts and fears he'd shoved aside started to creep in. Kendall took a deep breath and closed his eyes.

"Don't," Ridge said fiercely.

Kendall reopened his eyes and met Ridge's intense gaze. "Don't what?"

"Don't you dare pull away from me."

Kendall blinked in confusion, then patted his strong shoulders. "I'm right here and haven't so much as moved a muscle."

Ridge lowered his head and ran his nose against Kendall's, nuzzling him before planting a soft, solitarily stingy kiss on his upturned lips. "Maybe you haven't pulled away physically, but I've watched you distance yourself emotionally from me for weeks now."

Kendall swallowed hard. "It wasn't intentional," he said. "Not at first, anyway. I wasn't aware you noticed."

"You've seen the drawings I've made of you. Those were all done from memory, by the way."

Kendall bit his lip to keep hope from bubbling out of him in a nervous giggle. "Even the one of me sleeping? You could've sketched it while I dreamed of you, and I wouldn't have known it."

"Stop watching so much true-crime shit," Ridge said, then cupped his neck and pressed their foreheads together. "Even the sleeping pictures were drawn from memory. You saw the attention to detail. Do you honestly think I didn't notice you picking up extra shifts nearly every day? Do you think I didn't feel the changes in your body? During sex, you couldn't hold me tighter, but afterward..."

"I pulled away," Kendall whispered. Instead of sprawling over Ridge, he'd kept to his own side. Kendall took a deep breath and leaned tighter into Ridge's embrace. "That was a completely subconscious decision."

"To protect yourself from me," Ridge said. "God, I hate that so much."

Kendall squared his shoulders, steeled his resolve, and put a little space between them. He didn't want to use sex to persuade or manipulate Ridge. "I know you didn't count on me showing up and throwing a wrench into your plans, and I'm sorry the situation with Stanton has caused trouble for you, but I..." Kendall's thoughts got tripped up, and he faltered before they could become words. *I think I'm in love with you. I think we could have a real future together. I will travel the world with you.* There were so many things he wanted to say.

"I submitted my resignation this morning," Ridge said. "It's partly why I'm so late getting home." *Home?*

"Why would you do that? Why not just transfer to—"

Ridge silenced his question with a kiss. "Before the mission, the chief asked for either my resignation or a transfer request."

"Because of me?"

Ridge stroked his cheek. "No, because of *me*. I was the one who let her down, not you. I essentially felt like she was asking me to choose between a life with you or without you. And I chose you."

Panic and joy surged inside Kendall, and it was hard to figure out which emotion was winning the war. "But you love your job, and you're so good at it."

"I'm good at many things," Ridge said huskily. "Doesn't mean I want to make a career out of them."

"No," Kendall said, shaking his head. "I will not be the reason you give up a job you love. If you want to transfer, I'll pack and go with you."

Ridge tilted his head. "You'd do that for me?"

"I'd follow you anywhere." His words were met with a dopey smile.

"What about your food truck?"

"We'll take it across the country. I have no idea what kind of permits and licenses that would entail, but I'm excellent at research." His mind started tallying the things he'd need to sort through.

Ridge chuckled softly. "Kendall."

"Hmmm?"

"Marks fed my resignation through the shredder. She said she wasn't standing in the way of love."

"Love?" Had Kendall spoken his earlier thoughts out loud? That was a fuckton of pressure to put on Ridge. They hardly knew each other. Love? It was too soon.

Ridge pulled Kendall into his embrace and trailed kisses along his neck. "No need to panic."

"I'm not," he said breathlessly.

Ridge nipped the tender skin where Kendall's pulse beat frantically. "Your pulse says otherwise. I see you. I want you. I lo—"

Kendall pulled back and stared into his eyes. "But we've only known each other for two months, and you've just gotten out of a relationship. We went from eye-fucking one another to living together. It's a bit of a leap, isn't it?"

"Does it make it less true?" Ridge asked, quirking a brow as he waited for Kendall's counterargument. When none was forthcoming, Ridge added, "It's okay if you're not ready to speak the words right now or slap labels on what we have. I'll figure out your feelings when you debut your next sauce."

Kendall grinned. "You'll eat my feelings?"

"Something like that."

Kendall couldn't deny the base ingredients for the next secret sauce had started to shift. He no longer wanted to punish; he wanted to…

"Adore. That's the name of my next sauce."

Ridge's rumbling purr rivaled the cat's. "I *love* the sound of that." He kissed Kendall for several long moments before pulling back from their embrace. "I don't suppose I can talk you into holding off on starting the sauce for a little while?"

Kendall took a few steps backward, tugging Ridge with him. "You have other things you'd like to do?"

"Uh-huh. And I need your help."

Ten minutes later, Kendall stood in the center of his bedroom, scowling. "This wasn't what I had in mind." He had to shout to be heard over the banging.

Ridge stopped hammering, then hung the second canvas. He stepped back to study his handiwork before adjusting each frame until he was happy. "There. Now I'm happy."

"I hadn't noticed," Kendall said as he trailed a finger over the erection poorly concealed by Ridge's pants. "You really like these images, huh?"

Ridge arched his hips, pressing into Kendall's caress. "You are by far the most exquisite person I've ever met. I'm not just talking about your looks and sex appeal. Those are only parts of the recipe. I love your heart." Ridge slid his hand down to cover Kendall's chest. "The one that's beating so hard for me right now." He pressed a kiss to Kendall's mouth. "I especially love the sass that comes from these sweet lips." Ridge nipped his earlobe and slowly dragged his teeth down the flesh until it popped free. "I adore how you listen so attentively and how deeply you care about the people in your life."

"Are you going to kiss all the parts you like?"

"Yes," Ridge said, but then pulled back. "I brought back a few things from Texas for you."

"Me?"

Ridge pulled out a leather cord necklace with a light blue heart pendant. "It made me think of your eyes."

Kendall smiled up at him. "I love it. Thank you."

"The salesman said you could wear it as a necklace or wrap the cord around your wrist a few times to make a bracelet."

"Or you could use it to tie me to the bed and fuck me."

"Oh, damn," Ridge said. "I should've bought two." He reached back into the bag and pulled out a cowboy hat.

Kendall accepted the gift but eyed it suspiciously as he traced the brim with his finger. "You want me to wear this?"

Ridge nodded and pulled a second one from the bag. "I have one too."

"So we can play ride 'em cowboy?"

Ridge's answering grin was full of wicked intention. "Yes, you'll need practice for where we're going."

Kendall tipped his head to the side. "And that is…"

"Montana. To meet my family."

Chapter Thirty-Three

IT TOOK A MONTH OF WORKING ASSET FORFEITURE BEFORE MARKS allowed Ridge out of the dungeon and another three weeks before she approved the vacation time he needed to take Kendall out west.

"What if they don't like me?" Kendall had asked during the flight. He'd been a nervous wreck since they'd woken up that morning. "Two weeks is a long time to be trapped with someone you don't like."

"They already adore you." His mother had texted Ridge a photo of the Christmas stocking she'd knitted for Kendall not long after he returned from Texas. He'd thought about showing it to Kendall to ease his nerves but didn't want to ruin his mother's surprise. Instead, Ridge lifted his hand and kissed it. "Everything will be fine."

His parents met them at the airport, and Cheryl Dandridge practically elbowed him out of the way so she could envelop Kendall in her arms and squeeze him tight.

"I'm so happy to finally meet you." They'd been texting and chatting on the phone for weeks, which was why Kendall's nervousness was so cute.

"Me too," Kendall replied, pulling back from the hug. He extended his hand to Ridge's dad, but Mitchell Dandridge wasn't having any part of that. He hugged Kendall and kept his arm around his shoulders as he led them out of the terminal.

"I'm going to want him back," Ridge said grumpily.

His mother giggled and looped her arm through Ridge's. "If you think we're bad, wait until Sierra gets a hold of him."

The next two weeks were the best of Ridge's life. Montana was on the precipice of fall, and the leaves were still flirting with the idea of changing colors. Though the temperatures dipped lower than what Kendall was accustomed to, he loved sipping coffee while sitting in one of the chairs Gemma had painted. Ridge usually found his mom sitting in the one beside him, a look of contentment on her face as they quietly watched the sunrise. Kendall took to ranch life and camping much easier than even Ridge had anticipated. Kendall had especially loved sharing a sleeping bag with him. He'd been nervous around the animals at first but quickly caught on to their eccentric personalities, and he especially liked Gus, the goat who thought he was a dog. Kendall loved sipping spiced cider or mulled wine by the fireplace as they played hours of board games. He'd started out laidback, but it only took a few days before the Dandridges' competitive personalities rubbed off on him.

"He's one of us now," Dad had said one night after Kendall trounced them in Monopoly.

"Yeah, he is." One day, it would be in name too.

And his mom had been right. Sierra and Kendall had become thick as thieves. They whispered, laughed, and danced like no one else was around.

"Stop pouting," Dad said the night before they were set to board a plane back to Georgia. "If you can't see how much that young man loves you, then you need to get your eyes checked."

"Yeah, he does." Kendall expressed his adoration with his actions, body, and words. "I'm going to marry him someday."

His dad slapped his shoulder. "I know you will."

Chapter Thirty-Four

Eight months later…

PIERRE TUCKED HIS PHONE AWAY AND SMILED. "DREW SAID A LINE is already forming. Are you ready for this?"

Kendall looked around the pristine interior of the truck they'd worked so hard to get ready. He smiled at the two line cooks, then nodded at Pierre. Kendall's Kickin' Chicken was moments away from becoming a reality. "The question you should be asking is if Savannah is ready for us?"

"Give them hell, kid," Pierre said.

Kendall straightened the custom apron Cheryl had made for him and rolled the concession window shade up. He stared in awe at the nearly thirty people who stood in line. The paper had run an article about them in the arts and entertainment section a few weeks prior, and apparently, it had generated quite the buzz. At the back of the crowd, Kendall saw some of the faces he loved most in the world, and he was nearly moved to tears.

"Welcome to Kendall's Kickin' Chicken," he said. "Who's first?"

Their team worked seamlessly, serving up the best wings and fries the city would ever know. Kendall not only felt it in his heart but saw it in the faces of his customers as they took their first bites. He'd served nearly two dozen people before his fan club arrived at the window. His biggest fan was first in line.

"Quit pushing," Eddie grumbled.

"Save some wings for us," Zack chimed in.

"Hey, fellas," Kendall said without tearing his gaze away from Ridge's gorgeous brown eyes. "Hi, baby."

"I'll take a dozen boneless chicken wings in Heartbreaker sauce," Eddie said, muscling in.

Kendall leaned forward and kissed Ridge's smiling lips before taking the rest of their orders. "Your food will be right out."

"Ridge better not get extra," Zack said. "I'll be counting."

His mother and Adelaide were the next to step up to the window. "Thank you for coming," he said as he hugged both women. Kendall couldn't believe the changes he'd witnessed in his mom in just a few months. She'd interviewed for the receptionist position at the private detective agency and had landed the job the same day. It had boosted her confidence, which kept her going on the darkest days. She'd known all along she wouldn't escape media scrutiny, which would only get worse when the trials started. The court of public opinion seemed evenly divided between those who thought his mom was in on the scam and those who thought she was just another of Stanton's victims.

Kendall told her not to read the stuff written about her in the paper or on social media sites. None of them knew the truth and wouldn't until she testified on behalf of the government. Even then, Stan's high-powered attorneys would do their damnedest to pick her apart. Kendall hoped Stan would do the right thing and work out a plea bargain, but he doubted Stan would do anything that included an admission of guilt. Kendall would worry about the trial when the time came. For now, he was just so happy to see his mom thriving and grateful for the chance they'd been granted to repair their fractured relationship.

"There's no place we'd rather be, honey," his mother said.

Adelaide nodded and smiled through her tears. "We're so proud of you."

Kendall covered his heart with both hands. "What can I get for you lovely ladies?"

Adelaide ordered the mildest wings on the menu while his mom went for the hottest.

"Mom, are you sure?"

"Oh, I'm positive. Bring on the heat!"

Mitch, Cheryl, and Sierra were next. Kendall's eyes filled with grateful tears. "I can't believe you guys flew in for the grand opening. Ranch work waits for no one."

"Well, we're a tight-knit community and pitch in to help others when needed," Mitch said. "Right here is where we were needed, so our friends are running things while we're gone."

Cheryl rose on her tiptoes, and Kendall leaned forward to kiss her cheek. "Nice aprons."

"Thank you," he said. "An extraordinary lady made them for us."

"My boo!" Sierra said, pulling a happy squeal from Kendall. She made him model and pose for pictures before they placed their orders. The girls went easy on the sauce, and Mitch begrudgingly ordered a grilled chicken salad with vinaigrette dressing.

"Never thought I'd see the day," Ridge said as he joined them.

His dad clasped his shoulder and said, "I have too much to live for."

The line seemed to stretch on forever, not that Kendall was complaining. It just made it hard to enjoy the expressions on everyone's faces when they took their first bites.

Most of the waiters and bartenders from The Cockpit dropped by to order food and offer encouragement.

"How's my favorite earthling?" Emmett had asked.

Kendall had responded in a series of squeaks that made his friend howl with laughter.

"What the hell was that?" Chet asked as he approached the window.

"Secret language only Emmett and I know," Kendall told him, then made introductions.

The two men eye-fucked one another for a few seconds before Emmett took his food and joined the others from the club.

Chet turned and stared after him for so long Kendall had to tap his arm to get his attention.

"Sorry," Chet said. "Who is that guy?"

"Emmett. He tends bar at The Cockpit."

Chet winked. "Good to know." Then he tilted his head and studied Kendall closely. "You look ridiculously happy right now. Doesn't your face hurt from smiling so much?"

Kendall shook his head. "Nope. You can be just like me someday if you try really hard."

"Well, I took the first step toward happiness today," Chet said. "I dropped Bobby Jack Dennison as my client and tendered my resignation at Elderwood, Johnson, and McClary."

"Whoa. What's next for the Bull Shark?"

Chet cringed. "I'm going to champion the underdog."

Kendall nodded. "Nice. I'm proud of you."

"That means a lot," Chet said. He turned his head and scanned the menu before placing his order.

"Be out in just a few minutes."

Chet stepped aside so Jonah and Avery could approach the window. Kendall had been so busy with final preparations that he hadn't been able to spend much time with his friends. They agreed to a double date the following weekend.

Travis and Seth stopped by a little while later. Kendall was happy to see his stepbrother living his best life but wished he'd been a fly on the wall the day Stan found out Travis had eloped to Vegas with Seth.

"Hey, guys," Kendall said. "Good to see you." He smiled down at the grumpy-looking pug sitting by Travis's feet. They'd recently adopted the little gremlin. "Hello, Lulu." The old dog blinked once but otherwise didn't acknowledge him.

When Kendall handed them their food a few minutes later, he held tighter to Seth's tray. "Remember, I get the final say on any videos about me from now on."

Seth smiled sheepishly and blushed. "I shut the site down a long time ago."

Kendall knew he had but still teased him about it. Seth had felt horrible about causing trouble for Ridge and felt even worse when Drew fired him over it. Kendall had intervened to get Seth's job back, and the younger man had learned a valuable lesson.

Colt and Carey stepped up next, and Kendall was glad to see the two lovebirds looking happy and healthy. Drew claimed the club had become boring once they stopped fighting their feelings for one another, but Kendall doubted it.

And speaking of the club manager, Drew smiled when he stepped up to the window.

"Checking up on your investment?" Kendall teased.

Drew shook his head. "Supporting a friend."

Kendall served several more customers after Drew before he caught a quiet lull. He wanted to mingle among his customers and find out what everyone thought about the food but focused on tidying up the truck and restocking supplies for the next rush.

"Excuse me," Ridge said firmly.

Kendall whirled around to see what was wrong. "Babe?"

Ridge's eyes glittered with adoration and orneriness. "There's a problem with my order."

Kendall snorted and approached the window. "What's that? You ate it too fast? There are no free refills, sir. Not even for the man I adore."

"Nope. I found something in my food."

Kendall's eyes widened, and alarm screamed through him. "What?" he managed to croak out.

"This!" Ridge said, holding up a platinum ring. "It was in my food. Are you trying to tell me something?" It took Kendall's brain a second to catch up since his heart was still pounding from the scare. Now it sped up for an entirely different reason. He glanced around and saw almost everyone had their phones aimed in their direction.

"What are you doing?" Kendall whispered as he reached for his boyfriend.

Ridge grabbed his hand, then dropped to one knee. "Pretty sure it's obvious. I'm asking the man I love to marry me."

Kendall's mouth fell open, and he stared at the face he loved so damn much. "Am I dreaming?"

"No, baby. It's all real."

Kendall tore his gaze from Ridge long enough to scan the crowd, noting the smiles on everyone's faces. Their mothers held hands while they waited for Kendall to respond. He imagined they were holding their breaths too.

"So, will you?"

Kendall met Ridge's warm, hopeful gaze again. "There's nothing in the world that would make me happier."

The crowd cheered as Ridge slipped the thin band onto his finger. Kendall dashed out the door of the truck and leaped into Ridge's arms.

"I called it," Zack said.

"*We* called it," Eddie countered.

"Idiots," Jess and Emma said.

"What are they talking about?" Kendall asked Ridge.

"After Zack and Eddie met you at Asher's barbecue, they wouldn't shut up about how perfect you were for me."

Kendall smiled up at him. "Well, they're not wrong. Now kiss me. Let's seal this deal."

And Ridge did.

Sometime later, it could've been five minutes or fifty, Eddie said, "Your boyfriend sure can cook chicken."

Ridge smiled. "*Fiancé*, Eddie."

The End!

Want to be the first to know about my book releases and have access to extra content? You can sign up for my newsletter here:
http://eepurl.com/dlhPYj

My favorite place to hang out and chat with my readers is my Facebook group. Would you like to be a member of Aimee's Dye Hards?
We'd love to have you! Go here:
www.facebook.com/groups/AimeesDyeHards

AIMEE NICOLE WALKER

Curl Up and Dye Mysteries
Dyeing to be Loved
Something to Dye For
Dyed and Gone to Heaven
I Do, or Dye Trying
A Dye Hard Holiday
Ride or Dye

Road to Blissville Series
Unscripted Love
Someone to Call My Own
Nobody's Prince Charming
This Time Around
Smoke in the Mirror
Inside Out
Prescription for Love

Welcome to Blissville Collection (Both M/M Blissville series)
Volume One
Volume Two

The Lady is Mine Series
The Lady is a Thief
The Lady Stole My Heart

Queen City Rogue Series
Broken Halos
Wicked Games
Beautiful Trauma

Zero Hour Series
Ground Zero
Devil's Hour
Zero Divergence

Sinister in Savannah Series
Ride the Lightning
Mr. Perfect
Pretty Poison

Savannah Standalone Books
Invisible Strings

Standalone Novels
Second Wind

Fated Hearts Series
Chasing Mr. Wright

Coauthored with Nicholas Bella
Undisputed
Circle of Darkness (Genesis Circle, Book 1)
Circle of Trust (Genesis Circle, Book 2)

Acknowledgments

First, I need to thank my husband and children for their constant support and encouragement. It's not easy living with a writer who often disappears into a fictional world for long periods of time. They do so many things to help me so that I can realize my dream. I love you guys more than words can ever express.

Many, many thanks to Susie Selva for her incredibly thorough edits and to Lori Parks for her keen eye during proofreading. These ladies are consummate professionals and an absolute joy to work with.

I want to thank Natalie of Butterfly Ink for this stunning image. I was smitten at first sight and had to have it for a cover. Thank you for making the world a more beautiful place with your art, Natalie. Matthew David is such a delight to know, and I've loved working with him over the years. He's so much more than a handsome face, and I truly appreciate all the wonderful ways he's supported my career. And much love to Natasha Snow for this gorgeous cover and to Stacey Ryan Blake for the stunning interior. The two of you always make my books sparkle and shine so beautifully.

I thank my lucky stars that I get to work with such wonderfully talented people.

xoxo
Aimee

About

AIMEE NICOLE WALKER

Ever since she was a little girl, Aimee Nicole Walker entertained herself with stories that popped into her head. Now she gets paid to tell those stories to other people. She wears many titles—wife, mom, and animal lover are just a few of them. Her absolute favorite title is champion of the happily ever after. Love inspires everything she does, music keeps her sane, and coffee is the magic elixir that fuels her day.

She'd love to hear from you.

Want to connect? All her links are in one nifty location. Click here:
linktr.ee/AimeeNicoleWalker